IRISH TIGER

ALSO BY ANDREW M. GREELEY
FROM TOM DOHERTY ASSOCIATES

BISHOP BLACKIE RYAN MYSTERIES

The Bishop and the Missing L Train
The Bishop and the Beggar Girl of St. Germain
The Bishop in the West Wing
The Bishop Goes to The University
The Bishop at the Lake

NUALA ANNE MCGRAIL NOVELS

Irish Gold
Irish Lace
Irish Whiskey
Irish Mist
Irish Eyes
Irish Love
Irish Stew!
Irish Cream
Irish Crystal
Irish Linen

THE O'MALLEYS IN THE TWENTIETH CENTURY

A Midwinter's Tale
Younger Than Springtime
A Christmas Wedding
September Song
Second Spring
Golden Years

All About Women
Angel Fire
Angel Light
Contract with an Angel
Faithful Attraction
The Final Planet
Furthermore!: Memories of a Parish Priest
God Game
Jesus: A Meditation on His Stories and His Relationships with Women
Star Bright!
Summer at the Lake
White Smoke
Sacred Visions (editor with Michael Cassutt)
The Book of Love (editor with Mary G. Durkin)
Emerald Magic (editor)

IRISH TIGER

A Nuala Anne McGrail Novel

ANDREW M. GREELEY

A TOM DOHERTY ASSOCIATES BOOK
NEW YORK

This is a work of fiction. All of the characters, organizations, and events portrayed in this novel are either products of the author's imagination or are used fictitiously.

IRISH TIGER: A NUALA ANNE McGRAIL NOVEL

A Forge Book
Published by Tom Doherty Associates, LLC
175 Fifth Avenue
New York, NY 10010

www.tor-forge.com

Forge® is a registered trademark of Tom Doherty Associates, LLC.

Library of Congress Cataloging-in-Publication Data

Greeley, Andrew M., 1928-
Irish tiger : a Nuala Anne McGrail novel / Andrew M. Greeley.
p. cm.
"A Tom Doherty Associates book."
ISBN-13: 978-0-7653-1588-5
ISBN-10: 0-7653-1588-2
1. McGrail, Nuala Anne (Fictitious character)—Fiction. 2. Women detectives—Illinois—Chicago—Fiction. 3. Older couples—Crimes against—Fiction. 4. Irish American families—Fiction. I. Title.
PS3557.R358I838 2008
813'.54—dc22

2007040875

First Edition: February 2008

Printed in the United States of America

0 9 8 7 6 5 4 3 2 1

— Cast of Characters —

Nuala Anne McGrail (née Moire Phioulaigh Ain Mac Griel), singer, accountant, fey, Irish Tiger

Dermot Michael Coyne, husband to Nuala Anne

Their children

Mary Anne (Nelliecoyne), age eight

Micheal Dirmuid (the Mick), age six and a half

Socra Marie, age five

Josef Porrig, age two and a half

Their hounds

Fiona

Maeve

Cops

Mike Casey

John Culhane

Terry Glen

Nikos Mashek

Clerics

CARDINAL SEAN CRONIN

COADJUTOR ARCHBISHOP JOHN BLACKWOOD RYAN

REV. GEORGE COYNE ("Prester George"), brother to Dermot Michael

Clients

JOHN PATRICK DONLAN

MARIA ANGELICA CONNORS

Persons of interest

LOUIS GARNER, classmate to John Patrick

JOSEPH MCMAHON, staff to John Patrick

CONGRESSMAN STERLING SILVER STAFFORD, onetime suitor to Maria Angelica

BROTHERS SABATTINI, brothers to Maria Angelica

Friend (and friend of friends)

DOMINIC

IRISH TIGER

— Prologue —

(Excerpts from the columns of the *Chicago Herald*)

Observed by Eyes and Ears of Chicago

The Eyes observed two of Chicago's most beautiful of beautiful people huddling at Ambria. John Donlan, CEO of Donlan Assets Management, and Maria A. Connors, CEO of Elegant Homes (and cover girl in a recent issue of *Chicago Market*). Were the handsome couple discussing corporate mergers or perhaps more intimate mergers?

. . .

The Ears hear that talk of a romance between John Donlan (Donlan Assets Management) and the gorgeous Maria Angelica Connors (Elegant Homes) reported a couple of weeks ago have caused a tsunami. In both families. "If he wants a fling with a woman like her only two years after his wife died, that's up to him. But he can't expect us to accept her," said an angry Donlan woman.

Eyes and Ears on Channel 3

ANCHORPERSON: What's happening in the controversial marriage of John Donlan and Maria Angelica Connors?

EYES AND EARS: It looks like it's not happening. The Donlans have their skirts in a twist because Donlan Assets Management has invested a ton of money in Elegant Homes. Ears hears that none of the Donlans will be in the wedding party or come to the ceremony in St. Frederick's Church. One of their nicer words they use for the gorgeous Ms. Connors is "shameless gold digger."

ANCHORPERSON: They're both grandparents aren't they?

EYES AND EARS: That's part of the problem.

Channel 3 News on Saturday Night

ANCHORPERSON: There were Catholic fireworks at St. Frederick's Church this afternoon. Father Michael Hennessy, the pastor of St. Freddy's canceled the Gold Coast wedding of John Patrick Donlan to Maria Connors. In a surprise announcement just before the service began, the pastor informed the stunned congregation that he had evidence that there had been a previous marriage of Ms. Connors in a Catholic church. Our Mary Alice Quinn was there.

QUINN: That's right, Clarice. It was supposed to be the most fashionable wedding in the autumn season here in the marvelous old German church. Father Hennessy spoiled all the fun.

(Interior shot of priest in a high German-style pulpit overlooking the congregation. Bride is radiant in a light blue gown.)

HENNESSY (*a smart and overweight young punk in a biretta*): I'm afraid that the bride has not been completely honest with the church. She was married at St. Lawrence parish in Oakdale, Illinois, by Father Thomas Hartnett while she was still a student at a non-Catholic university. This marriage was before her alleged marriage to her late husband, in which she lived in sin for many years. Her attempt to marry again here today makes her liable of the punishment of canon law.

(Quick shot of the shocked bride and groom. Cries of outrage from the congregation.)

QUINN: Ms. Connors made a statement as the bridal party left the church.

(Dissolve to exterior shot of bride and groom emerging from church, she wearing a mink coat over her gown. Both are ashen. Media swarm around them with microphones.)

MEDIA: Maria Angelica, why didn't you tell the priest about your prior marriage?

MEDIA: Did she tell you about it, John?

MS. CONNORS (*stony-faced but in control*): My only previous marriage was to my late husband, Peter James Connors, God be good to him. We will talk to our attorneys to seek relief from this defamation . . . Now if you'll excuse us we have a wedding dinner to attend.

QUINN: A young woman, presumably from the groom's family who would not give her name, had a different view.

YOUNG WOMAN: She's a whore! Serves Jack Donlan right!

QUINN: So there you have it, Clarice, a controversial wedding becomes a controversial banned wedding. We haven't heard the end of this story. The next scene will probably be in a courtroom.

ANCHORPERSON: A modern Romeo and Juliet in Old Town, Mary Alice?

QUINN: Romeo and Juliet as grandparents, Clarice. Very attractive grandparents.

Channel 3 5:00 News on Sunday Night

ANCHORPERSON: The Catholic church has apparently lifted the ban on the marriage of two high-powered Chicago executives. Our Mary Alice Quinn is at Holy Name Cathedral interviewing Coadjutor Archbishop John B. Ryan.

(Cut to steps of cathedral. Blackie does not look like a coadjutor archbishop. He is wearing black jeans and a Chicago Bears jacket.)

QUINN: That's right, Clarice. Archbishop Ryan has just told me that Sean Cardinal Cronin has administered the sacrament of matrimony to John Donlan and Maria Angelica Connors in a private ceremony in the cathedral. And the cardinal is now having supper with them in the rectory. How can he do that?

BLACKIE (*blinks behind thick glasses*): As we all know, Mary Alice, a cardinal prince of the Catholic church can do just about anything he wants. In this case he determined that there was indeed no evidence to support the claim of a prior marriage. Therefore he apologized to the couple and offered to bless their marriage which the bride and groom administer to one another in a Catholic church. They accepted the offer, if I may say so, with considerable joy.

QUINN: Is that a rebuke to Father Hennessy?

BLACKIE (*sighs loudly*): One could suggest that due diligence in such matters might have led one to determine whether there is or ever was a parish named after St. Lawrence anywhere near Oakdale, Illinois, or whether there was in the last four decades a priest in the Rockford Diocese named Thomas Hartnett. It might have required as much as two minutes to make such a determination.

Channel 3 5:00 News on Monday

ANCHORPERSON: The controversy about the wedding between Chicago tycoons John Donlan and Maria A. Connors continues, as one would expect these days in the courts. Our Mary Alice Quinn has been following the story.

(Cut to Daley Center Plaza.)

QUINN: Clarice, Tony Cuneen, the husband of Evie Donlan, filed a suit this afternoon asking that he be appointed conservator of the trust funds for his wife and her two sisters. The funds which are currently under the control of Donlan Assets Management. He also asked the court's authority to remove all stock in Elegant Homes Inc. from these trust funds.

CUNEEN (*combative and nervous*): My wife and my sisters-in-law are anxious that the trusts which will provide college tuition money for their children not be diverted to purposes which might endanger their solvency. None of us in the family have any idea of how the monies in the three trusts are invested. We would like to have some accountability, especially in view of the current controversies in the family.

EVIE: We don't want that strumpet to have any control over our children's future. We don't want her near any of them. She might be contagious.

QUINN: So, Clarice, the fight gets dirtier. No comments on the suit yet from either Donlan Assets Management or Elegant Homes Inc. Back to you, Clarice.

Channel 3 5:00 News on Tuesday

ANCHORPERSON: Another chapter tonight in the battle of the Donlans and the Connors. Our Mary Alice Quinn is in the offices of Meyer, Meier, Major, and Suarez.

QUINN: Jaime Suarez, who is acting for John Patrick Donlan, made a brief announcement this afternoon.

SUAREZ (*tall and handsome, thick black hair edged with grey*): I'm Jimmy Suarez and am acting today as Mr. John Patrick Donlan's attorney. I feel called upon to make a statement with regard to the suit filed yesterday against Mr. Donlan by his son-in-law. He is, as you might suspect, on his honeymoon and in any case would not want to make any public comment. As to the three trust funds for his daughters. Each of them received certified quarterly statements since reaching their majority which list both the contents of the funds and the gains and losses and provide charts of the net gains since the funds began. If they can find any copies of these reports, they will note that consistently over the last two decades, the trusts have grown at a rate exceeding the Dow. They will also note that there is not and never has been any admixture of the common stock of Elegant Homes Inc. in their trusts. I have sent copies of the quarterly reports for the last four years to Mr. Cuneen's office. But that there may be no confusion in the future, Mr. Donlan has ordered me to hand the trusts over to the appropriate officials at the Chase Bank. We will move tomorrow to quash the suit.

QUINN: What about the mixing of Elegant stock with the trust funds?

SUAREZ (*charming smile*): That will be a matter for Mr. Cuneen to discuss with the trustees at Chase. I should probably say that anyone who has studied Mr. Donlan's methods knows that he has several different investment products, the most famous of which is his Frodo Fund. He shifts investments in and out of that fund with great care. Other securities that he might acquire go into other products. On some occasions he also acquires other securities which he invests in his other products. Some time ago he acquired stock in Elegant Homes for one of his real estate funds. A review of *The Wall Street Journal* pages of the last several months would show ELG, as it is called, has done very well. Whether it will ever be added to the securities in Frodo is an open question. I would add by the way that as someone who was involved in the acquisition of ELG stock I can testify that he made the decision to acquire those securities before he met Ms. Connors.

QUINN: Do you think, Jimmy, that your clients have been defamed?

SUAREZ: In my opinion they certainly have. We have yet to decide whether to seek relief.

— Dermot —

THE COUPLE walking up the stairs to our house on Sheffield Avenue reminded me of Lladro statues—handsome, perfectly shaped, well dressed, flawless. And so fragile that a sweep of my hand might shatter them. A Lexus limo waited for them in front of the house. At the wheel sat Sergeant Gabrielle Lopez, of the Chicago Police Department, in her off-hours with Reliable Security. If Gaby was on the job, then someone thought the couple was in danger. The dark sky glowered at all of us who were stupid enough to be in Chicago after the middle of November.

"Jack Donlan," said the man, poised, urbane, wavy black hair with just a touch of white—an ad for a men's magazine of a decade and a half ago. "My wife, Maria."

"Archbishop Ryan sent us," said the tall, slim woman in a mink coat. "He said you didn't want nobody that nobody sent."

The light of an imp flashed quickly across her face as she repeated the old Chicago political cliché.

"Dermot Coyne," I said shaking hands. "Come in, as my good wife would say, before you catch your death of cold."

It was my good wife they wanted to see, the legendary singer and puzzle solver, and not her loyal and brave spear-carrier.

Earlier as I had entered our master bedroom and discovered herself in red and green lace lingerie in honor of the coming holidays, I gulped as I always do when I see her, especially if she is partially dressed.

"Well, didn't I tell you that they would call us?"

I had been running the dogs and my two older children at the dog park. Even the elderly Fiona had better wind than I did. They had bounded up the stairs to the second-floor entrance and down to the playroom on the ground floor where my niece and our nanny, Ellie, would preside over them and their two smaller siblings.

"Who would call us?" I demanded putting my hand on her bare shoulder.

"Och, Dermot Michael Coyne, give over," she replied, leaning against me. "We have business to do. The lollygagging can come later."

"Promise?"

"If I don't, it doesn't matter, does it?" She returned to arranging her long and formidable black hair in a bun on the top of her head. She was putting on her business mode. "And meself telling you that them poor folks would call us and I not needing any more of me hormones chasing around in me bloodstream."

"What poor folks?"

She smelled of soap and perfume and promise. I didn't remove my hand from her shoulder, but I refrained from attempting further progress. My wife is easy to seduce, but I had grown skilled through our years together at reading the proper times and places.

"Them poor folks that German shitehawk over at St. Freddy's wouldn't let marry and the poor woman so lovely in her blue gown and her gorgeous boobs."

My wife had an Irish woman's fury at injustice, especially when a woman was a victim.

"Jack and Maria Donlan . . . Blackie must have thought it was a case for a fey Irish woman."

"Doesn't your man say I'm the second-best detective in the whole city of Chicago?"

"As I heard him, he said best."

I kissed the back of her neck and slipped away. Her black pants suit was on the hanger. Over a white blouse with silver jewelry, she'd be ready for heavy lifting, an Irish professional woman. Indeed, a veritable Celtic Tiger. The Donlans would find a major ally against their enemies. And poor Dermot would have to find his spear and sally forth to battle.

You knew what you were getting into.

And not a moment's hesitation either.

"And yourself leaving without hooking me bra?"

"I thought you'd never ask."

Me wife and herself looking like an Irish goddess and blue eyes which could skin the flesh off your face if she were angry at you and a voice that hinted at distant bells ringing across the bogs was in high dudgeon these days—indeed stratospheric. The new president of the TV network which had presented her Christmas specials every year—hereinafter known as "that frigging gobshite"—had canceled this year's production and terminated her contract. "Many people," the said gobshite had observed, "think it is not correct to have so much religious music at Christmastime. Such songs ruin the holiday season for those people who have no religious belief and resent having such music imposed on them. Moreover, popular reaction to the series has been slipping over recent years."

This was frigging bullshite, my woman insisted. The ratings were higher than ever last year, indeed higher than all other Christmas specials. He also canceled the concert without consulting Nuala's agent or without negotiating payment for a cancellation fee. Then when another network tried to pick up the performance, he said that as he read the contract, Nuala Anne couldn't perform for anyone else but he didn't have to pay her. She didn't give a friggin' damn about the pay, but she had prepared twelve numbers from six different religions so that *Lullaby and Good Night* would be politically correct.

So the matter went to court. In Chicago, much to the dismay of the media lawyers from Los Angeles.

When my Nuala is in dudgeon, she becomes an Irish Tiger, though we in the family are not targets but audience. We try not to laugh. The Donlans had come at a good time. Her aroused fury would be aimed at their enemies too.

In the parlor I took our guests' coats and hung them in a closet, barely covering my gasp at the sight of Maria's lovely body pressed against a maroon knit dress. Without her mink coat she looked like a timeless Sophia Loren. I must not gape too much when my wife joined us. Her husband was wearing a three-piece black suit of Italian make, no casual for him. Both of them looked like models in a high-class magazine picture of Milanese fashions. Surely they exercised and dieted and went to spas, but their striking beauty was almost certainly genetic luck. I knew enough about human nature that those not so fortunate would envy and resent them, especially Maria. No woman over fifty had any right at all to look that timeless.

My wife, given to running down the stairs when she was in a hurry, descended with regal grace. I introduced her to both of them. She and Maria sized each other up quickly and bonded immediately as women sometimes do.

"Would you ever like a wee drop of something to banish the cold or maybe a small drop of Barolo?"

"There's enough Northern Italian in me," Maria said with another flash of her impish grin, "for that to have some appeal, but I'll settle for a drop of tea . . . black." Jack nodded with a smile, not nearly so exuberant as his wife's smile.

Her dark skin and flashing brown eyes suggested the Levant, wherever the hell that is, probably some place just outside of Palermo.

Stop undressing her before Nuala notices.

"My husband has cured me of the terrible Irish habit of polluting tea with milk! I'll put the kettle on and I'll be right back." She left with the same dignity with which she had descended the stairs, though, knowing her as I did, I was sure she wanted to bound. Left to her own desires, my Nuala Anne bounds rather than walks.

"We've seen her on television of course," Jack Donlan said softly, his normal tone of voice. "But she's even lovelier in person."

"And herself with four kids and a career and a house to manage and a laggard husband to be given instructions!"

"Fey too?" Maria Donlan said, asking a question.

"When she comes back, she'll have slices of Irish bread and jam which she made earlier because she knew you'd ask for tea. She predicts the gender of children even before they are conceived. You get used to such things after a while. Archbishop Ryan calls it a neo-Neanderthal vestige."

A small laugh around the room in honor of Blackie.

"He is a most unusual man."

"A very holy man."

"And a very smart man, according to my brother the priest."

The couple were patently, as Blackie would say, in love. They could not take their eyes off each other. Sitting on our antique couch their hands frequently touched. Somehow this infatuation did not seem inappropriate, even if they were over fifty. Age had nothing to do with it, nor their physical perfection. A man and a woman had every right to fall in love again or for the first time. As a sixty-five-year-old colleague on the Exchange said, "I get on the elevator with her, my legs turn to water, and I forget she's my wife."

Don't pretend you don't know the experience, boyo.

Nuala reappeared with the tea tray, distributed the cups, saucers, and the plates with the soda bread and jam, and placed the cozy on the Galway teapot, all these rituals performed with maximum West of Ireland ceremony.

"We'll let it steep for just a minute longer. We Irish know just how long it takes tea to steep."

She poured it and we all sampled it.

"The soda bread is excellent."

"Thank you, sir, and didn't I make it meself."

"Her mother always says," I added, "that the best Irish bread is made in the house where it's served."

Then, just as we were about to turn the conversation to the reason for their visit, a strange apparition took place. Two large, snow-white animals, bronze age remnants, pushed their way out of the door leading to the ground floor, and without looking at Nuala who had forbidden such intrusions into the parlor, walked to Maria Donlan's feet, sat on their haunches, and raised their right paws.

"Maria Donlan," my wife said, "may I present our two resident doggies, Fiona and Maeve. They are absolutely not supposed to be here, but I presume they know what they're doing."

She lifted an eyebrow in my direction, as though I were somehow responsible for their violation.

The dogs shook hands with their new friend. She hugged them and told them they were wonderful, which of course they knew but were glad to hear again. Thereupon they lay down, definitively in charge, both with their huge muzzles at her feet.

"You'll think I'm crazy, Jack, but I've always wanted one of these creatures."

"No reason why you shouldn't," he said quietly.

"This is all very serious," my good wife said grimly. "Very serious indeed."

"How so?" Jack Donlan asked.

"Fiona, our matriarch here, was a police dog in her youth. She sometimes has an instinct that someone is in danger."

"And you have Reliable Security looking after you? I noticed that one of their operatives was driving your limo."

"Sweet child," Maria said softly.

"And a crack shot," I added.

"We've had some threats. . . ." Jack said, his voice trailing off. "Very serious threats. Filled with hatred . . ."

"I agree with Archbishop Blackie," Nuala said. "There is serious evil at work here."

Then, as if the tension were not already turning creepy, Fiona stirred herself, rose from the floor, and began to howl. Maeve, not to be outdone by her mother, joined in the cry. The hounds of hell were loose.

— Dermot —

I GLANCED out the window. An old Chevy had pulled up in front of our house. Three men in black overcoats and grey fedoras emerged, each of them holding a big club of salami. It looked like a scene from the Capone era, called up from the nineteen twenties by an evil wizard. They strode toward our stairs, undaunted by the howling hounds. But then, someone threw open the door of our house and the great white monsters, howling with rage, emerged and rushed down the stairs followed by a banshee—a woman spirit, also howling and waving a club of her own.

That's my wife. She shouldn't be doing that.

A smaller woman spirit followed, aiming a small camera at the invaders.

That's my daughter. She shouldn't be doing that either.

I punched in Mike Casey's number on my cell phone.

"Casey . . ."

"Mike, tell Gaby to drive the car back around our corner. We have visitors from the nineteen twenties. Tell Culhane to get his people over here too."

I realized that I should play some kind of subsidiary role. I grabbed the snow shovel on the porch and dashed down the two flights of stairs, almost slipping near the top. My personal seraph intervened.

Just as I regained my balance, the invaders scurried back into their car. Their movements were frantic and clumsy. Two of the three fedoras were lost in the rush as well as all the salami clubs. The bad guys made it in the nick of time. They slammed their doors shut just as the white monsters arrived. The woman spirit pounded on the windows of their car with her camogie stick, a weapon used in the woman's version of hurling. Hadn't my wife been all-Ireland when she was in high school?

The weapon smashed the back window of the car just as it began to move. Nuala got a jab at one of the thugs. The hounds circled the car yowling and yipping, snarling and screaming. Nuala called them off, lest the terrified invaders might hit one of them. Obediently they sat next to her and continued to howl.

Some one of these days our neighbors would complain.

I should remonstrate with my wife about taking chances. She would argue that with her doggies and her camogie stick there were no chances involved.

"What are you doing here?" she demanded of her elder daughter.

"Taking pictures of them and their car. I got the license number," our eight-year-old said proudly.

Gaby's Lexus sped around the corner, police siren crying out in dismay.

"The rest of the flying squad is ready for action," I said, pointing up the stairs. The three younger children, commanded by Ellie, stood on the porch, each of them holding some kind of weapon or would-be weapon.

"Nelliecoyne," Nuala said, suddenly sounding very weary, "go upstairs and help Ellie get your brothers and sister back downstairs."

"Yes, Ma!"

"Dermot love, I know what you're thinking. I'm a terrible eejit altogether. . . . Would you ever calm down our guests and tell them that I'm not always that crazy."

"Only when someone attacks your house."

The dogs sniffed at the salami clubs and turned up their noses in disdain. Not their kind of food.

Several squads from the Sixth District arrived on the scene. Their cars are doubtless programmed to come to our block automatically.

Captain Cindasue L. McLeod of the United States Coast Guard materialized from down the street in a USCG sweat suit, her forty-five service revolver, bigger almost than she is, at the ready.

"What in tarnation you uns a doin' down hyar on a quiet Sunday afernoon?"

"Jest, a stirrin' up the shite, Cap'n ma'am."

Our two guests, eyes wide, were watching us as we climbed the steps.

"It's part of our campaign to force the people of the neighborhood to put us under peace bond."

"Anyone want a small splash of the creature? . . . Ellie, would you wet the kettle again?"

"They were going to attack us with those sausages?" Jack Donlan asked.

"Old Capone gambit . . . clumsy . . ."

I poured splasheens for the guests and filled the jar tumbler for my wife and me.

"I'll never eat salami again," his wife murmured. "I see why the archbishop sent us to see you. You have a formidable team."

"Who were those men?" Jack said as he accepted the jar I gave him (a Waterford tumbler, but still a "jar" when the creature is poured into it).

"Lowlife thugs for hire. Very amateurish. Those who are out to make trouble for you are clumsy and stupid. But not undangerous."

My virtuous wife was calm and serene when she came from her conversations with the cops.

"Sorry for the interruption. . . . Please pay attention to the hounds. They are very proud of themselves. . . . Dermot, you have treats?"

I gave her the treats and she rewarded the dogs who were then assigned to the backyard to run off some of their energy. Of course, they expected embraces and praise from our guests.

"You don't have to persuade us, Jack and Maria, that you have enemies out there. Maybe you could tell us something about yourselves and your lives."

— John Patrick —

COMING HOME from my wife's burial at All Saints Cemetery, I realized that an oppressive burden had been lifted. I was choked with painful grief. I had loved her. I had failed her. I would miss her always. Yet I was finally free of her mean miserable family. I could move out of their neighborhood, buy a co-op somewhere along the Gold Coast, one with a swimming pool, and relax into a solitary, almost monastic life. It would be a struggle to keep Faith's grieving family at bay, but I hated them so much that it would be easy. My eldest daughter, Evie, was already married, my second daughter, Irene, was engaged, and my youngest daughter, Mary Fran, was in first year at Loyola Medical School and living out in Forest Park, near the campus. I had protected them as best I could from the family. They would be on their own now. I was getting out.

My in-laws are mean, miserable, overweight drunks. Faith was the only one who was an alcoholic, but her unmarried sisters—Hope and Charity—her mother, Eulalia (aka Lallie), and her father, Guy, and her grandmother Evangeline were all drunks, woozy from drink at the end of the day.

I found myself furious at them once again. Their behavior at the wake and the funeral was one long boozy, hysterical bash in which the principal theme was that I had killed Faith. As expressed by the enormous Evangeline, if I had not persuaded the "poor kid" that she was an alcoholic, she would not have drunk so much and would not have piled up her Lincoln Town Car on Magnolia Street returning from her mother's birthday party while I was away in Washington.

"You never gave a damn about her," Lallie, her mother, screamed at me as she fell on her daughter's body at the funeral home.

Her father, in addition to being an enormous fall-down drunk, was a pious fraud. A huge man, he was a crooked lawyer who interfaced between the more corrupt elements of real estate trade and the local governments. The Feds had questioned him often and the media had labeled him "Mister Fixer." But none of the many United States Attorneys for the Northern District of Illinois had found enough to indict him, much less to persuade him to testify—or wear a wire—against some of his "business associates." Despite his reputation for adroit maneuvering on LaSalle Street, he was without influence in his own family. Like me he simply avoided conflict with his daffy, and half-tuned, women. He had an office somewhere near the county building, but did his business in a string of bars and restaurants in the heart of the Loop, none of them places where he and I might encounter one another and be embarrassed by our inability to find appropriate small talk. For my part I usually hung out at the Chicago Club or the University Club, just off Michigan Avenue. Though he was well known in the parish as a shady operator, as well as a perennial officer in the Holy Name Society, a trusted head usher, and chairman of the parish finance committee. When he lumbered down the aisle with the collection basket, I thought to myself that I wouldn't trust him as far as I could throw him.

My three daughters were loyal to me at the wake and funeral, protecting me as best they could from the family and easing me into the head of the procession into church.

Evie even whispered into my ear as I drove her and Tony, her husband, home from the final explosive night of the wake, "The next time you marry, Dad, choose a different kind of family." Given what subsequently happened that was a strange comment indeed.

"I'm sure I'll never marry again, hon."

Marriage seemed so easy in the early nineteen seventies. One went to Notre Dame to study economics, met young women either there or from St. Mary's across the road or from Barat in Lake Forest, danced with them, fooled around with them (the meaning of which was expanding even then but not nearly so far as it has now), fell in love with them, decided to marry while we were still in graduate school (MBA at Loyola for both of us because it was right around the corner), and settled down for a life of happiness together. Faith was a lovely, affectionate young woman, brimming with energy and enthusiasm. Her family was a little strange, but most families are. At least they knew how to have fun, which is more than I could say for my own careful, responsible parents.

Neither of my parents drank. They were both only children born late in the lives of their own parents. I had no experience of drunks when I was growing up save at teenage beer bashes. I was not sensitive to the signals that a person had moved from jollity to intoxication. I did not realize that Faith's parents and grandparents as well as her older sisters were "tuned" at the end of almost every day. They were, after all, capable of getting up the next morning and going off to work in their offices in the city or county bureaucracy. Faith hardly drank at all when we were dating and then courting during our last years at Notre Dame and Barat. Yet she became an alcoholic and they were merely lushes. I could have protected her from her fate. I should have protected her. Ignorance is not an excuse. Or maybe it is. I don't know. She seemed a cheerful, charming, and pretty young woman. Her family were all vulgar. She was not and I was marrying her, not them. We didn't have to live with them.

Again in my ignorance and inexperience I didn't know that very few young people are able to exclude their families from their lives.

Nor did I have any knowledge about what we would later call postpartum depression and what it can do to a woman's body and soul, especially if a woman has three children and an interlude of PPD—postpartum depression—after each birth. I didn't realize that the other women in her family would close in on her like a swarm of worker bees around an ill queen and exclude me as for all practical purposes a drone. Nor did I understand that they would try to "cheer her up" with a steady diet of booze.

Finally I didn't understand how different women are from men. I still can't claim any comprehension of that matter. One autumn evening while my daughters and I were having supper at an Italian restaurant on Walton Street after we had witnessed a disastrous defeat of Notre Dame by Michigan I tentatively raised the question. "Daddy," one of them said, "how can you be so totally chauvinist? Women and men are basically the same. The argument that we are different is just an excuse for patriarchy."

"When it comes to enjoying sex, there is no difference between us and guys. We both want all we can get."

Mary Fran, who usually avoids arguments with her sisters, blew up. "You guys are full of shit. That stuff is just hardcore feminist propaganda. In our profession we know that men and women have endocrine systems that are radically different. Men don't go into postpartum depression after a baby is born."

The argument turned into an attack on Mary Fran because it was alleged that all doctors, even women doctors, were ideological chauvinists. Mary Fran won easily because she had the facts. She explained why the hormone oxytocin made young women easy targets for predatory males.

I phoned her the next day and asked about postpartum depression. She explained it clearly and concisely. I was silent.

"Mom have it?" she asked softly.

"Three times."

"Dear God! The poor woman! . . . Is that why . . . ?"

"She became an alcoholic? Her family tried to cheer her up with booze. It seemed to work. . . . Perhaps I should have stopped them."

"No way, Daddy, no way. Stop blaming yourself."

"This oxytocin stuff . . ."

"I call it the crush hormone. Gets activated when we form a crush on someone and reinforces the crush. It's a bonding chemical in most vertebrates. Generates desire and trust, sometimes dangerous."

"Disappears after marriage?"

"Stimulates mother's milk too, ingenious and untrustworthy. Probably helps in renewal of married love in humans, like you and Mom often did."

If Faith's family had only left her alone. . . .

"I knew so little then. . . ."

"Nobody knows anything much when they're young."

Mary Fran wanted to be a psychiatrist and apparently was already working on it.

"I'm surprised that you noticed."

"I was probably the only one that did. . . . Daddy, stop blaming yourself. They were determined to get her. She was the only one of the three that was beautiful. The other two put on weight to take them out of the mating game. Mom broke the rules, she broke ranks, she didn't care what she was doing to her older sisters, damn them all."

"That's too simple, hon."

My daughter was not a certified psychiatrist yet. She shouldn't even be thinking such thoughts about her family.

"Sometimes, Daddy, reality is simple, tragically simple. . . . You're not getting any oxytocin jolts are you?"

"I'm too old for a crush, Mary Fran."

"No one is ever too old to fall in love."

I went back to a report from one of my researchers on a new stock. They thought it might be a good bet. Oxytocin would surely distract me from making investment decisions for my clients. I did not want to fall in love again. It was too dangerous. Marriage was dangerous too. I'm good at calculating odds and hence a good gambler and a good asset manager (as we call investment managers these days—I would not even consider the title "wealth manager"). I was not going to gamble on marriage again. I would go through life alone from now on. That would mean a certain amount of loneliness and also a freedom from the problem of sharing my life intimately again with a woman. Even in the best possible circumstances that was a risky business. One had to negotiate personal differences, learn to read the other's mind (not what she said, but what she meant), strive to be sensitive to her moods, read the complexities of her sexual needs, and the anxieties and fears which plague her life. Then if one had been modestly successful at acquiring these intricate skills, one could still fail miserably at the crucial times in her life.

There was no reason in the world to think I would not fail miserably again. I had made my contribution to the continuation of the species. I had fallen into the tender trap once. I need not do it again.

There were costs to this monastic style, especially loneliness at the end of the day when there was no one to talk to. Maybe I should be a monk. Or join the Jesuits . . . I'd be eighty before they ordained me. . . .

Nor could I pretend that I was so disillusioned with marriage that I did not find women attractive. That was the wound that might be original sin. With all my wisdom and all my determination, I would have to maintain an iron discipline against their appeal, especially because my money and power might make me attractive to them.

Faith and I began to work immediately after our honeymoon, which was fun, but somehow disappointing. Neither of us knew much about sex, to say nothing of marital sex; nobody does, it turned out. I went to work for my father, who had just changed from an investment broker to an investment adviser.

"Whatever we call it, Jackie, it's the same game. We bet and our clients bet with us that over the years we will keep their profits anywhere between five and ten percent over the Dow."

"And their losses," I said.

He laughed that quiet little laugh that meant I had made the point.

"We won't talk about those, Jackie, no gambler does. But there's not going to be another Great Depression, not for a long time."

Dad was an interesting man. His own father had been a Pullman conductor on the Chicago-to-New Orleans line. Dad had been born in 1914 and went to St. Ignatius College as it was called in those days to study accounting. He began to work as a messenger on the Chicago Board of Trade when he was eighteen, in the depths of the Depression. He joined the Army on December 8, 1941, and rose to the rank of lieutenant colonel. He never talked about the war or explained why he had won the Distinguished Service Cross at Bastogne during the Battle of the Bulge, the last desperate charge of the German army in about the same place that the Kaiser's army had launched its final attack in 1918.

He came back to Chicago with his secrets and the money he had made in poker games and opened his broker's office in the old Conway building across the street from what is now the Daley Plaza. He never bothered to get a seat on any of the exchanges but would call his orders into brokers on the floor.

"You didn't have to be very smart in those days to know that all the money people made during the war would flood into the economy like a levee break in the Ole Miss."

A lot of returning GIs, having money to invest for the first time in their lives, heard rumors about the brilliant poker player colonel. He made a lot of money for them and for himself.

He also went to night school at Loyola up at Lewis Towers and got himself an AB in accounting and then a law degree.

"When you have enough money you can buy your own lawyer, Jackie," he told me. "Until then a man has to do it himself."

Did I seduce Faith or did she seduce me? We used to argue about that and laugh at the rituals of the springtime of love. Those were sweet times, nonetheless. Almost thirty years of marriage. If we had another thirty years . . . Even twenty . . . Even ten . . . We might have made something out of it.

But that was nonsense.

I was adjusting to being alone. Indeed I had been alone much of the time when she was still alive. Lust would diminish through the years, would it not? I compared my own marriage with my father's. In 1950, when the war in Korea had just begun, he married an Army nurse whom he'd met in Germany after the war. I would learn later that they had written daily letters to one another for six years. I was born three years later, right in the middle of the Baby Boom, the only child they were able to have. They were quiet, gentle people. In their own undemonstrative way they were deeply in love with one another and that love spilled over to absorb me. Nothing in our big house on Balmoral Street prepared me for the conflicts and the agonies and the failures of my own marriage. I presume they had to adjust to each other as every husband and wife must, though maybe not. For them simple goodness and affection might have been enough. Were they just lucky? Or did they learn somewhere wisdom that I had never acquired?

While I was finishing my MBA, I worked in my father's office, studying companies in what we would now call research. He nodded in appreciation at my summaries. "You have the green thumb, Jackie. Good instincts. Beware of them. They'll usually be right, but when they turn wrong, you can get yourself into real trouble. Never trust an instinct completely."

I didn't know what he meant then. Now I do.

My parents met her family only at the rehearsal dinner at the Lakeshore Athletic Club. They were too polite to say anything, but I could tell by their eyes that they were horrified.

"Faith doesn't drink at all," I said.

"And she is not in the least vulgar," my mom said.

They lived long enough to know and adore all three of their grandchildren. They never left our neighborhood for Florida and did not buy a summer home in the Dunes, much less Door County, like many of our neighbors.

"We're a half a block from the Lake," my father explained to their friends, "and we have all our books and records here in the house."

He drove a Chevy all his life and rode the Howard Street L down to his LaSalle Street office every morning. I was pretty much in charge of the office when Mary Fran—my mother's name—was born. (My in-laws were furious at the choice and whispered loudly about their displeasure.) Dad would read the papers, glance at the ticker (which he called the screen), mutter a few suggestions, and then ride back home to spend the day with Mom, maybe to go to the "movies."

"Old gambler knows when to back down," he said with a laugh. "Let the young gunslingers take the chances."

He died in 1986 of a stroke. Mom died five months later of a heart attack. They died as they lived, quietly, gracefully.

I was on my own with three daughters and an alcoholic wife who had been fired by Lilly, Smith because of her drinking. Her increasingly eccentric sisters blamed me. If I had not forced her to work and if I had left her alone (by which they meant not slept with her) she would never have become a heavy drinker.

When she began to work Faith was hired at a much larger brokerage—Lilly, Smith—doing the same thing I was doing.

"They're pretty high over there on your young woman," Dad said to me one day. "They tell me she's as bright as they come and they generally don't like women around their shop."

It was the middle nineteen seventies, however, and even a stuffed shirt firm like Lilly, Smith had to hire some women. When she told them that she was pregnant, they took counsel with one another and decided to tell her that they wanted her back after the baby was born. I was proud of her but uneasy. Yet she was one of the generation of young women who believed they could have everything and I had enough sense not to argue against her choice. I would have lost anyway.

Faith's first pregnancy was a nightmare, sickness almost every day. Childbirth was long and agonizing, then depression and a long struggle back to health afterward. Her family blamed me for making her go back to work, though I had done my best to talk her out of it. I wanted to move out to a suburb like Hubbard Woods or even River Forest to escape from them, but she argued that she had to live near them to prevent them from killing themselves.

"I'm the only sane one in the family," she insisted. "I can take care of them and watch poor little Evie at the same time."

"And hold down a job too?"

"I'm supermom," she laughed. "I can do anything."

In principle she could have done a lot of things easily, but the PPD, as we would call it now, came back after her next two pregnancies. She wanted a son the worst way. Her doctors were skeptical, but she insisted.

"God is playing tricks on me," she insisted. "I have to produce a son. I grew up in a house with two sisters and it was hell on earth. Women are mean to one another."

She began to drink heavily during the depression after Irene's birth. Stubbornly she went back to work before she felt better. They fired her after the first month.

"She needs help," the senior partner at Lilly, Smith confided to me in the pompous tones which are essential to a man in his position. "A long vacation, a good therapist, and maybe some AA."

She did go to a psychiatrist and we did take a vacation. She came back from the Caymans pregnant with Mary Fran. Same scenario—depression and alcohol. She fired her therapist, quit AA, and sank into an emotional swamp. I persuaded her to try a mental hospital in Evanston where they helped women out of such messes which were not their own fault, as I put it. Invariably she followed my advice, indeed enthusiastically, and praised my patience and kindness. I was such a wonderful man. She didn't deserve a husband like me.

Her family turned to obscene phone calls when they found out that I had barred them from visiting her. Looking back on those days in the early eighties when the Reagan Revolution was transforming American life and repudiating us Boomers and we ourselves were buying the gospel of greed, I realized that the country was in revolt against the intensity of the sixties radicals. It was also turning to a vision of human life which preached that happiness came from wealth and possessions. My daughters laughed at all the funny clothes and the stupid demonstrations of my era (even though I never wore funky garments or protested against anything). But their laughs were affectionate. They were convinced that their mother and I were "cool." And were on their side. Their bonding with Faith was intense and inviolable. They were the ones who talked me into suggesting the Betty Ford Center.

Why not?

By then she had slipped into what the doctors had been calling a "manic depressive syndrome" and later be called "a bipolar disorder." She spent six months at Betty Ford. I would leave my office at noon on Friday and fly to California to visit her and return on the Sunday night red-eye. I did my best to be both mom and dad to the kids and they tolerated that, but none of us fooled ourselves, I was no mom, at least not a mom like their mom. But I was still "cute" and "cool" and sometimes even "adorable."

She came home a "new woman" as she proclaimed herself. She went to AA every week and begged me to permit her to revive her old work skills. She also went to all the kids' activities at Sacred Heart parish.

"You don't have to hire me," she explained. "I'll just sit in my office here at home and explore companies for you."

"Fine," I said. It seemed like a good idea. She soon proved herself as good a researcher as her bosses at Lilly, Smith claimed she was. It was the era of the dot-com bubble and a legion of madcap start-ups. Faith thought it was all nonsense.

"A lot of people are going to get hurt," she said, "and you and your friend Frodo are not going to be among them."

By that time Frodo had achieved a certain fame, which my father's son that I was, I did not like. I told myself that I would not believe the good things *The Wall Street Journal* said about me. However, I rented the office next to mine in the Conway building, fixed up the two offices so they looked mildly prosperous, and hired a couple of assistants.

Faith prospered at her desk, recommending several new stocks for my increasing variety of products. She went home early in the afternoon to be with the kids, though her family leaned on her the way they could that she should be home with them all the time, just as their mother had. By definition, any idea I had for my wife was wrong. However, those months when we shared both home and office were the happiest time in my life.

The Frodo Managed Fund (FMF) was my pride and joy; some of the stocks in it I had inherited from my father, so Frodo spanned the generations. It became a legend in wealth management. Some years it ran a full ten percent above the Dow. It was of course an instrument in gambling. My investors bet that they could trust me to deliver a presentable profit every year. And I bet that my instinct and sense of the markets could achieve that goal. The riverboat gambler in me loved the contest and the instincts, both of which I had inherited from my father. If the instincts started to fade I could go into the business of being a floating corporate trustee, not that I didn't have some personal money protected in the safest of safe havens.

The so called "dot-com bubble" was a merry time for us three-piece-suit bettors. I sensed it was a bubble and protected my friend Frodo from most of the trolls lurking in the bushes and the alleys. When the bubble burst my clients and I felt that we had been kicked in the stomach by an NFL field goal kicker. But, because I had taken a good hard look at the cards, we survived and bounced back quickly.

Unfortunately for Faith the bottom fell out of one of the stocks she had persuaded me to take on. It was the only truly devastating loss for Frodo, my fault rather than hers. I had very little doubt about it when I decided that Internet food markets would certainly prosper. Dumb! I told Faith not to worry about it. She had warned me of some of the possible downsides of the stock. The buck at Donlan Assets stopped at my desk. I never blamed a researcher who sold me a lemon.

My reassurance was not enough for poor Faith. She had to blame herself. When I arrived home (riding the L as my father had) I found the three daughters crying in the parlor. Mommy was sick in the bedroom and grandma was taking care of her.

"Well, I hope you're proud of yourself," Lallie shouted at me. "Look what you've done to her."

I ordered Lallie to leave the house immediately and never come back again. She called the wrath of God down on me as I forced her out the door. My daughters swarmed around me and hugged me.

"She's a terrible woman," Evelyn informed me. "Thank God you came home."

"Any time she tries to get in here when I'm not around, call me at the office. . . . Also if Mommy comes home sick again."

They solemnly promised.

She went to an AA meeting the next night but it didn't help much. I told her the job would always be waiting for her at my office. She replied with a bitter self-hating laugh. A week later she whispered to me one night, "I think I'd better try Betty Ford again." This time the effect of that splendid institution lasted only a couple of months.

I tried to persuade her to help me set up a new Nasdaq fund (I called it DOT), which was for the high rollers among my clients, including myself. Faith had read *The Wall Street Journal* every day at the Betty Ford. I never consciously gambled for high stakes with clients' money unless they wanted me to. But I had no scruples about gambling with my own. In truth I was much more of a high roller than my father would have tolerated.

So I made a bundle for all us high rollers with DOT, including Faith, for whom I put a bundle in our joint investments. "We'll make a killing on it," she said to me confidently and she was right. We went to Ambria in the Belden-Stratford Hotel on New Year's Eve to celebrate that we had made enough money to pay for the college education of our kids. She refused to appear again in the office, but continued to provide me with first-rate research. Our interludes of happiness lasted longer, but they were never permanent. The final one ended when she attended her mother's birthday while I was in D.C. I felt certain that they invited her to the party just so they could prove to her once again that she was not an alcoholic.

The light went out of my life. She was a lovely, brilliant woman and good bed partner. I would miss her forever. As I have said, I was glad to be rid of her family, but I would have gladly put up with them and with her problems, if only she had survived.

I was paralyzed by grief and guilt for the year after her death. Her daughters insisted that it was not my fault.

Two years later, firm in my informal vow of celibacy, I was looking over the research on Elegant Homes, feeling very dubious about a start-up corporation from Oakdale, Illinois, formed by a woman real estate person. The prospectus looked good, however, and Jim Leavy, my most brilliant research guru, suggested we ought to think it over for DOT. I do three sessions with my staff about each research suggestion. Then I do one thought session by myself in which for the first time I look over all the papers.

Joe McMahon, my research director who keeps his eye on start-up stories, brought the project to me from a lawyer in Rockford. While I trust Joe's good sense, Rockford is downstate—which is to say any part of Illinois beyond Cook, Lake, and DuPage counties. Rockford is in fact north of Chicago but it still is downstate and good Chicago Democrat that I am I don't trust downstate. I had never heard of Oakdale and have rarely been west of the DesPlaines River. The ELG project had a lot going against it, i.e. Rockford, downstate, luxury homes, a real estate woman, all of which raised warning flags.

Joe is a rotund little leprechaun of a man who went to work for my father fresh out of high school. He is an absolute genius at separating good buys from bad buys and is a pleasant if eager man with whom to work. He cannot make decisions or even recommendations. My father paid him well for a man who had not attended college (just as he had not), but not what he is worth. When I took over I gave him a big raise to what he was worth and continued raises and bonuses through the years. He always seemed grateful but hardly surprised. He's in his middle seventies and may or may not want to retire. I know nothing of his personal life, but he has two sons about my age, both of them MDs of whom he is very proud. His wife died (of cancer) I think ten years ago. I was surprised when I went to the wake and funeral in Bridgeport by the crowd and the grief. She must have been a remarkable woman. I regret that I never met her. Somehow I had gained the impression that he did not want me to meet her. As far as I can tell he is very devoted to me.

The proposal was that instead of the firm going to a bank to float the IPO, DAM would undertake to acquire a large block of stock at the IPO asking price. Since the stock would presumably shoot up in the first week, we would make a tidy sum of money. The company would be protected from underwriters' fees. And everyone would be happy.

It is not the sort of venture that I would normally make. The bubble of the late nineties became a bubble precisely because too many people engaged in such crapshoots. ELG properly belonged in a hedge fund in which the truly high rollers played with chips worth millions of dollars. I don't do hedge funds because there is too much money involved, too much uncertainty, and too many ruthless investors. Joe McMahon has been pushing me for years to edge in that direction. Each time I decline with thanks.

I wouldn't let ELG within a light-year of Frodo. The loyal fans of Frodo would think I had lost my mind. Jim argued that because much of the strength of the concept of designing boutique homes was dependent on specialized software that enabled clients to design splendid homes online before a single spade of dirt was displaced, it might well belong in the DOT fund, which I had renamed Samwise. Besides there were so many odd stocks in Samwise the customers wouldn't notice one more madcap toss of the dice.

I didn't like the proposal, however. Real estate markets are notoriously volatile. The data from ELG made a persuasive case that luxury and quasi-luxury markets were more stable. People with lots of money or moderate amounts of money consistently bought special homes. ELG's contribution to this market so far had been to provide a range of choices in such homes that would be environment-friendly, attractive to men and women of good taste, and easy on the purchasers' time. ELG was not for those who wanted to spend most of their time for a year or more agonizing over the details. Rather it was for those who were in a hurry but wanted a home that would have their own imprint on it and confirm the discrimination of their owners. Moreover because ELG had market power in the areas where it had offices, they could virtually guarantee that builders would finish their work on time. In an afternoon or two you could design your house and decorate it on a computer, make your down payment, and move in a year later.

An appealing idea perhaps for those in a hurry, but also a comment on our speed-crazy culture. So too, however, to be fair, were asset management services like mine. Yet could any good come out of Oakdale, a suburb of Rockford out in the prairies? Moreover it was a start-up created by a woman real estate agent, albeit one with a good technical team. The prospectus was well done and had cleared my technical team. I couldn't base my decision on my residual sexism, could I?

I turned over the last paper in the file. The woman stared up at me—Maria Angelica Sabattini Connors. I gulped. It was a color photo cover of a magazine called *Chicago Markets* that did puff pieces on local entrepreneurs. Ms. Sabattini was unquestionably beautiful—dark skin that suggested the Mediterranean, perhaps Lebanon or North Africa, brown, smoldering, and intelligent eyes, a hint of a smile which implied mystery and perhaps romance, and a delicately carved face that could haunt a man for the rest of his life, especially if loneliness made him susceptible to haunting by such a one.

I sighed and turned the magazine over. It would be most unwise of a man in my situation to become involved even in a business relationship with one like that. I was overcome by the temptation to read the article.

Nonetheless I had to know more about her. There was little in the article to support my romantic fantasies—how could there be romance in Oakdale? The youngest daughter of an Italian immigrant from Tuscany and an Irish American GI who worked as a mechanic at a garage in Oakdale. Homecoming queen at Oakdale High School, Miss Kishwaukee County, a year at Northern Illinois University, married high school star quarterback who had attended Notre Dame. Like any Catholic kid in

Chicago I knew the names of all the Notre Dame quarterbacks for the last two generations. Peter Connors wasn't one of them. Rabbit in an Updike novel?

Went to work for the Connors family real estate and development company at nineteen. Mother of two daughters and two sons. Named president of firm when she was thirty. Won a national award for a high-scale development along the Rock River. Involved in civic and artistic activity in Oakdale; led committee which rejuvenated the town. She and her husband inherited the firm, renamed it Elegant Homes. Has been refining the concept for years and expanding it beyond Illinois. May go public soon with a listing in Standard and Poors. Vivacious, charming, witty. Rebounded from her husband's death three years ago with the usual clichés about how much she missed him. After her children were raised went back to school in computer science at NIU. Earned a master's degree. Has designed much of the software for the new Elegant.

A lot of shallow stuff about the firm, covering some of the material that was in my file.

And pictures. Maria Angelica as a sumptuous Miss Kishwaukee County. Maria Angelica with her four kids. A still sumptuous Maria Angelica at a benefit ball in Chicago in a black gown that showed just enough to be provocative and not enough to be immodest. Did she look fragile in that picture? I glanced again at the cover. Yes, there was a hint of vulnerability, or at least my brain, now perturbed by racing hormones, thought so.

I threw the magazine in my wastebasket and closed the file. Then I realized that my secretary, Elfrida, would check to make sure that I had looked at it. Better not to give that woman any hint of my reaction. I retrieved the *Chicago Markets* issue, placed it in its proper place at the end of the file, and put it in my out-box.

I had to leave in ten minutes for my weekly tennis match at the Racket Club. Still I sat motionless at my desk, thoroughly ashamed of my adolescent reactions to the woman. My reactions, however, remained the same. Was I so hungry for womanly flesh that innocent pictures could fill my imagination with a stew of lubricious fantasies? No way could I enter into a business relationship with that woman. My team had set up a meeting to discuss our purchase of their stock for Samwise. I would cancel the meeting.

For a couple of decades four of us Loyola grads had played tennis every Thursday—two matches of two sets each. We purported to be equally skilled. In fact, over the long haul, I had won more matches than anyone else, though I was the only one who counted, and that secretly. My competitiveness in the assets management game marked, perhaps blighted, my whole life. The day I had fixated on Maria Angelica Sabattini my need to win, now driven by my male hormones, was fearsome. My friends suggested that I was about to make a "killing" in the market.

After our showers, I went into the dining room for a salad and a glass of iced tea with Lou Garner, a financial adviser on the North Shore. Neither the cold water nor the frugal meal calmed me down.

Lou, moderately successful in a tough market, was an incorrigible gossip. He kept up with all the rumors in the financial services world, especially the scandalous ones.

"Are you really going to hop into bed with Maria Connors?" He demanded.

"I gave up that behavior when my wife died," I said primly.

He was unembarrassed.

"Didn't mean it literally but with her it usually comes to the same thing. She sleeps with anybody that can promote her career and then dumps them when she's got what she wants out of them."

"That's her reputation?"

"Everyone knows it's true. . . . Hey, one year at DeKalb and the daughter of Sicilian immigrants and from Oakdale? Gimme a break. . . . She's really vicious, but so far it's worked."

"One would think the reputation would catch up with her."

"It will eventually, I suppose. . . . But stay away from her."

"I am forewarned."

My team does excellent due diligence work. They do not screen, however, for Jezebels.

Back in my office I phoned Mike Casey, a former police commissioner.

"We're involved with a project that would imply a relationship with one Maria Sabattini Connors from Oakdale, Illinois, a firm called Elegant

Homes Incorporated. We would in effect be taking a long position on her firm. Would you be able to run a screen on her . . . ?"

"Reputation, trouble with the Feds, record, that sort of thing?"

"Yes . . . She has a reputation of being promiscuous in her business dealings. I mean that in the strict sense of the word."

"That you don't need. . . . I'll be back to you in a couple of days."

I was relieved. I could tell my staff, all very eager on a project they thought was right down our alley, certain confidential matters had arisen that made our taking a position in ELG inappropriate at the present time. They would not press me on the point.

Mike Casey called me back on the following Tuesday.

"The woman is a chaste and modest matron, Jackie. There are rumors in the financial services community in Chicago, based on envy. But out in Oakdale, a place everyone knows everything about everybody and they don't particularly like beautiful and successful Sicilians, they'll tolerate no criticism of her. The sheriff out there in Kishwaukee County, a shrewd old bird, told me Chicagoans had dirty minds. Which may be true. 'Chaste and modest matron' are his words."

I thanked him and went into another fantasy tailspin. A chaste matron was even more of a potential delight than a woman out of an Eric Ambler novel.

"Eric Ambler" dated me.

Nothing would happen at our meeting or at any other event as we added her to Samwise. I would certainly decline to accept a position on her board of trustees.

— Maria Angelica —

I DRESSED very carefully for my meeting with John Patrick Donlan—competent, professional businesswoman—somber grey dress, loosely fitting, longish skirt, one turquoise pin, hair severely combed back, hardly visible makeup. My due diligence had revealed that Jack Donlan was generally thought to be a "gentleman," not known for hitting on women. However, widowers in their early fifties are often a problem, especially for a widow in the same age range. I have had enough experience with men hitting on me to cope with them, though it's always distasteful—an occupational hazard for a woman who is thought to be attractive.

There had been one love in my life, my high school sweetheart and husband, God be good to him. The sex in that relationship left a lot to be desired because poor Peter Connors knew very little about women. However, I had learned that most men know very little about women. Real orgasms, as opposed to fake ones, are few and far between. It doesn't take very many to produce four kids. As our marriage went on, sex became unimportant, for me because it wasn't much fun and for Pete because it required too much of him as had everything else in life.

I was very frank about sex with my sons while they were growing up, about how a man should love a woman. They were surprised and grateful. Peter Junior told me how important my lecture was in their marriage. Vicki, his wife, told me in an awed whisper that my son was a great lover. That made me very proud.

I don't recommend the celibate life to anyone, except a priest or a nun. I tell the latter that they don't know how lucky they are. They laugh at me. Uneasily.

My husband was a loser. Is it possible to love a loser? Not to pity him, but actually to love him?

I fell in love with Peter in a high school crush on a hero. I learned early on that he was not much of a hero. He threw the passes that brought the championship to Oakdale. But he was terrified before every game that he might blow it. In fact, he went through high school and all his life afraid of personal failure—as well he might have been. His father, Michael Reed Connors, was a great bear of a man, all-American tackle at Notre Dame. He didn't like me at first because I was a Sicilian but he came through the years to respect me and be grateful for my love and care of Peter. His mother, Violet Egan, was a nervous timid little woman who had, I'm afraid, shaped Peter's soul. She resented me all her life because I cared for that soul much more skillfully than she could.

Peter needed to be cosseted, propped up, sustained. I knew that the summer before he went to Notre Dame with expectations that he would be another Paul Horning or Angelo Bertelli. I hoped and prayed that he live up to his own skills. It would have eased his path through life. Alas for all of us, that goal, while within his athletic skills, was not within his personality skills. He never stopped being homesick. "I don't like it here," he said to me often on the phone. He couldn't face personal conversation with me or write letters. Everything was on the phone.

Against my parents' wishes, I had enrolled at NIU as a day student, riding back and forth on a bus. I did well enough my first semester to earn a scholarship, which didn't make them happy. I should be earning money for the education of the rest of the family—that is, the boys in the family.

The spring football practice at the Dome (as my kids call it) was a disaster. Peter was cut from the team. He came home a broken man.

NIU signed him up. He was second string during his sophomore year and did pretty well. We dated often. Peter was proud of me and the reaction of his athlete friends who were not bad guys. Old Michael Reed Connors was smart enough to comprehend that I was responsible for his son's improvement.

"I used to think you were the problem with him, Maria," he said in a tone which for him would pass for gentle. "Now I see you are his only hope."

I thanked him.

I began to work in their real estate office after school and bought a car with which I could commute over to DeKalb. Mike, as I now called him, was proud of me.

I also was making enough money to pay for my brothers' education. Still I didn't please my parents and understood that I never would. They had not wanted a daughter people thought was beautiful. That was not good for a young woman.

Peter tore cartilage in his knee during a game in which he threw five touchdown passes for the Huskies, a record which still stands. It was a career-ending injury. The coach lamented the loss of such a promising player. I realized that Pete's career ended in the nick of time.

We were married in the parish church the following autumn by the bishop of Rockford. It was a big wedding with a huge reception at the country club for which I paid with money that Big Mike had slipped to me. My parents were embarrassed by the whole event. We went to Europe for two weeks on our honeymoon and then on return we both went to work for the firm.

Sex between us was not much, though we managed to produce four adorable kids, two boys, two girls. They tell me that on balance I was not a bad mom—always with wicked grins, which have become their trademark when dealing with me. We sent them to the Catholic school in Oakdale and Oakdale High, then on to what they now call the Dome. I was never much of a Catholic and they are Catholic fanatics in a laid-back, comic way. The oldest three are involved in the ACE program from

Notre Dame in which they teach in Catholic schools in impoverished neighborhoods after graduation and Clara, the youngest, intends to go the same route. I've become a much better Catholic because of them.

My husband had little aptitude for the family business. Big Mike made him president of the firm and me the vice president—inside and outside persons. He would sit in the front office of our storefront and chat with those who would drop by, take customers or influential folk or cronies to lunch at the country club, pick up all the local gossip which might affect our business, maybe even scare up some rich customers. I would do all the work and create our new ideas. I never resented this division of labor. Both roles were important. I liked running things and he liked talking. He never pretended that he was in charge and on the contrary praised me to his buddies as a genius at our game.

Oakdale had been a camp for Chief Black Hawk on the Kishwaukee River when Illinois troops, including young Abe Lincoln, were driving the Fox and Saux out of their Illinois homeland. Then it became a trail post on the road between Chicago and Rock Island, and later a station on the Rock Island Railroad and a commercial center for the surrounding farms, prospering as the farms prospered and suffering when the farms suffered. When the Rock Island ended its passenger service after the Second War, the town went into eclipse, the parks declined, and the storefronts on Chicago Avenue, as we called our main street, turned shabby and almost derelict. Donlan Development was a happy exception.

My premise through the years was that Oakdale, even almost halfway across the state, was a satellite of Chicago, only an hour by expressway from the Oak Brook complex and maybe an hour and ten minutes at the most from O'Hare. Our future lay in being a desirable exurb, "boonie," for Chicago. So we developed a plan for sprucing up downtown and building high-quality homes in the empty spaces and elegant developments outside of town along the Rock and Kishwaukee rivers. There was some opposition from the local establishment, which had never quite adjusted to the end of the Great Depression. Big Mike won them over—after I won him over, which was easy because he approved of me. We had Chicago Avenue declared a historic district and pried loose some state money to refurbish it. We built a four-star hotel downtown with an inside/outside pool and a courtesy link to O'Hare—a quiet rural Illinois setting, we alleged, for weary travelers. We opened two excellent restaurants, one in the old railroad station, and persuaded the country club to permit visitors to play golf for an appropriately exorbitant fee. My husband organized a campaign to improve the course and we made a large contribution to the fund. I became president of Oakdale Civic Association and a member of the revived Kishwaukee County Democratic Organization. There were nice articles in the travel magazines and in one airline magazine. I loved the image of travelers reading it as they circled over O'Hare.

Urged on by my zealous Catholic children I also became chair of the St. Cyril's financial council, which approved an expansion to the Catholic school which I had never attended.

My brothers, Jimmie and Paulie, were a problem. They had founded a construction company which might have done a lot of work for us. Unfortunately their bids were sloppy and unreliable and their work was often shoddy. My parents were furious at me because I wasn't willing to "help your brothers out." I had sold out, they shouted, to old man Connors.

"I'll be eager to help them," I replied curtly, "when they submit proper bids and do professional work."

"You're not loyal."

"And this is not Sicily."

Actually we were not Sicilians. But we were very poor Tuscan dirt farmers, which may be almost the same thing, though my mother and sister and I looked like aristocrats born on the wrong side of the bed.

Instead they built a new riverboat gambling complex outside of Rockford with ties to the Chicago outfit. My brothers, overweight bodies stuffed into expensive Italian suits, seemed to fit right in. Then the Chicago mob made them an offer they couldn't refuse. They would continue to manage the casino and take a percentage from the profits, but the "boys" owned it.

My sister, Gina, moved to Chicago, got a job as a nurse at Northwestern, and married a rich doctor. We drifted apart, though the last couple of years after I had opened an office in Chicago, we'd have lunch occasionally and became if not quite friends, at least pleasant siblings.

"I don't want either of those guys in the store," I told my husband and father-in-law, "and I don't want either of you to associate with them at the club. They're bad news. We're Caesar's wife."

They didn't argue. They never argued with me when I laid down the law, which I did rarely. I also told my kids to stay away from their cousins.

"Get real, Moms," my elder daughter, Marissa, admonished me with the required crooked grin. "We're Florentines, not Sicilians."

"Sienese," I insisted.

"Whatever!"

The idea for Elegant Homes slowly developed through the years—designer homes that you could create for yourself with our software. It caught on quickly. My instinct seemed correct that some of the newly affluent Boomers would want their own tasteful and environment-friendly home that they designed and furnished themselves on the Net. We provided the alternatives and the builders and the decorators, who dared not be tardy or go over estimates.

"You gotta go ahead with this," Big Mike insisted. "It will make a lot of money and a lot of people happy."

"Fersure," my husband agreed.

I noticed that I didn't age much through the years. I had managed to slide through menopause rather easily. My children told me that I embarrassed them by being a "dish."

"I can drink three malts every day if you want."

"Won't do any good," Clara replied. "It's in your genes, like your mother. Only you're not a wicked witch."

My husband got along fine with the kids. They figured he was another kid like themselves. They were not far from wrong.

He deteriorated slowly through the decades, so slowly that I would notice only when I'd recall the difference between birthdays. A hint that his world was disintegrating came five years ago when he withdrew from the annual country club golf tournament, which he had won twice when he was in his twenties.

"Just too tired," he sighed. "Mar, you go out and defend the family honor."

I had never played in the tournament because I did not want to humiliate him. It was silly because he knew how good I had become while I was working on the golf course modernization. I've won it twice since then, but only after he had died.

Peter began to go to Mass every morning. Clara or I would drive him down the street to St. Cyril's. Usually we both would go with him. My children had made me a good Catholic. My husband made me a devout Catholic.

I refused to think about his death, though deep down I knew he would be lucky to live to be sixty. Big Mike once said to me in a choked voice, "I'll outlive my own son. It's all my fault."

"The doctors say that his depression is genetic, not psychological."

"I didn't help matters by pushing him so hard in high school and college."

"That's what fathers do. You weren't worse than anyone else in this town."

You'll have to take care of him when Peter dies, I told myself with Italian fatalism. But I didn't think it would happen so soon. . . . Nor that Big Mike would die a year after.

I awoke a couple of nights after our thirtieth wedding anniversary. Beside me in bed—better a sexless bed, I often told myself than an empty bed—Peter was twisting and turning restlessly. Then he doubled over and cried out in pain.

"I'm dying, Maria! Call the ambulance! Oh, please call the ambulance! Now!"

I had made a deal with Ladislas, the director of our town ambulance service, that I would call him on his top secret number when we had an emergency, and just tell him my name. He would come immediately. I had precoded his number in all my phones.

"Laddy, it's Maria."

Then the rectory, "Father Matt. It's Maria."

"I'll be right over, Maria."

"Hold my hand, Maria, PLEASE!"

"I love you, Peter. I always have. I always will."

"Best wife a loser like me ever had."

"You're not a loser, Peter. You never were."

Then Big Mike.

His whiny wife answered.

"Do you know what time it is, Maria . . . ? We both need our sleep."

"We're taking Peter to the hospital."

"Can't it wait till the morning?"

Miserable little bitch.

"Put him on!" I shouted into the phone.

She whimpered but put Mike on.

"We're taking him to the hospital, Mike. He may have had a heart attack."

"I'll meet you there . . . ! How bad is it?"

I hesitated.

"Pretty bad?"

"I think so."

The ambulance wailed outside. I put on a sweatshirt and jeans and grabbed a raincoat. Then back to my husband. I held his hand with all the passion I possessed.

"I love you, Peter. I love you with all my heart and soul."

"I didn't deserve you, Maria. But I'm happy you've been with me. You have to get yourself another husband."

"Don't be silly. . . . I better open the door."

The paramedics eased him out of the bed and carried him gently down the stairs. I trailed behind, cell phone in hand. Pete's young wife, Vicki, whom he met during their term in ACE, halfway through her first pregnancy, answered the phone.

"We're taking Dad to the hospital, hon."

"Oh, Mom, how awful!"

"How bad is it, Mom?" Pete was on the phone.

"Pretty bad. We're putting him in the ambulance. Father Matt is here and is riding down the street with us."

"We'll be right there."

"Let Vicki drive. You call the kids. Tell them not to be reckless driving home, especially Clara."

"I'll tell her to wait till morning. She usually does what I say."

"You must marry again," Peter pleaded with me, clinging to my hand.

Father Matt performed the Last Rites with sincerity and grace as we rolled down the street to St. Angela's Hospital. Big Mike and Pete and Vicki arrived at the same time. Just inside the entrance of the hospital thunder growled above us and lightning danced across the sky, my husband sat up on the stretcher, his face glowing, his eyes bright.

"I'm here, Jesus," he said with a strange laugh. "Please take me home."

Then he fell back on the stretcher, closed his eyes, and died.

None of us said anything. In fact it would be months before we allowed ourselves to speak about that last half minute of his life.

I was numb through the wake and funeral, unable to weep, hardly able to speak. I thought I had prepared mentally for his death, but I knew nothing about grief.

The wake and funeral were overwhelmed by strangers, men and women I had never met and did not know, but who worshipped the legend of Peter Connors. My brothers and parents did not appear. Gina and her handsome doctor drove in from Chicago. My kids steered me around and whispered instructions in my ear. After the burial in Oakdale Memorial, they urged me to go away for a couple of weeks. Instead I went back to the office the following Monday morning. Life went on and so did the firm. So too did Elegant Homes, my firm.

Denial and grief continued for a year. Mourning will never end. I was finally able to ask myself whether I had been happy, whether I would do it all again if I had the chance, whether I had any regrets. I didn't know the answers and I still don't. I do know that I had been a shallow and naïve young woman who knew nothing about life or marriage and who was unaware that she had other choices. I also concluded, after several conversations with Father Matt, that I had been a good wife and a good mother, a conclusion on which Big Mike and my kids vigorously insisted. I had not failed completely in these responsibilities. In that hardly dramatic and minimal conviction, I found solace.

I also decided that I would not try marriage again, it was far too demanding a venture to attempt more than once. After my required year of mourning, I put away my widow's clothes (always fashionable, mind you) and began to act like a responsible aging grandmother. "Men are going to start hitting on you, Mom," my adorable Vicki informed me.

"Vick, men have hit on me all my life. They didn't pause for more than a moment or two when I had a husband or when I was wearing black. The only problem is that none of them are the kind of men I wouldn't mind hitting on me."

She and my son both laughed, as did my grandchild, who laughed all the time. They didn't realize that I was speaking the literal truth. I had had it with men.

Or so I thought.

— Maria Angelica —

WE HAD, I told myself, nothing to lose by going public with Elegant Homes. We needed more money to spread our software and offices around the country. If the shares went up, my children and I would make a tidy sum of money, enough maybe for my grandchildren's college education and for me to retire to my native Sienna some day. Actually I don't think we are Tuscans, more likely Lombards or Goths or some other barbarian crowd.

Nor did I resist the idea of offering a large block of our stock to Donlan Assets Management. I had some money in Frodo, which had paid for my kids' long residence at the Dome. Jack Donlan apparently knew what he was doing. His accountants and lawyers swarmed over our offices both in Oakdale and Sears Tower.

"Very smart people," my son, Pete, who ran the Oakdale office now, observed. "If they think we are a good investment, a lot of other people will too."

"He makes mistakes like all of them."

"Not very many."

"His Frodo fund paid for your education."

"I told them that. . . . I don't know whether he knows you're a client."

"I'm sure that wouldn't affect his decision."

Finally the day came when he and I would meet. Apparently we had passed all but the final test—his meeting with me. Was I the kind of person who could be trusted to protect the stockholders' wealth he had put in Samwise, his more speculative fund. I didn't like the idea of the test. I wore a conservative navy blue suit with a single oak pin. I had not removed my wedding ring for two years. I solemnly resolved that I would choke all my wisecracks.

So my lead-off remark was, "It doesn't seem to be a level playing field—three Irish speculators and one Sicilian widow."

"Tuscan, as I remember."

"You read the article? I hope you didn't take any of it seriously. Actually we are Sienese, to be honest, from a little farm on a hill outside of Siena. Probably Goths or Lombardi or some other primitive Bronze Age tribe."

"Some of the genetic research suggests that the Etruscans were a Celtic tribe."

"Then you have one female Celt against three male Celts. Be forewarned that you're outnumbered."

"My late mother, a lieutenant colonel in the United States Army, would have agreed completely."

"Smart woman. Presumably you inherited her intelligence."

Our colleagues around the room laughed nervously at the banter. I was an idiot.

John Patrick Donlan was what my daughters called totally cute. Slender, maybe five foot eleven, pale baby blue eyes, curly blond hair with a faint touch of white, a quick, heart-melting smile, a three-piece dark grey Armani suit, gleaming white shirt, and a blue tie with a thin pattern that sort of matched his eyes. I warned myself that I should keep my mouth shut and that I should not let myself drift into a crush on this man. Those baby blue eyes had a veneer of cold steel.

He was a strong man with a tough, disciplined body and an aura of integrity that suggested moral strength. I would not fool him. Indeed every time his eyes focused on me, I felt vulnerable, even naked.

A handsome African-American woman drifted into the room with tea and coffee and Belleek cups and saucers.

"This my assistant, Elfrida Jones, Ms. Connors. Elfrida, this is Ms. Maria Connors."

"Hi, Elfrida."

"Hi, Maria."

I had an ally in the room.

"You take tea, I believe, Maria."

"Black as midnight on a moonless night."

"Elfrida is the one who put the relevant issue of *Chicago Markets* in my file."

"We used models for the swimsuit pictures," I blurted, feeling my face flame.

"I very much doubt that, Ms. Connors," he said with a matching blush.

Stop, you fool. Shut your big mouth. And banish all those errant thoughts.

"Now tell me a little about Oakdale. I'm afraid I don't know much of Illinois west of the DesPlaines River."

"So we took down the rusty old statue of General Atkinson who led the American forces and put up a monument to Black Hawk. Almost no one knew who General Atkinson was."

"That would doubtless please the faculty from NIU—Northern Illinois—who live in town."

"The symbolism would be lost on them. They think a Black Hawk is a hockey player."

"You always have the last word, don't you, Ms. Connors?"

Those steel blue eyes probed me, body and soul.

"Only when I'm awake."

He smiled faintly, as though impressed.

"Now could you tell me three good reasons why I should not become involved with your enterprise?"

Ah, now was the real test.

"The first reason is that Elegant Homes depends on a sufficient level of prosperity in our society and a management class that wants homes that honor what the art critics and the environmentalists say, but do not have the time, and perhaps the talent, to build such homes. If our economy should collapse, then we would certainly go down with it."

"As would all of us."

"A second reason is that there might be something inappropriate about earning a living off such homes while there are still homeless people on our streets, minorities living in slums, and young couples who cannot afford homes of their own. We must vote for reforms that diminish or eliminate such injustice. When we do that in fact, we strengthen the economy instead of weakening it."

"Spoken like a good Democrat."

I permitted myself a first taste of the tea. Spiced.

"The third reason is that you might want to consider serious doubts about whether you want a babbling woman like me deciding the fate of your investment."

"I would never dare to think that, Ms. Connors. You must excuse me for declining to serve on your board for the present. I have a marriage coming up in my family and that will consume a lot of time. Later perhaps . . . However, I would urge you to assemble a good group of outside board members."

"May I ask you in another year?"

He considered carefully.

"Of course," he said with a slight nod of his head.

He signed the document in front of him on the desk and passed it across to me.

I raised an eyebrow to my lawyer, who smiled.

"I've vetted it. If you want to read it . . ."

"Too excited."

I pushed the document across the desk. Both lawyers applauded. We shook hands all around, thanked one another, and departed. There was no offer of lunch, thanks be to God. As we were walking out of his tastefully antique office—I must get some slides of it for our repertory—he followed me.

"I have a check here, Maria, for the agreed price. Do you want to accept it and sign a receipt?"

"You better give it to my lawyer. I'd spend it all in one place."

I left the building, my heart beating, my head throbbing. I called Pete on my cell phone.

Vicki answered.

"Tell your husband I passed."

"Hooray! . . . Was he cute?"

"In a button-down way. No big deal."

But it was a big deal.

— John Patrick —

MARIA SABATTINI had invaded my imagination and refused to depart. I would get over her, I told myself, it will just take time.

Why get over her? Because if I did not I would fall in love with her and have to marry her. I was determined that would not happen.

She was not only beautiful but she was intelligent and funny and admirable. She was still wearing her wedding ring, which meant she was not available, did it not?

It had been my intention to take them all to lunch at the Chicago Club. The lawyers both expected the invitation. Had either of them told her? I had also told them that I would be ready to serve on the board of Elegant Homes where I could keep an eye on the efficiency of the staff. Yet I had changed my mind. They would want to know why.

Would she want to know why?

Because I was scared of her? That would be the behavior of a coward. Could I say that I was afraid of her? She had not tried to "hit" on me, a word the origin of which my daughter had to explain to me. Rather she had dismissed the meeting and my role as the Grand Inquisitor as silly and acted as if money and success were not at stake. She had decided to be her normal self, intelligent, fearless, and funny.

Was she not a woman to be pursued? Did I want to pursue her?

She was not the fetish woman I had made of her after reading the article. Rather she was the kind of woman you had to respect as well as desire. I was not at the age of life to take on such a task. I was not ready for the challenges of matrimony. And marriage to Maria Sabattini Connors would be all challenge, despite the obvious advantages it would involve.

My first wife would have said that God had seen fit to proffer me a great opportunity in addition to the gains that would arise from having part ownership of Elegant Homes. God would be upset with me if I waived such an opportunity.

Was God telling me, "Bed the woman while there's still time. Don't let her get away"?

I will not marry again, I insisted. Been there, done that.

I reached for my phone to call someone, I knew not whom.

I picked up the phone and there was Joe McMahon.

"What did you think?" he asked.

"I think you were right, we made a very good deal."

"I know that. . . . What did you think of her?"

"Apparently a very intelligent woman."

"Is that all?"

"Clearly attractive."

"And just a little crazy?"

"I wouldn't say that. She was obviously nervous and covered it up with wit."

"We should keep an eye on her."

"Not I."

Joe, I told myself, was not a matchmaker.

Or was he.

I did not want to share my life with a woman, any woman. Certainly not one larger than life.

That's where I left it. On the day of the public offering the shares opened twenty percent above the floor. They fell fifteen percent the second day and ten percent more the third day. The *Journal* had a heavy-handed article about frivolous corporations. By the end of the second week, the share price was thirty percent above the initial offering and stayed there. The *Times* weighed in with a feature article about Maria Angelica, as she now claimed was her name. "Rural Woman Reads the Signs of the Time" was the headline. "Claims to Be a Lombard or a Goth. Build Your Dream House Online."

That kind of publicity you can't buy. I was not worried about my investment. Neither article mentioned my involvement. Publicity I don't need. Then, however, I began to suspect that God was conniving against me. It was a moderately hot Chicago day in August. It had been a listless summer for me. None of the other acquisitions we looked at seemed interesting. My funds were doing well, Samwise was prospering in great part because of ELG. When I was a kid I loved summer. I would run down to the beach at Montrose, swim, read, and then swim again. I'd buy an ice cream bar on the way home, joke with my parents at supper, and then read some more. I bought a little beach house in the Dunes where we would go on some of the weekends and for a week in August. After we married and before my wife's serious problems appeared, we'd spend two weeks over there with our daughters, much to the resentment of her family. They wondered why they were never invited to visit while we were at the beach. The answer was that there was just enough room for two adults and a child or two. There was no room for a bunch of overweight people who would be drunk by one in the afternoon. My wife begged me to keep them away.

Later I took up sailing because my doctor urged me to find recreation that was more relaxing than my tennis obsession. I bought a thirty-two-foot sailboat, berthed it at Montrose Harbor, and took sailing lessons. My teenage daughters thought it was cool and wanted to take lessons too. We had a lot of fun, especially during the summers Faith was away at the Betty Ford Center. The *Mary Fran*, named after my mother and my youngest daughter, was a kind of a hangout for the kids and their friends. My mom absolutely refused to board it even at the dock.

"That's no boat for you to be driving around," she warned me. "It looks as unreliable as the old woman after whom it's named."

Nonetheless she and my father would walk down to the edge of the park to watch us sail by.

"She's a pretty boat, Grams, once you get to know her."

"Well, your pa is a rich speculator so he's entitled to a pretty boat."

Her problem was that the boat would give a "bad example" to others.

Since Faith died, I used neither the boat nor the cottage, though I had paid to maintain both and had remodeled the cottage so that my daughters and eventually their families could use it. I felt not the slightest desire either to sail or drive to the other side of the Lake.

I was acting like a worn-out old man.

Grief, I told myself, maybe I'll just have to live with it.

I remembered fondly the summer days when my father and I would walk over to the Italian Village on Monroe, eat pasta Bolognese, and drink a bottle of Barolo—in memory of his days in Italy after hostilities had ended.

"They're a strange, wonderful people," he remarked. "Just the opposite of the Irish. We are generally pretty happy but pretend we are morose. They are very sad but do a wonderful imitation of happiness."

Why not?

I turned right at Clark and walked two blocks to Monroe.

Did Maria, or Maria Angelica as I must call her, fit that model?

Suddenly, as I thought of her, she appeared in front of me, in green sundress, and carrying a matching bag, strolling down Monroe Street like she was on the Champs Elysées—which I'm sure she had never seen—and totally unaware of the admiring glances that trailed after the sundress that outlined the shapes of her body.

"Maria Angelica," I murmured, as we almost collided, "green goddess of summer."

"Jac— uh, Mr. Donlan . . . What are you doing here?"

"Walking down Monroe Street to the Italian Village, a right I have by virtue of my voter registration in this city, which is more than I might say for you."

I had taken her completely by surprise.

"What Italian Village?"

I pointed at the sign down the street.

"My late father, God be good to him, and I had the custom occasionally on a hot summer day to eat a bowl of pasta there and drink a bottle of Barolo."

"I never knew it was there. . . . I must have walked by it a hundred times."

"Every Chicagoan knows about the Italian Village. You must learn these essentials or you'll earn the reputation of being a hick."

"Exurbanite . . ."

"Congratulations on the wonderful publicity in the name of all those who have invested in Samwise. . . ." I took her arm. "Surely you will join me in disposing of a bottle of Barolo in celebration of the good fortune of Samwise?"

"Jac— Mr. Donlan . . . This isn't a good idea!"

She was breathless, but she did not resist my directing her across the street.

"It's Jack, or if you wish, Jackie, and yes it is."

"No, it's not."

"On some occasions there is an obligation to test something that seems not to be a good idea, but which in fact may well be."

We were at the door of the Italian Village. I released her arm to give her a chance to decline my invitation.

She took a deep breath, sighed, and murmured, "I just love Barolo," and recaptured my arm.

This is your idea, I said to God. I hope you know what I'm doing. I warn you that I will pursue this woman and learn all I can about her. I doubt that anything I learn will dissuade me. Okay?

There were no signals from heaven that the deity demurred from this game plan.

I will, however, pursue her slowly and gently and with all due respect.

"I was surprised that the *Times* didn't have a picture of you."

"They wanted one the worst way. I refused. I am not a sex object."

"You certainly are not, Maria Angelica. You are a very beautiful woman and for that you should be thankful to God and not intimidated by either envious women or lecherous men."

I am certainly invoking God often. I should also plead with Him to help me. This is an art that I never learned.

"You are leering at me now, Jackie."

"I am not, Maria Angelica. I wouldn't dream of leering at you."

"You're fantasizing about taking off my sundress."

"Guilty as charged, but only respectfully and reverently."

"Sometimes the fantasy is much better than the reality."

"I'll take my chances."

She relaxed and grinned.

"You're winning all the exchanges today, Jackie. I warn you, it won't last."

"I'm duly warned and I'm sure it won't last."

"Do you miss your father?" she asked cautiously as we arranged ourselves at the table and I ordered the Barolo.

"He was not just a father, but a teacher, a mentor, and good friend and never tried to run my life."

"You've been very fortunate. My parents and my two brothers won't speak to me, haven't for years. My sister, Gina, and I are friends, but we don't see each other often. My brothers have a construction firm. They are sloppy in their proposals and sloppier in their work. Everyone thinks that because they are family, I owe them business."

"Ethnic standards."

"I couldn't do it. . . . I wouldn't do it. My father-in-law and his father had created a reputation for integrity that I could not violate."

We ate our pasta and consumed our Barolo and toasted each other every couple of minutes. She told me her life story, candidly and without any show of emotion or occasional flashes of wit. I realized then how vulnerable she was and promised the deity that I would always protect her—but only when she wanted to be protected. Her romance with Peter Connors was the stuff out of which Verdi operas were made—beautiful and bittersweet.

"Now you know all there is to know about me, Jackie. Not much of a story really. I tell myself that I was a good wife and a good mother, not perfect, but I tried hard. I probably saved the family business."

"And remade Oakdale and created Elegant Homes."

"I guess so." She was close to tears.

"There is always a sense at a certain time in life that the youthful dreams, especially the romantic ones didn't come true, but for all the heartbreak something was accomplished. That is consoling, but it does not justify acceptance."

Who was I of all people to say that?

"That's an improper comment, Jackie. It presumes an intimacy between us that does not exist."

Strike one.

"I don't presume any intimacy, Maria. I was not reflecting on your experience but on mine."

"I'm sorry. . . ." Her shoulders slumped. "Too much Barolo. I feel too vulnerable . . . a little scared too."

"I'm not hitting on you, Maria. And, when I'm thinking seriously about that, I'll give you warning so you can exercise due diligence."

"If I want to . . . I've told my story, now do you want to tell me yours?"

"Fair is fair."

So I told her my story. She had the right to know it anyway. Moreover, shared memoirs strengthened bonds. As I told her about Faith's family, her lovely face tightened with rage.

"Those bitches! Evil people! They killed that poor girl because she found a husband and her sisters didn't. . . ."

"I don't make that charge."

"That's up to you! I make it. Small, passive-aggressive, mean-spirited people like that make me want to puke!"

"I tell myself I should have done more to protect her. . . ."

"She knew that you did all you could. . . . I wonder that you would never become involved with a woman ever again. We are such nasty, petty, miserable people. . . ."

"Not all of you! . . . And I'm not sure that I'll ever marry again."

She just grinned.

"Walk me back to Sears Tower, Jackie. I'm so tuned that I'll get lost. . . . Never should drink a half bottle of wine at lunch."

She took my arm and we walked slowly back to Wacker Drive and Sears Tower.

"It was good to talk to you," she said.

"Likewise."

"Would you be interested in another adventure that we probably shouldn't do?"

"In for an inch, in for a mile."

I wasn't quite sure what that meant.

"I don't suppose that out there in the prairies, you ever did any sailing?"

"We have lakes in the prairies."

"Lakes with a small *l*."

"What other kind are there?"

"Here in Chicago we have the Lake with a capital *L*."

"So I'm told."

"You never crewed on a lake with a small *l*?"

"I certainly did and on a twenty-two-foot boat that our firm owns."

"I have a boat on Lake Michigan. I haven't used it in a while."

"How big?"

"Thirty-two feet."

"That's a yacht."

"It has three staterooms and a head and will sleep twelve, though it never has. It can do the race to Mackinac though it also never has."

"You want me to crew on that monster thing?"

"I'm inviting you to come for a ride tomorrow. I bet you never saw the skyline from the Lake."

"We really shouldn't do it, Jackie. It's a workday."

There are other and better reasons for not sailing the *Mary Fran*.

"The winds are forecast to be light and we can have a nice leisurely sail, perhaps drop anchor and swim."

"No Barolo?"

"I permit myself and my crew only one can of beer. . . . Your virtue will be under no assault."

"I make no promises about yours. . . . What time?"

"I'll get there early to make sure everything is in working order. I'll meet you on the deck of the yacht club about eleven?"

"I haven't said that I'll show up."

"That's true."

"Well, I guess. I'll be there. . . . I reserve the right to change my mind when I see the boat."

— Maria Angelica —

SO THE next morning at a quarter to eleven, courtesy of a taxi, I stood on the deck of the yacht club, covered with suntan cream, and stared in amazement at the busy harbor and its panorama of yachts, most of them covered up though it was August. I was early because I'm always early, an obsession I did not learn from my parents. I was wearing cutoff jeans and an NIU sweatshirt over my brand-new and very modest two-piece black swimsuit. I had purchased both swimsuit and new boat shoes late Thursday afternoon when I had recovered from the Barolo. Grandmothers, no matter how well preserved, should not wear bikinis—at least not in ordinary circumstances. I was carrying a shopping bag with a cover-up, a change of clothes, and four sandwiches, four cans of Diet Coke, and a box of oatmeal raisin cookies. I felt very much like a hick from the prairies, especially compared to the well-dressed people that strolled around the harbor. The shopping bag is the best I can do, folks, I'm a hick from the prairies. I leaned against a wall and tried to pretend I wasn't there.

Jack Donlan showed up promptly at eleven o'clock, wearing khaki shirt and slacks and a matching baseball cap with gold braid and the words *Mary Fran* on it. My heart jumped at the sight of him. He was so cute. Careful Connors, real careful. You don't want to be that way so soon.

"Good morning, Captain," I said with a salute. "Sea-person Connors reporting for duty."

"Good morning, Maria," he said, brushing my cheek with his lips. "You look gorgeous, as always."

My heart did several more leaps. This was not good.

He took the shopping bag from my hand.

"Sorry about the matched luggage, I didn't bring any of my sailing gear in from Oakdale. . . . I have some food in there. . . . I assume you have refrigeration on board. . . . This Lake is bigger than Oak Lake."

Mary Fran was a lovely boat: black hull; teak decks; polished bronze hardware; electronic winches; bulkhead dials reporting radar, wind, water temperature, and air pressure; and three comfortable cabins.

Jack helped me into the boat.

"She's beautiful!" I said.

"We had a lot of fun on it," he said, a touch of sadness in his voice.

"You haven't used it the last two years."

"Kids were busy with other things, marriage, family, courtship."

"Father Matt, our pastor in Oakdale, says it's all right to own an expensive boat, so long as you use it."

He laughed.

"Father Matt is right, but *Mary Fran* earned me money the last two years by appreciation. Paid for her upkeep."

He gave me a thin khaki life jacket and a cap, both labeled with the boat's name.

"Rule on this boat is everyone always wears a jacket. Regardless. I note that you have already smeared suntan lotion on yourself. That's another rule."

"And you've got chains to put me in if I disobey any rules?"

"Bread and water."

He instructed me on my duties on the craft, easier than on the *Maria Angelica* because of the electronic winches.

"Any questions?"

"No sir, Captain, sir."

He pushed a button on the bulkhead and a fan cleared the hull of gas.

Then he pushed another button and the auxiliary motor hummed confidently.

"You buy the best, don't you, Captain, sir?"

"For my wife and kids, only the best," he said, the touch of sadness back in his voice.

If this turned into a memorial voyage, it would be a big mistake.

"Cast off the mooring lines!"

"Yes, sir! Right away, sir."

He laughed.

I had him. You don't dare be a sourpuss on a boat ride with me!

"Sure does beat an outboard!"

Mary Fran slipped out of her berth and eased her way into the channel, uncrowded on Friday morning. In a few minutes we were out of the harbor and on the gentle waters of the enormous, scary Lake. With a very scary captain.

"Raise the foresail!"

I pushed another button and the foresail flapped in the breeze. Jackie turned off the motor. *Mary Fran* hesitated, not quite sure what to do. He eased the wheel around and the jib caught the wind.

"Raise the main!"

Another button to push and the boat surged forward, knowing now what she should do.

"Wow!" I exclaimed. "Totally cool!"

"A good boat. She does what's she told."

"Unlike most human women!"

I kept him laughing all the way down the shore beyond Navy Pier. The breeze was offshore, consistent, and moderate. Ice cream cumulus clouds were moving slowly across the sky.

"You want to take the con?"

"You mean drive this boat? Course not!"

I moved over to take his place.

Mary Fran, not at all sure about this new pilot, hesitated and I moved the wheel gently. She settled down like a trained horse. Good girl.

"You have the touch, Maria Angelica."

"It's a lot easier than doing the rudder thing."

I had been so bemused by the skyline, the boat, and captain, my captain, that I had not noticed I was hot and hungry. The thermometer said eighty-six.

"Would you excuse me for a moment, Captain, sir?"

"Certainly."

"Permission to go below."

"Of course."

I removed the sandwiches, Cokes, and cookies from the fridge, took off the life jacket, shed the Huskies sweatshirt, slathered my self with suntan lotion, put on the life jacket, and climbed back into the cockpit.

"Grandma in a bikini!" he gasped. I mean literally he gasped. This might not be a good idea either.

"It is not a bikini," I said primly. "It is merely a very modest two-piece swimsuit. Grandmothers," I repeated my own principle, "no matter how well preserved, should never wear bikinis unless for a very special occasion. Here's your sandwiches. They should distract you from staring."

"What would a special occasion be?"

"A honeymoon or something like that."

As soon as the words were out of my mouth, I regretted them. Jack, however, guffawed.

"I'll try to remember that."

It was my turn to feel a flaming face.

"Very good sandwiches," he said, saving both of us.

I wasn't trying to seduce him, not really. Only in the long run.

Back at Navy Pier, I steered us into the calm water behind the breakwaters.

We lowered the sails. He pressed another magic button and an anchor slipped into the water, gripping bottom after a long time.

"Permission to swim, sir?"

"You note the temperature of the water?"

"Sixty-four."

"That's cold."

I shrugged my shoulders.

"Do I have to wear the jacket?"

"Stay within twenty yards of the boat!"

I kicked off my jeans, tossed aside the life jacket, and dived in from the gunnel. It was a longer way down than a jump from the *Maria Angelica*. When I hit the water, I thought I would die, it was so cold. I surfaced, shivering and, I suspected, blue.

"Piece of cake," I shouted.

"I can see that."

I swam maybe a hundred yards back and forth, just to prove I could do it. My poor body adjusted reluctantly to the water temperature. Finally, it was time and past time to stop. I swam to the side of the boat. Jack tossed a rope ladder.

"I have to climb that?"

"Only way."

I tried twice and failed, took a deep breath, and clambered up to the gunnel. I was too weak to force myself over it. He took me in his arms and lifted me on to the deck. Very strong arms.

For a brief moment I was powerless in those arms. My face flamed. Then he let me go, reluctantly I thought.

"You're a tomboy, Grams," he said, throwing a huge towel around my shoulders, one that announced it was from the *Mary Fran*.

"And proud of it," I gasped, still shivering.

"The barometer is falling. We'd better get out of here."

I glanced at the western sky. A line of black clouds on the horizon was moving right toward us.

"That wasn't part of the prediction."

I pulled on my cover-up and my boat shoes.

"Sometimes on humid days weather cells blow up without warning. NOA weather radio hasn't picked it up yet."

"Let's get out of here," I announced.

We lifted the anchor, raised the sails and gave *Mary Fran* free rein. The wind continued to be offshore but picked up to sixteen knots. The harbor was three miles north of us. We were flying along at six knots an hour and were almost at the harbor mouth when the rain hit us. The lines on the main sail jammed. I climbed up to the top of the cabin and lowered it by hand, without being told. The jib went down easily. Then we turned into the harbor and a gust of wind rocked us. I clung to the mast for dear life and shouted for the joy of the contest. Jack helped me down and returned to the wheel. I collapsed on the floor of the cockpit.

"You okay?" he yelled.

"Never better!"

Then the lightning and thunder started.

"You and your big ideas, Jack Donlan!"

"Wanted to see what kind of a sailor you are."

The auxiliary motor brought us to our berth. We covered the sails in the driving rain, secured everything that needed to be secured, and walked as quickly as we could to the clubhouse.

"Buy you a hamburger?"

"Great idea."

I went to the women's room, tidied up, put on my change of clothes, and joined him in the bar.

"You okay?" I asked captain—my captain—who was nursing a beer.

"I wouldn't want to be hit by one of those in the middle of the Lake."

"You'd need a crew like me out there to survive."

"Maria Angelica, you're too much."

"I've been told that."

"Instead of fear, you were shouting with the joy of the battle."

"I could turn out to be dangerous. We don't quite have storms like that on Oak Lake. . . . By the way, you're really good at that sort of thing."

We laughed together again, finished our beer and burgers, and he drove me back to Millennium Towers. I ached in every bone and muscle of my body. I had to get back in condition. It was now a serious issue.

"Next Friday?" he asked at the door of my apartment.

"Only if you promise more serious action."

He laughed again, kissed me with some vigor, and departed.

This was courtship?

Whatever it was, it went on till the middle of September when we sailed the *Mary Fran* to her winter storage on the river. I wanted to cry. We had great fun. I would miss her. As for her captain, I had no idea what was going on in his head.

However, I had great stories to tell my children back in Oakdale on Saturday morning.

"Has he made a move, Mom?" Clara demanded.

"Nope."

"Will he?"

"Honestly, hon, don't know."

"Do you want him to."

I hesitated and then told the truth.

"I haven't made up my mind."

Just the same, after I had waved a sad good-bye to *Mary Fran*, I paid a visit to an elite lingerie store and bought a fresh supply, in case I needed it. We had been very careful that our late summer sailings were very cautious ventures—as far as our courtship was concerned. Both of us were concerned about stirring up strong emotions too early. Too cautious? I don't know.

The next week there was an opera. My invitation came in a phone call two nights before.

"Would you like to attend *Turandot* this week?"

"Why not?" I said.

I loved to listen to opera music, but I'd never once in all my life been to a sure-enough opera.

There wasn't even enough time to find a script and read it. I had yet to learn about the supratitles they use at the Lyric.

Supper at the Graham room was lifeless at first. Then he asked the question that was on both our minds.

"What are we doing, Maria?"

"Well," I said, pretending to weigh my words carefully, "one might say that we are at the early stages of tentatively beginning something folks might call a courtship."

"How do you feel about it?"

"Interested, obviously, and scared silly."

Time for honest talk.

"Me too . . . It's happened too quickly for me to grasp. . . . It's a serious business."

"With serious risks," I added.

God knew how often I had pondered the risks in rides back and forth to Oakdale.

"I have the feeling that if we go on like this much longer, there will be no escaping. . . . Only a fool would want to escape from you, Maria. . . ."

"I understand the fear," I assured him. "The other side of the coin is the fear I might lose the opportunity of my life. . . . I kind of enjoyed those boat rides."

We both laughed. I would have to lead him into laughter for the rest of our lives. Would that be bad?

Not necessarily.

"Might we need a hiatus to be sure?"

"I'm sure that's a good idea. . . . How long, do you think?"

"Two or three weeks maybe?"

"Is that all?"

"No more, certainly."

My mind was not completely made up, but it was more made up than his. I should say something wise.

"Jackie, take as long as you want. I don't want to cause any pressure."

Well, not any unfair pressure.

"I knew that's what you'd say. Thank you . . . That you're that kind of woman increases the pressure."

"Naturally."

And we both laughed again.

His good-night kiss was not quite violent, but it certainly was vehement. So was the touch of his fingers on my breast.

"No pressure at all," I gasped.

As I was falling asleep, I said to myself, "Maria Angelica, there is no such thing as the perfect permanent lover, but you could do a lot worse."

Like the time you almost went to bed with Chip McConnell, who was the running back on Peter's high school team. Dear God, thank you for stopping me.

I have to ask myself whether I might be slipping into a similar disaster.

— John Patrick —

I TORMENTED myself with worry for the next three weeks. I reminded myself that I was a speculator, a gambler, a risk taker. I firmly believed my father's dictum that certainty is not possible either in love or the stock market. You play the odds, he used to say. And how do you figure the odds in love? I would ask in return. You just know, he'd sigh. Like I knew with your mother the first time I saw her.

I was overwhelmed by Maria Angelica the first time I saw her. I continue to be. She is fun—fun to talk to, fun to banter with, fun to laugh at, and fun to yearn for. But so was Mandy Clifford, the national TV reporter. At the last minute she dumped me because I was a Catholic and wouldn't divorce my wife who at the time had been six months at Betty Ford on her third session there. After Mandy walked out on me, I realized that it had been foolishness from the very beginning. I would have become her boy toy. Yet at the time it looked like a good risk. My daughter's oxytocin, I guess. Yet I felt about Mandy the same way I feel about Maria. How can I figure out what to do? Mandy was a nasty person. She loved to obliterate people she was interviewing. That troubled me at the time, but I paid no attention to it till she turned on me and tore me to shreds. What troubles me about Maria? Her laughter? It suggests she's never serious, but her life story shows just how serious she can be.

I agonized for three weeks, sleeping poorly and not listening as carefully as I should to my staff. They knew something was wrong, but they would never have guessed. ELG stock, in the meantime continued to climb, not wildly but steadily. Good investment. Better than I thought it would be.

Finally, on impulse, I phoned her.

"Maria Connors," she said crisply.

"Jack Donlan."

"I knew someone by that name once."

"I wonder if we could have supper at Ambria this evening. Pick you up at seven o'clock?"

She should have bawled me out for the delay.

Instead she said, "Good, I've been waiting for an occasion to wear my brand-new black lingerie!"

— Maria Angelica —

I DID not mention the subject at hand when I climbed into his Lexus. I was scared again, not that he would say that he didn't want me, but that he would say that he did. I was fully prepared to rebuff him if all he did was hit on me. That was unlike my Jackie, however. He would rather affirm his eternal love for me and then lead me off to his apartment. Unless I said, no, not yet.

I wouldn't do that to him. I loved him too much. If he told me that he loved me, that would be for the moment as good as a marriage vow. He'd been without a woman too long. The only sensible thing would be to give myself to him completely. I had never done that before. What would it be like? Scary—like clinging to the mast of *Mary Fran*.

And fun too—of a terrifying variety.

"I'm sorry I kept you waiting."

"You had less than twenty-four hours before I took out my personal phone book and drawn a big black line through your name."

"Really?"

"No, a red line!"

"I'm glad you're not angry. . . ."

"Who said not angry, 'white man'? . . . Do you realize you could have lost the best crew you'd ever get for that silly old boat of yours? A woman has her honor to consider, after all."

We kept up the banter until we left the outer drive. Then at the stop light at Lincoln Park West, he crushed me in his arms. Preview of coming attractions. Yet very gentle and very sweet.

"You plan on raping the poor chaste matron, even before she drinks half a bottle of Barolo?"

When we were shown to our table, I noted that an uncorked bottle of Barolo was already waiting for us. Nice touch.

After we ordered, Jack Donlan began what would be for him a painful conversation. I resolved that I would not make it more difficult for him by any smart-ass remarks.

"I must begin by apologizing for taking so long. I made up my mind this morning that I was acting like an idiot. . . . How long did you ruminate?"

Mistaken word!

"I bought some Wrigley's gum so I could chew on a cud and decided the next morning that I love you very much and can accept the possibility of sleeping in the same bed with you for the rest of my life. . . . You don't snore, do you?"

"I don't believe so. . . . You would be perfectly right if you just got rid of me. . . ."

"Perfectly wrong."

He reached into an inside pocket of his brown Armani and produced a small box. Pure corn! And I was from the prairies. . . .

"Whatcha got there?"

It was the biggest diamond in all the world . . . well not quite, but certainly satisfactory.

"The standard response," I said, "is that you shouldn't have spent so much money and I hope you didn't have to sell the *Mary Fran* to pay for it. . . . But it is beautiful. . . . Too beautiful for the likes of me, but I'll wear it anyhow."

Then, without any planning, I began to cry. How like a woman!

"Don't cry, Maria!"

"Tears of joy," I sniffled.

"I'll love you always," he said, again displaying little creativity.

"You'd better!" I replied and then broke down completely as he put the ring on my finger. It was indeed huge.

I'd better say something memorable.

"I guess we're engaged, huh?"

Maria Angelica being memorable.

"That's a fair assessment of the situation."

"I'll try to stop making my idiot remarks."

"If you do that, I'll take the ring back. I fell in love with you in the office that day because you were beautiful and you had a wonderful gift for wit."

"Oh," I said very quietly. "I hope it doesn't dry up."

"Not a chance."

I was floating toward the sky. We were a pair of happy kids.

"Second childhood," I said, "is better than first."

"Experience helps us enjoy it more."

Under the table his knee touched mine. I quickly pulled back.

"Sir, are you hitting on me?"

"Yes, ma'am, but it's all right because we're engaged."

"That's true. . . . Incidentally I reject out of hand the vulgar phrase *get engaged*, as in 'Jack and I got engaged last night.'"

"I think I can remember that."

I moved my knee back in contact with his. He rested his hand on my thigh. That was very nice.

"I want to say something serious, affianced one."

"I await your words, madam."

"I have learned through the years that if a woman is going to give herself to a man, she should be a total gift. So at this minute, halfway through the roast beef and more than half through the Barolo on this our engagement day with our knees touching and your hand pleasantly on my thigh, I give myself to you totally and completely, John Patrick Donlan. Henceforth I am yours and you can do with me whatever you want."

He gulped and his hand tightened on my thigh. Grandma in delirium.

"I will always treat you with respect and reverence, Maria Angelica Sabattini Connors."

"Naturally," I said dismissively. "Incidentally that is, though now officially permitted, a strong grip you have on my thigh."

He moved his hand up and down, as though he owned me and everything about me. I wanted to shout with pleasure.

"Strong thigh," he observed.

"All the better to squeeze you with, my dear."

We went back to my apartment and he carried me triumphantly inside.

"I have the feeling that the captive matron will be violated in this cave."

"Count on it," he said, absorbing me in a total kiss.

So we began the dance of consummation. I had expected that it would be a clumsy and awkward waltz as we began to discover one another. It was not that way at all, however.

It was an exquisite pleasure as he slowly undressed and aroused me.

"What's your fantasy now?" I demanded through lips tightly pressed together.

"I've violated the modesty of a chaste suburban matron. . . . But as I progress I see how regal and graceful she appears as I strip her, I perceive that she is perhaps a grand duchess or maybe even an empress."

"I want to be a high priestess."

"Virgin high priestess?"

"Yes but very horny . . ." I gasped.

"Who am I? A pagan high priest?"

"A desert warrior," I whispered, "who has kidnapped me from the temple and has made me his slave."

We were both laughing in this exchange, but the laughter was no more than erotic background music.

We melted together and soared, floating above the ordinary world of problems and fears into a state of body-wrenching pleasure where multicolored surprises waited with promises of wonders unimagined. I was ecstatic with victory. He was mine forever. Then we slipped back into the world we had left behind, but it was now a place of peace and tranquility where a good night's sleep was possible. I wanted to proclaim my victory but was too weary with joy to speak

"Jackie Pat," I murmured, "you're pretty good at this kind of thing, just like sailing the boat. . . . You're a keeper. Don't ever think of trying to get away."

"I wasn't," he was able to murmur.

" 'Cause I'll never let you go."

That seemed to settle that.

"And you should watch some old Valentino films to see how desert warriors treat their slave women, not that you were all that bad at the game."

— John Patrick —

IN THE days and weeks to come, I had expected the ordinary stresses and strains of intimacy to rear their mean little heads as we rushed from our work to our beds, either at her apartment or mine. Yet while we bantered constantly, we did not squabble. It helped that we were both fastidious neatniks. Moreover my wife, as I had come to define her in my own mind, seemed possessed by the conviction that it was a wife's responsibility to keep her husband happy. I suggested once, very gently, that there was no such obligation in our relationship.

"I always spoil my boy kids rotten," she replied.

I wondered if I would ever grow weary of her brash "last words."

Probably not.

She enjoyed sex and seemed ready at any time I was ready and even if I were not.

However busy we were during the day, at night we lived in an indolent and luxuriant paradise. Then we visited Ambria for a second time and the news of our romance made it into the media.

"Looks like we'd better get married," I said to Maria.

"I suppose I gotta make an honest man out of you."

Then my eldest daughter, Evie, phoned me on my private line in the office, her voice tight with rage.

"Dad, what the hell are you doing to our reputation?"

"Whose reputation, Evie?"

"Our family's reputation. Why are you letting yourself be seen in public with that whore?"

"That's a harsh word, Evie."

"It's the only word to describe her. Don't you know her reputation?"

"I've looked into her reputation. There's nothing in it of which she or I should be troubled."

"Then, Daddy dear, you're an asshole."

I was in a nightmare. None of my daughters had ever spoken to me with such disrespect.

"My investigation was carried out by a highly respectable agency."

"Then they're full of bullshit. . . . Look, I've talked to the girls and they agree that if you want to have a fling with her, screw her every night, and carry on with her in public, then go ahead and do it. But if you marry her, which is what she wants, we will never accept her and you will no longer be part of our family. I will not permit that woman to be near my children."

I hung up.

A few minutes later, the phone rang again.

Irene, my second daughter, did not waste any time on preliminaries.

"Why the fuck did you hang up on Evie?"

"I don't like your language, Rene."

"We don't like your behavior, Dad. How dare you humiliate us by appearing in public with that hooker?"

Different words, same party line.

"She's not a hooker."

"You're full of shit. If you dare to marry her, we'll disown you."

"That will be your problem."

I hung up on her too.

I waited a few minutes for Mary Fran to call. Evie had a powerful influence on her sisters. She was the oldest, the most articulate, the most determined. She bitterly opposed Mary Fran's decision to be a psychiatrist. Mary Fran did not argue, but she ignored her sister, which created a permanent state of war between the two sisters.

I concluded that Evie had seen the piece in the Chicago *Herald* and jumped to a conclusion. This would mean a long and bitter conflict because, once Evie made up her mind, she was not likely to change it.

A dam burst inside me and sadness swept through me. It was all too good to be true.

It got worse that night. We went over to St. Freddy's to make arrangements with the new pastor for a wedding the week after Thanksgiving. The housekeeper informed us that Father Hennessy would not see anyone who had not made a previous appointment. I informed her briskly that I had lived in the parish since my baptism and had made major contributions to it and that I demanded to see the pastor. I wondered if my daughters had put in the fix against us.

She shrugged and left us standing in the hallway. I led my fiancée into an office. A half hour later, Father Hennessy, a large young man wearing a cassock and a biretta, stormed into the office. We stood up.

"You rich people are all alike," he said. "You assume that the priest must be at your beck and call. To talk to your parish priest is a privilege, not a right."

"We want to arrange for a wedding."

"So I am told. . . . When will this wedding take place?"

"In the week after Thanksgiving."

"Typical . . . I must inform you that it is impossible."

"Why?"

"Because the guidelines require six months' preparation for marriage, including a Pre-Cana conference."

"Father, Ms. Connors and I have both been married before and we are in our early fifties. I assure you that we do not need a Pre-Cana conference."

"Nonetheless you attend one if you wish to be married here. . . . Are you living together?"

"I fail to see that's your business, Father."

"It is my business because I have made it a rule that no couple who are living in sin may be married here."

"We are not living in sin, Father," Maria said calmly. "Are you living in sin, Father? We will not be married by a priest who has a partner."

"Do you live in this parish, young woman?"

"I live in Oakdale, Father, and I am old enough to be your mother, who clearly did not teach you good manners."

"Then you must marry in Oakdale. That settles the matter. I ask you to leave the rectory."

"Father Matt from our parish has agreed to perform the wedding ceremony."

"Father Matt will in fact not preside over the ceremony. I do all the weddings in my parish. I bid you good evening."

He stomped out of the office.

A chill wind blew across the Lake.

"Did the Vatican Council ever happen?" I asked.

"Only the first one . . . What do we do now?"

"I call my friend Cardinal Sean Cronin tomorrow. He will straighten that fat slob out."

"The shortage of priests must be serious if men like that are appointed pastors."

The cardinal congratulated me on my forthcoming marriage. "I met the woman at some kind of civic event. She is clearly a very special person. I'm happy, Jack, that she has found a special spouse. Now tell me what that idiot at St. Fred's said to you."

I described our visit to the rectory in careful detail.

"That young man will end up shortly as a hospital chaplain if he doesn't grow up. . . . Let me call you back."

"There are no Masses scheduled for the Saturday after Thanksgiving. . . . Can you imagine how many couples he's driven over to Old Saint Pat's? You deliver the documents to Father Lulu, a wonderful young Filipino who will shortly be the next pastor—baptism, confirmation, death. He will fill out the forms. Father Matt is authorized to preside over the wedding ceremony. If you have any more problems let me know."

And that was that. Cardinal Cronin was one of the more liberal American bishops, but he is not afraid to use power to protect the layfolk from crazy priests.

Okay, we'd be married (*get married* was banned just as *get engaged* was) at St. Freddy's and Father Matt would be the officiant. But we'd have to fight our way through my family. That would be very unpleasant. My daughters were choosing to assume the role of my in-laws. I permitted the family's influence in my first marriage. I permitted them to kill her. I would not tolerate similar behavior from my daughters. They thought they could disown me. I would disown them first.

I called Maria on her personal line.

"Sabattini," she said with a thick Italian accent.

"Johnny Pat."

"I've slept with a lot of men who call themselves that."

"I had a phone conversation with your very good friend Sean Cronin."

"Darling man."

"The St. Freddy's problem is solved. Father Matt has the cardinal's permission to preside. . . ."

"I'll vote for him in the next conclave."

"Let's have lunch at the Chicago Club and I'll tell you the details."

"I can't go there."

"Why not?"

"I've never been there before. I won't know how to act."

"Noon, Maria Angelica."

"They'll all stare at me."

"They are too old to be the staring kind."

I then hung up, having the last word. That was the only way I'd ever have the last word.

They did stare, however.

"The cardinal did not say those things about me."

"He did so."

"He never said that I was beautiful."

"He did so. . . . But now I have something serious to talk about."

"We're in love, Jackie Pat, and we're going to make love tonight and we're going to be officially united by the Catholic Church. What could be serious?"

"My daughters."

She put down her salad fork.

"I was afraid they might not like me. Kids don't like stepmothers."

"That would be an understatement."

I recited my conversations of the morning.

"They don't know me."

"They think they do."

"Can I win them over?"

"Evie is the problem. I don't think she has changed her mind from a snap judgment in all her life."

She swallowed nervously.

"They threaten to disown you if you marry me?"

"Literally."

"That's not fair."

"Of course it's not . . . I've told you how their aunts and their grandmother and their great-grandmother define reality so it fits their suppositions. Apparently my daughters inherited that propensity."

"What will you do, Jack?" She pushed aside her salad.

"Eat your lunch, Maria Angelica. It's expensive."

She laughed and did what she was told.

"They killed my first wife. I won't let them kill you."

"I'm different." Her chin went up in defiance.

"They can't disown me, because I will disown them."

"Take away their trust funds . . . ? You wouldn't do that. It would be vindictive."

"They inherit their mother's fund. They can live off that."

"They'll hate you forever."

"They already do."

"Can I meet them? Persuade them that I'm not a whore or a hooker? . . . See, I've eaten my salad!"

"You shouldn't have to go into the lion's den."

"Lionesses . . . Are they really serious?"

"They get carried away by their rhetoric and can't admit that they've changed their mind."

"Do they believe that they can intimidate you?"

I thought about it.

"They know how much I love them. . . . Yes, they probably think they can. They're wrong."

"I know that. . . . They can make the rest of your life miserable. . . ."

"And yours too, if I let them."

"I still want my shot at them. Get it over and done with."

"You may have to adopt me into your family, Maria Angelica."

"Oh, we already have done that. . . . I even got a unanimous vote."

I had spent Labor Day weekend in Oakdale, not a little taken aback by the fact that it was a lovely little place and the people seemed very much like Americans. Her bright and handsome kids seemed to like me at once, even Clara who, her mother had warned me, was very suspicious of Chicagoans. Maria told me later that after dinner, Clara had demanded to know if her mother was sleeping with me. Maria denied the charge, which wasn't true then.

"Well," she said, "you're crazy if you don't. He's totally cute and a total keeper."

"A young woman of excellent judgment."

Conversation around the table was a tournament in which five very quick people fought desperately for the last word. They didn't know they were doing it, much less that they were imitating their mother, though Clara and Marissa knew that I was amused and competed vigorously with each other.

I explained to them all that I was not really an investor nor even a speculator. I was a gambler. . . . A riverboat gambler who bet with other people's money as well as my own that I could earn them more money every year than the Dow Jones index could.

"Ever fail?" Pete asked.

"Sometimes, but only in the years when the index went even lower."

"Vegas?" Marissa, fresh home from her first year in ACE, Notre Dame's peace corps, and a radiant clone of her mother, asked.

"I've never been near the place. People are reckless down there. I am not a reckless gambler. I win some and I lose some, but I win a lot more than I lose."

"Timing is very important in gambling, isn't it?" Clara asked, pushing what I suspected had become her new agenda.

"It's the whole show."

She smiled in satisfaction. I had heard her message, clever little witch.

I laughed all the way home as I recalled the day in all its rich sending and receiving of messages. I promised them all a ride on the *Mary Fran* first time out in spring.

"He's a very stern captain," my love said. "Very authoritarian."

"A good captain has to be that way," Clara said, now completely on my side.

Now poor Maria would have to face a much more hostile bunch. We sat at the table in a private dining room in the Four Seasons Hotel, sipping from a glass of Barolo, waiting for my daughters who were already half an hour late.

"A couple of sips for eloquence," Maria commented.

"This is not a good idea," I said.

"No, but it is necessary."

There was a tentative knock on the door; a guest but a hesitant guest. I opened the door and my youngest, Mary Fran, came in.

"Hi, Dad, the others are downstairs, drinking and plotting against you. I couldn't take it anymore. . . ."

"Maria, this is my youngest daughter, Mary Fran. . . . Mary Fran, this is Maria Connors."

"I knew, Mary Fran, that a young woman who lent her name to such a lovely boat must be very beautiful. I know now my expectation was not wrong."

"Thanks, Maria." Tears cascaded down my daughter's face, as the two women embraced. "I wanted to tell you that I was on your side, but I'm afraid I'll have to desert the battleground."

"A wise decision, Mary Fran. We'll get to know each other at other times and other places."

The two hugged each other and Mary Fran hugged me.

"I guess you will have to make some choices, Mary Fran," I said.

"It's about time. I've already done it in my head. The choice is easy. The action won't be."

"In your own good time, hon. There's no rush," Maria said soothingly. So far she had made all the right moves. What, however, could she do against angry drunks?

"Who's down there?"

"Great-Grams, Grandma and Grandpa, the aunts, Evie, and her weasel of a husband, poor Irene and her irrelevant boyfriend—they all hate you and want to get even with you for different reasons, mostly that you're a success and that you and Mom had a happy marriage, regardless. I know I should stay and fight them, but I don't have the stomach for a drunken Irish wake."

"I walk out on Italian fights too," Maria assured her. "Your father can take care of himself and I can take care of the two of us."

"Irene follows Evie, as always, but what is Evie so angry about?"

"Dad shouldn't marry a woman so much younger than he is."

My lover laughed.

"Hon, I'm two months older than he is."

"Yeah, but you are much more beautiful than Irene and presumably stuck up. . . . I better run before the Huns storm the gates."

"I wish we could ask her to be in the wedding party," I murmured, as Mary Fran, still weeping, left the private dining room.

We sat again at our empty table and watched men and women in their Sunday garb entering the gothic Presbyterian Church across the street.

"I'll call her at the hospital during the week and invite her to join Clara and Marissa as bridesmaids. She won't be able to do it, but after the wedding she'll come over to our side. . . . Is she right? Could your oldest daughter be jealous of me?"

"She's always been possessive. And Irene has followed her around like a little puppy."

"Hard cases, Jack. It will take a long time, but I'll win them over."

"I'd never bet against you."

No one knocked, but the door burst open and my family entered bearing with them the thick aroma, not of a cheap bar, but of an elegant lounge—a sure sign that they had signed my name to the tab. They staggered into the room, their obesity taking over all the free space.

"Maria Angelica," I began calmly, "let me introduce you to my late wife's family and my own. . . . Faith's grandmother Evangeline Clifford Fahey."

Grandma had collapsed into a chair and was busy pouring Barolo in a water tumbler.

"Why don't you leave our family alone?" Grandma Fahey demanded as she put two ice cubes into the wine. "We don't need anyone like you."

"I'm not sure that I need anyone like you either, Grandma. In any case I'm not marrying your family. I'm marrying John Donlan."

"Faith's father, Guy O'Meara . . ."

"You're all Republicans out there aren't you, Mrs. Connors?"

"In fact, Mr. O'Meara, Kishwaukee has gone Democratic in the last two elections because of the influence of NIU and Rockford. Our town has historically been Democratic and as chair of the Oakdale Democrats I intend to keep that tradition alive."

Guy was protected partially from the family nuttiness by his political obsessions.

"Not far enough away for us," Lallie snorted. "You'd better be careful of this fellow, young woman. He killed my daughter when he got tired of her and he'll do the same to you."

"My mother-in-law, Eulalia Carmody O'Meara, commonly known as Lallie."

"My sympathy, Ms. O'Meara. And I don't believe you. I have read the records of her accident. She should not have been permitted to leave your house alone in the condition she was in, especially since her husband was in Washington and could not be expected to drive her home."

So I wasn't the only one who did preliminary investigations.

"Faith's sisters, Ms. Hope O'Meara and Ms. Charity O'Meara."

The two aunts had both aged since the burial scene at All Saints Cemetery—and put on more weight. Moreover they were both on the fringe of the fall-down state of Irish intoxication.

"Fucking bastard," Charity said, her voice slurred, not a response that was in keeping with her name.

Nor was her sister's barely audible "cocksucker," an appropriate word from someone called Hope.

"It is not worth answering them, Maria. They won't remember tomorrow what you said. . . . Finally my daughters, Evelyn and her husband, Anthony Cuneen, who is an attorney at law, and Irene and her 'boyfriend' Christopher Riordan, who is an aspiring filmmaker."

And, I did not add, is alleged to be heterosexual, even though he does his best to exhibit a gay persona.

"I was hoping," my beloved said, in a dangerously meek voice, "that you young women would be part of our wedding party."

"Where did you get your boob job?" Irene asked, on a signal from her sister. I had a strong urge to strangle them both.

Maria dismissed her with an amused laugh.

"I'm afraid I have to blame my Tuscan genes for my figure. There's not much one can do about them. I've never had any cosmetic surgery. Only pretty good makeup. I could recommend it to you if you're interested, though it tends to be expensive."

Chris Riordan, who may not have had a shower for the last week, yawned. He did not realize that he should memorize the scene, which might have been drawn from one of Eugene O'Neill's plays about Irish drunks. The scene was now set for the end-of-the-act performance by my firstborn daughter, the light of my life, my pride and joy.

"We will not, Ms. Connors, accept positions in your wedding party. Nor will we appear at the ceremony itself, which is probably sacrilegious. To be candid, we don't like you. We don't want you. We will not accept you as, God forbid the word, our stepmother. You are a strumpet, a whore, a hooker, a cunt, a punch card. I would not let you near my kiddies for fear they would pick up some hideous disease from you. . . . Dad, you have shown incredibly bad taste in your choice of a woman. You disgrace and humiliate us and our mother. If you go ahead with this hideous marriage, we have no choice but to disinherit you. Permanently. From the day of your marriage you will simply not exist for us. You can try to take our trust funds away from us. My Tony says that you will not be able to do that. But fuck the trust funds and fuck you too."

"You might also have called me a drab, a blowen, or even flattered me a bit and used the word *courtesan*. . . . *Heinous* would have been a better adjective in the context, more Catholic." My bride would have the last word, would she not?

"Do you have anything to say, Dad? We are all prepared for fervent denials. We reject them out of hand."

"No response at all," I said. "I will not play Lear to your Goneril, now or ever."

"What your father means"—Maria stole the final word again—"is that you can't excommunicate him because he has already excommunicated you. I assume you have sent up the ticket for your bar amusements, a charge which excommunication does not cancel. This time."

They all exited silently.

"I suggest," she continued, "that we have our dinner sent in, and another bottle of wine and then return to your house for whatever amusements are available to us on a lonely autumn night."

— Maria Angelica —

WE DID just that. It was a memorable night of love for me. Sex with Jack was better than I imagined it could be, but the ultimate pleasure had still escaped me. However, that evening with the full moon bathing both of us with its inviting glow I plunged over the edge into abandon and the depths of pleasure. . . . So this is what it is supposed to be like. . . . Sometimes . . . I must remember the way down, so I can come back. . . .

Then Jack was speaking to me, the sound of fear in his voice.

"Are you all right Maria! Wake up, please!"

"I'm all right," I sighed, "but if it's just the same to you, I'd rather not wake up. . . ."

"What happened?"

"Abandon, I think. Sometimes women lose consciousness for a few minutes. . . . It is not serious. . . . But, oh, Jackie dear . . . It was so wonderful. . . . Thank you . . ."

"Can I get anything for you . . . ?"

Poor dear man, he was so worried about me. . . . He really does love me. . . . Like most men he is afraid of the depths of womanly orgasm.

"I just want to lay here with you, naked in the moonlight and bask in all the warmth. . . . It beats the Cayman Islands. . . ."

He wrapped his arms around me and pulled me against himself, as though he were afraid he'd lose me again. Poor dear man.

"You could bring me a large glass of iced tea, spiced kind please, heavy on the ice, a touch of lime."

When he returned I had pulled myself into a chaise and tossed a towel around me, not so much out of shame as pride. His naked body was very beautiful in the moonlight. Mine . . . all mine.

He reclined next to me and gave me the iced tea.

"Hmmm . . . Good."

"Sweet and tart . . . Just like you . . ."

I caressed him gently.

"You want more?" he asked, astonished.

"Not right away." I touched his lips gently with my own, tasting his strength and goodness against the tea.

"Those poor people," I said.

"You feel sorry for them, after the terrible things they said?"

"They are so lonely, no joy in their lives at all."

"That's certainly true. The O'Mearas are filled with pride and bitterness and drink. They'll never escape. . . . It's my daughters I worry about."

"Don't worry, Jackie Pat, I'll get them back for you."

I must have fallen asleep then. The next thing I knew it was morning and I was in bed, curled up in my lover's arms as the sun peered above the horizon to warn me that there was more to life than fun and games, though they were fine too.

You know the rest of the story. After the nonwedding banquet we walked over to the cathedral to protest to the cardinal. The sweet teen at the door whose name was Megan told me that the cardinal was not in but Archbishop Ryan would see us. A funny little man with pale blue eyes behind thick glasses, he was wearing black jeans, a clerical shirt, and a Chicago Bears Windbreaker.

"Ah," he said, "you have fallen into the hands of idiots, clerical idiots. I will make a phone call that should clarify matters. Forgive me while I don my clerical persona and call the cathedral rectory in our suffragan see to the West, Northwest in point of fact, though it is politically 'downstate.' "

The darling little man assumed an expression of mock pomposity.

"Yes, this is Archbishop Ryan calling for Cardinal Cronin. May I talk to the monsignor . . . ? Ah, good afternoon, Monsignor . . . The cardinal has directed me to call you to seek information. We have a situation here which he wishes to resolve promptly. . . ."

He grimaced at his role of the ponderous ecclesiastic.

"Yes, Monsignor, I appreciate your willingness to cooperate. . . . My first question is whether there has ever been a parish in honor of St. Lawrence in Oakdale or anywhere in the adjoining communities. . . . Yes, I see . . . My second and last question is whether in the last half century or so there has ever been one Father Thomas Hartnett in your diocese. . . . Yes, I will wait till you check the necrology. . . ."

He put his hand over the phone and rolled his eyes.

"Yes, Monsignor . . . Indeed, well that resolves our little problem. . . . The cardinal directs me to thank you and to convey his fraternal greetings to your ordinarius. . . . Yes, Monsignor, but the pleasure has been mine.

"Hooray for our side . . . as I expected you have been victims of a foul and, if I may say so, sloppy plot. . . . Can you gather your wedding party together tomorrow morning? . . . Good, Milord Cronin will be pleased to offer a nuptial liturgy in one of the side chapels in the cathedral tomorrow morning at nine-thirty. I would suggest that if you require an explanation of this nasty and messy plot, you contact this young woman. . . . Her name may be familiar to you. . . . She sings. . . . Yes, that one . . . she also has considerable talent at disentangling puzzles. . . . Oh, yes, I will be present for the liturgy to, uh, assist Milord Cronin and, if it pleases him to say a few words that might be appropriate for the occasion."

The next morning the cardinal said the nuptial Mass, a choir of teenagers led by a young woman named Crystal sang. The wedding party was there and Mary Fran whom Maria had seen coming out of Mass at St. Freddy's and dragged over to the dinner, where she seemed to bond quickly with Maria's kids. My Cordelia.

After he had read the Gospel, the cardinal, tall, handsome, and charming, said a few words to us about how the Church should be judged by this service instead of what happened yesterday.

"I could preach for you and maybe put our lovely choir maidens to sleep. Instead I am going to ask my helper archbishop to tell you why God made strawberries."

The nice little man was wearing a white alb. Only a gorgeous silver St. Brigid's cross around his neck suggested that he was anything more than a random deacon who had wandered in.

This is a story I first heard from a Cherokee princess. My Cherokee brogue isn't very good, so I've changed it to a brogue and a setting I know a little better.

Once upon a time, long, long ago, there was Earth Maker and First Man and First Woman. They lived in a whitewashed stone cottage on the edge of a green field with a silver lake and a road leaving over the hills and out beyond. First Man and First Woman were very much in love and very happy together. Earth Maker was pleased with himself because it appeared that his experiment of creating male and female had been a huge success. Oh, they argued a few times a week, but never anything serious.

Then one day they had a terrible fight. They forgot what they were fighting about and fought about who had started it and then about what the fight was about.

Finally First Woman was fed up. You're nothing but a loudmouth braggart! she said and stormed out of the cottage and across the green field and by the silver lake and over the hill and out beyond.

First Man sat back in his rocking chair, lit his pipe, and sighed happily. Well, at last we'll have some peace and quiet around here. The woman has a terrible mouth on her.

But as the sun set and turned the silver lake rose gold, he realized he was hungry. Woman, he shouted, I want my tea. But there was no woman to make the tea. Poor First Man could not even boil water. So he had to be content with half of a cold pratie (which is what the Irish call a potato). Then as a chill came over the cottage and First Man felt lonely altogether, he sighed again, let his pipe go out, and felt he needed a good night's sleep. He didn't light the fire because, truth to tell, he wasn't very good at such things. First Woman did all the fire-lighting in their house because she could start fires in a second.

The poor fella shivered something awful when he pulled the covers over himself. Well, he told himself, she did keep the bed warm at night. He didn't sleep very well and when he woke there was a terrible hunger on him. Woman, he shouted, I want me tea! Then he realized that there was no woman and no tea. So he had to be satisfied with the other half of the cold pratie.

Well, he was sitting in front of the cold fireplace, puffing on a cold pipe, wrapped in a thin blanket, when Earth Maker appeared.

Let me see now, said Earth Maker. This is earth and I made ye male and female. And you're the male. Where's herself?

She's gone, Your Reverence.

Gone?

Gone!

Why's she gone?

We had a fight!

You never did!

We did!

And she left you?

She did, Your Reverence.

You're a pair of eejits!

Yes, Your Reverence.

Do you still love her?

Oh yes, Your Reverence, something terrible!

Well then, man, off your rocking chair and after her!

She's long gone, Your Reverence. I'll never catch up with her.

No problem. I can move as fast as thought. I'll go ahead of you and slow her down! Now get a move on!

Poor First Man, his heart breaking, trundled out of his chair and down the path across the green field and by the silver lake and out beyond.

Meanwhile Earth Maker caught up with First Woman. She was still furious at First Man. She walked down the road at top speed, muttering to herself as she went.

The woman has a temper, Earth Maker reflected. But that fella would make anyone lose their temper.

So to slow her down, said "ZAP!" and created a forest. Didn't she cut through it like a warm knife cutting through butter?

Then Earth Maker "ZAP!" created a big hill. Didn't she charge over the hill like a mountain goat?

So ZAP, Earth Maker created a big lake. That'll stop her, he said to himself.

It didn't stop her at all, at all. She charged into the lake and swam across it, Australian Crawl.

I don't know where she learned the stroke because Australia didn't exist way back then. But she knew it.

Och, said Earth Maker, there are problems in creating women athletes, aren't there now? Well, the poor thing is hungry, so she'll slow down to eat. ZAP. There appeared along the road all kinds of fruit trees—peach trees, plum trees, grapefruit trees, apricot trees (no apple trees because that's another story).

What did First Woman do? Well she just picked the fruit as she was walking and didn't slow down a bit.

Sure, said Earth Maker, won't I have to fall back on me ultimate weapon. I'll have to create strawberries!

ZAP!

First Woman stopped cold. Ah, would you look at them pretty bushes with the white flowers.

As she watched didn't the flowers turn into rich red fruit?

Ah now isn't that gorgeous fruit and itself shaped just like the human heart?

She felt the first strawberry. Sure, doesn't it feel just like the human heart, soft and yet strong and firm. I wonder what it tastes like.

Sure, doesn't it have the sweetest taste in all the world, save for the taste of human love?

Well, she sighed loudly, speaking of that subject, I suppose the eejit is chasing after me, poor dear man. I'd better wait for him.

So didn't she pick a whole apron full of strawberries and sit by the strawberry bush and wait for First Man.

And finally, he came down the road, huffing and puffing and all worn out.

This is called the strawberry bush, she said, pointing at the bush. And doesn't the fruit taste wonderful? So she gave a piece of fruit to First Man, like the priest gives the Eucharist.

Oh, says First Man, isn't it the sweetest taste in all the world, save for the taste of human love. So they picked more strawberries and, arm in arm, walked home to their whitewashed cottage by the green field and the silver lake and the hill and out beyond. 'Tis said that they lived happily ever after, which meant only three or so fights a week.

Now I want all of you here, especially Maria Angelica and John Patrick to remember every time from now on when you taste strawberries, that the only thing sweeter is the taste of human love. And remember too that love is about catching up and waiting and true lovers know how to catch up and wait.

So that's our story, Nuala Anne, I hope it didn't bore you. . . . There's people out there that wanted to stop our marriage and now want to ruin it and maybe kill us. I'm afraid that both of us are not as scared as we should be. . . . And as we saw a few minutes ago we have hired ourselves very classy angels. . . . I take your point, Dermot, seraphs.

— Dermot —

"WELL, DERMOT Michael Coyne, what would you be after thinking about the afternoon show?"

"I thought the dogs were wonderful and weren't you smashing altogether and yourself swinging your camogie stick like you were a fifteen-year-old again!"

"Give over, Dermot Michael! That's not what I meant!"

Give over is Irish English that is more or less equivalent to *get real*, though it implies that the addressee is also a bit of an eejit.

My lovely wife and I were engaging in a new ritual we had inserted in our lives. We were sitting on a couch in our master bedroom, wearing robes, and sipping a small splash (a splasheen) of Baileys, though on other nights it might be a swallow of Bushmills Green, and discussing the events of our day. It was an interlude of peace and recollection marking the end of the chaos of the day and anticipating the wonders of the night, sleep, and perhaps love. It was supposed to constrain us not to retire with any resentments against each other. It was herself's idea of course and like all such, altogether brilliant, by her own admission. She argued that it had increased not only the frequency of our "messing around" and the quality. We ended the ritual with a decade of the rosary.

"And your older kids swarming up the stairs with their softball bats and meself swinging the snow shovel, faith we could have repelled the whole Brit parachute regiment, couldn't we? No one pulls up in front of the Coyne house and looks suspicious and the dogs howling like they were auditioning for *The Hound of the Baskervilles*. We scared them shitehawks!

"And me daughter thought to bring her camera and take a picture of their friggin' car and get its license plate number."

One of the rhetorical rules of our happy union is that when one of the kids does something "brilliant altogether," it's her offspring and when one goofs up, the child becomes "mine."

"The whole business suggests that the plot against our new friends is clumsy."

"Reckless and possibly dangerous . . . And them poor folks just beginning a brilliant new marriage . . . And don't think, Dermot Michael, that I didn't notice all the attention you were paying to the woman."

"I was only imagining myself at that age and having such a gorgeous spouse."

"Och," she said with a sigh, the typical West of Ireland sigh which sounds like a severe asthma attack. "Doesn't she have pretty boobs? And herself experiencing full orgasm for the first time. . . ."

"Ah," I said, figuring that if my wife could predict pregnancies before they happen, she could also sense the quality of a woman's orgasm after the fact.

"Some of us never experience it at all, the trick of it, as you well know, is for the poor woman to yield to her body's demand for total abandon of which she is afraid. Sometimes she even passes out for a moment. . . . But her pleasure then is much greater than that of the eejit with the pent-up hormones who's riding her."

"So I have been told."

"Sure you don't even remember when it happened to me for the first time, do you now?"

"Woman, I do. It was in Limerick town . . . and you scared the living daylights out of me when you passed out."

I had the day marked in my calendar and gave her a present on the anniversary.

"Sometimes you see a woman on an elevator and you can tell where she's been the night before."

"And where's that?"

"In the antechamber of heaven, where else . . . And meself praying to God that her eejit lover will remember how it went . . . and that he shouldn't expect it all the time . . . So we have to protect them both, poor dear people, from those who want to destroy their love, isn't that true, Dermot Michael?"

"Woman, 'tis."

"Those gobshites in the car weren't the people behind it. Commander Culhane says that they are just thugs sent to harass them, like all the phone calls and the anonymous e-mail. But the evil people behind them are really dangerous. Sloppy maybe but that makes them only more dangerous, doesn't it now?"

"I think the real plotters—conceding for the moment that there's a plot . . ."

My contribution to the resolution of the mock attack on Sheffield Avenue was to call Mike Casey on my cell phone and tell him to tell Gaby Lopez to drive around the block before I had grabbed the snow shovel and belatedly joined our mob. They would have fled quickly enough anyway, the Devil himself would have run from the howls of our hounds.

Afterward, terribly proud of what they had done, they returned calmly to the first floor to play with the kids.

"Dermot Michael Coyne, there is a plot, haven't I told you so?"

"Woman, you have . . . They're probably playing it all by ear, taking advantage of the opportunities that come up. . . . Empiricists . . . I can't imagine what they're up to. . . ."

"They want to destroy Jack and Maria and we have to find out why."

"They both said that if their marriage becomes a media sensation, it could destroy their businesses. . . . Is that true, Dermot?"

"His asset management funds depend on investors' confidence in him. I can't imagine Frodo or Samwise tanking but he might have to sell them, though he'd collect enough to live the rest of his life in total comfort. Her venture is new and promising, but fragile. It's on the bubble. It could come under assault from suspicious customers and disappear into the night."

"So tomorrow morning, don't you have to go out to Loyola Medical School and interview this Mary Fran person and find out where they heard all the misinformation about Maria Angelica and whether they passed on that fake letter to the gobshite at St. Freddy's?"

"Wasn't I thinking the same thing meself?"

"And we must say our decade of the rosary tonight that them gobshites and CTN (Consolidated Television Network) back down. Or that the judge gives us . . . What do they call it?"

"An emergency order. Our guys made a strong case about catastrophic harm. The judge will grant the order. They'll appeal and we'll need the Seventh District to grant their own emergency. The CTN people are dumb enough to try the Supreme Court. That will be a waste of their time and money."

"I still don't like it."

"What you don't like, good wife, is staying out of the fight."

"Och, sure, Dermot Michael, don't you have the right of it."

We said the rosary. It was her turn to lead. The tone of her voice suggested that the deity was receiving his instructions.

Then we would make the rounds of the bedrooms. Both the boys and the girls were sleeping soundly, the former under the watchful eye of Fiona and the latter snoozing under the surveillance of Maeve. Both would slip into the master bedroom in the course of the night, nudging the door open with their big snoots.

"Well," I said rising from my knees, "I don't suppose there'll be any riding tonight."

"Go long with ya, Dermot love, after the sexuality oozing around our living room today, I won't permit you to dream about that woman's boobs all night long."

"Well then." I pulled off her robe. "I'll have to find an alternative subject for my lascivious dreams, won't I now?"

— Dermot —

"EVIE CARRIES a lot of anger," Mary Fran Donlan said in the calm tone appropriate for a Freudian therapist in her middle fifties or a newly ordained priest. "She is angry at our mother whom she adored for being an alcoholic and then for dying too early in life. She is angry at the O'Mearas for killing her and at Daddy for permitting them to kill her. She is angry at me because, as she thinks, Daddy named the boat after me, when it was really his mother's name. She is also furious at me because she thinks I'm prettier than she is. She is angry at the Church because it is there, inviting anger. She's angry at her husband because he is a creep with no confidence in himself and lets her browbeat him. . . . I'm sorry, Mr. Coyne, for lecturing. . . ."

"Dermot," I insisted. "Mr. Coyne is my father."

"Actually, he's Dr. Coyne." Her brief smile would have melted an ice cap. "He's one of the nicest men in this place. And Dr. Coyne asks questions just the way you do, Mr. Coyne . . . Dermot."

We were sitting in a cubicle for students doing their clerkships at Loyola

University Hospital and Medical Center in Maywood. There was room for a small metal desk on which there were two paper cups filled with coffee (black), two uncomfortable metal chairs, and us. In her shapeless green coat and without any makeup, she looked like a pretty, natural-blond teenager playing nurse and not the beautiful young woman that Maria Angelica had described.

"A deeply troubled young woman," I nodded in agreement.

She smiled slightly in acknowledgment that I was giving a therapist's response.

"Yet her fury turns her into a dynamic leader for any cause that happens to come along. Back in the days when Daddy was young she'd have marched on the Pentagon alongside Norman Mailer. She has charisma and charm to spare, all driven by her rage at the O'Meara family and at the O'Meara inside herself. . . . Now look at me! Analyzing my sister like I'm a teaching analyst at the institute! And I'm really only a third-year med student."

The "institute" was the Chicago Institute for Psychoanalysis founded by one of Freud's pupils, Franz Alexander, and not to be confused with the Art Institute or *The* University.

"But you hope to be one some day."

"Maybe," she shrugged. "I'm not sure I buy all that Freudian stuff. . . . Anyway she's very angry at Maria because my stepmom, as she is now, is a perfect target—another O'Meara and yet a non-O'Meara."

"And too beautiful by half, as the Brits would say."

"And she has laid-back kids like Evie wishes we were. . . . Well, she doesn't know the kids yet, but wait till she does."

Before I drove out to Maywood on the Congress Expressway (as we Democrats still call it), my wife and I took our three oldest children, accompanied by the two dogs, across the street to St. Josephat school. I wondered if they might some day become a viper's tangle of conflicts that would be our fault. Nelliecoyne (aka Mary Anne) was four years short of her chronological teen years but had already become a certified, card-carrying preteen, especially in her ability to be acutely critical of her parents' inconsistencies. She and her mother argued constantly, though with little anger.

"You and Ma banter, Da, me and Ma argue. It's the way we bond."

"Ma and I," Nuala Anne corrected her.

"Yes, Ma," she said with a sigh almost as loud as her ma's.

She was also fey like her mother, "even more than I was at her age, the poor dear little thing."

So Nelliecoyne and her ma often communicated without the benefit of words, especially when I was the subject. That alliance against me would become stronger as the years went on.

The Mick, named after me Micheal Dirmuid, was all boy, soccer, baseball, Cub fan, Bear fan, Bull fan, Notre Dame fan, even Marquette fan. He loves to play with trucks. He also loves to paint. Just as his sister carries a camera all the time, he has a sketchbook in his pocket and would translate that sketch often to a computer graphic.

Socra Marie, at the moment leading her two doggies into the little band of kindergarten children who screamed with joy every morning at the sight of the huge white beasts, was our miracle child. Impatient to get into the world, she left her mother's womb after twenty-five weeks and was so tiny I could hold her in one of my hands. She entered the world with a determination to stay with us that was barely strong enough to ensure her survival. But she made it and finally came home with us, still tiny and still filled with vitality. By the time she was two her energy made her a tiny terrorist who, with great éclat, broke or spoiled everything she could get her hands on. She also wore "gwasses," which hung askew on her little nose but never quite fell. She tried her best to be a "good little girl" but her ongoing celebration of life precluded such a transformation till she went to preschool. She charmed teachers and classmates alike and calmed down a bit because she perceived that was necessary to her charm. But the mania was still there just beneath the surface. "Teacher says I'm an adorable handful," she had told us proudly.

Last of all came two-year-old Patjo, who was described by one of my sisters as "just like his father, big, strong, good-looking, and useless."

Such comments infuriated the child's mother, but I never did dispute them. I did hope that Patrick Joseph would graduate from college at the appropriate time instead of failing at both the Dome and Marquette. But

I also hoped he would never let his studies interfere with his education. Herself agreed completely.

"Haven't I been saying all the time that you're the best-educated man I know, Dermot Michael? The poor little fat punk will be blessed if he ever knows all that you know."

"I was a fat baby too."

"See, I'm always right."

"Yes, you are."

I wasn't sure about what, but it didn't matter.

So I kissed the kids good-bye and patted the two hounds who never liked to see anyone go away, and themselves not being sure we'd come back, and kissed Nuala and off I went to Maywood and meself knowing that I would think of her all the way.

And recall the images of our love the night before. If we were to avoid the family mess that had overwhelmed Jack Donlan it would be Nuala's doing not mine.

"So you believe that your sister will never accept her new stepmother?"

"I don't think so."

"And where does that leave you?"

Mary Fran considered that question for a moment.

"I'll have to make up my mind, won't I? Evie was furious at me because I sneaked into the Church for the wedding and that I then went to the reception."

"You went to the Mass at the cathedral?"

"I didn't know about it. I'm sure the others wouldn't attend."

"All three of you were there outside of St. Freddy's?"

"Evie said we should see how vulgar she looked. . . . I didn't think she looked vulgar at all. I thought she was gorgeous . . . and that Daddy was a very lucky man."

"And to hear what the priest said when he ordered them out of the church?"

"That was as much a surprise to us as it was to everyone."

"Might Evie have received it from someone and passed it on to the priest?"

She thought about that.

"I doubt it, Mr. Coyne, uh, Dermot. She would have lorded it over us as soon as she received it. It might have come from the same source as the original letter but not through us. Evie was ecstatic. She said it proved she had been right all along."

"And what did that original letter say?"

"You have eyes just like your father's."

"Even when I'm playing my role as a private eye?"

"Asking questions for your adorable wife."

"The last one of which you have not answered."

She opened the single drawer in her desk.

"I scribbled a copy of it when Evie wasn't watching," she said as she handed me a single sheet of computer paper. "She wouldn't let the original out of her hands. It was a scrawl on a lined page of notebook paper."

Your new mom is a whore. Out in Oakdale everyone knows she screws every man she's working on a deal with. They keep count of her victims. There's twelve of them that are common knowledge. She didn't take over that company because of her intelligence. She's a regular punch card. The guys she fucks know her reputation, but they can't keep their fly zipped when she puts out. She takes a lot of money away from them because they can't think straight. She's already taken from your asshole father and she'll clean him out before she's finished. She'll take your inheritance if you don't watch her every move.

It was, I thought, not so much an obscene letter as a letter from someone who was trying to give the impression that she was a truck driver. I used the word *she* advisedly—a proper woman trying to sound dirty.

"Can I take this?"

"Sure."

"What do you think of it?"

"Maybe a jealous middle-age woman pretending to be a truck driver . . . Evie should have torn it up and thrown it away. But she was looking for dirt. It was all she needed to organize the family against Ms. Connors."

I slid the paper into the pocket of my trademark yuppie navy blue blazer. I'm not a real yuppie because real yuppies don't flunk out of college, do they? But it's a helpful image when I am carrying the spear for Nuala Anne. A nice, wholesome-looking professional wouldn't be mixed up with Bronze Age superstition, would he?

I thanked her and gave her my card, which carries just my name and my e-mail address. It does NOT say "Spear Carrier."

"Working for that dangerous daughter-in-law of mine . . . Mother of my favorite grandchildren?" my father said when I stuck my head into his office to pay my respects. "Let's see—to give them their Christian names—Mary Anne, Michael, Sarah, and Patrick."

My folks have never been able to get their tongues around Socra Marie.

"Trying to earn an honest buck in the garden of good and evil."

"Well, that young woman is one of the best students we've had here in a long time."

Dad was telling me that he knew what I was doing around the Med Center.

"Maybe you should go to work for herself," I responded.

We both laughed.

The theory in the family is that Nuala Anne is the nice girl I brought home from Ireland who had forced me to grow up, though not nearly enough. They don't propose it to her anymore because those luminous blue eyes of hers turn as dark as storm clouds rushing in from the North Atlantic. The myth of shiftless Dermot will never die. Just as well. When I hear it from my sisters, I reply, "At least I taught her to wear shoes."

On my way back to East Lincoln Park (a more pretentious community name than "DePaul") I drove through my own "old neighborhood" River Forest, just to convince myself that the Italians hadn't ruined it yet.

(When I was young, the Irish in our suburban enclave were considerably upset at the migration of Italians from their "old neighborhood" on Taylor Street. They would "ruin" the neighborhood, it was whispered. In fact they were zealous in their home and landscape improvements, though their exuberant Christmas decorations were deemed "tacky." Which just goes to show you.)

That reminded me that I should talk to my old friend and classmate Dominic. A man who was clearly connected but clean. This meant that the money for his electronics firm may have had some shady antecedents but Dom himself was not involved directly with the outfit and that he used no outfit thugs to promote his electronics firm. I have his private number in my cell phone and he responded immediately. "Dominic."

"Hey, Dominic, it's Dermot! What's happening?"

"Hey, Dermot, what's happenin'? I hear that your beautiful wife is gonna cream this Triple A crook from Hollywood?"

"It's going down today, Dom. It looks like we're going to win."

Triple A was the name the Chicago media had assigned to Archibald Adolf Abercrombie, the president of Consolidated Television Network who was trying to stifle the Nuala Anne Christmas show. A tall, dynamic, and totally bald man, he treated Chicago media and Chicago judges and lawyers as though they were ignorant peasants standing in the way of progress. Not a particularly wise stance for somebody engaging in litigation that was dubious at best.

"Hey, Dom, you hear what went down in front of my house over in Lincoln Park yesterday?"

"No, I didn't hear. What happened?"

"A couple of individuals in a stolen car pull up to the house and get out carrying what looked like baseball bats or maybe large salami sausages. You know what certain kinds of people used to do with those?"

"Dumb! Dumb! I can't believe anybody would do that in Chicago these days, much less to you and your family. I've told you often that the friends and my friends respect you and admire her greatly."

"Yeah, well, it was kind of a mess. Our wolfhounds got angry and howled and you know what it's like when wolfhounds start howling. These individuals climbed back in their car and pulled away. We got their license number but the car was stolen."

"Sincerely, Dermot, I'm sure that no one who is a friend of my friends would do that kind of thing but let me find out. Okay?"

"I sincerely believe you, but I'm just asking that you check it out to see if your friends know who was behind this caper."

"Yeah, yeah, Dermot, I understand. We'll look into it. And I sincerely assure you that whoever was doing it won't do it again. They'll be warned off. You can count on that."

"I'm happy to hear that, Dominic, and I sincerely believe what you say. Tell the friends of your friends we don't want to complicate this one. I'm on what went down at the marriage between the Sabattini woman from Oakdale and our very good friend here in Chicago John Patrick Donlan."

"He was born with the gift of laughter and the sense that the world was mad."

So Dominic had read *Scaramouche?* Strange world.

"You got it, Dom."

"Oh yeah I heard about that. Really a strange one. So you're working on that case?"

"Trying to straighten it out a little."

"Sabattini, I've heard of them. She's supposed to be totally clean and a very nice lady. Her brothers are no good, no good at all punks. . . . Yeah, and a fake letter in church? The punks have been watching too many episodes of *The Sopranos*."

"The brothers might not be involved. . . ."

"Yeah, but they know about it. Just a few quiet words whispered into their ears. They're such lowlifes that even a whisper from the friends of my friends will scare the shit out of them, you should excuse the expression. Pleasure to help you, Dermot."

"I sincerely trust you and believe you, Dominic. Let me know what the friends of your friends are able to unearth."

The Outfit, as we call them in Chicago (or sometimes "the boys") are a group of serious businessmen. Some of their businesses are legit and some are not and some are somewhere in between. Crime interferes with business. So they try to keep a lid on crime as best they can, other people's crime. Like Blacks and Latinos and punks from out of town. It also brings in the Feds who are not very effective in their periodic campaigns against the Outfit, but who can create inconveniences. If they discover that punks, from out of town or Chicago, are messing around without asking permission, they are extremely upset. If you have good relations with them, they'll keep you informed about what's going on and what's going down. One deals with them through intermediaries and communicates in a kind of code. They'll do favors for you without necessarily picking up a marker.

So Dominic might say to me (though he never has), "I don't think I can help you on that one, Dermot. I sincerely wish I could."

That means the wiseguys are involved and to mess around could be dangerous.

Or he might say (as he sometimes has), "My friends tell me that their friends are aware of the situation and are taking care of it."

That means exactly what it says and adds the suggestion, "you'd better stay out of it."

Or yet again, "Please tell your friends that we'll clean up the mess."

When you agree to pass on the message they will have picked up a marker.

That meant that the cops should stay out of it (or the state's attorney, or Mike Casey, or even the Feds).

The Feds pretend that they eschew such communications with sworn enemies. But they engage in them as much as anyone else. It eliminates a lot of mess.

The boys take good care of me because I saved Dominic's life when we were in high school, which gives me a kind of unlimited marker. I don't use it much, in part because the thrill could become addictive.

I turned on the car radio to pick up the noon news.

Harold Hastings was reporting, one of my favorites because he is skilled in very mild African-American English, a creative and humorous dialect that deserves more respect.

"Triple A got himself canceled this morning in the Dirksen Federal building. The National Bureau of Standards obtained a permanent injunction against the man so he could not interfere with their production of the Nuala Anne McGrail Christmas special this year. Old Triple A canceled the series, which had another year to run on its contract. NBS picked it up with considerable enthusiasm as you might imagine. The tycoon of CTN came to town to block such a switch. He didn't want Ms. McGrail on his network or anyone else's and he was not about to negotiate a termination agreement with her production company. As Federal Judge Ebenezer Brown commented in granting a permanent injunction, Mr. Abercrombie's lawyers should explain to him contract law. Even in Hollywood you cannot terminate a contract short of a termination date and still control the other party of the contract. Mr. Abercrombie announced that they would immediately appeal the decision. 'It's our show. If we decided not to present it, we will not permit anyone else to present it. *Christmas with Nuala Anne* is dead, permanently dead.'

"Gerard Mooney of the Chicago firm of Moody, Mooney, Meany, and Mularky, who represented NBS, remarked that ole Triple A must never have heard the story of the Dog in the Manger.

"Mary Anne Coyne, a spokesperson for Ms. McGrail, said that the immensely popular singer was unavailable for comment because she was practicing songs for the special."

Mary Anne Coyne was not a spokesperson for her mother.

I punched in the Heart Line Number intended for exclusive use of meself and me wife.

"Nuala Anne McGrail's line," my daughter informed me.

"Are you Ms. McGrail's spokesperson?"

"Is that you, Pa?" she said with a giggle.

"Possibly."

"I'll get Ma."

A louder giggle.

"Dermot, we beat the nine-fingered shitehawk!"

"The shitehawk in the manger . . . Woman, you're violating the child labor law!"

"She's your daughter!"

"You hired her!"

"I have to practice me singing. Won't I be talking to you when you get home? . . . Did you like me 'dog in the manger' line?

"Wasn't it grand!"

"Love you, spear-carrier!"

She hung up.

Bitch.

Go long with ya, you're proud of her!

— Nuala Anne —

"I'M SORRY to disturb you on a day which is so important to you," Maria Connors began hesitantly.

"Och, don't fret your soul about it," I replied, slipping into me ma's reassurance style. "Hasn't poor Mr. Triple A dug himself into a hole which his stockholders won't like at all, at all, so we'll probably win, perhaps even with enough time to get the show together. It was supposed to be the last one anyhow. Sure, I've been thinking all year that this would be the last one anyway. We maybe need a rest from it, but NBS wants a two-year commitment. . . ."

"You must be a very busy woman, Nuala?"

She was wearing black trousers and a fluffy white blouse over the waist with a thick black belt holding the whole thing together. She was beautiful altogether and her boobs were firm and perfect underneath the blouse. But what was the point in hating her?

I was holding me youngest in me arms. He was about to fall asleep, an impulse which, like his father, he rarely resisted.

"Handsome little guy," she said.

"They say he's lazy, just like his father, but me Dermot is anything but lazy. He's just laid back, as this little punk . . . I think I'll put him down now. He won't bother us again."

I hummed me favorite lullaby, the Connemara, as I carried Patjo up to his room. . . . *Blow winds blow* . . .

Maeve had followed me upstairs. It was her turn to supervise the boys' room.

Fiona, and herself napping, was lying at Maria's feet.

"Sweet, sweet dog . . ." she said, stroking the massive head.

"And a lifesaver too sometimes . . . How's business?"

"So far, so good, down a little bit maybe, but it's Monday morning and the holidays and our usual yuppie clients are busy on other forms of consumerism."

"Don't be a cynic, Maria, you're not one, not anymore."

"You see too much, Nuala Anne," she said, blushing. "I have a story to tell you, however, that may have an impact on the puzzle. I haven't told it to Jack yet, but I will this evening. He deserves a warning of what might happen."

Now I may be a tad fey, and I may see auras around people's heads—Maria's was a kind of dusky rose gold—but a confessor or a counselor or a spiritual director I am not and I'm not sure I want to be.

"He'll love you just as much as he did before you told him and maybe more."

"It's about my affair, fling, fall from grace whatever with Congressman Stafford of our district. He lost in the election a couple of weeks ago. Kishwaukee County, which has had a lot of war casualties, beat him into the ground. Oakdale went overwhelmingly against him, though he never won a majority from our voters."

"And yourself the precinct captain, aren't you?"

"I always campaigned against him even before our fling. Since then I have worked even harder, though I realized that it might be risky. . . . You may not have seen any pictures of him. He's a big, good-looking man, broad shoulders, long gray hair, big smile, oozes charm. I always thought the charm was a bit sinister. I should have been wary, but I wasn't."

She paused, stopped petting Fiona who protested by raising her head. Maria renewed the affection. Someday, I thought, I'm going to be as grown up as she is and won't I be about ninety?

"Anyway, one weekend five years ago, his office in D.C. called and suggested we have dinner on Saturday night at the country club. He had good news for me. I was suspicious. He was married and his wife, a smartly dressed woman about his age, had decided, unlike the current congressmen's wives, to live in Chevy Chase. Sterling Stafford nonetheless flew back to his district a couple of times a month. Maybe that ought to have made me suspicious. He had enormous power in Congress, lots of lobbyist money, and was close to Newt Gingrich when he was Speaker and a leader in the impeachment of Clinton."

"Nice man," I said.

"The news was really good. He had made a deal which would bring some major grants to his district for historic preservation and development. I needed good news. My poor husband's decline was accelerating. We were no longer making love, though we hugged and held hands. I didn't think I was any more deprived sexually than many women my age who were in unsatisfactory marriages—which seemed to me most of the women I knew. Their favorite conversational topic was how inadequate their men were in every respect. My plans and projects and big ideas and little crusades seemed useless and boring. Only my kids kept me going. They were fun and they let me have fun with them.

"I drank too much wine that evening in the club. Sterling didn't push his luck which was wise because I would have smote him with righteous anger as my evangelical friends say. His kiss good-night was too forceful but it stirred up emotions and sensations that I had not experienced in a long time and expected not to experience again. . . . That's when my adultery began."

"It began," I said firmly, "when you went to bed with him."

She was weeping now, a thin line of tears slipping down her cheeks. She hugged a delighted Fiona as though the wolfhound promised salvation.

"We drove up to Rockford in his wife's Cadillac the next week for dinner at an expensive and elegant steakhouse—probably the only one in town. I drank too much and surrendered all thoughts of resistance. Sterling pawed me all the way back to his home on the Kishwaukee, one we had built for him. I knew what would happen and I no longer cared. He had said nothing about the appropriation bill for our grants and I didn't care about that either. Nor did I care about the animal heads and the gun racks with which he had ruined our design for the parlor. No wonder, I thought, that his wife stays in D.C. He carried me upstairs to the master bedroom which was one of our standard models. He began to remove my clothes, none too gently, and to kiss me with increasing brutality. One of those kind, I thought, but it doesn't matter."

"Why did you get out?"

"How did you know that!" she exclaimed, startled.

"No way you were that drunk or lonely."

"I heard the camera running."

"Camera!"

"There was a vague sound of something whirling—even, mechanical, implacable. I was on a soundstage. Like I say, I knew the room and I looked at the corner where one might hide a camera. Sure enough! I pushed the bastard off me, dashed across the room, picked up the camera, pulled out the tape, and threw the camera at him. It hit the bastard in his head and stunned him for a moment. I grabbed my dress, ran down the stairs, and seized one of his shotguns."

I applauded.

"I hope you shot him!"

"Och, Nuala Anne McGrail Coyne, aren't you the violent one!

"He stumbled down the stairs, stark naked, and dazed. He called me a lot of names, the mildest one of which was 'tease.' I told him I would blow off his balls if he came a step nearer to me. I wouldn't of course, but I would have hit him on the head with the butt of the gun. I could see the safety was on the gun. He was still woozy. The camera was a good weapon. I picked his car keys off the mantel where he had deposited them when we had come into the house.

"He collapsed into a chair and rubbed his head. 'You hurt me, bitch.' 'Not as much as I will if you get out of that chair. Now I'll tell you what you're going to do. You're going to take some aspirin and sleep this off. Then tomorrow morning at ten o'clock you drive into the parking lot behind our store in your Taurus. You will bring the rest of my clothes in some kind of suitcase, enter our front door, and deposit it inside the door. I will throw this key at you and you will get into your wife's car where this gun will be on the backseat, minus the bullets, and drive home. You can have one of your guys pick up the Taurus. And that's the end of it. I have the tape and I'll write up an account of the evening. I will place the tape somewhere where you won't ever find it. I won't blackmail you and you don't try to have me killed. And we'll call it even. Clear?' "

"Quick thinking," I said.

"Salespeople have to think quickly."

"He called me some more names and then groaned and held his head. I was ready for him the next morning with one of my father-in-law's guns, not loaded. 'Just put the bag down and leave.' "

"He tried to make peace?" I said.

" 'Maria, it was all a terrible mistake. I beg you, please forgive me.'

" 'It certainly was a mistake. I won't use this against you. Just get out of here and leave me alone.' He begged some more and I raised the gun and he dashed out.

"He phoned the next day to apologize again and promised that he would tell no one."

"Damn well better not," I said.

"The money actually came through for our project. I publicly thanked him for his support. We chatted amiably on the rare occasions we were together in public. He looked like a whipped little puppy dog."

At the word *dog* Fiona perked up her ears to see if she were under discussion. She rearranged herself and went back to sleep.

"And a frightened one at that!"

"Yes, he did seem scared."

" 'Tis yourself who needs a drop of the creature."

I left the room and came back with two jars of the finest. She had suspended her weeping and repaired her makeup.

I glanced out the window. A reliable limo was waiting.

"*Slainte!*"

"*Slainte!*" she said in return, not pronouncing the word properly at all—most Yanks can't.

We both sipped our drinks. She shuddered, but she needed something strong, didn't she?

"So," I said, "when did the adultery happen? Did you give him a second chance?"

I knew very well she hadn't.

"I drove up to Rockford to go to confession. I couldn't tell Father Matt. The priest said that I had intended to commit adultery and that was already a mortal sin of adultery. I had to say all fifteen decades of the rosary."

"Bullshite! You never really intended to do it, else why would you be looking for a way out and hearing that friggin' camera? He would have had to rape you and I suspect you would have beat him up while he was trying. . . . You never went to Catholic schools?"

"My parents said we couldn't afford it."

"Well, if you did, you'd know it was no sin at all, at all."

Nuala Anne McGrail, mother superior, confessor, and doctor of the Church.

"If you want to know what I think, you should forget it all together . . . though it's a great story."

"I have to tell my husband."

"Why ever would you do that?"

"They say that Sterling Stafford is very bitter over his defeat and is talking about getting even with his enemies."

"If you ask me, and I know you haven't, he still regrets his lost opportunity. So you tell Jackie and won't he laugh like I did!"

"You will tell Dermot, won't you?"

"We'll find out what your man is up to. I suspect he's still terrified."

"You're a wonderful confidante, Nuala," she said, her eyes shining.

And the woman a good twenty years older than meself, even if she didn't look it. Wait till I tell Dermot!

"I don't understand why sex is so important to women my age. We're not likely to produce more kids. There is no need for us to stay married so that our kids will receive an education. I thought I was through with it till I met my husband. Now I'm like a raging inferno."

How fortunate for your man.

" 'Tis the discipline, isn't it now?"

"Discipline!"

" 'Tis! Sex is great craic, but only if we can learn the discipline of being sensitive to our lover. All the time. No complaining about him to our women friends. Same for him. We learn how to respect everyone by respecting our lover. And if we're not generous to him, we won't be generous to anyone else and we'll be miserable human beings, won't we? So sex at any age civilizes us, at least if we want to keep up the craic. Lots of times it isn't easy because the other is often a friggin' amadon. But that's the way they are. Women can be eejits too, you know, friggin' onchucks."

"We have to learn how to preserve our lovers?"

" 'Tis true and if we can do that we have learned how to be good in all our relationships."

"The lover is paradigmatic?"

"Isn't that what himself, the little archbishop says and doesn't he know everything about it and himself an outsider."

We drained our jars, she put on her Brit trench coat and walked down to the car, meself with her lest she fall. She hugged me again.

"I'd better go home and prepare myself to be generous to my lover, not that it is difficult these days. . . . I must learn to understand him better. . . ."

"Ah, no, that's useful, but the trick of it is to understand yourself better."

She nodded, as if she got it. Smart woman that she was, she surely got it.

"Come on, Fiona, we've done a good day's work," I said and we walked up the stairs together.

— Dermot —

"WHAT'S HAPPENING?" I asked as I ambled into Jack Donlan's office.

He glanced up and smiled, a smile which me wife had said would break many a married woman's heart if she were Irish. Not mine of course, she had added.

He stood up briskly and shook hands.

"A cup of tea?"

"A touch of it," I said. "It's been a dry morning."

Waiting in the doorway, Elfrida said, "I'll make it, Mr. Donlan. You don't know how to do it for an Irishman."

I thought of pleading that it was me wife that was Irish.

"To answer your question, the Dow, Nasdaq, S and P are all nervous. Frodo and Samwise are no more nervous than anyone else. The lightning is still up there, but so far so good."

"You think that will continue?"

"Until the other shoe falls."

"What's the other shoe?"

"The next phase in the plot."

"You think there is a plot?"

"Dermot, as a gambler, I have to deal with probabilities. If it looks like a duck and walks like a duck and quacks like a duck, it's probably a duck—eighty-five percent probability. Maybe it's a South American pigeon which is invading our shores. This affair looks like someone—singular or plural—is out to get either Maria or me. They are hasty and clumsy but so far they have proven themselves skillful at seizing opportunities."

"You are remarkably calm about it, sir."

He shrugged, a hint of Celtic fatalism.

The good Elfrida returned with tea and buttered scones and admonished us to let it steep for a while. I immediately captured one of the scones and swallowed it whole.

"One wins some and loses some. I won Maria, I might lose Frodo, but with enough cash to live luxuriously for the rest of our lives. As my father used to say, don't fight the Holy Ghost. I might sail a boat round the world or do something else constructive."

"Who are the plotters?"

"I don't know. I'm trusting you and your wife and Mike Casey to figure that out. I think my family is involved, but only as unwitting tools. . . . Have you managed to find any evidence about that?"

He poured tea for both of us. Perfectly steeped, as I knew it would be. Like me wife he must have a stopwatch in his head for such matters.

"This is a copy of the letter they received," I said, passing it across his desk. "The original was crudely scrawled on a lined page torn out of a notebook."

He glanced at it and shrugged again.

"I would say probably an outburst from a hysterical middle-aged person, likely a woman. Just the sort of screed that would appeal to my family."

He gave it back to me.

"They certainly made a lot out of it," I suggested. "Would you suppose that she knew how they would react?"

I sipped the tea. Delicious.

"Milk?" he asked.

"As I tell the woman of the house, I never pollute perfectly good tea."

"Or maybe the one who sent the letter had a shrewd guess about what they would think anyway of a new stepmother. . . . I never would have thought that adult women would so resent another woman in the master bedroom. . . . Shows how much I understand women, doesn't it, Dermot?"

"Me wife, who knows about such primal things, tells me that the mystery of the parental bed is both fascinating and terrifying to kids as they grow up."

"Mary Fran gave you the copy, I suppose? Where is she?"

"She understands that she must make a decision and knows that she will choose you and Maria but hesitates."

"Spirit is willing, but the flesh is weak, eh?"

"A colleague of yours made roughly the same allegations, did he not?"

"Lou Garner, a classmate at Loyola University, real estate, loves to gossip, but is not vicious, means no harm by it . . ."

"A rival?"

"On the tennis court . . . Otherwise a friend. He came to the wedding and the reception and was very gracious in his congratulations. I don't think he is capable of conspiracy, but then what do I know?"

"Either he made up the allegations or they are free-floating rumors up and down LaSalle Street."

"I thought they were the latter, the sort of remark which is made about a woman who is beautiful and successful. I asked Mike Casey to investigate."

He opened a drawer in his desk and with the unerring instinct of the man who knows where every document is, removed a file folder and handed it to me.

Three typed pages of notes, which I read quickly.

"When is her feast day?" I asked, returning the file to his desk, still opened.

He chuckled.

" 'Chaste and modest matron' summarizes it all, does it not? I'll confess that I found the prospect of bedding such a one to be, how shall I say it, appealing. I hope that does not make me sound like a degenerate."

"If it does, then much of the human race is degenerate."

You think herself is a chaste and modest matron?

Among other things.

That's why you fuck her in the kitchen?

Once in a while when no one else is around.

I shook off the murmurings of my everpresent Adversary and returned to the discussion with my client.

"You might mail this report to Mary Fran. It would confirm her inclination to admire your wife."

He considered the folder and glanced up at me.

"Better you send it to her. It will then appear in a more neutral context."

"Good idea . . . Now, would you give me permission to talk to Lou Garner?"

"Why not? I would have a hard time thinking of him as a suspect."

A classmate and a foe on the tennis court who was not nearly so successful as you? Gimme a break.

I gathered together the remnants of our morning tea, but Elfrida intervened to prevent servile work by such an important man. As I left the office I observed that John Patrick Donlan had returned to the eternal flow of stock reports on his big computer screen and rejoiced that I had withdrawn from that casino.

I hurried home in the hope that I might find me wife in some domestic situation in which she could play the role of the chaste and modest matron.

I was out of luck. There were vehicles all along Sheffield Avenue, including a Channel 3 TV truck. Several small ones were thundering up the stairs. Nuala Anne was having a party. Celebrating our victory in court.

The parlor was swarming with people, rug-rat people and grown-up people, neighbors and their kids like Peter and Cindasue Murphy, kids from school who were in Nuala's chorus, teachers from the school, the priest from the rectory, my sister Cindy and her husband Tom Hurley who was one of the lawyers for NBS and parents of Ellie, TV technicians, me wife pouring tea, me older daughter and son offering Coke or water, Ellie and Danuta serving scones, Socra Marie hugging anyone who looked like they needed a hug, and the hounds proudly sauntering around as if they were in fact the cause of all the celebration.

"All right, quiet please! . . . Are you ready, Nuala? . . . You can put the teapot down for a moment. . . ."

The ever-present Nelliecoyne removed the pot from her ma's hand. In a red and gold Marquette sweatsuit me wife looked every bit the surprised yuppy matron.

I was proud of her, like I usually am.

"Nuala," Mary Alice asked, "would you have any comment that you seemed to have won the case and your Christmas special will air again this year on NBS?"

"Winning is better than losing, as we Irish know because we've lost so often in our sad history. And isn't it NBS who had the injunction lifted, so didn't they win? And isn't the decision on appeal and no one knows what this new bunch of lawyers will do? So it's still early days, isn't it now? But it's time for a preliminary celebration anyway. . . ."

"Isn't it true, Nuala, that Ireland is now the richest country in Europe?"

"Och, 'tis, but we don't like to talk about it for fear of hurting the feelings of your poor Brits. All that proves is that the Irish win in the long run but they have to wait a thousand years. . . . And we only have a couple of more days?"

"Do you have any comment on the fact that Mr. Abercrombie will appear in all the papers tomorrow morning as the dog in the manger?"

"I'm just happy that you Yanks are all familiar with Aesop's fables."

The kids began to sing the Connemara lullaby.

The camera turned on them. They sang more loudly.

"Great!" Mary Alice gave the cut sign. "Now let's rush this, guys, so we can get down to the studios in time to get it on both five and six o'clock."

The TV folks exited loudly. The eating and drinking and talking and singing went on. In Ireland, they would have called it a comeallye, though there would be liquor on the premises.

"This wasn't me idea," Nuala assured me as she pecked at me, uh, my cheek. "It was your sister and her husband and their daughter and themselves, terrible people altogether!"

"It was worth a celebration," I said, returning the kiss.

"Did you find out anything?"

"We better talk about it later."

"Sure, don't you have the right of it, Dermot Michael, like you always do."

My cell phone rang. I walked into our library and closed the door.

"Dermot Coyne," I said tersely.

"Hey, Dermot, it's Dom, what's happening!"

"We're having a little celebration."

"I heard you won the case."

"They're appealing."

"Them appellate judges are no good, Dermot. I hope you got a good one. . . . Say, I talked to my friends. Their friends tell them that none of our people were involved in that caper that went down yesterday. The guys who put out the contract were punks. They were told to get out of town and not come back. My friends said that their friends assured them that there wouldn't be any more trouble and that I should tell you that they still have enormous respect for you and your wife."

All very neat.

"Where were these guys from?"

"Somewhere in Wisconsin. They're back there now."

"And the guys who pulled up in the stolen car?"

"Already gone, back to St. Louis."

"No one from Oakdale?"

"Like I told you, my friends' friends don't like the Sabattini bunch at all but this is not the way they operate."

I found that reply unsettling. It probably meant that the wiseguys had no evidence and had not investigated that angle with any great care. Probably however, the wiseguys would keep an eye on them. As far as I was concerned Maria Angelica's brothers were still on the suspect list.

"I assume they'll watch them."

"Dermot, the friends of my friends always watch guys like them that are crazy and are too close to Chicago. Someday they'll go too far and then it's zero for them."

"Thanks, Dom, thanks a million . . . You'll let me know if you pick up anything more."

"I promise you that sincerely, like I tell you, you are a man my friends respect."

I never have been able to figure out why they respect me. The wiseguys have no reason to be afraid of me or of Nuala Anne. But they get nervous when they get near people that seem supernatural.

I went back to the parlor. Nuala, as is her wont, was giving orders. I noted that Cindy and Tom were not looking happy.

"All right, folks, it's getting dark outside, and all the kids should be going home. We'll continue this party on another day. Mick and Nelliecoyne, will you take the doggies downstairs so everyone has protection going home?"

"Yes, Ma!"

"Now, everyone goes right straight home, understand?"

"Yes, Miz Coyne."

Only in the context of St. Josephat school is she Miz Coyne. If she's not, how can she be Nelliecoyne's mother? At other times Miz Coyne is my mother.

"We had bad luck at the Seventh Circuit," Tom Hurley reported as Nuala was ushering the kids down the stairs, lest anyone fall. "There is only one man on the circuit who might give us trouble, Rick Rowbottom. And that's who we got. Anyone else would have thrown the dog back in the manger. Rick delayed a ruling till tomorrow morning so that he could study the case and that's very bad news."

Cindy and her daughter were in the kitchen putting together a supper. They were getting along very well, much better than they would in their own kitchen. Nuala's idea to hire her as babysitter had been, as usual, wise.

Cindy stuck her head into the dining room where her husband and I were setting the table.

"He defines narcissism. He imagines that he is the best lawyer on the circuit and that the pretentious and self-important opinions he writes are going to be cited for the ages. Now he has another chance to primp and preen and perform on a high-profile case about which there is no serious question of law at all. He'll delay a decision until the matter is moot on the grounds that there are very serious—his favorite words—matters of law at issue. He is a pimp and a prick!"

"Mother!" her daughter protested from the kitchen.

That's my sister Cindy, never one to be guilty of excessive moderation—five words beginning with a *P* leading up to prick, alliteration with a vengeance.

"What will you and Gerry do, Tom?"

"We'll go into Rowbottom's court tomorrow assuming that obviously he will sustain the injunction while he reviews the serious matters of contract law at issue. He will suspend the injunction until there is a full review of the issue. It's a matter of national importance and a full review is essential, especially because media law is extremely complicated. We will be astonished and then outraged. It is a simple matter of contract law, that every second-year student in law school could answer. He will be offended, which is good because he says stupid things. He will set a date for argument sometime after Christmas. We will yell that the issue will be moot by then because the program is scheduled for the week before Christmas. He will reply that the majesty of the legal process cannot be subservient to the television schedule, especially when that is dependent on a religious feast. He will be very proud of himself for having introduced the church/state issue. We will announce that we are appealing to the full circuit and storm out in high dudgeon, just like Nuala Anne when she's upset, to say nothing of my wife."

"Rick ought to be locked up," Cindy cried from the kitchen.

"Then we'll go down to the chief justice's office and scream bloody murder. This kind of grandstanding is what gives appellate courts a bad name. Can you see the headlines tomorrow—'Judge keeps dog in the manger!' You can imagine what that will do. He will try to calm us down. We will repeat the argument. He will say, 'Religious feast, did that asshole really say that?' and we will say it's all on the record and he'll say we should appear before him first thing in the morning and ask for emergency relief. He'll set up a panel of justices that will have an emergency hearing and a decision by the end of the business day tomorrow."

"Are you sure that it will work out that way?"

"Not certain. Probably."

"The chief justice hates Rick's guts." Cindy arrived with salad. "There's enough problems in the circuit without his muddying the waters. . . . My daughter made this salad and it's scrumptious. . . . Where's Nuala?"

"Out with the dogs," I replied, "taking her choir kids home."

The front door opened and the white demons thundered into the house, followed by the "big kids," followed by their mother. Then the "little kids" appeared from the playroom.

Socra Marie, now always a self-designated spokesman for her little brother announced, "Patjo says he starving."

"Downstairs, doggies," she ordered. "You were wonderful!"

She had to hug both of them.

"Nelliecoyne, Mick, feed them please."

"Yes, Ma."

"Thank you . . . Dermot Michael, I need a drink!"

"Yes, Ma."

Much later, when the Hurleys (save for their daughter) had gone home and the kitchen and dining room cleaned up and the kids put to bed, and Danuta had driven off in her Honda, and Ellie was studying sociology in her room—herself and meself had settled in with a "splash" of Baileys—we sat at the window overlooking Sheffield Avenue for our end-of-day conversation.

"Dermot Michael, I may die before morning."

"Woman, you will not!"

"I am too old for days like this. . . . Anyway, tell me what happened."

"I want to go on record as claiming that I am too old for days like this too and I'm a lot older than you."

"Five years."

"Five and a half."

We sipped our Baileys.

"You first," she said. "I have a wonderful story for you."

I recounted my conversation with Mary Fran.

"Poor child. She'd find Maria a wonderful confidante."

"I'm sure she will eventually."

"Is that something of which you are sure or that you know?"

She laughed my favorite Nuala Anne laugh, wicked, fey, impish—a leprechaun child.

"Sure would I be saying it so confident like, unless I knew it?"

"Here's the copy she made of the letter that led to the big family fight."

Nuala Anne looked at it and frowned, turned it over to look at the other side, and then frowned even more deeply.

"It's a copy of a note scribbled on a lined page torn out of a notebook."

"Hmm."

"It ain't what it pretends to be. It's very evil."

Rarely does she slip anymore and say *ain't.* It's not accepted American usage anymore, though herself insists that it is a perfectly "daycent" word.

"Oh," I said.

"It's someone pretending to be a hysterical middle-class woman, pretending to be vulgar. But that's not what it is at all, at all."

"What is it?"

"Evil."

Then I told her about my first conversation with Dom.

"I've never met the man, but I don't like them."

"He's not a Tony Soprano type."

"I hate that program," she said firmly. "I won't let me kids watch it. It's evil."

"The outfit imposes some social control here that otherwise wouldn't exist."

"So did the lads in Northern Ireland . . . Did he call back?"

"He did."

I repeated his message, almost word for word.

"Wisconsin, St. Louis. Your friends on the West Side are not telling us the whole truth, are they?"

"They know more than they're telling, that's for sure. Their own guys are not involved. And they've warned off the outsiders. But that doesn't help us much. Our friends are safe for the moment. We'll tell Mike Casey to keep a close watch on them."

Then I told her about my visit to Jack Donlan's office, about the nervousness of his funds and about his tennis friend Lou Garner. Then I gave her Mike Casey's three-page report about Maria Sabattini Connors. She read the document carefully and grinned.

"Chaste and modest matron, fersure!"

"In my experience they are great craic in bed."

"And yourself with great experience of them kind! You're supposed to mail this to Mary Fran? Good idea. They'll all come home eventually. And before you ask, Dermot Michael Coyne, let me say that now I know that."

How does one not know something and then know it?

Don't ask me. Am I fey?

Darn good thing for all of us!

"Dermot, since we're too tired to do anything but sleep, would you ever bring me another little splash of Baileys?"

I had been thinking the same thing.

"She came to see me this morning," Nuala informed me when I returned with two brandy snifters, her eyes twinkling mischievously.

"Who came to see you this morning?"

"The chaste and modest matron."

"Why?"

"To confess an act of adultery."

"She never did!"

"That's the way I talk."

"Did you give her absolution?"

"Dermot Michael, I did not. Wasn't there nothing to absolve?"

"Why did she tell you?"

"Because she thought we should know it."

"Are you going to tell me?"

"I might just," she grinned and yawned.

The story of Sterling Stafford was wild.

"So you see your chaste and modest matron is also a warrior queen, maybe descendant of Granne O'Malley."

"Jackie Donlan is an even more fortunate man than he realizes," I observed.

"We'll have to charge your man extra for our fee. Doesn't the woman think that I'm her confidante now?"

We don't take fees. If people ask how much they owe us, herself always says, "Give whatever you want to the charity of your choice and don't complicate me income tax returns."

I don't know what that means, but one of the advantages of marrying a woman who is, as she says, a "chartered accountant" is that she does our tax returns, which, as she avers, "They'd never dare question."

"She'll call me in the morning to tell me whether your man has thrown"—pronounced *trun*—"her out of their apartment. . . . Well, we've made enough on Samwise, so I suppose we can't complain, can we?"

"Does he know you're a client?"

"He didn't say, but then he wouldn't."

"That's his high-risk fund! I didn't know you were a high roller, Nuala Anne McGrail!"

She yawned loudly.

"Didn't I marry you?"

" 'Tis true . . ."

"Dermot love, I'm going to bed now. Tomorrow night we can say two decades of the rosary."

I tucked her in like she was a little girl. She was already asleep.

Poor kid. One moment she was sitting in O'Neil's pub off the College Green and the next moment, almost before she knew it, she had a lecherous husband, four kids, a big house, a couple of demanding careers, and a major court case.

I was tired too, but, unlike me wife, I couldn't wipe out the stimuli of the day. I walked the house for another hour trying to sort out the problems before I slipped into bed next to her. As I disappeared into the magic world of Nod, she took my hand.

Thank you, I whispered to the deity.

About time you said that.

— Nuala Anne —

I BEGAN the day peacefully enough. I brought the big kids over to school, along with the dogs. I then glanced at a picture on the front page of the *Herald*, depicting Triple A in a manger labeled "Christmas," and reading his comment, "Judge Brown is typical of the subhuman hacks that suck graft out of the city for the Daley administration." I settled down to practice my lullabies for my younger son who stopped playing with his trucks long enough to climb into my lap and grin his idiot grin, which is an imitation of his father's grin. . . . Och, me Dermot isn't an idiot and neither is Patjo.

The first call was from Cindy Hurley.

"There's bad news and good news. The bad is that Judge Rowbottom lifted the injunction this morning and scheduled a hearing after the first of the year. He's preening around the Dirksen building like he's just been named to the supreme court. The good news is that Judge Brown has held Abercrombie in contempt of court and sentenced him to a week in the Federal lockup. The marshals arrested him when he came out of the

Hilton this morning. His lawyers are going crazy. So are the media. Don't miss the noonday news! Gerry and Tom are appealing this afternoon as planned. Funny thing is that George Bush the First appointed Ebenezer to the bench and he's a Republican. I'll keep you informed."

I'd spent too much time in the courtrooms of this litigious country to regret that I was not part of the scene. Cindy was a lawyer. She loved every second of it. If we lost the case, the Christmas specials were dead. I could still sing me songs to me own kids and we'd get out a record anyway.

Ellie came in about ten from her class at Loyola, all excited about how wonderful college was. She took me son from me arms. Faithless one that he is, he deserted me without protest.

"Come on now, little punk, your ma has work to do."

"Didn't you and your ma get along well enough in the kitchen last night?"

She sighed, a bad habit that she had picked up from me.

"My mom is okay, Aunt Nuala."

"Learned a lot, has she now, since you walked out on her? Sometimes parents grow up in a hurry, don't they?"

"Like you say, Aunt Nuala, mothers and daughters bond by fighting."

Aunt Nuala was becoming an authority to be quoted.

The next interruption was a call from another one of those who had decided I was a trusted confidante.

"You were right, Nuala, as you well know. Jack was wonderful. He told me that he always knew I could take care of myself, but now he was absolutely certain!"

"Brilliant."

Me husband says that *brilliant* is the superlative of the Irish adjective *grand* and the comparative is *super.*

"He laughed at my description of my 'destruction' as he calls it of Sterling and said he wasn't sure he wanted a shotgun rack in our apartment. I felt like a fool for ever doubting his reaction. He also said to pass on the word to you and Dermot that Sterling is a bad 'un and that we should keep an eye on him."

"Me man has already passed that information on to Mike Casey."

"He made me promise not to throw a camera unless it was one of those small ones."

"And you replied . . ."

"Oh, that there were always objects around the house that you can throw at an obstreperous husband. . . ."

"And then you had a lot of fun?"

"We did that, Nuala Anne . . . I still feel like a fool for being scared of him . . . I'm a very lucky woman."

"You're not the only lucky person in the family, not even the luckiest."

I went back to my annotations of the working script for our problematic show. It had started out as fun, now it had become a heavy burden, even without the eejits in the Dirksen building.

I heard the hounds barking, their we're-going-out-now bark. Danuta was making lunch and watching the rug rats and Ellie was picking up the older kids to bring them back for lunch. No cold lunch in the school for Ms. McGrail's kids.

The phone again.

"Nuala Anne."

"I wonder if I could speak to Dermot?"

She sounded teary.

"I'm sorry, Mrs. Coyne. This is Mary Fran Donlan. We have more problems, I'm afraid."

"Och, isn't Dermot Michael out hunting the bad guys. He mailed something to you this morning. . . . I'll try to reach him on his cell phone."

"I'm afraid that my dad had Tony Cuneen, my brother-in-law, fired from his law firm, just as he was about to be named a partner. It's not fair. Tony is a good lawyer. Okay, he made a fool of himself about our trust funds. . . ."

"And on television."

"We were all upset. . . . We should have known better."

"What did they say to him?"

"They told him that the managing partners didn't think he would be comfortable in the firm. . . . They didn't throw him out on the spot. His contract doesn't expire till February first, but he can't appear in court for them again. So he's free to look for another job. . . . But who would want him?"

"You're after being sure your dad is behind this, are you now?"

"Who else might it be?"

"I don't know your father very well, dear, but wouldn't I be thinkin' that he's not the kind of man who takes revenge that way?"

"I know, but Evie is certain. . . ."

"She's always certain, isn't she now?"

"She says that woman drove Dad to fire Tony."

"Might she not have a fixation on that woman?"

Dead silence.

"You're right, Mrs. Coyne. I think I've made a fool of myself again."

"Mrs. Coyne is me mother-in-law and a grand woman altogether. I'm Nuala."

"I'm sorry, Nuala."

"Wouldn't it seem to an outsider that your poor brother-in-law disgraced the firm by his remarks on the telly and that his firm really had no choice? And that maybe your sister is the one to blame? Would you want to hire a lawyer, no matter how gifted, who behaved so foolishly?"

Silence.

"I never thought of it that way, but you're right of course."

Poor beaten little girl child. Her sister was a bitch.

"Me Dermot hasn't checked in yet, but won't I try to get him on the cell phone and tell him what's happening. I don't know what we can do about it. Probably nothing at all, at all. But we'll try."

"I'm sorry I've made a fool of myself, er, Nuala. I should have thought for a minute and realized Dad would never do anything like that."

"He seems a very decent man to me. . . . *Decent* is Irish for good and honest and kind."

"He is, oh, yes, he is."

"Well, maybe you and your sisters should try acting that way toward him."

"Maybe we should."

"I'll call me Dermot."

I tried again. No answer. He was obviously very busy. I thought about it. What the hell. If people treat me like a friggin' parish priest, maybe I should act like one. I pulled out my phone book and punched in Jack Donlan's phone number.

"Mr. Donlan's office."

I put on my professional face and the voice to go with it.

"This is Ms. McGrail calling. May I speak to Mr. Donlan."

"Certainly, Nuala Anne. Just a moment please."

Good enough for my professionalism! I switched my face.

"Wouldn't you be Elfrida now?"

"Yes, ma'am."

"Well doesn't me husband say that you make better Irish tea than I do?"

He'd never said that, but sometimes a compliment doesn't hurt.

"You know what Irish men are with their blarney!"

" 'Tis true!"

"Good morning, Nuala, it's good to talk to my wife's confessor!"

Speaking of blarney!

"Ah, no! I don't have the power of absolution, only the power of listening, so wouldn't I more properly be called a spiritual director?"

"Whatever, you were a big help to her yesterday and I'm grateful."

"Won't I be after adding a charge to me fee?"

"I'm a very fortunate man, just how fortunate I keep learning."

I sighed my Connemara sigh.

"Well, I have a bit of a problem for you this morning. . . . Your son-in-law has been fired by his law firm. . . ."

It was his turn to sigh.

"I was afraid they'd go after him, poor kid. He's a good lawyer, top of the list for partnership until my daughter dragged him into court to protect their trust funds. . . ."

Danuta appeared at the door of my office with the frown she uses to indicate the food is getting cold. I raised the finger that said I'd be right there.

"And isn't she blaming you instead of herself?"

He was silent for a moment.

"And her sisters agree?"

"Not Mary Fran."

At least not after I had a quiet word with her.

"Thank God for that!"

"And yourself having no markers at all, at all at the firm?"

"You're a desperate woman, Nuala Anne McGrail!"

"And yourself picking up the Irish idiom quickly enough."

"As a matter of fact, I have several markers over there. They probably dumped him as a favor to me. So it won't hurt them to take him back, another year as an associate and a promise to never appear in a case with his wife. . . . Doubtless he'll be happy to keep it."

"Won't he have to rein in that one?"

"I've never been able to do that."

Then I thought to myself, the marriage will fall apart. Hasn't me poor Dermot saved our marriage a couple of times by shouting at me? . . . I shiver at the thought of losing him, poor dear man.

"After this escape, he may have learned a lesson."

"I'll call him now and ask what they said when they terminated him. Then I'll call them to pick up my markers. . . . I owe you a lot of favors, Nuala."

"In a whole lifetime you won't be able to pick them all up. . . . Now don't I have to eat my lunch before me housekeeper fires me."

I sighed again, with satisfaction for a good deed. That poor little bitch was asking for lifetime heartbreak.

Danuta appeared again with a plate of salad.

"Everyone watch TV," she complained.

In the kitchen all the kids, Ellie included, were watching Mary Alice Quinn on Channel 3.

"Yesterday's dog in the manger has become today's bird in the jail. This morning Judge Ebenezer Brown ordered Federal marshals from his courtroom to arrest Archibald Adolf Abercrombie and bring him to the courtroom to face charges of contempt of court."

(Pictures of three marshals trying to muscle Triple A into the Dirksen Federal building.)

"Judge Brown, a Republican appointed to the Federal bench by the first President Bush, asked Mr. Abercrombie if he had made a statement contemptuous of the court yesterday."

(Picture of Abercrombie coming out of the building yesterday.)

"Judge Brown is typical of the subhuman hacks that suck graft out of the city for the Daley Administration."

Mary Alice again.

"Under advice of his attorneys, the so-called dog in the manger refused to answer. Then Judge Brown solemnly sentenced him to a week in the Federal lockup. Mr. Abercrombie announced that he would appeal and that he was sure the appellate court would assert his right to freedom of speech about an incompetent and retarded judge. Judge Brown extended the sentence to three weeks in the lockup."

Pictures of Triple A emerging in shackles, still struggling with the marshals.

"We asked Tom Hurley, one of the lawyers representing NBS which wants to produce the Nuala Anne Christmas special what impact he thought the imprisonment of a celebrity Hollywood mogul would have on the case."

(Tom Hurley relaxed and confident with a leprechaun's twinkle in his eyes.)

"Out in Hollywood the bosses of Kosmic Entertainment might begin to wonder whether the entertainment Mr. Abercrombie is providing for us in Chicago is worth the cost."

"Didn't an appellate court judge deliver a setback to your case this morning, counselor?"

"A temporary setback, Mary Alice. Judge Richard Rowbottom lifted the injunction we had won from Judge Brown and set a date for a hearing on our motion for January third. We intend to appeal that decision this afternoon. Obviously January third is after Christmas."

"If Mr. Abercrombie is the dog in the manger, what would that make Judge Rowbottom?"

"Well, if Judge Rowbottom is successful in his ruling—and we confidently expect a reversal—then some people, certainly not including me, might think that he wants to be the Grinch who stole Christmas."

"Mr. Hurley is well known in the Chicago area as the husband of celebrity trial lawyer Cynthia Hurley."

Then there was a commercial about a weight-loss diet. My children and my niece were exchanging high fives and I had to join in. Slapstick entertainment for Chicago.

— Dermot —

"LOU GARNER," Mike Casey told me, "is both sleazy and slippery. Jack Donlan should find himself another tennis partner. He has his fingers in lots of minor little development deals and light clout with some aldermen with whom he drinks a couple of times a week. He always has a deal in the works and usually makes some money when the big players buy him out to get rid of him. He pretends to be one of the big players, but he never will be."

"Not enough money."

"Money is not the problem in that world. Not enough smarts. He skates pretty close to the edge. The Feds have him on their radar scopes but he's too small-fry for them to bother about unless they want a slam-dunk conviction to raise their conviction rates. They'll get him eventually of course."

"Is Jackie Donlan involved?"

"No way! Much too smart. I told him that he shouldn't pay any attention to his gossip about Maria Sabattini. Garner is a bottom prowler on

LaSalle Street, always trying to soak up gossip that he can use for one of his capers. I wasn't surprised that we were able to clear her."

"Chaste matron?" I said ironically.

"Absolutely."

I called Elfrida to make sure her boss, somewhat reluctant for me to corner his high school and college friend, had set up the appointment.

"I don't like that Lou Garner," she said, exercising a woman's right to criticize her employer's friends. "He's no good at all. Shy, shifty, too suave. Be careful of him, Mr. Coyne."

"Woman, who's this Mr. Coyne?"

She giggled. "Dermot!"

"That's better."

I was to meet Mr. Garner at his office in Andersonville, a North Side neighborhood whose name reveals its Swedish past and high quality of its Swedish bakeries. His office was on Clark Street, just off Foster Avenue, near St. Gregory's Church. He would be happy to talk to me as we toured some of his North Side properties. He would reserve a parking place for me behind his storefront office and we would drive around in his "jalopy."

I'm West Side Irish—indeed River Forest Irish which is the worst kind—and I know very little about the North Side. While I am in constant verbal combat with the South Side Irish (who tend to be unenlightened White Sox fans), I usually deny that there are North Side Irish, only Germans and Swedes whose closeness to the Polish Corridor along Milwaukee Avenue is their only claim to Catholic virtue. It is not a stance that is likely to please anyone. I do believe, however, that the Italian influence on the West Side has civilized us West Siders and that those of us who do live in enclaves on the North Side are not positively affected by the dour Germans and the silent Swedes. My bedmate is baffled by all of this urban village talk and points out that she and our children are all North Side Irish. I deny this and insist that she is Connemara Irish and our children are Lincoln Park Irish. She throws up her hands in dismay and proclaims that I'm an eejit. Which in these matters is true until you've been around Chicago for a couple of generations.

I parked my ancient Benz behind the storefront with a huge "Garner" sign hanging out over the sidewalk, like it was a funeral parlor. Next to my car, looking very imperial, was a silver BMW X-5. Classy and a little boring, I told myself.

Lou Garner met me at the door. He was not what I expected, not an overweight gum-chewing, heavily scented man with razor cut white hair. Rather he looked like someone who might belong in the Racket Club with John Patrick Donlan—a little taller perhaps, sharp but handsome features, conservative and expensive dark blue, but not quite navy, suit, gleaming white shirt and a tie with stripes which suggested an obscure English regiment. His pale blue eyes did, however, look a little shifty. And his radiant geniality suggested that I would not want to buy either a secondhand car or house from him. He spoke in staccato outbursts, like an AK-47. Me bedmate would have instantly tagged him as "a bit of a gombeen man." His office was indeed part of an old Jewish funeral parlor, spiffed up with modern Danish furniture.

"The old Mercedes yours?" he asked easing the BMW out of its parking place as it purred softly, a jungle cat eager for the chase. "Great little car, should be a classic in a couple of years, probably appreciating even now."

"My wife owns a Lincoln Navigator. She figures it will be useful, if the English should come down from Toronto and try to repeat the Fort Dearborn massacre. We'll all need tanks then."

He didn't say anything in reply.

"I figure," I went on, "that they'll try to land at Loyola Beach, like the opening shots in that flick *Flatliners*."

My loony words had stopped him cold.

"I also figure that the Jesuits will yield land till Broadway and then hold the line till the Cub fans pile out of Wrigley Park with their axes and pikes."

"The Broadway-Clark corridor," he began his spiel, "is critical for the redevelopment and expansion of the North Side. You have to view it as a funnel coming out of the loop and the Magnificent Mile and channeling all the excitement and vibrancy of Downtown right through to Howard Street and beyond into Evanston and Northwestern University. It will become the exclusive place to live and work and play and absorb art and culture. It has two critical assets—Lake Shore Drive and the elevated lines. . . ." He babbled on and on, doubtless trying to weary me and turn me away from the subject at hand. People do that, blond kid in a blazer, clearly not very bright. You overwhelm him with talk and you have no problems.

"Lake Shore Drive," I said, "is no good unless the mayor is able to extend it beyond Hollywood up to Howard Street and Calvary Cemetery, maybe even up to the Bahai Temple. Sheridan Road is a joke, always has been. So is Evanston. Prohibition started up there. Women's Christian Temperance Union. You sell all the old homes in Evanston to upwardly mobile Blacks, great market! And they're welcome to it. What you have to do is lure the Winnetka and Lake Forest folk to come down the Drive to the Loop and Michigan Avenue and Grant Park. Then they'll see all the high-rises, the old ones and the new ones you'll probably build and want to live in them when they have empty houses on their hands. Or even Balmoral or Lincoln Park, they're one step or two away from slums. Look at them in the winter when the leaves are off the trees. Your corridor is good for what it is, shops, offices, car dealers, that kind of thing. All high class of course. But face it, Lake View is finished. How long have you known Maria Angelica Sabattini?"

"For a long time, twenty years maybe," he stumbled. "Not well, but she's a hard one to miss at real estate meetings and conferences. You know what I mean?"

"Yeah, though I suppose it depends on your tastes. Nice tits, if that's what you're interested in. . . . So you were surprised when your buddy Jack Donlan invested in her company."

He had pulled off Sheridan Road and parked where the road turns left to circle around the Loyola campus. We were looking at the Lake, grey and somber on an early December afternoon. I shivered, though I wasn't cold.

"Well, she didn't seem quite his type, I don't mean physically." He stumbled again. "They're obviously a striking couple, right out of an issue of *GQ*, people can't take their eyes off them. I mean corporately. Tell you the truth, the idea of people designing their homes on the Net and then a national office supervising the construction and decoration sounds like another dot-com bubble sort of thing, know what I mean? . . . It seems to be working out fine so far. Old Joe McMahon has done a pretty good job scouting out firms for Jackie. And to give Jackie full credit, he has an instinct for a good deal."

"But you warned him about her?"

"You hear things about her, know what I mean? You hear things about women who are successful, huh? Especially if they got looks. So there's always talk along LaSalle Street. I understood that he hadn't met her and he wouldn't until Joe McMahon and the lawyers worked out a deal. But, hell, there are pictures of her everywhere and Jack is lonely. His marriage was a mess, know what I mean, kooky family and she'd become a fall-down drunk. I always regretted not warning him about her family. He was head over heels and I didn't want to make him angry, so I kept my mouth shut. Big mistake."

"So you figured you'd not make the same mistake this time?"

"Something like that, know what I mean? He's lonely, they're together a lot on business, she's gorgeous, she's a widow looking for a guy, he's a great catch. I was right on that, wasn't I?"

"It would appear so."

"I warned him. He wasn't offended. He did an investigation and she came up clean, as clean as any woman her age can, know what I mean? So first thing I know we're getting a wedding invitation. I'm surprised and I keep my fingers crossed. Then I hear his kids are against it and I get uneasy. . . . Marriage is a tough slog, know what I mean?"

"Do I ever!"

I would not report that part of the conversation to me wife.

Better not.

"You gotta have a wife that understands you and stands by you, regardless. Sex holds people together just so long. Then you gotta have shared values and commitments, like my wife and I have, and good kids too. Poor Jackie married the first time essentially because he wanted to get laid. It didn't work. I think he'd be more careful this time, know what I mean? I'm sure he's getting a lot of action and I say good for him. More power to him, but, like I say that wears off. The kids won't come to the wedding. There's that nightmare over at St. Freddy's and all the publicity. Hell of a way to start a marriage. I met her the first time at the dinner at the Four Seasons. She knew who I was and understood what I was doing, more than poor Faith ever did. Anyway Maria was charming and gracious and I thought, well, maybe it will work out. But I notice she has a tongue on her, know what I mean. Funny, real funny, always has a final comment that makes you laugh. I tell myself that Jackie who is a very serious guy will get tired of that after a while. Then she might be just a little too much. Like I say, sex is the most important thing a couple of months before the marriage and the least important thing a couple of months after. Know what I mean?"

"Do I ever!" I lied again.

Liar.

Shut up.

You think he's abnormal. Ever think you might be?

No.

Yes you do.

"You know who the people were who warned you on LaSalle Street?"

"You know what it's like with those things, someone says something in passing and you hear it and kind of remember it, but you can't call back the face. I do remember the guy saying that one of the victims was the Congressman out in that district, what's his name . . . ?"

"Sterling Stafford?"

"Yeah, that guy . . . Well the word is that she let him screw her into the next county and then dropped him and he's never been the same since."

Threw a camcorder at him, actually.

"He's married, isn't he?"

"Yeah I saw him concede on television. She was lurking near him. Not bad for their age, but I don't know."

Bingo!

"Come on, let's have lunch, there's a great steakhouse up on Sheridan Road. I made a reservation."

I resolved firmly that I would have fish.

He couldn't let the topic go. After I had ordered my Alaskan salmon, so called, he returned to it.

"I sure hope she's nice to him, long run I mean. Poor Jackie is a fragile guy and he's been hurt enough, know what I mean. She could destroy him, eat him alive like they say she did to Stafford. That's what a lot of women do. Can't blame them. They have to get as much as they can, before it's too late."

"Does she seem like she's the kind to do that?"

"No, but Jackie was probably the biggest catch she ever encountered, that's the way those kind of women are."

As I drove down Clark Street toward Fullerton, I decided I didn't like Louis Garner, one bit. His elegance was an expensive veneer of class for a man who was quite incapable of being anything but vulgar. He would have been suspicious of Nuala reading her world economics book that night at O'Neil's on College Green and her dismissal of me as a "focking rich Yank" when all the time she was thinking that she might have to fall in love with me. She's still embarrassed when I remind her of it.

"And yourself taking off me clothes in that dirty imagination of yours!"

Those issues were irrelevant, however, to the present case.

When I pulled up to our prefire (Chicago Fire) house on Sheffield, the same crowd of cars were lined up, plus a network van from CTN. So we'd won the case? Well good on us.

You let that gombeen man interfere with your normal good disposition. Don't rain on their parade.

Your metaphors are worse than ever.

As I walked up the two flights of stairs—Chicago houses in those days immediately after the Civil War had their entrance on the second floor because the first floor was a sea of mud—I heard singing, not lullabies, but drinking songs and also the happy howling of wolfhounds.

My daughter Nelliecoyne emerged and waited for me on the little porch at the top of the steps. She gave me the thumbs-up sign and then shouted ecstatically when she hugged me, "We won, Da! Poor Ma is so happy and herself pretending that it was no big deal!"

In the parlor, me good wife, tears flooding her face, which in turn glowed with light, was talking to the camera.

"Well, the Grinch didn't steal Christmas, did he now, and himself, poor dear man, furious at his colleagues . . . The fight is a shame altogether. I don't like fighting at all, we Irish women are a peaceful and forgiving people. We have to be because our men require so much forgiveness. . . . Christmas should be a peaceful time. I'm sorry we had to protect our Christmas songs and themselves again from all over the world. I hope they do a little bit to bring people closer together. The children for whom lullabies are sung deserve a world where people are closer together. So we'll all pray that the people who hear the songs will feel more peaceful. . . . I'm going to ask the kids to sing our Arab lullaby."

While they sang the marvelous little number, mostly wordless exclamations of joy, Tom Hurley and I drifted into the library.

"The panel restored the ban on the injunction?"

"They did indeed do that and with withering sarcasm for the attempt to moot the issue with gobbledygook incantations—the chief justice's very words—about church and state."

"That's the end of it, I hope?"

"Not at all, Derm, not at all! After the hearing in January, we'll go back to the district court for relief from the damages done to the show by Mr. Abercrombie's defamatory comments about it and for his gross violation of NBS's contract. If herself wants to quit after next year, that's fine. I don't think they're fun for her anymore, but we can't let a raving maniac ruin it and leave a bitter taste in everyone's mouth."

"They'll settle, I suppose?"

"Yeah, they'll settle and they'll put a lid on Triple A. . . . And your sister and I will be able to buy Christmas presents for our kids. . . ."

There was another dinner, for which Nuala had laid in supplies of hamburgers and hot dogs and much toasting. My heart was not in it at all. I was worried about the Donlans and the forces of evil I saw swilling around them. If I could sense converging threats, what might Nuala see. How did you prepare a Christmas concert and protect good people from crazies?

We said last night's decade of the rosary before our conversation. Nuala poured a "jar" of whiskey for each one of us. Solemn high conversation.

"So tell me about the gombeen man who made you come in with such a long face?"

The woman doesn't miss a thing.

You just noticed that?

So I told her about Lou Garner, Jack Donlan's great friend.

"Wouldn't he love to destroy him! All his success and fame and now Maria!"

"That about summarizes it."

"And the gobshite thinks he fooled me husband too?"

"The curly haired yuppie in the blazer!"

"And Sterling Stafford apparently is talking about Maria?"

"Maybe he was talking about her before she whupped him and then lied to cover up what really happened."

"Do you think so, Nuala Anne?"

"What do you think?"

"He sounds like the kind of man who broods about his failures in the seduction contest, especially when the woman makes a fool out of him. Then he gets drubbed in an election and he broods some more. Then he reads about a wedding and he explodes, but he's not too smooth anymore and does some clumsy things."

"He's giving a talk down at the Union League Club tonight. The subject is the 'Republican Revival.' . . . Nine-fingered shitehawks! They're properly beaten and already planning a way to sneak back in."

My wife had never paid much attention to Irish politics, save for denouncing the leadership as amadons. However, she had been strongly influenced by my mother's intense loyalty to the Democrats.

"If our man Barak wins the election," I mused, "they'll need a new senator from Illinois two years from now. Sterling is a little long in the tooth, but that would be a spectacular comeback."

"And Maria is out there with the film of his trying to rape her. She'd never use it. . . . She hasn't looked at it herself. . . . But she's still got it, in case she should ever need it."

Film is pronounced the Irish way as though there were a *u* between the *l* and the *m*.

We were both silent, nursing our jars cautiously because we knew they'd weaken our thinking.

"The problem is, Dermot Michael, that none of these things hang together yet. There's a pattern out there, but all they tell us is that someone has a grudge against Jack and Maria, but they're inept. . . . Maybe someone whom she once hit in the head with a camera. . . . I'll ask Mike Casey to go down to the Union League and listen to your man."

"Good idea . . . You've got a TV special to jump-start. . . ."

"That's what you Yanks call a slice of cake."

"Piece of cake."

"Isn't that because you eat it with your fingers! . . . When do you think they'll reinstate that gobshite Tony Cuneen?"

"Huh?"

"Och! Dermot! And meself only a tad over thirty and losing me mind altogether . . . I forgot to tell you!"

She told me about the call from Mary Fran and her conversation with Jackie and "that sweet little Elfrida kid."

"I think you should probably see a doctor or take a long rest. Yourself with four brat kids, a gobshite of a husband, and a court battle with some bad people, and you forget that you save a young man's career and marriage by a single phone call."

She was blushing and, having to decide between laughter and tears, opted for laughter.

"Would you ever fill up me jar again?"

"Woman, I would not!"

"Then you'll have to make love with me or I won't sleep at all, at all."

"Well, it's been a long, hard day, but I guess I might manage it."

I snaked my hand up her thigh. She groaned in response.

I took her in my arms and warned her, "I'll probably have to kiss you everywhere tonight."

"Isn't it what you would do to a poor woman who is losing her mind! . . . Do you think they have reinstated Tony yet?"

You weren't even thinking about screwing her tonight and now you're acting crazy.

There's a lot of sex in this case and it's festering in my head.

"Dermot Michael Coyne," she gasped. "You've taken off all me clothes and we're not in the bedroom yet. . . ."

"Who needs a bedroom!"

"Och . . . DERMOT!"

— Nuala Anne —

ME POOR husband is a heavy sleeper and after a small jar and a bit of serious loving, he sleeps like the room has fallen on his head.

I love him so much. I'm glad I decided when I came to Yank land that I wanted to spend the rest of my life in the same bed as he.

However, I have to keep one ear open at night in case there's any noise in the kids' rooms. The dogs are watching, but what's the point in having a mother unless she is listening for your sounds at night?

Me husband doesn't know all me secrets yet, but the ones he doesn't know, don't matter much. I hope he never becomes bored with me. Well, I can probably come up with some more secrets if I put what's left of my mind to it.

I was only half asleep when the phone rang. Isn't the phone ringing at night the most terrible sound altogether? You're after wondering if someone is dead. . . . Dermot was next to me in bed, the kids were in their rooms . . . me ma or dad . . .

"Nuala Anne," I said, as crisp as if I was wide awake.

"Blackie . . ."

Real trouble.

"What's wrong?"

"Our friend John Donlan is in the emergency room at St. Joseph's Hospital. He has been beaten brutally. . . ."

"Brigid, Patrick, and Colmcille! He isn't dead, is he?"

"No life-threatening injuries, concussion, maybe some internal injuries. They're doing X-rays and scans. A little concern about the concussion . . ."

"Maria is there?"

"Oh yes, she drove off the perpetrators with a golf club. . . . She is, however, somewhat stressed, as they say."

"I'll be right over."

"That would be a good work. The situation here is somewhat problematic."

I jumped out of bed, put on black jeans, a black sweatshirt, my black leather jacket, and my black boots. Granne O'Malley goes to war at night.

Well, you have to look the part, don't you?

I grabbed a sheet of computer paper and a Magic Marker.

Dermot Michael. Jack injured. Off to St. Joseph's. Call me on my cell.

The woman you slept with last night.

Maeve followed me downstairs.

"You coming with me, girl? Okay, but you have to act right, understand?"

I jumped into me Lincoln Navigator, the hound right behind me. The thing about me car is that in a crisis situation it provides a certain gravity.

I know St. Joseph's better than I'd like to. For four months we were there night and day, taking care of our little neonate, whose survival will always seem to me to be a miracle. "You sang her into life," the resident told me. Socra Marie and I still go over there a couple of times a year "to sing for the babies" as she says.

Now she even sings on key sometimes.

I pulled up to the emergency room driveway—cop cars, Reliable cars, ambulance, Blackie's cute little Smart Car, thank God no TV vans. I jumped out of my SUV—the license which announced "Nuala"—and walked in the door, my hound tagging along with me. Two young Latino attendants and a pretty African-American nurse waited at the door.

"The archbishop said you should go right in, Nuala. . . . And who is this lovely lady?"

"This is Maeve."

Mavie politely offered her hand.

"Maeve, you stay here with this nice woman. If we need help, we'll yell."

"Archbishop Ryan said that you would come in a big red SUV with a big white dog, he didn't say how pretty you are, darlin'."

The hounds love adoration and when the two attendants Juan and Rodrigo cautiously joined the group, she was ready to settle in for the night.

The corridor outside the emergency room was crowded with people—Mike Casey, John Culhane, the commander of Area Six detectives, two detectives, both women, two cops, both men, several people in hospital gowns looking serious and a screaming Evie Cuneen and her befuddled husband Tony. Neither Blackie nor Maria were present.

Naturally I walked up to the two senior police officials. In me old country I'd avoid the Guards like they were Brits and we were still under occupation.

"Mike, how is he?"

"Nuala! I didn't hear you come in! He's still unconscious, likely concussion and possible internal injuries. They are a little worried about the concussion."

I don't like hospitals at all at all. I spent too much time in this one with my darling little tiny terrorist. At night they are especially gloomy. St. Joseph's, being a Catholic hospital, was so clean that you could eat off the floor. Still these were places where life and death met under bright lights with the whole world dark outside and the smell of antiseptic dense in the air. Purgatory must be something like this—purgatory where you know for sure that things would somehow improve.

"Two thugs managed to sneak into his building and trapped him between the elevator and the door to his apartment," John Culhane said.

"Gangbangers probably. It's not clear that they wanted to kill him. Amateurs, probably, though as the superintendent points out, getting into that building would have been very difficult."

Mike Casey hadn't been superintendent of police for a long time, but it's like a governor or an ambassador here in Yank land—the title is lifelong.

"His wife heard the ruckus outside, grabbed a five iron, rushed out into the corridor, and assaulted the perpetrators. They fled for their lives. She may well have saved her husband from far worse injuries. They were unsheathing knives when Maria entered the fray. Jack was covered with blood when they brought him in here, only it wasn't his blood."

"*Mulier fortis*," I remarked.

"We picked up a couple of individuals on Clark Street, one of them bleeding," Commander Culhane said. "They may be the perps. Both high on crack."

"Amateurs of a sort," Mike Casey added. "Someone else must have provided them with the means of access to the building."

"Is that hysterical woman his daughter?" Culhane asked. "She's making reckless charges against Ms. Donlan. And her kid is wailing. No one needs that here. . . ."

"It will be a pleasure to shut her up," I said.

I strode over to Evie and shook her.

"Shut up, you crazy little bitch. You almost ruined your husband's career the other day on the telly. Your poor dad bailed him out. If you don't calm down, he'll be chasing ambulances for the rest of your life."

She glared at me, hate darting from her eyes.

"That isn't true, is it, Tony?"

"Yes, it is, Evie. They told me this afternoon I'd have another year of probation. If I appeared in public with you again, I'd have fifteen minutes to leave the offices."

His face was dark with despair. His little son continued to wail.

"Why didn't you tell me?" she asked, her body caving in on itself as though she had been hit in the stomach.

"I've been trying to tell you all afternoon. I couldn't get by your hatred for your father's wife."

She leaned against the wall of the hospital corridor and slowly slipped to the floor. She curled up in a knot and began to wail. The child, in his father's arms, joined in. The little guy could have been cute under other circumstances, a clone of his grandfather.

"Get them both out of here, Tony, before she does any more harm."

Holding the child in one arm, he lifted his wife with the other.

"Thanks," he said to me as he struggled to bring his pathetic little family to the lounge at the end of the hall. The next stop, I feared, would be the divorce court.

Okay, I was a bitch on wheels, but it worked. I had cracked open her cocoon of hatred, perhaps for only a few minutes.

The door to the emergency room opened and a young woman, blond with gentle eyes and a kind smile, came out—along with the archbishop. Blackie was wearing his usual uniform—black jeans, a black turtleneck shirt, and a Chicago Bears Windbreaker. Since they made him an archbishop, he remembers more often his silver St. Brigid's pectoral cross and his New Grange silver Episcopal ring, both made by his favorite cousin Catherine Collins who does gorgeous sunbursts.

The young woman, who looked like she was sixteen, was wearing the standard green hospital clothes. A student nurse, a nurse's aide?

"Doctor Reynolds," Blackie announced, "will discuss Mr. Donlan's condition, which thanks be to God and the Blessed Mother, may not be as serious as was first thought."

The child was an MD?

"Mr. Donlan was a victim of a savage attack. He suffered a brain concusssion of moderate severity and lost consciousness for a period of time. However, he is regaining consciousness now and brain scans show no serious malfunction in his brain. He was able to recite not only the names of his own family, but of Ms. Donlan's family. There was no evidence of internal injuries in our CAT scan, but there is a chance that some may show up in the next couple of days. There may also be some bruised ribs. The assailants apparently did not know how to inflict anything more than cosmetic injuries which can readily be repaired. Mr. Donlan is a very fortunate man. I would ask the police to give five or six hours for further recovery before they attempt to interview him. I trust that his personal security protection will remain here with us. It may also be several days before he should attempt to return to work. He will awake tomorrow with aches and pain in most parts of his body. Thank you."

The crowd began to disperse.

Blackie motioned me toward the emergency room.

"We're waiting for you and your daughter to visit us again. Whenever she comes to neonatal, I go upstairs to listen."

"Thank you . . . Maybe we can sneak over in the next few days to try some of our Christmas lullabies."

Good practice for the kids from Josephat.

"Just a minute, Nuala Anne." Mike Casey, looking for all the world like Basil Rathbone playing Sherlock Holmes in the films me ma loved, though she had only seen a few of them. Holmes the savior, Holmes the powerful, Holmes the total Brit.

"I did wander over to the Union League Club with my good wife, Annie Reilly. To escape from purgatory I did listen to Sterling Stafford and did not become ill. It was, however, the same old stuff—Ronald Reagan won the cold war because he had courage. If we can be courageous we will bounce back in the next election, old-fashioned American values, no substitute for victory, keep faith with the troops, no substitute for victory, international terrorist conspiracy, if troops come home too early, terrorists will come right after them, prosperity depends on cutting taxes, Democrats are traitors etc. etc. etc."

"He's running then?"

"Oh yes he's running, said Senator Obama is a foreigner, should not be permitted to run."

"Any chance?"

"Not that I could see. He's too long in the tooth and too confused. His wife is pushing him hard. She was sitting there beaming. Democrats stole the election. We'll be back."

"Suspect?" Mike asked.

"Our client hit him with a video camera! Threw it at him!"

"He has a lot of grudges. We'll take a closer look. . . . Maybe send Dermot over to talk to him . . . Interesting politics out there in Kishwaukee County."

"I've been thinking of that. Press credentials?"

"Didn't I tell you he had signed on as a stringer at the *Herald*? Just in case you don't want to sing anymore?"

Inside the emergency room, his face black and blue, with streaks of red, a couple of teeth missing, a bandage on his head, and his chest taped, John Patrick Donlan still managed to look chic, with just a touch of a smile on his swollen lips.

"Hi, Johnny Pat," I said.

"Hi!"

"Who is she?" Maria Angelica in blue slacks and a dark blue and green sweatshirt, demanded.

Maria had endured a horrid experience. She was also very tired. Yet her verve was undiminished and her beauty as radiant as ever.

"Isn't she the McGrail woman," Jack whispered, "and herself a bit of a witch."

"Where did the Dow finish?" I asked.

"Around 12,000, near a record."

"See, Jackie," his wife said, "nothing wrong with your brain."

"He's just resting a little," the Latino nurse said with a smile, glancing at the brain scan on its monitor. "Which you should do, Mr. Donlan."

"I'm afraid that if I go to sleep again, I won't wake up."

"The effects of the concussion are wearing off, sir. You'll wake up all right."

"I know I've asked you this before, but have I had a stroke?"

"Didn't Archbishop Ryan tell you that you had not?"

"And," I added, "would himself not tell you the truth, and a holy bishop he is?"

"My dad used to say, trust everyone but always cut the cards!"

"Where's . . . Dermot?"

"Isn't he back at house with the kids and all of them such sound sleepers, they didn't hear the phone.

"The dogs heard and didn't Maeve ride over here with me?"

"You left the poor dog outside?" Maria protested.

"The poor dog is in the lobby charming everyone in sight."

"We're going to move him upstairs in the morning," Maria said, "perhaps into intensive care. He'll have aches and pains all over, but it seems that he has a high tolerance for pain. . . . He'll need some dental work. . . ."

"If this isn't heaven, I'd love to walk down LaSalle Street with a cane . . . create a sensation."

"So long as I'm on your arm, it's all right."

He shut his eyes as if about to sleep.

"Steal the show."

Someone knocked gently on the door.

I opened it—a nurse's aide who belonged in grammar school.

"Are you Mrs. McGrail?"

"That's me ma. I'm Nuala Anne."

"I've seen you on television," she said shyly. "Is that gorgeous white dog yours?"

"She's not making a nuisance of herself?"

"We should add her to the staff. . . . You remember that obnoxious woman you threw out of the corridor? Well she and her kid were back there wailing and the dog . . ."

"Maeve walked over to play with them?"

"It was incredible! In just a few minutes they were both laughing and smiling and the woman was hugging her husband. . . ."

"And me hound was strutting around like she owned the hospital?"

"She's so lovely. . . . Anyway the young woman asked if she could visit her father. She promised she'd be good."

I glanced at Maria Angelica.

"Evie?"

"Herself."

"Why not?" She lifted her arms in a magnificent Italian gesture of fatalism.

"Daddy! Daddy! Daddy!" Evie screamed and fell on her knees next to the bed. "I'm sorry, I'm sorry!" She grabbed his limp hand. "I am a spoiled brat, an ungrateful bitch. Tony says I've become my own hate and he's right! I'll regret as long as I live what I've done. Please, give me one more chance! Please!"

"Limit up!" he murmured with his wisp of a smile.

She looked up at a thunderstruck Maria.

"You too! The little good in me wanted to love you! I beg for one more chance . . ." She struggled to say the word, "Mom!"

Maria of course had the last word.

"I already have two daughters. A few more will just add to talk in the kitchen!"

Evie scampered to her feet and rushed to the door.

"I love you all! Thank you!"

At the door, she touched my arm and won me over finally.

"Great dog! Really great!"

Jack Donlan closed his eyes.

"Would you sing him a lullaby?" Maria asked.

"Won't I sing a couple?"

Actually I sang the whole repertory for the Christmas show. The smile remained on his face. Poor dear man would have a lot of pain in the next couple of days—teeth, face, ribs. He was entitled to a pleasant night's rest.

"Brava," said the young doctor standing behind me at the door. "He's sound asleep now, helped by the medication and the music. He'll be fine tomorrow, except for all the bumps and bruises. His brain looks great. We'll keep our eyes open for internal injuries. Home the day after tomorrow, please God."

"We'll have guards here all the time. If he can't walk twenty yards down a corridor without getting into a fight, we'll have to protect him all the time."

We'd better push ahead with our work. What kind of morons would beat a man as they beat Jack? Someone who hated him a lot.

Me cell phone beeped.

"Nuala," I whispered.

"Meself . . . How is he?"

"Pretty good, nothing too serious. They'll keep him around tomorrow to check for internal injuries. Sleeping peacefully. A lot of things happened."

"I didn't hear the phone."

"Good thing you married a light sleeper."

"Maeve went with you. . . . She's not around here."

"Stole the show. She's snoozing right outside of the emergency room now."

"Fiona is pacing anxiously and your elder daughter is wondering where you are."

"Tell them I'm coming home right away and that they both should go back to bed."

I suggested a decade of the rosary for Jack and led it, of course. Then I kissed poor Maria good-bye. "Call me in the morning.

"Come on, girl," I told Maeve who had managed to break the rules and sneak up to the door of the room where I was, her primary responsibility. "They're waiting for us at home. . . . And quietly!"

She restrained her impulse to bound. Nonetheless when I opened the door of me Navigator, didn't she jump in before me. The night's work was done and it was time to go home.

— Dermot —

NUALA ANNE had crashed completely when she returned from St. Joseph's last night.

"He'll be fine in a few days," she said as she shed her boots, jeans, and sweatshirt and tossed them in a disorderly heap on top of her black leather jacket, behavior utterly untypical of my fanatically neat wife.

"Maria and Evie made peace," she said as she snuggled beside me in her underwear. "And the puppy stole the show, as she always does."

Then she was in whatever precinct of the land of Nod to which fey mystics go when they crash out. I folded her into my arms, a place she likes to be when she returns from East of Eden. Or in her case perhaps West of Eden.

About eight o'clock I went downstairs to make her breakfast. Ellie was feeding the kids who were in a wild mood, though they were not quite at the food-throwing stage.

"Ma came home late from the hospital last night," Nelliecoyne informed me. "She was there alone."

"Except for Maeve."

"Maeve went to the hospital with her?" the Mick said. "Totally cool."

"Maeve should be chaplain at the hospital," I said.

"Maeve stays here," Socra Marie insisted as she slowly consumed her dish of fruit.

"And you, young woman, finish every bit of that delicious fruit."

"Yes, Da!" she said with a loud sigh.

There were logistic problems. Ellie had a class at ten thirty. Danuta's hours were irregular. Ellie would take the kids across the street to school, but someone had to take care of poor Patjo—who looked anything but poor as he devoured all the food in sight.

"Patrick Joseph," I commanded, "don't you dare eat Socra Marie's breakfast."

"Yes, Da."

"Your ma might come downstairs and catch you."

"Yes, Da."

"You can leave right after you dump the kids, Ellie. I'll cover for the punk."

I then brought herself's breakfast upstairs—tea (so strong you could walk on it), orange juice (a full-to-the-top glass), oatmeal (steaming hot), and three slices of toast with the crusts cut off.

I gave the crusts to Patjo who made them disappear instantly.

My wife was sitting, freshly showered and smelling of soap, at the breakfast table in the master bedroom, chin in hands and staring glumly at the gray autumn.

"Lake effect flurries," she said. . . . "Sure, Dermot Michael, aren't you a paragon of a spouse! . . . The oatmeal is hot, is it?"

"Woman, would you look at the steam coming off it?"

She touched the mess with her index finger and withdrew it quickly.

" 'Tis hot!"

She then gave me a play by play account of the dramas at the hospital. Maeve appeared, stretched contentedly, and lay down for a morning snooze at my feet."

"Good dog, Maeve," I said.

The hound sniffed in contentment.

"And yourself now having two women in your cult group?"

"Och, Dermot, won't she be on the phone this morning? And meself with a Christmas show to prepare. And I have no choice about her, do I?"

"You don't! You open your big mouth and you have another dependent. . . ."

"So does poor Maria Angelica, a battered husband, and a newborn child . . . Dermot, what would you be doing on this terrible day?"

"I was planning on fantasizing about my adventure last night."

She flushed.

"Heathen."

"Well, ravishing an Irish goddess is an event to remember, isn't it now?"

"An experience you've never had before . . . Aren't you going to pour me tea?"

"Yes ma'am."

"Why don't you ride down to the office of Donlan Assets Management and see what this fella Joey McMahon is like? Didn't he start this whole friggin' mess? Besides, you can read all them silly reports on the computer and tell how DAM is really doing?"

"Yes ma'am . . . Do you think it possible that your new friend Evie might be faking her personality transformation?"

"I do not. I was there, Dermot Michael. It was all quite transparent and moving. . . . 'Course we'll have to see what happens."

"And what about former Congressman Stafford?"

"I don't like the man, Dermot love, and I wonder if it is a coincidence that poor Jackie was attacked the same night he was giving a lecture. . . . Yet from what Mr. Casey reports, he's a loser."

"Losers can be dangerous!"

"Well that's for tomorrow. Joey McMahon for today . . . Och, the friggin' phone."

Someone from CTN about today's practice. Me wife turned on her charm.

I picked up the breakfast tray.

She put her hand on the phone and kissed me, revealing a notable amount of décolletage, enough to sustain me through the day.

"You're a grand lover, sir, and a desperate husband altogether."

What more could you ask, idiot?

Energy, stamina, hormones.

Give over, you're getting a lot more of her than you deserve.

'Tis true.

— Dermot —

THE OFFICES of DAM were peaceful the morning after my ride through the North Side. Joe McMahon was presiding with a sure touch in Jack's office. He confidently assured all callers that "the boss" is fine. Highly strong guy. "He'll probably be home tomorrow. You know the Irish! We all have hard heads! We got a computer over to St. Joseph's so he can watch the indexes. Both Frodo and Samwise slipped a little in early trading, but they're doing fine now. No, this stuff isn't doing any good, but not much harm either. Yeah, I'll tell him you called."

Despite his smooth responses to the phone calls Joseph Xavier McMahon seemed woefully out of place at John Donlan's desk. A short, round man in an off-the-rack grey suit with patches of hair around a bald head, a constant frown and darting eyes, he did not look like the market wizard he was alleged to be.

"The last time this happened was when the old fella died. He had stepped back from the business and Jackie was running it with the same intelligence as the old fella and a lot more flair. He was out in California at the place where his wife went to dry out. I'm here by myself and I don't even know whether I have a job and people are calling me from all over the country. Jackie flew back of course and commuted to Los Angeles on weekends. Tough times for all of us, but things settled down and his poor wife came home all bright and shiny. I asked him whether I still had a job the first day he was back. 'Of course you do, Joey,' he says to me with a puzzled look. 'As long as you want and with a lot more money than you're getting.' That's the kind of man Jackie is."

"You've been here how long?"

"Fifty-five years come next June. I came when I was eighteen and I'll be seventy-three next month. Old enough to retire. No reason to do that. My sainted wife is dead, my two fine sons are highly successful doctors at opposite ends of the country. I'll die in the harness."

"And you started out as an office boy and a clerk?"

"Yeah and the old man was a tough guy to work for. Demanding, ridiculed your mistakes, but a great teacher . . . I loved the old bastard."

"And when did you start making investment recommendations?"

"First year I was here. The old man made fun of me. But he wrote them down in a notebook. I kept on making them, he kept on ridiculing them, but he also followed my advice sometimes. When I was twenty-three, twenty-four, he said to me one day out of the blue, 'I've followed some of your hunches, Mac, as you've probably noticed. We made a lot of money on them. So I'm promoting you to the title of investment adviser. Your job is to find good investments. I'll pay you a hundred dollars more a week.' He was a hard man with the buck, but that's what comes of growing up during the Depression. 'Course I got raises later on, and especially when Jackie came on board. But I've been contributing highly to the success of this firm for a hell of a long time. I tell myself that they couldn't have done it without me!"

"Could you have done it without them?"

"All I needed was a college education and a little bit of class. But I went to work here straight from DeLaSalle High School, because we couldn't afford college. In our neighborhood you didn't acquire 'class,' not unless you went to college and for a lot of us even if you did go to college. That's why I sent my own kids to Yale and Princeton. That's why I'm happy they didn't marry a girl from the neighborhood or move back into it. The neighborhood girls they were dating were good kids, but not the right kind. I had to be candid with my guys about where that would end. They didn't like what I said at first, but they followed my advice. I'm sorry that I don't see them more often, but they probably had to break away from me too. I have no regrets. . . ."

His words were spoken brightly but his face was sad. We were no further removed from the immigration experience than he was, but River Forest is in another world, compared to 42nd and Wentworth. And an MD father was different from a streetcar motorman.

We were both silent for a moment.

Then Joey McMahon hastened to clarify his vision of his own impact on the firm.

"But, hey, I don't want to minimize the importance of the old man and Jackie in this firm. It's one thing to come up with the bright ideas and it's another to take full responsibility for them. I don't have to do that. . . . Every one of my bright ideas has to pass two scrutinies, mine and the boss's. If it's still a bomb the boss has ultimately to blame himself. Sometimes I'm wrong, sometimes the boss is wrong."

"No one keeps score?"

"The old fella did. Kept a chart in his office. Jackie doesn't do that, but with that memory of his he knows. They have made a lot more money by following my leads than they've lost. We all know that. I don't have my reputation as a wizard for nothing."

"What's your technique?"

"You worked on the CBOT for a time, didn't you? How did you do? Make a lot of money?"

"A ton of money, mostly by mistake. I quit when I was ahead. Turned it over to investors I trust more than I trusted myself, including this firm."

"You were just lucky? What about the longtime players?"

"They all had theories, but it came down to instincts. I didn't and don't trust mine."

I was not cut out to be a gambler. Only one big gamble in my life and I made it that night in O'Neil's pub on College Green. I was a winner that night.

That's what you say.

That's what I know.

"Yeah, that's it all right. Instincts. I read everything I can get my hands on, pursue hunches. Poke around. Mine are still good, real good . . . I weigh the pros and cons, let them percolate around in my head and then make a recommendation—strong, not so strong, and maybe. Mostly the boss buys only the strong ones. Only once did he go for a 'maybe.' Biggest risk he's ever taken. Spam catcher on the net. Good deal so far."

"What's the history of the Oakdale company?"

"A lawyer from out there comes in to see me. Highly reputable man—Langford Greenwald. Sounds crazy to me. Yet I do due diligence and it seems to be one of those new projects that might just catch on. It has three negatives—Oakdale, real estate, and a woman CEO. Don't get me wrong, I'm no chauvinist, but you still raise your eyebrows. I poke around a lot and I bring it to the boss. His reaction is the same as mine—dubious, but let's check it out. Finally it depends on both our instincts. His are more in favor of innovation than mine. Just the opposite with the old fella. He didn't like new things, which is why we weren't hurt by the dot-com bubble as much as other guys."

"The woman was a problem?"

He hesitated.

"Not really. She's a real dish of course, but she's also highly smart and honest and works hard. Better bet than a lot of men with bright new ideas. Like a dummy I didn't think he'd fall in love with her. It would have been a good deal if he had cooled it. Now, well, you see what's happening."

"And what is happening . . . ?"

"Controversy. In our business controversy is death. If this keeps up, the boss will have to step down. Maybe even sell the business at a huge loss. A big price to pay for a bit of fluff."

"Do you mean he should have considered the bad publicity beforehand?"

"He should have considered the possibility. If he told me he would get the hots for her, I would have said, forget the deal. Highly risky. He should have figured it out himself or wait till the publicity over the deal died down."

"You told him that?"

"It wasn't my place."

"I see your point. . . . But surely you must have been aware of the danger. . . . Jackie is still a young man. His first marriage was very difficult. He is lonely and unhappy. If a smart and beautiful woman should come his way . . ."

"Maybe I should have seen it coming. I had too much respect for him to think he'd go down that path."

"I see . . ."

His ordinary dour face changed to a look of grief.

"I've learned that marriage is a sacrament, no matter how tough it might be. If you lose your spouse, the sacrament is still there and you should respect it. I loved my wife and always will, even if sex didn't mean much to us after all those years together. A lot of women tried to land me after she died. I didn't give them the time of day. They wanted my money anyway. I had to be faithful to Barbara. After a while it wasn't hard. Lot less complications. I was wrong to think that the boss would operate the same way. . . . He should go to Mass every morning like I do. That's a big help."

His eyes filled with tears, a loyal follower deeply disappointed by his hero.

"Uh-huh."

"There are a lot of things more important in life than sex, like loyalty to your family and your colleagues and your friends. I was really disappointed in the boss at that wedding, none of his kids there and then the cancellation. I suppose Cronin didn't have much choice about doing the wedding Mass himself the next day. There's clout everywhere, even for a highly respected cardinal. Then this business last night . . . I don't know, I simply don't know. . . ."

"You believe the firm is in serious trouble?"

"A half a step away from it . . . You're a serious investor, you take one look at pictures of that woman and you know something fishy is going on. . . . You figure pretty soon she'll be running the firm. It's like Hillary Clinton . . . One more scandal and you'll hear the pitter patter of rodent's feet scurrying off the ship. . . . The boss has chosen pussy over loyalty."

Outside, in the Daley Plaza I phoned home.

"Nuala Anne."

"ET calling home."

"So?"

"He's one very creepy character. His last words, just before I fled, were, 'The boss has chosen pussy over loyalty.' "

"I suppose a lot of men will think that way. If only Maria were ugly, then women wouldn't envy her and men wouldn't demean her."

"I take your point. . . . What's happening in your life?"

"Phone calls . . . Panic from the CTN people . . . They need to panic to do their jobs. I don't."

"Ah, soul transplant!"

"Friggin' gobshite!"

"If there is enough order in the house in this new modality, I thought I might drive out to Forty-second and Parnell, find a pub, and have a bite of lunch."

"Go on, letcher, Danuta is here and Ellie will be back from school after lunch. The punk already wants his afternoon nap, lazy loafer. I'll drive over to the soundstage for a run through. The moms will bring the kids down after school and we'll do it again."

"I'll be back in midafternoon in time for my nap."

"Isn't it meself that needs the nap?"

"The ashram on the phone this morning?"

"I've always been a little sister, Dermot love, I don't quite fit in this big sister role."

"You'll play it well though."

"I love you, Dermot Michael Coyne."

"Not as much as I love you."

"Gobshite!"

My sexy Irish Tiger was tired. She needed a vacation. In a warm place. And winter coming to Chicago. The idiot Brit poet who said that if winter comes, can spring be far behind didn't have to live in Chicago.

In fact the Christmas show would be a splendid success. The producers from CTN would quickly discover two things: the Chicago freelancers my wife used as technicians and musicians and singers were pros and Nuala Anne was the boss, especially if she wore her boots and her black leather jacket.

Still she had to worry about it in line with the ineluctable Irish conviction that if you didn't worry yourself into sleepless nights about things going wrong, they surely would. God might be good and generous and eager to smile on your parades, but the fates were something else again.

— Nuala Anne —

HARDLY HAD my beloved spear-carrier ridden off in his chariot to do battle with this Joey McMahon person, when his private line rang.

"This is Dermot Coyne's private wife. Mr. Coyne is away. You can probably leave a message with me. I usually remember them."

I had a headache, needed a couple hours more of sleep, and was in a generally foul mood.

"Hey, Nuala, it's Dominic."

"Hey, Dom, what's happening?"

I did a little acting when I was at Trinity College Dublin—me Dermot said I'm acting all the time, which is probably true. I love to play the moll with Dom.

"Certain individuals I know want to pass on a message to Dermot about what went down last night."

"Yeah, we were expecting a call. We were upset, as I'm sure your individuals understand."

"Yeah, they want me to tell Dermot that they deplore the incident. Also the cops got the right perps."

"One feels safer when one knows the cops did a good job."

"Uh, yeah, and they say that the punks were freelancers. . . ."

"Gangbangers on crack."

"Right. They want Dermot and his friends to know they are trying to find out who the real perps are. Punks from out of town probably. Clumsy like the gangbangers."

"Clumsy punks can do a lot of harm, Dom."

"The individuals I'm in contact with know that . . . they were impressed with what Mrs. Donlan did to the punks. She's a brave woman."

"Tuscan, Sienna."

Why did I say a thing like that? Maybe me Dermot is right, I am a shite kicker.

"Brave and beautiful people . . . Well, I have to get back to work. . . . Looking forward to the Christmas concert . . ."

"Don't we have a Neapolitan lullaby this year?"

"Hey, that's great! My kids will love it."

What was the point in that conversation? I thought as I hung up. I'd pass it on to Dermot, who could probably interpret it better than I could. I was sure that Dom and his family were likable people, good neighbors, fine Catholics. But there was an aura about them of the IRA Provos at their worst. Then the phone rang again.

It was the third call as I tried to make a list of the "must-do" matters for the session at the soundstage. The most important challenge was to shut up the CTN producers who would want to mess around. The technicians and the musicians were all right, but the new folks in town from Hollywood would surely want to throw their muscle around, especially about the filming of Christmas lights at the Daley Center.

The first call was from a timid Evie.

"Mrs. McGrail . . ." she said tentatively.

"Ms. McGrail is me mother and isn't she off in Ireland enjoying the benefits of the Irish Tiger? And Ms. Coyne is me mother-in-law and herself a wonderful and sweet woman putting up with a screaming fishwife like meself . . . I'm Nuala Anne."

She gulped.

"I want to thank you for last night. . . ."

"Och, didn't me hound Maevie do all the work and herself all curled right next to me in me study?"

The good dog Maeve perked up at the sound of her name and shifted closer to me for some petting.

"You saved my marriage and maybe my life. I will always remember that. . . ."

"You saved it yourself, child."

"That's what Mary Fran says. But you and Tony and the dog woke me up. . . . Mary Fran says that I should see a shrink. She says I have a lot of hate for my mother who left us when I needed her the most and I've got to work that out of my system. So I have already called the woman she's recommended."

" 'Tis good, but don't let the woman violate your common sense."

"I won't. . . . I probably need a spiritual director too. . . ."

Brigid, Patrick, and Colmcille! It was like I had hung out a shingle.

"Wouldn't that be a good idea?"

"I, uh, wonder if I might come over and see you sometime . . ."

I didn't need any more kids. I already had four.

"Wouldn't I be willing to share a drop of tea with you. . . . Though we'd better ask Maeve to join us?"

"Wonderful! There's no rush! I know you have a TV program . . ."

"Sure that's no problem at all, at all. . . ."

Liar.

Fiona ambled in and curled up next to her daughter. Often when me husband isn't around they both set up camp in my study, in case I need help or protection.

"How's your da keeping?"

"He's sore all over and wants to get back to work. Mom won't let him even think about going home till tomorrow. . . . She's such a fine woman. . . . I can't believe I hated her so much. . . ."

"Well, child, overnight you have a ma, a shrink, and a loudmouth spiritual director. . . . All ready for a new life!"

"A second chance . . ."

"Don't wait for a third one!"

"I won't, believe me, Nuala Anne, I won't."

Good on you!

The two hounds were sniffing uneasily. I reached into the drawer of my desk where I hide a box of their treats. As soon as I touched the door they were on their feet, mouths open, eyes begging. I removed four treats.

"Oldest first!"

I offered one to Fiona who took it from my hand with great delicacy and then inhaled it altogether. Maeve had not yet learned such delicacy.

"Gentle, gentle," I warned her.

Poor thing, she tried hard. But still a puppy.

I repeated the process and they both reclined again on the floor, content up to a point; well aware that I never went beyond two treats.

They were big dogs, I assured myself. I wasn't spoiling them, was I?

The phone rang again. This time Maria Angelica.

"How's your old man keeping?" I asked.

"He's edgy and uncomfortable and wants to go back to work. . . . His daughter, well, our daughter, came to visit this morning. She is a very sweet child, terribly conflicted now, but I think she'll be all right, thanks to you and that doggie of yours. . . . Remember, I have an option on her first puppy."

" 'Tis only fair," I agreed. "Mind you they are terrible nuisances altogether. Shed a lot of hair, smell terrible, make demands, eat a lot . . ."

"As bad as human children!"

"Ah, no, not that bad, at all, at all!"

"Still they become part of the family, don't they?"

"Me Dermot says that's how they domesticated us. They ensconced themselves in our families and were so cute we couldn't get rid of them. 'Tis the way of things. . . . You'll keep your fella there for another day?"

"Or two! The doctors are still cautious and he's not in any condition to go back to the office. . . . Oh, that Eyes and Ears person called and asked if it was true that there had been a reconciliation. I told them that I would not deny it."

"Good on you!"

"Well, I'm going to ride over to my office and make sure the firm still exists."

I opened my notebook, waited for the phone to ring again, and started working on a "must-do" list.

I was uneasy, anxious. So were the hounds who were now stirring restlessly. I knew that something bad was going down. . . . What?

Nuala Anne, you frigging eejit!

I grabbed me black leather jacket and me camogie stick.

"Come on, girls, we have work to do!"

The hounds bounded up, ready for action.

We thundered down the stairs.

"Is yourself here?" I shouted at Ellie.

"I am, Aunt Nuala!"

"You're in charge. The doggies and I have to prevent a murder!"

We rushed down the stairs and jumped into me Navigator.

— Dermot —

IN MY venerable Benz, I exchanged my blazer and tie for my own black leather jacket, unlike Nuala's BLJ, even more venerable than the Benz. It was the perfect uniform for a pilgrimage to Back O' the Yards, which is south of the Yards as opposed to the "Royal Borough" of Bridgeport which is east of the Yards, an essential distinction, if not to all Chicagoans, and least to those who live in the eleventh and twelfth Wards.

The bar I chose—Mike's in bold green and gold letters—was an old storefront just down the street from Joey McMahon's residence. It was filled with a well-mannered, if boistrous, lunchtime crowd. It was a modern layout, if by modern you mean what was modern when aluminum and red plush were in fashion. There was even an elaborate jukebox in one corner, though it did not appear to be operational. The place was spotlessly clean which suggested to me Polish rather than Irish ownership. The only smell was disinfectant. It would have suggested a waiting room in an older hospital if the conversations were subdued. However, the talk was often loud as was the good-natured laughter. The clientele knew one another and enjoyed the constant bantering in which friends engage. The room was decorated with pictures and banners from the Chicago White Sox. Just behind the bar was a very old picture of a football team.

I walked up to the bar and gestured at the one empty place. The bartender, a red-haired, freckle-faced mick about my age but eight inches shorter with a constant smile and shrewd green eyes, said, "Why not?"

"You really have the best hamburgers on the South Side, like the sign says?"

"Wouldn't say it, if it weren't true, would he?" one of the fellows at the bar said. He was a giant of Eastern European origins with whom one would not want to argue, unless one happened to be an ex-linebacker.

"Is he Irish?" I asked.

Everyone at the bar laughed.

"Takes one to know one," my Slavic friend agreed.

I don't look like a linebacker, exactly. I quit my high school team because I didn't approve of the ethics of the coach and won a wrestling championship, which confers much less prestige. At the Golden Dome I was a walk-on because they thought I looked like a linebacker and were willing to take a chance. I walked off after the second practice. "Not vicious enough," I said to the linebacker coach. I settled in, determined to learn a lot, which I did, but not in the subjects that I was supposed to study. So I flunked out after my sophomore year to the tune of many complaints from Holy Cross Fathers that I was wasting all my talents. I did bring a lot of trophies home from intramural sports and became something of a legend because of my refusal to volunteer for any varsity teams. I then went to Marquette to study theology for the next two years and learned a lot, but did not pile up enough credits to graduate. So I appeared at the Chicago Mercantile Exchange where I lost a lot of money and then made it all back and much more on a single trade. Whereupon I retired and went on a grand tour of Europe, ending in Ireland. In O'Neil's pub on College Green, one rainy, misty night I met this gorgeous young woman and that was that, save for the novel and the books of poetry I wrote. I also became Watson to her Sherlock, Captain Hastings to her Hercule, Flambeau to her Father Brown. My wife beats me in golf, we are evenly matched in tennis, and I can beat any punk in the neighborhood in basketball.

Nonetheless, I could take the big guy that might be looking for a fight and, after a quick glance, anyone else in the room.

"I hear you don't make them medium rare on the South Side."

"Not for South Siders, but for aliens, I can try. No cheese on it. No junk, just a bun with a little bit of butter. Large, medium, or small?"

I feigned astonishment.

"Large, naturally!"

More laughter.

"Nineteen Fourty-Seven Chicago Cardinals—Trippi, Harder, Angsman, Chrisman. Only one championship, but still the greatest."

"You're not that old," said a gentleman on the other side of me, with an Italianate wave of his hand.

"Despite their present lamentable condition in the desert," I continued, "they are the oldest professional football team in America—called among other names in their South Side existence, the Morgans after Morgan Street, the Racines, after Racine Avenue, the Normals after the stadium at Chicago Normal where they played, the Cardinals after the faded University of Chicago maroon jerseys they bought, briefly the South Side Cardinals before they became the Chicago Cardinals, but that after they joined the nascent National Football League with the Green Bay Packers and the Decanter Staleys who, as we also know transmuted themselves into the Chicago Bears. While they were the South Side Cardinals they won a place in one of Jimmy Farrell's Lonigan novels."

"You play football?"

"For a couple of years in high school!"

"Where did you learn all this stuff?"

"I didn't learn much in the colleges I went to, but I did learn to read."

I also learned somewhere along the line to call up Wikepedia from my wi-fi utility in any local Starbucks and read about the Cardinals when I was venturing into an old South Side neighborhood.

"The mayor"—pronounced *mare* of course—"promised us he'd bring them back. Hasn't done it yet."

"The Mare or Mare Rich?"

"Both of them."

"I'm sure they tried."

"It all went down when Old Man Bidwell died," the retired cop said, "and those creepy sons of his got involved."

"And doesn't me wife, who is fey, predict that they won't be winners again till they come back where they belong."

"What do you?" the Slavic gentleman demanded.

"Financial services racket . . . We've got four kids and we need a new home. I'm out here looking for a home. She wants to live in a real neighborhood."

That was the only time in the conversation that I had wandered to the far edge of truth. Herself wanted a neighborhood all right. But she had one. I did look at the homes in Back O' the Yards because the time might come when we'd have to expand our own home and I was interested in how they did it out here. Odd constructions, but functional.

The men around me joined in boosterism.

"This is a great place to live, clean, stable, peaceful."

"Integrated too . . . Look around this bar. Everyone lives here, whites, Blacks, Latinos, Russians, Armenians, Muslims . . . No sweat."

"Good schools, great parishes, near the loop on the Orange Line . . ."

"DeLaSalle, Ignatius, UIC . . . the river . . . Lots of clout with city hall."

"Everyone keeps up their places, great Christmas decorations."

"I was over looking at Bubbly Creek, pretty place. . . . Till you think about what's at the bottom of it. And while I was there, it kind of bumbled. Kind of scary!"

"Did you smell it?"

"I don't think so. I took a good deep whiff. Nothing much."

"Nothing like when the Yards were still working."

Silence, as if in memory of the Yards and all it had meant to this area before it had become a dormitory suburb inside the city, despite its legendary stench.

"We got a guy who hangs around here a lot," the bartender said, "who's in financial services and claims to be a big success. . . . Joey McMahon . . . Know him?"

Aha, it finally came up and it had taken a long time.

"Hell, yes. He's a genius. Works for Jack Donlan. Lots of people say he is the genius behind the firm."

"Well, he certainly thinks so," the retired cop observed. "I'm not sure he's all that smart. He shouldn't be coming in here all the time and talking about how dumb his boss is."

Bingo!

"That sort of thing," I said piously, "is never a good idea."

"He thinks this marriage problem the boss has will force him to sell out and Joey will be right there with his ton of money."

Bingo again.

"Those things happen," I continued in my pious mode. "Never good to talk about it."

"Joey has been waiting so long that he can just taste it," said the bartender. . . . "Hey you want another hamburger?"

"Don't ask . . . Best one I've ever had on the South Side."

Now that is a lie! You were so busy tricking these guys that you didn't even taste it.

Go along with ya.

You don't fool me when you talk like her.

"I figured you'd like it, the way you ate it."

He promptly set about making another.

You blew that. You should have praised him earlier.

I wouldn't make mistakes like that if you'd shut up.

Fortunately Mike the proprietor was still interested in talking about Joey.

"I don't think Joey is smooth enough to run a big-time firm like that, is he?"

"Never can tell . . . What's the scandal?"

"This woman he's married. She's supposed to be a little shady. . . . Joey takes credit for bringing them together. You know her?"

"Yeah, met her a couple of times. You'd turn your head when you pass her on the street. Italian, Sophia Loren type. But, hell, she's a grandmother and as far as I can see a very nice person."

"Joey," the cop said, "is full of more bullshit than anyone in this neighborhood. My friends over at the precinct say they think there's some kind of plot going down. I tell Joey that he should keep his mouth shut."

"If he's had that much experience in what we do in financial services, he should have learned that long ago or he'll never learn it."

I bid my new friends "see you around" and slipped out.

"Next time you come in, bring your fey wife. Maybe she'll have some predictions about the White Sox next year."

"Yeah, I will. She might just know something."

But she'd never play that kind of game, even if she did. Wouldn't even tell me about the Bears and the Super Bowl.

Nice guys. They'd make good friends. But don't claim you're special or they'll eat you alive. Good neighbors. Too bad they're South Side Irish.

I told them that my name was Mike McDermot—close enough to the truth.

I drove over to the parking lot at Comiskey Park as we call it (not U.S. Cellular Field) and called Nuala on her personal office phone. No answer. Maybe she had already left for the first "walk through" of *Lullaby and Good Night*. I left a message. I tried her cell phone too, though she tended to be a bit of a Luddite about that annoying bit of machinery. No answer. I left a message there too. I felt a little uneasy. I should have called her before I went into Mike's bar.

— Nuala Anne —

AS I thundered down Fullerton, I decided it would be a good idea to tip off Mike the cop. My puppies and I might need some help. I pushed his button on my car phone, a machine I normally dislike.

"Mike Casey."

"Meself here. I'm driving toward St. Joseph's Hospital. Something bad is going to happen to Maria Donlan unless me and my doggies stop them. You and Commander Culhane should get some of your people over here to clean up the mess after we're finished."

"Nuala," he shouted, "don't do anything crazy!"

"Give over!" I said. "Meself crazy!"

We'd have all the advantage. The would-be perps would be terrified by the hounds. And meself with me club. I worried a little about Fiona. She was long in the tooth for a fight, but she was in good condition from all her running in the park. I went through the stoplight and turned right onto the Inner Drive. . . . People don't usually want to argue with a Navigator.

The dogs knew we were going to have a fight and the memories of ancient battles encoded in their genes began to stir. One of my ancestors must have been a woman warrior, one of those who charged naked into battle with clubs and the dogs. This caper would not require such extreme measures. I hoped me camogie stick wouldn't break the first time I hit one of the perps with it.

A half block away I saw the snatch going down right in front of the main entrance to the hospital. Three thugs in ski masks, all kind of small, were dragging Maria toward a car.

"Hang on, girls," I told the dogs and rammed the car into which they were trying to pull Maria. Another thug came tumbling out of the car. I pulled back from the car and then hit it again, pushing it over the curb and turning it over on its side. I turned off the ignition and opened both doors of me battle cruiser.

"Go get em, doggies!" I ordered. Almost instantly they bounded out of the car and hit two of the guys in the ski masks, knocking them to the ground. The dogs went immediately to their throats and sunk their teeth into the flesh, just enough to terrify them. Screaming what I thought might sound like the battle cry of an enraged Irish warrior woman I charged the two guys who were trying to manhandle Maria. She was clawing, scratching, kicking them, distracting them from me assault and me cry. I swung me camogie stick and banged it against the bigger of the two of them. He released Maria and crumpled to the ground. The other one let her go and reached for a gun in his rear pocket. I hit his male organs with a mighty swipe of the hook of my stick and pulled the gun away from him as he fell to the ground. I conked him on the head just for good measure. I retrieved the gun, some fool German thing, and slid what I hoped was the safety into place.

A crowd of people were assembling at the hospital entrance to watch the fun. I noticed that I had stopped my yelling. So I began again as I turned to the dogs' two prisoners. One of them was trying to free a knife from his belt. I hit his hand with me stick and it went flying to the ground. He reached for it and I stomped on his hand. As he pulled his hand away I scooped up the knife and held it in me right hand, shifting the gun into me left hand which also held me camogie stick

I pointed the gun at the bad guy's head.

"Try something like that again and I'll blow your focking brains out. Both of youse relax real nice and me doggies won't cut out your focking throats unless I tell them to. If you mess around with us, you'll be dead in less than a minute. Me doggies love to . . ."

Almost said "kill." But that would be a signal to the doggies to kill them.

". . . drink human blood."

Tony Soprano, where are you when I really need you?

I realized that I was out of control. Nuala Anne didn't talk that way in public. Nor did she ruin her vocal cords right before a big concert.

Two big uniformed hospital guys were disarming the first of Maria's assailants who had staggered to his feet. Two other guys were searching the other attacker, taking away his guns and knives and pulling off his ski mask as he struggled to regain consciousness.

A good thing I didn't kill either of them. It wouldn't look good before a Christmas special, would it now?

The growing crowd was cheering, had been cheering for a while. Hey, assholes, this isn't a movie.

"Step back, please, the police are coming."

I was still totally out of control. But I sounded polite, amiable, a sophisticated woman of the world who with her wolfhounds and red Navigator broke up capers and then retired for a martini before supper.

I know meself well enough to know that if I begin to have such fantasies I am really out of control.

Then a cop, not the cops, showed up, a single cop in a single patrol car.

"Ma'am," he said as he waddled toward me, his holster open, his radio in his hand, "I will have to arrest you for disorderly conduct. Please give me your weapon and release those two individuals."

"If I release them, eejit, they'll go after your throat instead of those perps."

"Ma'am, you're under arrest for disorderly conduct. Now please give me your weapon."

The crowd, now counting nurses, doctors, and other hospital staff types, booed loudly.

Good show, Nuala Anne. You'll never live this down.

"Those frigging perps were trying to kidnap Ms. Connors," I explained.

"We can discuss that all down at the station, ma'am. I'll have to cuff you now."

I lifted my left hand with what I would learn later was a Lugar in it and pointed it at his ear. I know what a safety is on a gun and I had slid it into place.

"Back off!" I shouted. "When this is over I'll sue you for false arrest, dereliction of duty, and attempting to imitate a police officer."

"Ma'am, you're compounding a felony!"

The cheering crowd was chanting. . . . What were they saying?

"Nuala! Nuala! Nuala!"

Me reputation as a sweet and gentle singer of Christmas carols was finished. Now I was irredeemably an Irish Tiger. Och, won't me Dermot be proud of me!

I hope.

"I said, back off, you friggin' amadon. When Commander Culhane arrives, I'll report you as a disgrace to the police uniform."

I had said the magic words. A tumultuous cheer from the audience.

"The dog is killing me," one of the perps pleaded.

"Only if you misbehave."

Oh, but the doggies, gentle peaceful souls that they are would so have loved to kill them. These stupid humans had dared to attack not one but two of their friends.

Then, thank the good Lord, before I could make even a worse fool of meself, the rest of the Chicago Police Department arrived on both sides of the Inner Drive, sirens screaming in agonized protest—squad cars, detective cars, Reliable cars, command cars, tech trucks, prisoner cars. John Culhane emerged from the first one, gun in hand. Mike Casey was in the second, his gun also in hand.

"Them two." I pointed at the two terrified perps. "Let 'em go, doggies."

Fiona and Maeve complied but stood next to them, growling dangerously. The crowd cheered wildly. The cops cuffed all four of the perps and loaded them into the prison wagon (called but never by me the paddy wagon).

"Doggies, here!" I commanded.

They ambled over to me, looking quite pleased with themselves.

"Sit!" I ordered.

They did, because they were perfectly behaved hounds of heaven. Far from being worn out, Fiona acted like she was the queen of all wolfhounds, immune to the cheers. Just like me.

But then they began to howl. In triumph. Wild cheers from the crowd. So they howled again.

"I thought it was a Christmas special," Mike Casey said. "I didn't know it was an episode of *Law and Order*. With a live audience . . . Do you want to give me the Lugar, Nuala Anne? You might hurt someone with it."

"Sure isn't the safety on it?"

"It's off," he said, flicking the switch.

"Just as well I didn't shoot that cop who was trying to arrest me for disturbing the peace."

The dogs stopped howling. They saw Maria and Jack hugging each other and himself in a wheelchair with robes and blankets.

"Go say 'hello' to them."

They bounded over to their old friends and embraced them both.

More cheers from the crowd.

"Shouldn't youse all go back to work? Isn't there a lot to be done before Christmas?"

Then they swarmed over me, demanding autographs. The hounds shook hands with everyone.

Nuala Anne can do no wrong, I thought. Even when she acts like a focking eejit, out of control altogether. However would I explain it all to me poor husband?

— Dermot —

I PULLED up at the soundstage on Racine and West Ontario. There was already a crowd outside. My Irish Tiger was a celebrity. Two cops stopped me at the door. I showed them my ID. That wouldn't do. Only relatives of the cast could come in. I showed them a picture in my wallet of Nelliecoyne. That was enough to get a faintly contemptuous wave from the cops.

Inside they were singing an Arab Christmas carol, a young Arab woman in long dress and veil was crooning to a baby in her arms. Nuala was singing the lullaby softly along with the mother, while the tiny choir—Socra Marie, Katiesue Murphy, and some of their class were watching the baby and his mother in mute admiration. Then at a signal from herself, they began to hum. In the background a couple of strings joined in.

"Them thar lil polecats a'singin like to call judgment day," Katiesue's ma, Captain Cindasue McLeod of the Yewnited States Coast Guard, whispered to me.

"How's it going?"

"Hit's a goin' long tolerable well. Your woman say happen you come in, I should a telling you what she done this hyar mornin'. Hit tonishin!"

Captain McLeod, some sort of gumshoe for Homeland Security, was from Stinkin Crik, West Virginia, or so she claimed. She spoke three Mercan dialects: Federal Bureaucratese, Plain English Talk, and Mountain Talk. With her friends and "plain ole folk" like her neighbors, she reveled in Mountain Talk—"hit a-bein' talk that thar Willy Shakespeare a talkin all-ta-time."

So she pretended that we war down ta hollor in Stinkin Crik by the ole hard shell Baptist church and recounted the events that morning in front of St. Joseph's Hospital. The hounds, who had been sleeping backstage, ambled up to me and sat on their haunches, doubtless aware that their praises were being sung.

I didn't say anything at the end of the story. My wife was still alive, so were the hounds, the kids were in various spots on the soundstage. All's well that ends well.

Cindasue ended the story in Plain English Talk.

"They were going to take Ms. Connors to a whorehouse, gang rape her, and throw her out in the street."

"Who paid them?"

"Some man paid them twenty thousand dollars in cash. They didn't know his name. Cops and FBI morons investigating, but they won't find anything. This hyar place a-crawlin' with security. Ya uns be careful."

"Shunuf!"

Two large and authoritative women in pants suits a size too small elbowed their way past us and pushed out on to the soundstage.

"I'm Ethel Showalter and I'm assistant director of the Cook County CPO, Children Protective Office. I'm closing down this performance."

My wife turned on her, eyes dark with rage.

"I don't think you are. . . . Cindy, will you take care of this witch and have security eject them?"

My sister, the redoubtable Cynthia Coyne Hurley, mother to our wondrous Ellie, appeared on the floor. Though I was technically not part of security I ambled over behind her, knowing full well that my sister could more than take care of herself.

"You're guilty of harassment, Director Showalter. I will seek an injunction against you in Judge Ebenezer Brown's courtroom in the morning and ask for punitive damages against you and the County of Cook. Please leave this soundstage immediately or I will ask security to throw you out."

"Federal court has no jurisdiction over us."

"If the Federal court makes this case its own by assuming jurisdiction, then it has jurisdiction. We will ask Judge Brown to confine you in the downtown Federal lockup."

My beloved Celtic Tiger was closing in on our little conversation, the two pooches acting as escorts.

"No way he'll do that . . . This soundstage is lousy with violations."

"Your choice of language is offensive. I have here in this manila folder all the waivers, permissions, contracts, and agreements into which we have entered for this activity and a letter from the secretary of labor of the State of Illinois stating that it is his considered judgment that we are in full compliance with the laws and regulations of the State of Illinois regarding child labor. You could have ascertained this compliance by a phone call to the State of Illinois building. . . . Young man, you're in charge of security, are you not?"

"Yes ma'am, Ms. Hurley, ma'am."

"Then will you and these police officers show these two women out of the building or direct the officers to arrest them?"

My Irish Tiger grinned wickedly and walked back to her podium. The doggies followed, looking reluctantly it seemed to me over their shoulders.

"We're leaving," Director Showalter snapped. "You haven't heard the last of this."

"Nor, Director Showalter, have you! Guard!"

"This way, please, Director."

Behind me, as I walked our two unwelcome guests out of the building, the hounds howled again. They had been doing that a lot lately. Bad habits!

The media were ready for them. Ms. Showalter was prepared.

"They are out of compliance in there," she snapped. "We will ask the sheriff to close them down."

As she departed the bank of microphones I slipped in.

"Our attorneys gave her a file with all the waivers, permissions, contracts, and agreements into which we have entered for this activity and a letter from the secretary of labor of the State of Illinois stating that it is his considered judgment that we are in full compliance with the laws and regulations of the State of Illinois regarding child labor.

"Our attorney also pointed out that Director Showalter could have ascertained this compliance by a phone call to the State of Illinois building and suggested that her harassment of the production might put her in contempt of the order of the Honorable Ebenezer Brown, forbidding all further harassment of the production."

"Do you think, Dermot, that Director Showalter is another Grinch trying to spoil Christmas?"

"They might need a whole Grinch floor over at the lockup pretty soon."

"Do you have any comment, Dermot, on the incident at St. Joseph's this morning?"

"I wasn't there."

I retreated quickly to resist the additional comment that I wasn't sure that I wanted to know what had happened.

I returned to the building with the hounds in tow.

My Nelliecoyne was singing the Connemara lullaby with perfect pitch. Nuala joined her on the first refrain, and the choir joined in for the second refrain.

"That's it," my wife said. "Well done, everybody. Same time tomorrow. We'll try to go through it all without any interruption."

Applause from everyone in the theater.

"They a-cheerin' like they cheered the li'l polecat down to St. Joseph's this morning. . . . Irish Tiger, shunuff."

Then me wife dashed into my arms and sobbed.

"Dermot!" she wailed. "I'm totally out of control."

— Dermot —

"DERMOT," SHE wailed for perhaps the fourth time that day, "I was totally out of control."

"Woman," I responded firmly, "you were not out of control. You just called up one of those personalities you stored away in your preconscious, one of those characters you know pretty well. I've seen her work several times, like that night in the alley in Dublin when those thugs came after me . . . surely you remember that?"

"Not at all, at all . . . I never did anything like that."

We were having our end of the day chat with the usual splash of the creature, this time a very large splash for herself who was so tense that I feared she might break if the phone rang again.

The last call was from Maria Angelica, complaining that her new family—her three new daughters acquired that afternoon—would not go home.

"I'm too old for this emotion," she had said.

"A lot of anger and guilt being discharged?" me wife had replied, in her psychiatric mode.

"They are sweet young women when given half a chance, but I'm not sure I'm up to them. You wouldn't want an extra daughter or two, would you?"

"Not at all, at all. Isn't it hard enough with the two I have? . . . How you keeping, Maria Angelica?"

"A little tense . . . Yourself?"

"Feeling no pain at all, at all. Just sitting here with my man and drinking the creature like they were locking it all up tomorrow!"

I returned to my discussion of the many faces of Nuala Anne.

"I don't suppose you recall the time you came charging down our stairs with the very same camogie stick and the very same dogs when those eejits were trying to beat me up in front of our own home and Cindasue coming down the street with her forty-five?"

"I don't remember that, at all, at all."

"You're the kind of woman I'd want behind my back when the lights go off in a room. I figure that when the lights come on, a couple of my enemies will lie smote on the floor."

"Nothing like that ever happened!"

"Not yet, but face it, Nuala Anne, when your friends and family are under attack they know they can count on you. . . . and the fire engine and the hounds of heaven . . . Doesn't it make me safe altogether?"

You're talking like her again.

Go back to your hole in the wall.

"Give over, Dermot Michael! . . . And don't I need another splasheen!"

"Not at all, at all! I have some special amusements to relax you and I don't want you to be fluttered."

"Well then let's get on with your silly games!"

"Not till we talk about the case."

"Well then report on what you did today while I was fighting off the barbarians!"

So we returned to our usual modality of my reciting almost verbatim my conversations with Joey McMahon and the guys at Mike's bar. I took my sweet time.

She nodded.

"He probably knows some bosses in the drug gangs out there. He could have turned them loose . . . what did those poor men tell the cops? Some man they didn't know gave them twenty thousand dollars in cash to kidnap and rape Maria? He wouldn't have done it himself. Too risky. But a man who knows his village as well as he does, would know a discreet go-between. . . . But Dermot, isn't this savagery? Terrible, terrible savagery?"

"'Tis. The Outfit which can be brutal and its upset would never put out a contract like that. . . ."

"Did you call your friend Dominic to thank him for the tip?"

"Sure . . . His friends say that their friends are furious. The police ought to do something about it. No one is safe in Chicago anymore. They're trying to ascertain—Dom's word—who put out the contract. I suspect that the perpetrator has vanished in the mists. He or they or she or whatever are clumsy but they're vicious."

"And they're getting more vicious. . . . Dermot, whatever will we do!"

A unusual plaint from herself!

"We'll do what we always do, we'll solve the mystery."

Silence.

"And we'll be careful. We'll stay close to our security people and we'll keep the hounds a little hungry, so they're ready to fight!"

"We'll not starve my poor little puppies. . . . Och Dermot, I've lost me sense of humor altogether. . . . And, Dermot love, as you Yanks say, I haven't a clue. None of it makes sense. . . ."

I didn't like that. At all, at all. If me wife's carefully tuned fey sensitivities hadn't picked up any emanations we could be in deep trouble. She certainly was in contact with Archbishop Blackie. If neither of them could figure out what was going down, we'd better invest in some automatic weapons.

"Your sis says the insurance company has to pay for the damage to me car. Isn't that nice and it being me own fault?"

"I bet she also said that your rate would shoot up or that they might even refuse to insure you at all, at all."

"She did . . . but, Dermot love, there were only a few bumps on the front, hardly to notice. I might just leave it that way. . . . Well let's run through our suspects. . . . The first ones that come to mind are those brothers of Maria. . . ."

"Small-time punks with big-time dreams who hate their sister. But we have no evidence on them and Dom says the Outfit thinks they're clean on this one."

She nodded.

"Then there's the Donlan daughters, but they have made peace, have they not? And with much weeping and phone calls to meself."

"Most unlikely suspects but they might know something."

"Something they don't know they know, is it now? Won't we have to talk to them again?"

Which meant that I would have to talk to them again.

"The next one on the list is Lou Garner," I continued, "a four-flusher who envies Jack Donlan's success and has some shady connections in the construction world. He's nasty but not violent."

"What's a four-flusher, Dermot Michael?" she said with a yawn.

"Someone who has four cards of the same suit in a poker hand but fakes that his hidden card is also in the suit and he's holding a flush which is five cards in the same suit. . . . A faker in other words."

"You must teach me that poker thing sometime, Dermot. I used to watch me classmates play when I was a young thing at Trinity College. I always knew what was in everyone's hand."

"Can you still do that?"

"I suppose so . . . I'm pretty good at predicting what your Bears will do on Sunday. . . . Why?"

"When we've solved this puzzle, we might go down to Vegas and win enough money to repair your Lincoln."

"Wouldn't that be cheating?" She yawned again. "Let's finish this conversation or won't I be too sleepy to satisfy your obscene needs?"

That would be most unlikely since she wanted lovemaking as much as I did.

"There's your man down at the office and out in the neighborhood?"

"Isn't he the prime suspect? I don't suppose you asked Dom to check him out?"

"Dom and Mike Casey both. He doesn't seem to be the kind of man that would have underworld contacts. But I'd bet he's a sneaky little guy."

"Still himself talking to people in the pub which is pretty clumsy and all this stuff being clumsy?"

"I agree that he's the prime suspect, but I want to know more about Sterling Stafford. He sounds like the kind of man who doesn't like to lose, either elections or women."

"You're not thinking of going out there by yourself, are you now Dermot Michael Coyne?"

Actually I was.

"I'll ask Mike Casey whether he can provide me a chauffeur for the ride out to Sunshine in Kishwaukee County. Tomorrow about noon."

"And meself with another rehearsal."

"It will be swarming with cops and Cindasue will be carrying her forty-five."

"It's not meself that I'd be worrying about."

"There are rumors about me kicking around in the empyrean?"

She pondered thoughtfully.

"Just wifely concern."

"Speaking of which, it is now time for an exercise of your wifely duties."

"Wifely rights . . . But not till we say our decade of the rosary and drink a toast to one another."

So we did both and what happened afterward exorcised at least temporarily whatever demons had been hounding my wife since her adventures in the morning.

— Dermot —

Memo
From: Michael Casey
To: Dermot Coyne
Subject: Sterling Silver Stafford
Representative Sterling Silver Stafford (Rep. Ill.) is your classic rural Middle Western Republican Congressman of the Reagan era. Not very bright, not very articulate, but very loyal to the party and never guilty of thinking for himself. Born in 1940, he inherited from his father, Fair Profit Silver, his hard shell Baptist religion, his good looks, his populist Republican style and his ability to go for the main chance. He also inherited his father's General Motors franchise in DeKalb and a thousand acres of prime Illinois prairie. Before running for Congress in 1984 (at the time of the second Reagan election, a Republican sweep) he had transferred his GM franchise to Rockford and transformed it into the largest Cadillac agency in Northern Illinois. He also increased his land holdings in Sunshine County to three thousand acres at the time when

the American farm belt was feeding much of the world. It was easy for him to get on the Agriculture Committee and not much more difficult to take over the subcommittee responsible for farm subsidies, a position which in the heydays of the Newt Gingrich Congress and the K Street lobbies, enabled him to become a multimillionaire. He played high school football at Sunshine High School but, despite his campaign claims he was never All-State. Indeed he was a perennial second string, though as his friends say, with a touch of irony, he sure did look like a football star. He was described in journals like TIME as a leader of the Farm Block, but in fact Sterling never led anything and was more a docile member of the Agribusiness Block. He sure did look like a congressman, however—white suit, white shirt, white shoes, black string tie, silver hair, rich baritone voice which could make the most unoriginal right-wing clichés sound like Gospel truth. He was compared to the late Everett McKinley Dirksen as a speaker, a comparison he reveled in, though he was not in the same ballpark as the "Great Ooze" when it came to oleaginous and shrewd statements.

He was twenty-six when he married Vivian Whitherspoon, a nineteen-year-old former cheerleader and stenographer at the Silver Cadillac agency. Their firstborn, Ron Silver, was born five months later. Vivie was a poor white trash country girl who wanted the good life. She hated Kishwaukee County and its memories of poverty and enjoyed the District and all its ceremony. She fit in perfectly with the rich white trash environment of the Reagan and Bush years, so much so that she rarely returned home on weekends with her husband or on recesses. Nor in Washington did she attend church with him at the upper end Southern Baptist Church where he occasionally preached on Sunday.

"Ole Ster" was a perennial candidate in the area around Sunshine and Kishwaukee counties, seeking membership on county boards, the State Chamber of Deputies, the State Senate, and even for Congress in primaries which he invariably lost to a popular veteran of World War II who was a natural on television and both smart and shrewd, claims that could never be made for poor "Ster." In 1984, however, the incumbent died two weeks before "Ster" was swept into Congress from which the wiseacres in that part of Illinois said he would be routed only by the same grim reaper who defeated his predecessor. Sterling Silver Stafford was just the congressman his constituents wanted, he looked like a senator, talked like a senator, and didn't say much.

He voted to impeach Clinton and, perhaps unwisely, gave a strong speech about morality and family values during the debate. Those who knew him both in the district and in Rockford and were aware of his constant and serial pursuit of attractive women—"don't matter none their age or sex"—thought he was skating on very thin ice and expressed the fear or the hope that the ice would sink beneath him. His reputation as a Don Juan made him attractive to a certain kind of woman who was desperate enough for one reason or another to take a chance.

His strongest opposition politically came from Oakdale Township, despite his home on the river inside the township and his membership in the Oakdale Country Club. His voting residence, however, was over in Sunshine in a palatial "family home" he had built on his vast farmland. It was an Oakdale member of the Oakdale Democratic Club (whose president was and still is one Maria Sabattini Connors) and a professor of English literature at DeKalb who finally defeated him with almost 60% of the vote in the 2006 election.

"Ole Ster," it was said, had not kept up with the times. Chicago was spreading into the prairies beyond the Fox River and Illinois was becoming a persistent "blue" state. The Iraq war, for which Congressman Stafford had voted enthusiastically, had turned sour. President Bush, whom he worshipped, had lost much of his popularity. Students from DeKalb picketed his office in Rockford every weekend. Local soccer moms were fed up with the rumors of his romantic affairs. Ordinary folk (i.e. white Protestants) didn't like the suggestions in Chicago papers that he might be indicted immediately after the election. As usual "Ole Ster's" campaign was perfunctory. Unwisely he wept at his concession speech as he said, "Ah reckon that eleven terms is a long time for any one man to live in a pressure cooker."

To the media after the concession, he denied any plans to run for the Senate.

"I reckon I could have beaten that African fella, if I had enough time to prepare a primary run. I was too busy doing a good job on my agricultural committee."

The editorial in the Oakdale *Democrat* suggested that "Ole Ster's" seat had been a lazy monopoly one term too long.

I have tried, Dermot, to keep my Democratic biases and my Irish sense of irony out of this memo. To sum up, Sterling Silver Stafford is a political dinosaur, albeit a relatively harmless one. He does not have a character that is capable of great good or great evil. He is probably too lazy to organize a major conspiracy, but he is a very bad loser.

I closed the file as my limo eased past the exurbs of Chicago, across the Fox River and beyond into more or less open farm country, brown, flat, and dull under the slanting rays of a sun moving ever farther away from us. The sky was cloudless blue and the temperature was in the mid forties. A nice early winter day, the kind that said, "Enjoy me because you will not see my like again for a long time."

Soon the fields would turn white, though that would not improve their appearance. Would it be a white Christmas this year? I hoped not. We would have to attend the Christmas Eve kids' Eucharist at St. Josephat's and the Christmas Mass at Old St. Patrick's where my wife sang in the choir, which, by definition could not do "O Holy Night" without her. Then we would double back to the cathedral to sing at the noon Mass—where she would sing solo "for all the furriners" and pay our respects to Cardinal Sean, Archbishop Blackie, and my brother Father George who was now the pastor of the cathedral so that Blackie would have more freedom to play his coadjutor role. Then we would venture on to the Congress Expressway for the final step in our pilgrimage to River Forest and the Coyne home, where my siblings and their numerous progeny (all of whose names Nuala would remember but I would not) would gather. Noisily. My "small ones" would yield second place to no one in their exuberance. My wife was, of course, one of the kids. I would sit on the sidelines and wonder where that quintet had come from and why, when the other brats began to whine, my bunch simply fell asleep, their mother included.

If it were a white Christmas, however, she would have to lead the whole pack outside for fun in the snow. On arrival in our Republic, Nuala announced that she didn't think she'd like snow all that much.

"Don't we do without it most of the time up in Connemara? I can't see why you Yanks insist on it."

When the blizzards came, however, you'd think she invented it. Wasn't it a wonderful time to play with your husband? And the doggies, and the small ones when they came along? Frolicking in the snow was not an option, a conviction enthusiastically embraced by her offspring, leaving poor Da to mutter that he needed a jar of mulled wine or a small cup of hot chocolate.

After fun in the River Forest snow we had to drive up and down the streets and admire the madcap decorations with which our neighbors—truth to tell, especially the Italianate neighbors—had created to celebrate the joyous season of the birth of Baby Jesus, as he was familiarly known to my kids. Dermot drove the Navigator on the trip, because as me wife announced, "You hardly had a drop to drink." Under normal circumstances she would drive "because everyone says I'm a better driver than you are, Dermot love."

Then finally home to Sheffield Avenue where the sleeping small ones had to be guided to their beds and the weary hounds had to be rewarded with several treats because, sure, isn't it Christmas Day?

Beginning last year weren't we up bright and early on Boxing Day (St. Stephen's Day as the devout Nelliecoyne would insist) to pack for a quick Christmas trip to her ma and pa. Wouldn't it be brilliant altogether for them to see the small ones this time of the year? It would indeed especially since Patjo was so adorable and himself named after me great-uncle. Thus had begun what my brother Prester George would have called an immemorial custom. Interminable, I thought. We would escape from one mad round of parties with family and friends in Chicago to a similar frantic rush in Carraroe.

Last year there had been an excessively white Christmas which clogged O'Hare and gave me family (herself included) a brilliant opportunity to prove that they could be as ill-tempered international travelers as anyone else and worse than most. Poor Da was the only one who had to keep smiling.

Even without the snow, this year's proof that you too can go home again would be difficult. Life was catching up with me good wife, the struggle over her Christmas special, the growing family, the Donlan case, the now almost legendary battle of Lake Shore Drive, the Donlan girls and their new mom—there was no upper limit to the responsibilities that me Celtic Tiger had collected. And she'd weep halfway across the Atlantic at the plight of the "poor doggies" who would not come with us this time and were not consoled by her promise that "won't you be able to come home with us in the summer?"

The doggies were farmed out to the Murphys down the street.

"My polecats are goin' ta think they a dyin' and a goin' to heaven."

We had "minded" the Murphy kids while their parents had spent time in the Cayman Islands. So they owed us and we picked up their marker.

Nuala protested that this wasn't fair—four kids for two. But she didn't protest too loudly.

She needed a vacation—away from the kids, from Mike Casey, from the Donlans, and even from Blackie Ryan. From everyone but me. I wasn't sure she'd agree and less sure that she'd relax.

When does a good husband try to draw the line? What does he do about an Irish tiger? A fragile Irish tiger?

My worrying ended when I saw a sign shaped like a large oak tree which informed me that I was "Welcome to Oakdale—Where Past and Future Meet!"

Maria Angelica's theme.

She must love Jackie Donlan a lot to shift her dwelling to Chicago, though she probably could cope with both worlds.

The town lived up to its theme. New restaurants and motels, mixed with restored homes and stores in a blend that was either miraculous or ingenious. It was not quite ready for national landmark status yet, but it was well on its way. No wonder that faculty from NIU were moving in. The newer homes may have been the first hint to Maria that there was a market for something like Elegant Homes.

The latest report on both the Donlans was that they were recovering "better than could be expected." The latest report from the forces of law and order was that they had all the perpetrators but none of them seemed to know who the contact man was other than "someone from out of town." My friend Dom reported that the friends of his friends reported that the guilty party was some "wiseguy" from Vegas who was "out of line." A message from one of the most important of the friends of Dom's friends warned him that he was so far out of line his misbehavior would be reported to the "Council" and that didn't mean the one in Rome either.

Apparently he was a person of such importance that the people on the West Side (many of whom live in places like Oak Brook or River Forest) would not consider putting him down without national authorization, unless they decided that they would lose all respect if they didn't.

This was high-level stuff. I asked Mike Casey about it.

"Your guy out there," he said, "was the one that warned you about the put-down on Maria?"

"Yeah," I said. "He has some friends who are friends to some people who are very important."

"Probably live right down the street . . . Dom is clean?"

"He's connected, but not involved in anything. . . . He thinks he owes me some favors."

"I don't like dealing with those people," he said with a sigh. "But sometimes it doesn't hurt to listen to them. They know we do some work for herself?"

"How would they not?"

"Yeah, so they figure you'll tell me. That's the way their convoluted Sicilian minds work."

"Our bunch has perfected indirection to its highest point in human history and we've done it without even trying."

Mike thought that was very funny and did not dispute the point. How could he?

"This is a neat little town," my driver, a young cop working for Mike on his day off, commented. "I bet it didn't happen by accident."

"No, Colm, it didn't."

"A smart woman with good taste?"

"You gonna go detective when you get out of law school?"

"I'll leave that stuff to your wife. I want to be a trial lawyer."

No one thought I did anything on me wife's little puzzles. That was grand with me. Grand altogether.

He was clearly from the South Side. He had two of the four characteristics required for trial lawyers in Chicago—he was short and gregarious. He had yet to put on weight and drink too much beer.

We pulled up at the congressman's "lodge," a sprawling brick house on the Kishwaukee River which despite its marvelous Native American name was a lazy and meandering creek.

"I'll wait outside," Colm told me. "Yell if you need me."

"I sure will."

I didn't expect any trouble, not from someone mulling the possibility that he could defeat Senator Obama, in the event that charismatic Chicagoan did not win a presidential election.

A security heavy with dark eyes and a high forehead met me at the door.

"Mike McDermot to see the congressman."

"He's expecting you, Mike. Have a seat in there in the trophy room."

The heavy looked me over and decided that he'd have no trouble taking care of me. He was wrong, but my glowing face and curly blond hair fool a lot of people.

The trophy room was patently, as Archbishop Blackie would say, the place where Maria Angelica had threatened to remove the congressman's genitalia with a shotgun blast, after she had knocked him daffy by throwing a camcorder so that it collided with his handsome, if outsized, head.

Good on you, Maria.

Sterling Silver Stafford appeared in the room with a certain flourish, clad in chinos, a brown corduroy jacket, and a bright red scarf wrapped around his neck. His large, classical head with its flowing white hair might well have been detached from his body and affixed to the wall where it would have fit in with the heads of somewhat lesser animals. Homo sapiens as king of the forest. However, he seemed relaxed and self-confident, quite the opposite of the grey and wounded veteran who had conceded victory to Mrs. Hallinan in the early morning after the election—not Ms. Hallinan, much less Dr. Hallinan.

"Good to meet you, Mike," he said with the usual friendly grin that had characterized his TV appearances and had created the impression that this nice man was probably a smart man too. "I don't see enough of your work, but I've been impressed by it."

The *Herald* had run a political commentary of mine once a month or so to confirm that I really was an investigative journalist. They even offered me a permanent job. I declined with thanks "for the present."

"Thank you, Congressman."

"Just Ster, Mike. Only judges, governors, and ambassadors get to keep their title after they step down."

"Some senators are trying to claim it for themselves."

"They'll never get away with it. . . ." He reclined in the very chair in which he had cowered when the shotgun was pointed at him. "I've asked for some coffee to be brought in and I thought we could talk till noon and then go over to the country club for a bite of lunch. Or are you a good Irishman, Mike, and drink tea?"

"I drink tea, Ster, though I'm not a good Irishman because I don't pollute it with milk."

A man who was either a Native American or an Asian, who had been hovering at the doorway, scurried away.

I noted a camcorder on one of the occasional shelves of books which provided décor for the room—the owner was not only a hunter but a student of primitive countries.

"Do you play golf, Mike?" he asked. "I've given up hunting for golf and would like to give all these heads away. They embarrass me."

"I swing a club occasionally," I said. "When I have the time. I don't exactly burn up the fairways."

There was a certain false modesty in that statement. My handicap at Butterfield is one and at Oak Park two. In the County Galway, I'm known colloquially as "that focking Yank who shoots even and wouldn't be permitted on the course if his wife weren't from Carraroe." I am very proud of that allegation.

"A hunter has to fight another animal, one that's inferior to him and doomed to probable defeat. A golfer, given certain minimal skills must face the worst possible enemy—himself, even one as good as Tiger Woods. . . . I suppose you want to know my view of the recent election?

"I am told that you said the other night that the election was neither a victory for liberals nor a defeat for conservatives."

"That's what I said and that's what I meant. The American people are in substantial part Christians and conservatives hence the Republicans should win almost every election. This time we were defeated by this damnable war. If the president had fired that fool Rumsfeld two weeks before he did I'd still be chair of my committee."

His face turned red in anger for a moment and then relaxed.

"I thought that you supported the war, Ster," I said as I nodded my head at the somber servant who had poured my tea. He looked like photos of Chief Sitting Bull (another head for Ster's gallery). I was willing to bet there was a gallery somewhere in his house commemorating all his sexual conquests too.

The tea was as black as midnight on a moonless night. So was the houseman's stare.

"Like every good American I was proud to see our country hitting back at the evil murderers who slaughtered so many of our fellow citizens. I felt we had to reestablish our self-respect and our power in the world, the only surviving superpower. Unfortunately we made some intolerable mistakes. The military leaders wanted us to go in with four hundred thousand men. That fool Rumsfeld thought he could do it with thirty-five thousand men plus special forces, air power, and Iraqi allies that the CIA had won to our side. I personally think that he was right about that. Such a quick strike force could have toppled Saddam Hussein easily. As a compromise he agreed to a little over a hundred thousand—too many for a military victory, too few for an occupation that could pacify the countryside. Now, when it's probably too late, we're arguing about twenty thousand more. . . ."

"What some people would call too little and too late."

"Not the words I would choose, Mike. . . . And I don't want to be quoted in that notebook of yours. . . ."

I inclined my head at his request for confidentiality.

". . . But materially correct . . . If we're going to go to war, we should go to war with all the power we have and to win as quickly as possible. That's common sense. . . ."

"It's what they called the Powell Doctrine, isn't it?"

"I don't particularly admire the former secretary, but any soldier with common sense knows that. Yet in Korea and Vietnam we did just the opposite for fear of offending the people with the casualties. Better to have heavy casualities for a few months than to dribble away your resources and the people's goodwill over four years. I thought that from the beginning. I admit that I should have spoken out. I was being a loyal team player. I'll never excuse myself for that. It would have been hard to dissent a couple of years ago. I guess I lacked the courage to go after the defense secretary. . . . and all those Jewish intellectuals he had around him."

"And the vice president? Didn't he have his own group of intellectuals?"

"I never liked the man. . . . I couldn't stand him, to tell the truth. Never give an angry man like him a little power. . . . He also has offended a lot of good Christians out here in my district . . . well, what used to be my district"—he laughed lightly—"by publicly supporting his lesbo daughter. Privately I don't mind. But doesn't the Bible say that the sin is an abomination in his sight?"

"I'm a Catholic, Ster, I don't know much about the Bible."

I had studied the scriptures for two years at Marquette and knew a lot about what God said and didn't say. Once I had the idea of becoming a Jesuit and going off to the Biblical Institute in Rome.

"You'd flunk out there too, Dermot," my brother Prester George had said bluntly. "You're not cut out for schoolwork."

He was probably right. However, I believe that I know a lot and did a good job as an autodidact even before I met me wife—and that was a whole education in itself.

"I finally came to the conclusion as I was trying to put the rest of my life together that the president isn't a very bright man. We all kidded ourselves on that. And he's as stubborn as a German farmer out here in Sunshine County."

I was silent for a moment. No point in jotting that down.

"In other words, Mike, we had a great opportunity after we got rid of that notorious sinner. And we blew it. And I'm partly responsible. . . ."

He reclined back in his chair and sipped his coffee. He was himself a notorious sinner. Yet his reverie seemed to disclose a man who, within his own limitations, was trying to be honest with himself. Or perhaps a man who was trying to persuade himself that he was trying to be honest.

"I made a lot of mistakes locally too. . . . You just came out from Chicago. You saw how the prairie which once separated us from the city becomes smaller every year. I came back here often and hardly noticed it, even though I was heavily engaged in the local modernization effort. We rehabilitated this town, so it was true to its past and yet a place to escape from the hubbub of urban life—especially the drugs and the crime . . . and the sex. . . ."

The kids at the local high school almost certainly had similar problems as did kids in Chicago high schools.

"And a good place for someone to catch a breath of fresh air between flights at O'Hare or maybe to schedule a small private professional conference in a restful environment. Maybe play a couple of rounds of golf between sessions. I am proud of the course at Oakdale Country Club. I put a lot of work into its development. We believe it is the best golf course west of Lake Michigan and we are hoping to get a major professional tourney here in the next couple of years."

"That's quite an achievement."

"I'm facing an obvious decision now. I've been offered a senior position in an important firm. . . ."

"On K Street?"

He frowned, not appreciating my insight.

"As a matter of fact, no . . . But right around the corner. I would like it. I'd still be playing in the big game. As much as I hated life in the district, I also loved the excitement, the drama, the challenge. . . . Something like hunting . . . Well I gave up hunting and I lost the big game in the district. Viv, my wife, would be happy to stay. She's winding things down in our condo now. She'll be home for Christmas and we'll make a decision then. Man and wife should not be separated for long."

Two days away from me own high-maintenance wife and I became your prototypical melancholy Irish male wondering where he'll find his next drink.

"Well, come on, let's go over and have lunch. Your driver can follow after us, can't he? Tell him I'll wind a bit through the town so he can see what we've done with it."

As he conducted his booster's tour of Oakdale, I tried to put together my thoughts about this not very bright but not uncomplicated man. He loved the town as much as Maria did. Or did he? Was this whole story an attempt to clear himself of suspicion? Or was it on the level? In his own way, twisted surely, did he also love her and hence want to add her beauty and talent to his collection? A strange kind of love.

I'd have to see what me wife could make of it.

The clubhouse was magnificent, reminiscent of Augusta, but somehow more decent and matter-of-fact. One could admire it and not suffer the temptation to dismiss it as reaching too far.

The course itself was not the best between the Great Lakes and the Pacific Coast, as he claimed while we walked a couple of holes. But it was damned good. He carried a seven iron and a bag of balls as we walked. (My Reliable followed at a distance, watching very carefully. He would make a good lawyer.) We came to the tee for the eighth. It was a par three with a narrow fairway which was mostly rough and woods between the tee and the green save for a ring of sand traps and a tiny pond in front of the green. He teed up a ball and slammed it. It went into the water. The second burrowed deep into a sand trap and the third lost itself in rough.

"Have a shot, Mike?"

All my deep macho competitive genes surged within me. The hormones coursed through my veins. I'd show the son of a bitch. A good investigator would have botched all the shots. But under those circumstances I was not a good investigator. I put my first shot three feet from the cup.

Ster chuckled softly. I glanced back at him. Amusement was already replacing rage on his face. Not in time.

"Great shot, Mike, you do play a little golf now and then, don't you! Can I interest you in a complimentary membership in the club. You'd be eligible for a shot at the championship tourney at the end of the summer. We'd make a great two-ball team."

I accepted the gift, but made no promises about the tourney.

"My work piles up then . . . so many of the older men are on vacation."

"Let's go in and have a drink on it."

"Only one . . . I have to take notes."

"One is my limit at lunch and only when I'm entertaining. One at supper too. Any more than that and I become dangerous."

Again I wonder whether this was true or part of an act.

At the lunch table I ordered bourbon on the rocks—Scotch is forbidden in our house and Nuala would want to know what I had to eat and drink for lunch, especially if she thought I might do some of the driving. He ordered a Caesar salad for lunch and assured me it was first-rate. It was, though I like my Caesar best when it was soaking in garlic dressing.

A symbol of the reformed Sterling Stafford? I didn't know.

"Another thing I missed out here was the importance of Northern. I remembered it as a kind of teachers' college and I didn't want to be a teacher. I got them a lot of grants and in return they gave me an honorary degree. I got them more grants and they asked me to give a graduation address that one of my staff wrote for me. Then somehow—I'll be damned if I know when—it became a great university, about where Champaign was when I was thinking about college. That was something I should have been proud of. And afraid of too. Great university means high-quality faculty. The way things are these days that means a lot of liberals. And that means a lot of Democrats. And a lot of Jews. They not only vote all the time, they campaign like Chicago precinct captains. You put them together with Oakdale and add the soccer moms and the Hispanics and you have the beginnings of a winning coalition. I was not unaware of them because they picketed my office every time I voted against something they liked—this damned global warming stuff, for instance. You add Iraq to the mix and I'm in serious trouble. There were a lot of other Republican team players in the House in the same fix. We murmured about it in private, but we still believed that the country was in a conservative mood and in favor of punishing the Islamofascists. We kept our mouths shut, confident that the president and his boy Karl Rove would pull the rabbit out of the hat again."

"They let you down?"

"Hell, yes! They didn't care much if a lot of us lost, but they thought their majority was safe. Turned out it wasn't and somehow that was our fault."

"The buck doesn't stop in the Oval Office?"

"Not for a long time."

He toyed with his salad but ate only some of it.

"So here I am, back in my district, hurting from defeat and wondering whether I should go back to the Beltway and play the game for the fun of it and not because I need the money or stay here with my farm and my country club and my national landmark little town—and it was the little town that beat me."

"Oakdale?"

He sighed again, not like the way my Nuala Anne sighs, but a sadness of real agony mixed with grief for the passing of the years.

"Not merely the voters here, they were never on my side, though this time they really turned out in force. But, you see, Mike, the president of the Oakdale Democrats was the woman behind the Oakdale plan. . . . What should I call her . . . ? The organizer and the creative genius . . . We were allies, not exactly friends, but I thought we respected each other. . . . That's the way it is in politics, I guess. . . . You won't put anything about her in the story, please?"

"Okay," I said, closing my notebook.

"We were never lovers, you see, though I often thought that would not be a bad idea, especially since Viv never came home on weekends. And my friend had a marriage problem of her own. Nothing ever came of it and I'm glad now of that. But it still hurts."

A quick flash of anger appeared in his dark eyes and then disappeared.

"I understand."

"Well, her marriage problem cleared up and she married a man in Chicago. She comes back often, but I don't see her. . . . Sometimes I wonder . . . But this defeat has brought me and Viv closer together than we've been in a long time. . . . So I suppose it's all for the best."

An expurgated version of what happened but a usable rationalization for a fractured ego.

"Maybe Junior did me a great favor when he didn't fire Rummy. Maybe I'm out of there in the knick of time. Maybe I should be proud of my achievements and let it go at that. Let the liberals run the country for a while and see how they mess it up."

At the door of the clubhouse, I introduced him to my man Colm, a student in law school.

"I always thought I might like the law," Sterling Stafford mused. "One thing led to another and I never did. I've concluded that I made a mistake. Lawyers have an edge on everyone in society."

"Only," my man Colm said, "because they make the rules where the edge is."

We all laughed.

"I'd know your friend was Irish," Ster said, "even if I didn't know his name."

I waited till we were out on I-80 before calling Nuala Anne.

"Nuala Anne," she said crisply, her artistic impresario face totally in place.

"Her husband."

"Och, Dermot Michael Coyne, aren't you a wonderful husband altogether to be calling and myself in a disaster area?"

"A frigging disaster, is it now?"

She pondered for a moment.

"I wouldn't go that far, not yet? But in all me life as a director, I've never seen a worse dress rehearsal or final run-through or whatever you want to call it."

"Did you cuss them out?"

"I'm an amadon as you know, Dermot love, but not that much of an eejit. I had a swarm of little girls, including poor Socra Marie and Katiesue. Didn't I tell them how great they were and how wonderful they'd be tomorrow night at the taping? And weren't some of the mothers angry at me for not going after them?"

"That's not your style, Nuala, except when you're straightening me out."

"Go long with you, Dermot Michael Coyne, I never give you a hard time save when it's for your own good and don't you know that?"

"What will it be like at the taping?"

"Won't they be friggin' brilliant? And if I made them cry, any more than they did, after tomorrow I'd have to be on the first plane to Shannon."

"Do you *know* this?"

"Would I be saying it if I didn't know? The small ones are winners! Now what did you learn about our gobshite friend out beyond?"

"Not what I expected at all, at all."

" 'Tis interesting . . . We'll have to talk about it tonight."

"You'll be too worn and frazzled."

"Don't be an eejit. . . . How long have you been married to me?"

"A couple of eternities . . . All right we'll talk about it tonight. . . . How are the Donlans doing?"

"Doesn't poor Jackie feel like he's died and gone to heaven and his wife and his daughters and his stepdaughters treating him like he's best thing since the invention of stock markets. The dentists and the plastic people have done him so that by Christmas he'll look better than new."

"And his company?"

"Still the value of the company is falling but not too badly, considering. Frodo and Samwise are standing firm. So's the ELG thing. If we can unknot this puzzle by Christmas, they'll bounce back."

"Will we? Can we?"

"Don't ever doubt an Irish Tiger. . . . See you at supper. Tell Colm to drive carefully."

Which I did of course. With a wife from the same ethnic background he assumed such a warning and would have been disappointed if it were not delivered.

At supper it emerged that the doggies were in, you should excuse the expression, the doghouse. They had misbehaved terrible altogether at the run-through, fighting with each other, and interrupting the songs with their infernal howling and chasing imaginary rats. That was unlike them. They had been banished to the Navigator where they howled all the more.

Me wife who looked thin enough and haggard enough to be hauled off to the emergency room herself was upset with the hounds.

"The kids," she said "don't know any better, but the puppies know they're supposed to behave."

The children were helped with their homework and put to bed as they sang songs to one another.

"You'll be brilliant tomorrow," she informed them. "Now just one more time through the Connemara lullaby and then off to the land of Nod."

Patjo and Socra Marie were most of the way there.

The hounds wandered into the songfest looking sheepish, if such a description can be applied to wolfhounds. Fiona, by reason of seniority, nudged me wife by way of apology. She embraced them both and produced a treat for both of them. The reconciliation was thereby sealed.

In our bedroom, after our showers, I recounted for herself my verbatim discussion with Sterling Silver Stafford aided by my notebook.

"Now isn't that the strangest thing!" she said, pondering my report. "What were you after thinking, Dermot Michael?"

"Wasn't I kind of thinking that he wasn't quite clever enough to make up the whole story."

"It's a story he's told himself many times and yet he can't quite believe it all. . . . He'd be happier if he filled in the blanks with the truth. . . ."

The hounds entered the room together, a rare enough event. Something was brewing.

"It's all right, puppies, I'm not angry at you anymore."

They cuddled up around her legs, and she patted them both. They were still restless.

My good wife began to shiver. She looked at me, her eyes wide with fear.

"Dermot! Someone's going to blow up my Navigator in the parking lot tomorrow night, just when people are coming out of the auditorium! Hundreds are going to die, including maybe us. We have to stop them!"

— Dermot —

WE BOTH froze. Nuala Anne has such intense warning experiences only rarely. They terrify her and frighten me as if someone is holding a gun to my skull. Something very bad was about to go down out there and we had to stop it. But we had only the faintest idea what it was and how to stop it. The warnings were vague and erractic and sometimes wrong. There was no way to be sure. Who would want to blow up her car and kill the people that would come to the taping, including, if John Culhane were to be believed, the mayor and the senator? Was it part of the Donlan puzzle which seemed to escalate every day? It had started out as a harmless item in a gossip column and now it threatened mass murder.

"Are you sure?" I asked, wrapping her trembling body in my arms.

"I'm sure the explosion is out there. . . . But sometimes it's wrong, never when it's this strong. . . . Och, Dermot love, don't I wish that I was never fey? Isn't it terrible altogether."

"Are you sure it's your Lincoln?"

"It looks like it. . . . Sure, I hope that we all of us die together, even the puppies."

"None of us are gong to die, Nuala Anne. We've beaten the bad guys before and we'll do it again."

"Ma! Ma!" Nelliecoyne rushed into the room in her Snow White and the Seven Dwarfs pajamas.

She threw her arms around her ma and sobbed.

"What's wrong, cara, what's wrong? Are them terrible Snow White dreams bothering you again?"

She had discovered an old Snow White tape and shown it to the younger kids, who loved it. Somehow it had scared her—though she was immune to nocturnal troubles after Harry Potter and the Ring books.

"The wicked dwarf is setting off a huge explosion, like a meteorite hitting our neighborhood! It blinded me for a few moments! . . . Oh, Ma, wasn't it terrible altogether! I knew I was dying! We were all dying!"

The two hounds rose on their hind legs as if to protect mother and child from impending doom. Poor Da could fend for himself.

This was the first time that the sight had affected both me wife and me oldest child. It was a major happening. I must do something. . . .

"All the dwarfs are good in the filum, darlin'. 'Tis the wicked queen who's the bad 'un."

"The queen wasn't in me dream at all, at all, Ma."

"And the dwarfs are good 'uns, aren't they?"

"Kinda dorky but they try to be good . . ."

"So it wasn't a true dream, was it?"

Nelliecoyne dried her tears on the sleeve of her pj's.

"No, Ma, it's not going to come true, but we have a lot of work to do."

"Your da and I always have a lot of work to do and we always get it done, don't we?"

"You're the greatest ma and da in the whole world! Katiesue's ma and da are real nice too."

"Then you'll go back to bed now and get a good night's sleep because we have the show tomorrow night."

"Yes, Ma."

"Did you wake up Socra Marie?"

"Och, Ma, the end of the world could happen outside our window and that one wouldn't wake up."

"Too true."

Ma and the small one went hand in hand back to the girls' bedroom. Me wife rolled her dangerous blue eyes at me as they went.

I had to do something, so I called my friend Dominic.

"Dominic," he said, polite as always.

"Dermot, Dom. Sorry to call so late."

"No problem, Dermot. Whole family is in bed, so I'm working on my taxes. What's happening?"

"We hear there's a contract out on us. An engineer is going to blow up our car tomorrow night in the parking lot after Nuala's show. Kill us and a lot of people!"

"Holy shit, Dermot. The mayor and the senator are going to be there. We can't let this go down. My friends won't permit it. That's all. They just won't permit it! . . . Is it part of this Donlan caper you people are involved with?"

"Probably."

"Okay, Dermot, thanks for calling me. I gotta get in touch with some of my friends right away."

"Thanks, Dom."

"You can count on us, Dermot. Tell your wife, my friends just won't let it go down. No way. Count on us."

"Thanks. We will."

"Your man?" Nuala asked.

She had come back to our bedroom, accompanied by the two hounds who had escorted her and Nelliecoyne back to the girls' room.

"Good idea," she said, filling our two Irish crystal tumblers with a large splash of the creature. "Last ones before the show wraps up tomorrow night."

"*Slainte!*"

"*Slainte!*"

My wife had rebounded. Once more she was the Irish Tiger, Granne O'Malley getting ready for a raid on the friggin' English.

"I'll call that nice Mr. Casey," she announced as she sat down at the desk to take charge. She gestured at the other phone for me to listen on.

Mike was always "that nice Mr. Casey."

"Hi, Annie, Nuala Anne here, sorry to ring so late, but you know what me husband is like. Keeps terrible late hours . . . Could I have a short word with himself.

"Hi, Mr. Casey. Sorry to trouble you, but we have reason to suspect that someone will try to blow up me little fire engine in the parking lot after the show tomorrow night."

"What kind of reason, Nuala? Ordinary or otherwise?"

He knew her well.

"Otherwise and very powerful . . . Aren't me poor doggies worried, but me poor little chile saw it in a nightmare. . . . A terrible explosion would kill all of us. . . ."

"And probably the mayor and the senator and their wives," I added.

"Hi, Dermot . . ."

My presence, of which he was certainly aware, was duly acknowledged. He could assume that I was sharpening up the spears which were what I carried in our joint operations. The spears (imaginary) would be useful should we encounter any vampires. Herself denied their existence. They were a silly English superstition, even if your man was Irish.

"I've already talked to my friend on the West Side," I said, nodding my head toward Taylor Street and beyond, which is de rigueur if you're talking about "the boys."

"Good idea. I'll call John Culhane and we'll be there for breakfast. . . . Lots of coffee, Nuala . . ."

"Tonight," she said bluntly.

"It's that serious? Okay, I'll ask John to call Terry Glen, the deputy superintendent. He'll be skeptical, but if we win him over, we'll have all the good guys on our side as well as the guys out on the West Side. Make the coffee anyway."

"Come quietly," I said, "and park in the alley behind the house. No cop cars."

"Won't we be letting you in the back door on the ground floor? You just have to walk down the steps."

So me wife and I put on our black jeans and our black sweaters and she tied her long hair up in a businesslike knot. We carried our black leather jackets and our ski caps and the sound monitors for each of the kids' bedrooms downstairs to the ground floor. The kids' playroom was in only mild disarray.

"Let's leave it as it is," she said, "so they won't think we planned all this. I'll take the soda bread out of the freezer and heat it up. You get the balls off the floor so no one will slip on them. Would you ever, Dermot love, turn on the coffee and teapot in the archive room?"

Me woman believed as a matter of faith that soda bread should be served fresh out of the oven. Then she saw her ma heat it up in the microwave we had given them for Christmas a couple of years ago.

The archive room was an L-shaped corner on the ground floor adjoining the playroom, but separated from it by a soundproof door. When we bought the house it had been a storage for old newspapers, some very old, and documents. We saved a few of the documents and papers, installed cabinets, paneled the walls, and provided a table with easy chairs around it. There was also a police radio scanner, a TV, and maps of Chicago on the wall and a bank of phones, a wet bar, a fridge, and coffee- and tea makers. I called it "the Situation Room" because Nuala had the room of that name from *The West Wing* in mind when she furnished and decorated it. We also had a bank of monitors from which we could survey the approaches to our house. I turned them on so we would be ready for the Chicago Police Department when they appeared. For the first time I realized that snow had been falling for several hours. The alley outside the house was already covered with snow. Four to six inches possible, the weatherman had promised, though most of it would be on the South Side and the southern suburbs.

A blizzard was all we needed.

The cops arrived just as Nuala descended with a platter of steaming soda bread. I opened the door and assured them that they didn't have to worry about tracking snow on the floor. I poured the coffee and tea and herself distributed scones, clotted cream, and jams and jellies, most of them imported from Ireland. There were four cops, Mike Casey, John Culhane, Deputy Superintendent Terry Glen, and Lieutenant Nikos Mashek, head of the bomb squad. Mike Casey acted as chair.

"As some of you know, the Sixth District has worked with the Coynes for some time on various puzzles and problems that have occurred in the district. Reliable Security has also worked with them in certain matters. We do not believe that Mrs. Coyne—professionally known as Ms. McGrail—is either psychic or fey. We do know, however, that she often puts together components of a problem in a way that escapes our skills. We have rarely discarded her insights and we have never been wrong in listening to her."

And so as the wind assailed our old wooden home and howled through the crannies and the snow continued to fall in our alley, we discussed the problem of whether we should cancel the taping of the Lullaby Christmas special.

"'Tis all part of the plot against the Donlans," she insisted. "It escalates each time. First it was just a leak in a gossip column, then it was a lie to stop a wedding, then an assault on Jack Donlan, then an attempt to kidnap Maria Donlan with intent to gang rape, now a car bomb in a crowded parking lot to kill hundreds of people. There is madness behind this escalation. The plotter grows increasingly angry as his clumsy schemes are foiled. He now plans mass murder."

"We should understand," John Culhane continued, "that Nuala's insights have never led us astray. When she senses trouble, there is trouble brewing, as we learned in the matter of the attempted kidnap in front of St. Joseph's Hospital. I believe we have to take this insight very seriously. The risks are too great if we do not."

Deputy Superintendent Glen, a tall, solid, charging-end person, was uneasy with the prospect of police involvement with what seemed a supernatural matter, as he should be. Reliable Security was a private company. If it wanted to take seriously the uncanny, that was its right, but the Chicago Police Department could ill afford the risk of media ridicule. The soundstage was not in Area Six's jurisdiction, but it could offer the usual protection for public events, though it would be better if Reliable Security took that responsibility. Ms. McGrail would be within her rights to postpone the taping.

My wife was calm and articulate. She would inform the network of a threat to the taping and recommend that it be canceled. Doubtless they would take her advice. They would have to say that there was a threat with which the Chicago police were not prepared to deal.

Sometimes when I watch my wife, I feel that I couldn't possibly be married to this beautiful woman and experience the evanescent desire that attacks a man's brain when he sees a beautiful young woman walking down the street. It would be nice to make love to her, but in a civilized society men don't do that kind of thing, don't even dwell on it in their imagination. Therefore I could not entertain lustful emotions in the present circumstances, whatever they might be.

No way.

The conversation was polite. Glen and Casey called each other "superintendent," though the former was only a deputy superintendent and the latter a retired superintendent.

In the repetition of the lines required in the discussion, Mike Casey played the role of the sophisticated Irish politician who sought in all disputed matters a sensible compromise.

"Reliable could always provide a security net around the soundstage and search every car that comes in. It would delay the event. It would be better if we could deploy a massive cordon of force."

"I can't see my way clear to doing that, Superintendent."

"And you're prepared to say that, Superintendent, if we should lose the mayor and the senator and their wives to a terrorist's bomb?"

"I don't think that will happen, Superintendent. . . . What's that noise?"

"It's our two Irish wolfhounds," I said. "They're retired police dogs. They've been upset all afternoon. They've been trained to sniff trouble."

Glen sighed patiently.

"You realize that you're asking me to accept the warnings of a psychic and the instincts of a couple of dogs?"

"I'm not a psychic," Nuala said. "I'm one of the dark ones."

"My wife means," I insisted, "that she's a mystic."

"Whatever!" He threw up his hands.

The dogs shut up. Nuala can tell them to shut up without speaking a word to them.

I consider that scary. She also sees the auras around their heads, halos if you will. I would consider that creepy if the halo around my head hadn't convinced her that she would have to sleep with me someday.

Or so she would later tell me.

"There is no way we can keep this out of the media," Commander Culhane insisted. "If we go ahead with a massive security cordon, it will be news and if the network cancels the taping, then there will be tough questions asked at the news conferences tomorrow morning."

"Mike, that's not for me to decide. What I need is a better reason for that cordon than signals picked up from the supernatural."

The dogs began to howl again.

"Well, then, I suppose that we'll have to take the bombs off me motorcar won't we?"

"Now?"

Lieutenant Nikos Mashek spoke for the first time, his quiet Slavic face shining brightly.

"How do you know that the bombs are in the car?" Terry Glen demanded.

"Weren't we after telling you that the hounds are police dogs? That car makes them nervous. It has all day long."

"We can't disarm a bomb here in the middle of a snowstorm!"

"Depends on the bomb, sir. I can inspect the car and see if there is explosive material on it. Then I can activate my unit and do whatever is necessary."

"Do you mean evacuate the whole block?"

"That's what we're trained to do, sir."

"How do you know that it won't explode while we're looking it over?"

"It hasn't blown up yet. If Ms. McGrail's suspicions are correct they intended it to explode tonight."

"It didn't explode when I was driving it home from down below this afternoon, it's not likely to explode now. They put the bombs or whatever into the car so that it would blow up during the concert tonight. There'd be no point in it exploding now. . . ."

"Unless they were careless or sloppy," the lieutenant said. "There's always that possibility."

Reluctantly the cops donned their overcoats. I helped me wife on with her black leather jacket.

"Well, Dermot, we'll go to heaven with all our kids, won't we now?" she whispered.

"They'll only let me in on your say-so."

"Sure, don't they know up there, that you're a livin' saint?"

"Let me calm down the puppies. Like I said they're police dogs. They love cops and they'll know you're cops and will want to be friendly. Tell them how wonderful they are."

In the kids' playroom, the hounds stopped howling and erupted in joy at the smell of cops. Perhaps I should say "other cops."

"Chill out!" Nuala ordered.

Reluctantly, they sat back on their haunches and awaited further instructions, troops prepared for battle. Superintendent Glen gingerly ignored them. Lieutenant Mashek patted them on their heads.

"Nice doggies," he said.

The hounds were delighted. They were working with cops again. If we were all blown up, they would go off to doggie heaven happy to the bitter end.

"You have the keys to your car, Nuala?" he asked.

Silently she handed a set of keys to him, keys to every room in our home and in a pinch a useful weapon.

"Superintendent Glen," he said at the door. "You've been on the force for how long? Twenty-eight years? How many members of my unit have we lost in that period of time?"

"None, Nikos," he said, "and we're proud of the unit's work."

"And no civilians?"

"Not a one."

"We won't break that record tonight."

"You'll be needing this floodlight." Nuala handed him a floodlight that she always kept in a closet on the ground floor. There were a few streetlights in the alley, not much use in the blizzard which was wrapping everything in a thick white blanket.

"You'd better stay in here," Nikos said to us, "until I come back from my car with my tools. In fact you can stay inside all the time. If the car should blow up, you won't be safe inside or outside."

He tried to push out the door to the alley but the wind resisted. I pushed with him.

"Thanks, Dermot," he said with a wicked grin. "I guarantee you there's no danger here, not much anyway."

"I am reassured," I said with a touch of irony in my voice.

He chuckled, a guy from the neighborhood, not this one, but a neighborhood somewhere.

The hounds gamboled out after him and leaped through the snow, ecstatic to be back on the force again and at the same time playing in the snow.

In a few moments Nikos returned carrying two small briefcases.

"Not many tools," I whispered to me wife.

"Hush, Dermot," she said to me, "isn't he a nice young man with two sons and a daughter on the way?"

She was showing off.

We walked to the Lincoln which was just a few feet away from the door.

"I've activated my night unit," he announced. "They'll be here soon. And quietly, like I told them."

Then he began to examine the car with some of his mysterious instruments, a medieval wizard plying his secret craft. Cautiously he opened the door of the Navigator and opened the hood. I was fingering my rosary. Me wife was peering over his shoulder. I stood next to her.

"Where are the explosives?" I whispered.

"Isn't it obvious? Aren't they in the boot? The puppies are letting him do his work and then they'll tell us all."

He examined the motor and the ignition and the gas tank with great care, moving an instrument like a long thermometer in and out of the innards of the car's machinery. Then he crawled under the huge vehicle and explored its underbelly.

My sweater and leather jacket were poor protection against the winds and the whirling snow. I was shaking with the cold. The snow assaulted the skin of my face. My feet were wet from the slush and the wind shook me from head to toe. My wife of course wasn't shivering at all, at all.

Finally, covered with snow and grease and looking like a circus clown, Lieutenant Mashek crawled out from under the Navigator.

"Sir," he said to the superintendent, "there are no explosives linked to the ignition and none in any of the usual places in the motor or under the car where they are usually placed. . . ."

The hounds bounded to the back of the car and growled at the fender. Then they howled.

"The boot," Nuala shouted above the wind and the wailing hounds.

In Dante's inferno, hell is a frozen place. I felt that I was in its antechamber.

We huddled over the trunk, Nuala, Nikos, Glen, and myself. I was hoping that I was in the state of grace as we used to call it and realized once again that the God of Jesus was not a hanging judge. The father of four children should not be out in a blizzard and himself watching a nerveless cop try to open the trunk of a car which, if the snarling hounds were to be believed, was filled with high explosive.

Nikos had put on thick gloves and was wearing the standard police armor, neither one of which would be much protection against a car bomb, one that might demolish our whole block on Sheffield Avenue. He inserted the key into the lock and turned it. But the key was somehow jammed in the lock and wouldn't turn.

"It worked yesterday," Nuala protested.

"Someone messed with it after you closed it," Nikos said softly. "Probably pried it open so they could put in the explosives."

"There'd be no reason for the explosion to happen before the taping this evening," Nuala said confidently. "Why waste all that effort on a block on Sheffield Avenue."

My Nuala Anne didn't seem at all frightened. But then maybe she could see things that I couldn't.

Nikos tried again. The lock wouldn't budge.

"Let me give it a try," my wife ordered. "I'm pretty good with contentious locks. . . . Just like contentious husbands."

We all laughed nervously, meself louder than anyone else.

The door, knowing as I did who was the boss, promptly sprung open.

I peered inside cautiously, as if looking at the explosives would set them off. A piece of tarpaulin covered a shapeless mass.

Nikos ran one of his little magic tools over the mass.

"As I expected there is no indication of an ignition device which would cause an explosion at this time. Everyone can relax."

"I'm shaking because of the blizzard," I protested.

Everyone laughed again.

Nuala clutched my arm. We would die together just as the ancient warriors, male and female alike, died together.

With a gentle and delicate movement, Nikos pulled back the tarp.

"Just kids' schoolbags," Superintendent Glen said, as though he were disappointed.

"Madrid," Nikos and I said together.

"When the jihadists destroyed the commuter trains in Madrid," Nikos explained, "they put the explosives in backpacks which did not seem to have any traditional ignition mechanism. They did not want them to explode before the proper time. Instead they used the insides of cell phones. When someone called the number, a simple device connecting the phone to the bomb ignited the explosive material. All the bombs went off at the same moment. With these pastel-colored backpacks, intended for little girls like my own, you need to ignite only one of the packs. When it explodes it will ignite all the others. You would have quite literally a blockbuster."

The hounds howled again, just for the record I suppose.

"This device—" he produced from his kit of surprises a slender instrument, about a foot long, with a scale running its full length. "—will measure each of the backpacks for the presence of metal, like a mobile phone mechanism. I will assume that like all crazy people, these morons had a sense of symmetry and that they chose the center bag." He touched the far left bag first and then the next one. He skipped the center and touched the final two. In each case, the instrument flashed on and off.

Then he touched the central backpack. His magic wand went crazy, flashing red lights and howling. The hounds not to be outdone howled in response.

"That's the bag with the ignition mechanism. Now, my last bit of magic, this camera is no ordinary camera. Rather it photographs the inside of the bag, penetrating the fabric around it. Moreover it produces a picture in thirty seconds."

He flicked a switch, the camera made whirling and swirling sounds like a small waterfall. Then it spat out a three-by-five picture. Nikos considered it carefully.

"You were right, Dermot. It is the same kind of mechanism used in the mass murders in Madrid. Note the lumpish material that fills the bag. That's the plastique, the plastic explosive. The bright red object as you can see is the innards of a cell phone. Someone dials the number, the ringer is activated and with it a current that flows into this blob of explosive and ignites it. The result is an exploding car bomb, or in this case an exploding truck bomb. In a crowded parking lot many, perhaps most of the gasoline tanks would explode almost at once. Instant mass murder. I am going to disconnect the ignition and remove it. In that way the truck bomb is permanently defused. . . . I presume, Nuala Anne, that during the rehearsal yesterday, they pried open the trunk, quickly dumped these bags into the car, and departed. It was a chance, but they are people used to taking chances. Fortunately for us, Fiona and Maeve knew that something was wrong and alerted us to the problem."

He patted the large heads of the great white dogs and they tried to lick his face.

"Chill out!" Nuala ordered. The dogs settled down on their haunches, panting happily.

"They were also taking the chance that you would not notice the bags and that your security resources here"—he patted both dogs again—"would not sniff something wrong. Their scheme was to mine the car when there was no one around, you would drive it home, and not activate the bombs. Then you would drive it into the parking lot this evening. They would be located somewhere in the vicinity. Once they saw this distinguishable vehicle, they would know that they could activate the bomb at their leisure and with a simple phone call kill hundreds of people."

"Well done, Captain," Superintendent Glen said.

"Lieutenant, sir."

"Not anymore."

"Thank you, sir . . . I will now remove the ignition device. I assure you that there is nothing at all dangerous in this exercise."

He removed a sharp knife from his bag of tricks, cut open the center bag, lifted the remains of a mobile phone, snapped the wire that fed into the plastique, removed the mobile carefully, and placed it in a transparent evidence bag.

Me wife loosened her compulsive grip on my right arm.

"If I may make a recommendation, Nuala and gentlemen." He began to assemble the tools of his trade. "When our bomb truck arrives, we will transfer the explosive material and bring it to our headquarters. I will drive this impressive vehicle to the appropriate lab and demand that it be swept for all available evidence. I would suggest that forensic teams finish their work in early afternoon and return the car to its present location. Then Nuala and Dermot could drive it over to the soundstage. In the meantime the force could search the neighborhood for the observation post of the perpetrators."

"I personally will direct the search," Terry Glen said. "Moreover we will throw a cordon of cops all around the soundstage and its environs. We will also search every car entering the parking lot—even the mayor's car."

"Having informed him earlier in the day of the situation," Mike Casey said with a laugh.

Terry Glen echoed the laugh.

"I'll tell him the whole story. He'll love it."

The police brass left us, their cars slipping and squirming down the alley. The big bomb squad truck arrived, lurching into the alley like a clumsy dinosaur. Some young cops examined the Lincoln repeating the steps that Nikos Mashek had taken. Then they loaded the backpacks into the truck. Nikos shook hands with us and the dogs, climbed into Nuala's car, and turned over the ignition. The Navigator started smoothly and followed the dinosaur down the alley and out on the street. Suddenly our alley was quiet. The wind subsided but the snow continued to fall, like your man said, on the living and the dead.

— Nuala Anne —

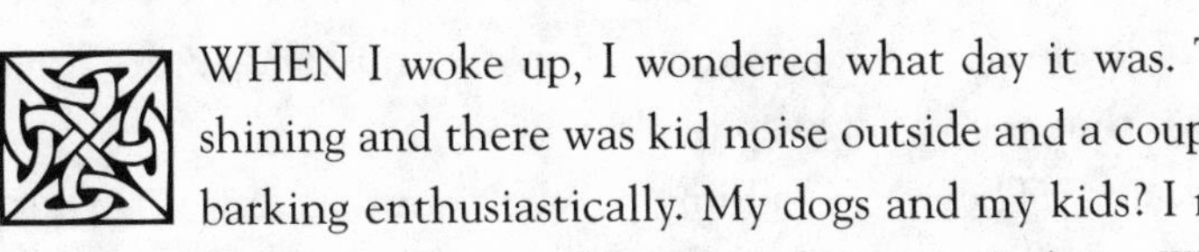

WHEN I woke up, I wondered what day it was. The sun was shining and there was kid noise outside and a couple dogs were barking enthusiastically. My dogs and my kids? I reached over to ask me husband what was happening. He wasn't there. Where was my friggin' husband?

We had slept in each other's arms all night, too weary to do anything more exciting. What day was it? If the kids were playing outside at this hour—my alarm claimed it was ten o'clock—it must be Saturday. Something important was supposed to happen on Saturday. What was it? Something very important. Nothing in court. Some test at TCD? No, I had four kids outside playing in the snow. I hadn't attended Trinity in ages. . . . What was it?

Then I remembered—the Christmas special . . . *Lullaby and Good Night* . . . I had a terrible nightmare about it. . . . A big explosion . . . Then I remembered it all and bounced out of bed. Had someone really tried to plant a bomb in my battered Lincoln Navigator?!

I put on me robe, stumbled over to the window, and peeked through the blinds. There was me friggin' husband out there rolling in the snow with me kids. Didn't he know we had a concert. The kids should be resting their voices.

Then the phone rang—the private line.

" 'Tis meself."

"Who else would it be?"

Familiar voice.

"It might be me friggin' husband and himself outside in the snow playing with me kids."

"You sound like you had a terrible night. . . . Or was it a bad run-through yesterday?"

"We were up terrible late altogether."

My memory started operating again.

The blizzard had been real. The bombs in the boot of me car had been real. The dinosaur truck had been real. I wanted to cry.

"Everything's all right?" Maria asked.

"Everything is brilliant," I said, crossing me fingers.

"My family," she said tentatively, "would like to come to the concert. By that I mean my five daughters and my poor, dear husband."

"And how is that good man keeping?"

"Much better . . . They've fixed him up so he's not reluctant to go outside. . . . You can get us tickets?"

"It's me own concert. Of course I can get you the tickets. Why don't you come over to our house."

"I'll be right over."

I hung up and thought about jumping into the shower. But the phone rang again. It was Dermot's private. We have a rule in our house—well, didn't I make it—that he can't answer me private line, but I can answer his.

'Tis only fair.

"Nuala Anne."

"It's Dominic, Nuala."

"Hey, Dom, what's happening? . . . Me Dermot is outside playing in the snow."

"My friends tell me that their friends have cornered the bad guys in a house on Ohio Street, Nine Eighty-seven West, right near your concert place. They don't know my friends are on to them. But my friends want to know whether they should put them down or leave it to the cops."

"I think me husband would say that it's better to leave it to the cops. Let me have Dermot call you back in five minutes, okay, Dom?"

"That's beautiful. But no more than fifteen minutes."

I put on me sweater and me jeans and me playing-in-snow boots and rushed downstairs, Dermot's mobile phone in me hand.

It was bitter cold, but the sun was shining brightly.

"Dermot Michael Coyne!" I shouted, instantly regretting the possible damage to me voice.

He knew after all the years of marriage that was a command.

It was bitter cold, so I stood at the top of our stairs staring down to the ground, waiting impatiently.

"Wasn't I thinking all along that I was sleeping in your arms, and yourself outside playing in the snow and ruining the voices of me talent."

And then, before we could get into an argument, I told him about Dom's call and gave him his phone.

"I'll see what Mike Casey says."

As he punched in Mike's number, I whistled me letcha-come-in whistle. The kids and the dogs froze in their tracks and then disconsolately gathered their snow things and trudged up the stairs.

"Youse can play all day tomorrow," I told them, "after church, but won't you be needing your singing voices tonight? Take off your boots and then inside with youse."

I always feel guilty when I use my boss voice with the small 'uns. They should not be afraid of their mother, should they?

The two puppies were the last ones up the stairs. They paused hoping for some sign of approval, as if they were saying, they weren't singing tonight, were they? I patted both of them and they charged happily into the house, doubtless working havoc with the parlor rugs. I followed them in.

"Downstairs with the lot of youse!"

"Ma," Nelliecoyne pleaded with me, "Da wouldn't let us shout."

"I know that, dear."

"You just wanted to remind us?"

"Just wanted to remind you."

Diplomatic little bitch, wasn't she?

Dermot was talking to his friend Dominic.

"My contacts at the department tell me that they'll collect the bad guys in early afternoon, so they'd appreciate it if your friends keep an eye on them until the contacts get all their players in place. They also direct me to say that they're very grateful for the cooperation of your friends. If anything happens over on Ohio Street, you might give me a ring. . . . Uzbekistan, that's an interesting innovation. I'll pass that on. . . . Our cars are clean now. . . . I appreciate your concern. . . . Once again thanks for all the help."

He smiled at me, the same smile which has melted me heart since the first night at O'Neil's pub. He pushed another button on his mobile phone.

"Mike? Dermot . . . The boys apparently have the bad guys under surveillance on the West Side. They say they're commandos from Uzbekistan. My feeling is that you good guys should proceed with caution but get them all out of there, one way or another, by four this afternoon at the latest. . . . Mike, don't give me that. Those Soviet-trained commando units traditionally bring mortars with them. It's an easy shot from where they are to the parking lot or to the soundstage itself. There'll be some activity there among the cops when the mayor's car shows up. . . . Or the senator's . . . Doesn't the Chicago Police Department have tear gas anymore? And what if the bad guys have gas masks? . . . You remember the Powell Doctrine? Right, maximum force! . . . Helicopters overhead . . . We're certainly not coming over in the red tank and we're not coming at all until that place is cleaned out."

"Trouble?" I said meekly.

"The friggin' cops don't get it. I've told them where the commandos are and they have to take them out now or they'll spread through the neighborhood shooting at anything in sight. . . ."

"Dominic's friends might be willing if the cops are not?" I asked.

Me Dermot's face brightened.

"Why didn't I think of that?"

He punched in Mike's button.

"Busy signal . . . I'll call Culhane. . . .

"John . . . What the fuck is going on with you assholes?"

I looked around to see if any of the kids were present to hear Da engage in cop talk.

"Don't they understand that they're black berets from Uzbekistan. They're tough, resourceful, and just a little crazy. If you're not going to use maximum force then don't bother. . . . I don't care what anyone says. . . . Look, my friends on the West Side are perfectly willing to take them out. . . . They will if I say so. . . . I want to hear in fifteen minutes or it will be St. Valentine's Day Massacre all over again. . . . What will they do? I don't know and I don't care. . . . Maybe they'll drive a truck bomb into the two-flat. . . . Fifteen minutes . . . Have your friend Terry give me a ring. . . . Or I'll call the mayor and tell him that the taping is canceled and why. . . .

"Woman," he said, as he hung up, "I want me breakfast. . . . No, wrong line . . . Woman, come down to the kitchen and I'll make you some breakfast. . . ."

Who was the Irish Tiger now, I wondered. Poor dear Dermot said I was. But I was frazzled and scarcely coherent and wasn't he giving out something fierce altogether. Normally I make breakfast because I'm up a little bit earlier, though Ellie does it often these days because she does her best studying in the morning or so she says. Danuta comes in around breakfast time and insists on making something healthy. But today Ellie is finishing a paper and Danuta doesn't come in on weekends. So I let Dermot make me favorite breakfast, oatmeal with brown sugar, apple juice, and toast with marmalade. He hates the very sight of marmalade which he says pollutes perfectly good toast. But this morning wasn't he slathering it all over.

"You didn't feed yourself, did you?"

This in the tone of voice that suggests that of course he had.

"Woman, I did and the chiles too."

"Aren't you a perfect whirlwind of a Celtic Tiger?"

"Woman, I am."

His mobile rang.

"Dermot Coyne . . . And the best of the day to you, Terry Glen . . . Ah, you want to thank me for the support. . . . I scared the big brass did I? . . . Well, good enough for them . . . Look, Terry, there may be only a handful of them and they may not feel like dying quite yet, but the CPD can't afford to be too little and too late. . . . Your very point? Lots of fingerprints on the bags? That will help. . . . Hey, sure enough, the tank is back in the alley where it belongs. . . . You'll excuse me, but our family will come over in one of Superintendent Casey's limos. . . . We're retiring the M1A1 tank until we find the time to fix the grille. . . . Me wife likes her cars to look sharp. . . . Yeah, she sure is . . . becomes more beautiful every day . . ."

"Dermot Michael Coyne, you are totally full of bullshite!" I said, blushing at the exchange of compliments. . . . "I have put some of that awful raspberry stuff on a couple of slices of toast for yourself."

"God bless you and keep you!" he says to me. He likes to talk like he's a mick when he's nothing but a friggin' rich Yank.

"And aren't you acting like you've become the Irish Tiger and meself a shattered wreck!"

"Well, you're going to have a nice long nap this afternoon and won't Ellie and I get the clan ready for the concert."

" 'Tis yourself who deserves the nap. . . ."

"I won't hear a word of it. You have to be your smiling self tonight!"

"I don't deserve a husband as good as you, Dermot Michael Coyne."

"As Archbishop Blackie would say, arguably."

Our eldest appeared, camera in hand.

"That cute Ms. Connors is here, Ma. She said you had tickets for her."

"Thanks, cara. Did you get a good picture of her?"

"Wouldn't it be impossible, Ma, not to get a good picture of her!"

"She won't stay long, Dermot love, and then I'll be off to the land of Nod."

"And not a minute too soon."

Maria Angelica was sitting in the parlor, in slacks and NIU sweatshirt, drinking a cup of tea and eating some of our remaining soda bread.

"That little imp of yours is a wonder," she said. "I have too many daughters of my own these days, but I'd be willing to trade any two of them for one of her. She did a wonderful portrait of me without my even noticing it."

"Better than the one in that real estate magazine?"

"No cleavage but sexier. I ordered a half dozen copies at five dollars each—a real bargain!"

"No trade! Won't she be supporting me in me old age . . . How's the old fella keeping?"

"He's fine, though the companies are slipping. Not too much yet . . . We can make love again which is nice. I lived thirty years or so without much sex and was none the worse for it. Now in sunset years I find a man I love and I can't get enough of him."

"Which he enjoys?"

"He's astonished. Can't understand why he's a sex object. I wonder if it will last."

"Why shouldn't it?"

"I've not been lucky with men."

"That's your old story. Now you have a new one. As long as you're good to him, you'll have a very happy marriage, even if he's occasionally an eejit."

"Such a sweet eejit," she said with a weak sigh.

Why should I laugh to myself at that? I had whispered the same words to meself about my poor, dear Dermot.

"And the daughters?"

"A lot of strong emotions trying to focus. It's working out, but like I tell them, I'm not a referee or an appellate judge, only a dorm mother."

"So you'll be needing seven tickets for tonight?"

"I will, if you have them."

"Sure, why wouldn't I have them? It's my show isn't it now? And won't I be glad when it's over!"

"It will be brilliant altogether, to use your terms."

"There will be a small party afterward backstage. Nothing stronger than a splash of Baileys . . . All you need is the tickets. Not long because we must get the small ones home."

"One more thing. My son tells me that my brothers are acting strange . . . laughing at the incident in front of St. Joseph's. They say that I'm finally getting what I deserve."

A light flashed in the back of my head. There was no time to investigate it, but it would stay there and I'd return to it tomorrow.

"Sweethearts, aren't they? Nothing will happen to you, Maria Angelica, as long as you have one of the Reliables around. It will all be over soon anyway."

I said that with more confidence than I should have. I knew, however, that it would be over by Christmas.

"Why do your brothers hate you so much?"

"Gina and I were popular in school, they weren't. I had good grades, they didn't. They're clumsy, I'm an athlete of sorts. I made it in the town's elite, they never had a chance. They're ugly and I'm not. My mother hated me and she loved the boys, she turned them against me. I was a traitor to the family. They were always loyal. It went on and on and on. They could do nothing wrong. I did nothing right. She spoiled them rotten. They've always been little boys who never had to grow up. When someone or something frustrates them, they react with rage. The mob in Chicago almost killed them."

"Not nice people?"

"I'm sorry, Nuala, you touched a sensitive spot in my memory. I try not to be angry at them. . . . I try to forgive them. I think I have and then someone asks about them and my fury comes back. . . . I don't think they're killers. Don't have the courage for that."

Somehow that information calmed me. I would have a good nap this afternoon.

I stopped at the door of Nelliecoyne's darkroom. The red light was off, so I knocked.

"Come in, Ma!"

"Ms. Connors said you took a real sexy picture of her and sold her a half dozen copies."

"Should I have? She insisted."

"Congratulations . . . We'll have to start charging you room and board."

"You'd never let Da do that," she said with one of her big grins. She showed me her first print. It was indeed very sexy. No way it wouldn't be at this time in Maria's life.

"Very sexy."

"She has beautiful boobs, Ma. Just like you."

"Are the other kids napping?"

"Not the Mick. He's drawing pictures. Aren't the young 'uns dead to the world, as I will be in a few moments."

"It will be wonderful tonight, cara."

"Of course it will, Ma."

So I went up to the master bedroom where me poor dear Dermot was waiting for me. I thought he might want to make love, but he took off my clothes and put me to bed with a promise.

"I'll wake you up in two hours, woman. We can't have you groggy tonight. Then we'll have our showers and engage in a little light focking."

"With you, Dermot Michael Coyne, there is no such thing as light focking."

Then before I knew it I was sound asleep.

— Dermot —

AFTER PUTTING herself to bed, I went back to the Situation Room and turned on the TV monitor of the CPD, which we weren't supposed to have, but we managed to obtain nonetheless. It picks up the same feed which goes into the superintendent's office. We didn't watch it much because the fare was usually pretty dull. I had no doubt that the top cop would be watching with great interest. Terry Glen's career was at stake. If he carried this caper off, then he'd be the next man. From what cops told me that would please the present boss and most of the force.

The monitor showed a quiet street in a very old neighborhood on the near West Side, some abandoned buildings, some vacant lots, some ancient brick two-flats, once superior housing for the emergent middle class, maybe a century and a quarter ago, back when the Cubs were winning championships a mile or so away at the old Playing Fields.

We were a half mile away in an unmarked van, probably an unprepossessing near wreck. Cars went by, looming large for a moment and then disappearing off camera.

My mobile rang.

"Dermot."

"Dominic . . . I hear from my friends in the neighborhood that they're pulling back out of sight. They'll see what happens and let me know. I'll be in touch with you."

"Stay out of there, Dom."

He laughed.

"Derm, you're the crazy one, not me."

As we talked a large, grey buslike thing lumbered down the street toward the camera. It stopped in front of what had to be the house where the commandos had established their command center. Instead of windows it had gun ports out of which automatic weapons protruded. No one fired from inside the house or from the armored bus. In case there was any doubt the blue letters on the side of the bus spelled out "Chicago Police Department—Tactical Unit 1."

Then a second and similar vehicle pulled into the alley behind the two-flat and clumped behind it. The gun ports opened and more automatic weapons appeared.

At the far end of the street, out of the line of fire, scores of police cars and other vehicles appeared and cops set up street barricades. Only a few cops left their cars. This was perhaps the combat infantry who would clean up the remnants after the battle was over. I had heard that the department had purchased some vehicles (pronounced always as *vee HIK ils*), but I was not prepared for the next grotesque monster—a broad, squat thing which looked like a heavily armored tank, with a squat pillar on top, a large artillery piece jutting from its front and two lighter weapons, looking like the Gatling guns from the Civil War or the Philippine Insurrection, poking out of recesses in the front. At the end of the pillar a radarlike device with a red light spun nervously. I was a couple of miles away, but the scene scared me.

The tank featured on its front a mammoth shovel which looked like a huge front loader. It wheeled around in front of the house and paused. The spinner on the tank spun furiously.

Then a man appeared in an open window on the second floor of the flat with one of those grenade launchers that we see on TV in the hands of Middle Eastern "militants." A puff of smoke appeared in the window and the grenade leaped out of its launcher. Suddenly the tank threw up what looked like a large steel hand, deflected the grenade, and hurled it back at the two-flat.

An incomplete forward pass. An agile cornerback like Mike Brown of the Bears.

Then a barrage of small-weapons fire erupted from the house, pinging noisily like hail on a tin roof against the sides of the armored bus.

"We're taking fire, sir," said a voice presumably from the bus.

"Well," said Terry Glen, "return the fire."

The Gatling guns on the tank rose from their recesses and began to eat into the bricks of the house. Then the automatic weapons in the gun ports on the buses opened up. The windows disappeared, some of the walls disintegrated, the front door vanished. Smoke poured from the house.

"Try the tear gas!"

A long arm appeared at the top of the tank, leaned over toward the disintegrating structure and, casually almost negligently, distributed several tear gas canisters through the available openings.

A white sheet appeared from one of the windows. Surrender.

"We know there are four of you in there. Come out of the house without your weapons and your hands in the air. If there are any missteps you will all die."

Then the command was repeated in a Slavic language. Russian. Best we could do.

"Ten seconds and we will begin firing again."

Four battered men, two of them wounded, staggered out of the remnants of the two-flat, hands over their heads.

"Get them in the bus and get out of there. The residence is filled with explosives."

A door opened in the side of the bus and a set of stairs unfolded. Four men in grey armor appeared and helped the prisoners into the bus and the stairs folded. The bus inched away from the wrecked two-flat and trudged down the street toward the camera. Suddenly there was a loud *whuf* as the building turned into a red and black fireball. The camera shook, the bus heaved to the side, and the strange tank thing rocked back and forth in alarm, its antenna quivering in the blast. Then a nozzle appeared from the top of the machine, spun toward the flaming two-flat, and emitted a thick stream of heavy liquid which turned into foam as it encountered the flames. The tank was prepared for absolutely any eventuality. A brilliant contraption altogether.

The fire was quickly snuffed out. No noisy Chicago Fire Department required. Then, as if offended by the temerity of the two-flat, the tank lowered its front-loader shovel and attacked the smoking ruins, reducing them in short order to a mass of rubble. Finally, it swept the remains into a neat pile, doused it again with foam, and then harrumphed back on Erie Street and, as if wiping off its hands in satisfaction lumbered toward the camera and then out of sight.

My mobile phone rang again.

"In case you're wondering, Dermot," Mike Casey said, "that monster, appropriately named Godzilla, operates completely on remote control. Tactical has been waiting eagerly for a chance to try it."

"And no media there to observe and record."

"Precisely . . . The only problem is that there were just a few terrorists. We don't know for sure what would happen if we had forty or so holed up in that building and they were real terrorists instead of out-of-work commandos."

"Either they would have surrendered or that monster—"

"We call it Godzilla."

"—would have stacked them up in neat little piles . . . I suppose your good friend Terry Glen will have a press conference on Monday and let the media take pictures of Godzilla from a safe distance, let it inundate them with foam."

"It does have a mind of its own. See you tonight. The boys in the blue uniforms will swarm on the ruins and dig out whatever they can. We'll have a thick cordon of them all around the soundstage tonight. Enjoy!"

I turned off the monitor just as a swarm of "civilians" tried to push against the police barriers to inspect the modestly withdrawing Godzilla. I checked my recording to make sure I could show it to Nuala before I destroyed it.

The word *modestly* reminded me of another Saturday afternoon responsibility I had.

Outside in the playroom, the kids, up from their naps and still in their pj's, were playing with their various amusements, the TV was playing *My Fair Lady*, and Ellie was teaching Patjo to read, an exercise he seemed to enjoy.

"Hi, Uncle Derm! Did you have a horror movie playing in there?"

"*Godzilla!*"

"I just love *Godzilla*," Socra Marie announced.

Nelliecoyne was working on a scrapbook of her pictures.

"Will Mr. Donlan and Ms. Connors be at the show tonight, Da?"

"They wouldn't miss it for the world."

"Good! I'll give her the copies of my picture. Ma says she looks real sexy."

"Ma would know."

Upstairs in our master bedroom, Ma was sleeping peacefully, looking like an innocent teen. Once again I found it difficult to believe that this beautiful woman was my wife and indeed the mother of my four rug rats. My desire for her surged as though she were a new conquest. Yet I felt sorry for the enormous burdens that had intruded into her life, mostly because of me. She shouldn't have to assume all the Christmas responsibilities that would weary her next week and then fly "home" on the day after Christmas. But then she wouldn't be Nuala Anne, the Irish Tiger.

She opened her eyes and saw me standing above her. Her face eased into a smile of adoration, which broke my heart every time I saw it. I didn't deserve that kind of love. However, since it was there, I might just as well take advantage of it.

"You're late for our tryst, Dermot Michael Coyne."

"Only two minutes."

"Sure, wasn't there a time when you'd be five minutes early."

"I didn't want to cheat you out of an extra minute of sleep."

"Well, make yourself useful and turn on the shower to just the right temperature and yourself knowing how much I hate a shower that's too cold or too hot."

— Dermot —

NUALA ANNE was radiant and relaxed as we drove in the Reliable Lexus from Sheffield Avenue over to West Ohio Street. She glanced at me occasionally and winked, sharing the joy of our marital love. She led the gossons and the colleens in singing some of their favorite lullabies which they would sing later in the evening. First the "Castle of Dromore":

The October winds lament
Around the castle of Dromore
Yet peace lies in her lofty halls
My loving treasure store
Though autumn leaves may droop and die
A bud of spring are you
Lullaby, lullaby,
Sweet little baby,
Don't you cry

I'd rock my own little child to rest
In a cradle of gold on the bough of a willow
To the shoheen ho of the wind of the west
And the lulla low of the soft see billow
Sleep baby dear
Sleep without fear
Mother is here beside your pillow.

Then they turned to their absolute favorite, the Connemara lullaby which all the mothers of Carraroe had sung to their daughters for generations and which according to family legend had kept Socra Marie alive in the hospital when she was too small to come home.

The childish voices were a pleasant background to my delicious memories of the amusements of our tryst in the shower and afterward. It had been a dangerous gamble on God's part to permit such pleasure to humans. It did bind husband and wife together but the bond was a two-edge sword which could so easily tear itself apart. Well, there was no point in being philosophical at the present moment, sometime in the next couple of days I must start the poem that had been hiding in my head, not quite ready to emerge fully blown like the mythical Venus on the seashell.

The car, even with its Reliable sticker, was searched thoroughly by apologetic but competent cops. Then we had to go through a door frame like the kind they keep at the Federal building and the county courthouse.

The rest of my family would go backstage. I hugged each one of them and told them that they were wonderful. Me wife hugged me and whispered, "Well, Dermot Michael Coyne, won't you do as a lover until someone better comes along?"

"See you later," I said.

"She didn't seem nervous at all," Maria Donlan murmured to me as I found my seat in the row in front of theirs.

"She's chilled out," I explained. "She refuses to worry on the day of a performance. 'Tis a waste of energy altogether."

I was nonetheless uneasy. We had done lullabies before and that special had been enormously popular. Now we were stretching for politically correct Arab lullabies, Sea Island lullabies, Russian lullabies, Chinese lullabies, African-American lullabies as well as Irish lullabies and the ones that everyone knew and loved. This did not mean that Nuala sang less but that she sang translations (that she had made) after the native singer and then the two joined together in a final chorus. It would be a tour de force if it worked. Moreover the kids and the Old St. Patrick's choir would background almost all the numbers. The choir was flawless of course. The kids were problematic. Not problematic, however, was Nuala. When she put on her Christmas special persona, she became the smooth, sleek, Irish Tiger whose rare mistakes carried on the performance. Her daimon at the Christmas special was flawless and carried the performers, the technicians, and the audience.

She left behind the barefoot lass from Galway and talked Trinity College Irish, patently Irish to the uninitiated, but all the wonderful diction of the West and its slang, not to say its vulgarity, left far behind.

"Good evening! It is good of you to permit me to visit your home again this year to sing my songs and help you to get in the mood for Christmas or whatever your midwinter festival may be. I promise you that I will intrude on your peace and quiet for only a little less than an hour and that my children won't be disruptive. This year we're doing lullabies again, singing some of the old ones and adding some new ones from all over the world. We'll begin with the favorite American Christmas carol, a blues carol written by Irving Berlin and sung famously by that great Irish American jazz singer Bing Crosby. I'm asking the kids from our Sheffield Avenue neighborhood and everyone in the audience here and at home to join in."

My Nuala can sing a song in its proper color no matter what's going on around her. She has the knack of carrying an audience, just as easily as she waves a hand at the Sheffield Avenue chorus. We sang "White Christmas" the way it ought to be sung—a blues carol. I was weeping at the end as was the mayor on one side of me and the senator on the other side—and most of the Donlan-Connors crowd behind me.

I relaxed. It would be the best special yet.

She glided from scene to scene and from performer to performer like a benign fairy godmother or perhaps a friendly local seraph. Her gracefulness permeated the performances, the soundstage, and I'm sure the millions watching.

And this was the same wanton woman with whom I had romped earlier in the day. Grace is indeed everywhere.

"I should tell you that the young mother and child are Arab Christians, Assyrian Catholics but their lullaby, I am told, has been sung by Arab mothers to their children, regardless of their religion, for thousands of years. Mary may have sung a lullaby like that to Jesus.

"Now as some of you might expect I'm an Irish-American and proud of both heritages. I'm from a place so far out in the West of Ireland that the next parish west is on Long Island. Out there in the town of Carraroe many of us speak the ancient Irish language, which was made to be sung. So I'm going to sing our own favorite carol in Irish and then in English. And I'm going to sing it to my youngest Patrick Joseph Coyne. . . ."

Applause for the little blond brat.

"We call him Patjo and everyone says that he's just like his father, big, blond, handsome, and laid back."

She sat on a chair and accompanied herself on the harp. Patjo, the little scamp, rested his head on her thigh just like he was going to sleep.

"Now we're going to sing it in English with his brother and sisters and some of the kids on the block. . . ."

On the wings of the wind, o'er the dark, rolling deep
Angels are coming to watch o'er your sleep
Angels are coming to watch over you
So list to the wind coming over the sea

Hear the wind blow, hear the wind blow
Lean your head over, hear the wind blow.

The kids sang as though they really liked the little monster (which they did) and blew like the wind with enthusiasm and, for them, wondrous restraint. And so it went, the show did not drag, her voice did not falter. Her grace did not fade, her charm did not wane. She was getting better every year. And not just in her songs either.

There was a brief five-minute break halfway through which Nuala used to talk about her own family.

"I'm delighted that for the first time people in my other country are watching this program on Irish television and that my mom and dad, me ma and me da, as we'd say over there, are watching it out in my home town of Carraroe, which is the most beautiful little village in the west of Ireland. *Nollaig Shona Duit* to everyone in Ireland and especially to everyone in Carraroe and especially my mother and father."

A panoramic slide of that lovely little village appeared.

"Now we're going to start the rest of the program with the second and last Irish lullaby—the 'Castle of Dromore.'" The kids rushed out, lined up smartly, and let their mother lead them. Socra Marie was off-key as always and won everybody's heart.

The program moved along briskly, not losing a beat in its tempo as it wound down.

"We have one last lullaby, maybe the most famous of them all, written by the great German composer Johannes Brahms. It's the theme of tonight's program. My daughter Mary Anne and I will sing in the original German and then in English and I want everyone to sing the English along with us."

Nelliecoyne appeared carrying her mother's small harp. She was dressed in Christmas red and green appropriate for an eight-year-old. Great applause and a nod of her head in return. She had a junior version of her mother's stage presence and a lovely little voice to which her mother deferred in the German version. Then "Lullaby and Good Night."

"Now that we're in German, let's end the program with the greatest of all Christian carols. Let us imagine that we are in Bethlehem honoring the Baby Jesus or our own most favorite new baby . . . but not so loud to wake him up."

The Sheffield Avenue choir, led by Socra Marie and Katiesue, scurried into position. Shaped by Nuala's restrained singing the program eased into a conclusion. Nuala turned to face the millions all around the world.

"Thank you for letting us sing in your homes again this year. Good night, Happy Christmas, and with the help of God till we meet again."

The ovation from the listeners rocked the building. Then they began to clap and demand an encore. Nuala hesitated, shrugged her shoulders, and took the small harp out of her daughter's hand.

"I'll sing one more song and that'll be the last one. . . . One cold rainy night a long time ago I was sipping a pint in O'Neil's pub just off College Green, minding my own business and studying my world economics book. An obnoxious Yank sat down at my table and tried to chat me up. He was kind of cute, but not very perceptive. So when the people in the pub started to shout for a song, I figured that was an excuse to dump this Yank. So I sang this song. The Yank, who obviously had no manners, just sat there at my table and stared at me. I haven't been able to get rid of him ever since."

So she sang "Molly Malone." After all these years it still makes me cry.

As the crowd left the hall and passed through the line of police guards, a few of us drifted back in to the bowels of the studio for a small splash of Baileys. The mayor walked next to me.

"How did you like our Godzilla?"

"She's totally cool and adorable," I replied. "I was disappointed that she didn't get to show off all her little tricks."

"It's nice to know she works," he replied.

My radiant wife greeted me at the door to the party room, with a plastic cordial glass containing a generous splash of Baileys and a broad smile, just short of a grin—still in control of the event with her grace and charm.

"Not bad," I said hugging her cautiously so as not to spill either of our jars. "Not bad at all, at all . . . You improve with age Nuala Anne McGrail."

"So do you, Dermot Michael Coyne, so do you!"

Her one arm hug became more insistent.

The Sheffield Avenue rug rats did not run wild. On the contrary, they behaved decorously as they accepted congratulations from their admirers, quite unfazed by the praise of the mayor and the senator and the various functionaries of NBS and Kosmic Entertainment. The president of the latter, a nervous but exuberant little man, was especially lavish in his praise of everyone.

"You're her husband, aren't you? . . . She's a delightful young woman. . . . Her performance was reviewproof. . . . Most of them will be good anyway. . . . We'll have DVDs out by the middle of next week. . . . I think we ought to make a film about her. . . . There'd be a tremendous market. . . ."

"You'll have to talk to her about that. . . . I'm not her agent, you know. . . . She acts for herself. . . . She's a tough one. All those West of Ireland women are tough. . . ."

"Still you're a very lucky man!"

"Tell me about it."

"You look good for yourself," I told Jackie Donlan a few moments later.

"My wife has had a lot of experience as a caregiver. . . . Also at managing a high-energy group of young women!"

"That project goes well?"

"It will take a little time for them to understand and adjust to one another, but they seem to genuinely like one another. They're going home tomorrow so we won't be running a sorority house anymore. . . . And my wife and I are going back to work on Monday. Maybe our lives will settle down. Christmas dinner in Oakdale next Saturday."

"Business is okay?"

"It would seem so. My eager little gnome, Joey, worries a lot, but nothing much will happen in the markets till after New Year's. Then the world will know I'm in charge again and we'll be okay. It will take some time, but we'll bounce back fine."

Only if we—well Nuala—can sort out the puzzle.

"Not an easy transition, Jack."

"Nonetheless, as you can imagine," he blushed, "a very welcome one . . . And we still have a honeymoon ahead of us, maybe in February."

"Best time to get away from Chicago."

In our family there were no vacations, save for trips to Grand Beach and Connemara and they weren't vacations. I'd have to work on that.

"Dermot love, I think we should get the chiles home. They're beginning to fade and we have a big week ahead of us. And Mass in the morning."

Only two Masses.

Indeed yes. A big week. Christmas shopping. Gift wrapping, tree decorating, carol singing, Aer Lignus to Shannon. Mad rush there. I'd get my annual cold. Then back to Chicago and back to school.

Ugh. I needed a honeymoon too.

We took the kids home and put them to bed and then staggered in our own room for a last little jar to calm our nerves then to bed for a quiet night.

"You're the best husband in all the world," Nuala whispered as she sank into sleep.

"Till you find a more resilient one."

She was, however, sound asleep as I was a few minutes later.

Still we have a puzzle to solve.

— Dermot —

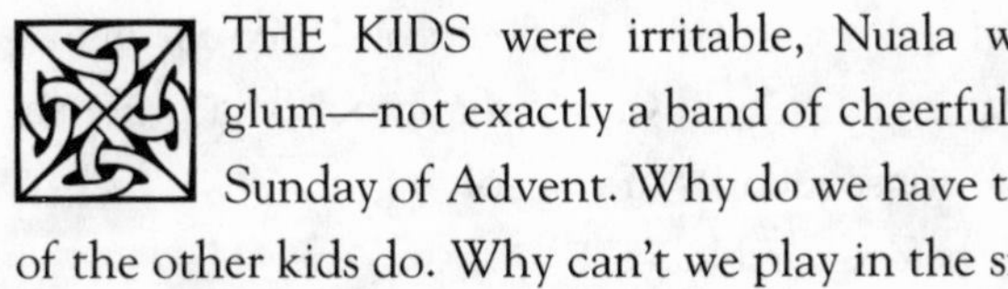

THE KIDS were irritable, Nuala was snappish, and I was glum—not exactly a band of cheerful Christians on the fourth Sunday of Advent. Why do we have to go to Mass twice? None of the other kids do. Why can't we play in the snow before it melts. Mass at St. Josephat is dull. Mass at Old St. Partick's is dull. Didn't we sing enough last night?

You're nothing but a bunch of heathens. You're lucky you can go to Mass in two churches. Stop fighting and pay attention to the priest. It is *not* boring. Dermot why don't you do something about your children?

I think it's *boring* too.

You should be ashamed of them.

It's not their fault. We're all worn out. It's just a letdown.

Da's right. We're all let down. It's natural after a big victory. Just like after a big volleyball game.

You're a little pagan and yourself with the use of reason.

I've given up the use of reason. Besides Da's right.

He is not!

He is so.

All of youse be quiet. I have a terrible headache.

That stopped them cold. The very thought that poor Da might be sick always silences the murmuring. What would happen to the family if poor Da were sick? I didn't use this tack of poor sick Da very often. It always worked.

But then we were back in the kitchen for our Sunday brunch which we all make together—blueberry pancakes, scrambled eggs, piles of bacon, Quaker Oats for Ma, soda bread, and maple syrup over everything and everybody. And lots of treats for the doggies who had been left alone last night. It is a family myth that we all make it together because Da presides over the effort, does most of the work, and prevents the younger kids from throwing syrup-drenched pancakes at each other.

Then the kids went to the playroom and Ma and Da to her study. (I have an office and she has a study, which is not to be confused with her music room where she has a piano. The next thing she'll be wanting is a "meditation" room. She also has an exercise room which I can use when she's not.)

"We may have to cancel the reservations to Shannon," herself said as she sank into her thinking couch. As always she approched a problem from the perspective of the consequences of not solving it.

"We have a whole week before we'd leave."

"The week before Christmas is not a time to solve puzzles."

" 'Tis true," I admitted.

"And ourselves knowing not much more than we did at the beginning."

I had been idly glancing through the Sunday papers. My article on Congressman Stafford had yet to appear. I saw a heading in "Eyes and Ears."

Peace on Earth for Donlans?

It would appear that the divided Donlan clan has decided to kiss and make up. The daughters of stock tycoon John Patrick Donlan (Donlan Assets Management) are now praising their new stepmother, Maria Angelica Connors (Elegant Homes). "We were not fair to Maria and we feel terrible about

> it. She's a wonderful woman, very sensitive and sympathetic and very, very witty. She and her kids are welcome additions to our family and they don't seem to mind us in their family. We're all going out there to Oakdale for Christmas." The combined families were in town for the taping of the newest Christmas special of singer Nuala Anne McGrail. Ears hears that all the reviews will be ecstatic.

I read the item for me wife.

"Just asking for trouble," she fumed. "They need a convoy of armored cars to get out there unless we can untangle this mess. . . . Well, what do we know about it, Dermot?"

"If we assume that from the false allegation at the wedding, to the bomb plot last night were the work of the same perpetrator, that person is a clumsy amateur who has access to some dangerous people, not approved by our friends out on the West Side, that he becomes more reckless each time he tries something, and that he knows how to cover his tracks."

"And why is he doing these terrible things?"

"He seems to want to destroy both their businesses, especially Jackie's."

"Why?"

"For some reason he hates him or maybe both of them. He's obsessed by his hatred. He started low key when he tried to ruin the wedding. Then when that didn't work he escalated."

"Mad?"

"One would think so."

"Does he have anything personally to gain by it?"

"Other than personal satisfaction, probably not. Unless it is Joey McMahon. He thinks that he could buy out the company and make more money on it than Jack. He's probably wrong. I suspect that someone else would buy it out first if it came to that. Someone with deeper pockets than Joey."

"Disgusting little rodent."

"True enough. But where does he get his troops? Even if there may be wiseguys in his neighborhood, they'd be afraid of offending the boys to say nothing of the political organization."

"He's been out to Oakdale, hasn't he?"

"To do some of the preliminary work on the deal."

"He might have heard about Maria's brothers and talked to them. Maybe a deal to get rid of both Jack and Maria . . . Drive them out of business and then do physical harm to them."

My Nuala would think of something like that.

"We don't have any proof of that. Ster Stafford might have used them as a go-between."

"Give over, Dermot Michael. Your version of the congressman tells me that he never recovered from being hit in the head by the camera our friend Maria Angelica threw at him."

"Yet he clearly worships her."

"He had a terrible way of showing it."

"For which I think he is genuinely sorry . . . In any case he is not smart enough to fake his admiration and regret. In a strange way, he seemed almost glad she defeated him in the election."

"Fair play to you, Dermot love, sometimes you're wrong about women, but never about men. I'd just as soon not leave him out of the game, though if you don't mind, I'd also like to call him tomorrow morning."

"Be my guest."

"Still. That leaves us with the possibility that the rodent, and Lou Garner and the brothers Sabattini might have entered a conspiracy against our clients, doesn't it now?"

"It does, though Garner is too clever a small-time gombeen man to mix himself up with anything as crazy as the assaults on our clients and then the attempted murder of our family and perhaps our neighborhood."

She considered this for a moment.

"So in this perspective we are considering, without any evidence, save for the characters of the people involved, the possibility that Joseph McMahon in conspiracy with Maria's brothers, is the solution to our case?"

"An eminently plausible thesis, love of my life. All we lack is proof."

"And also any conviction on my insight that this theory is correct."

"Alas, 'tis true."

"We should ask that nice Mr. Casey if he knows of any evidence at all at all of any link between them recently."

Mike the cop is always that "nice Mr. Casey" when I'm expected to call him. So, loyal spear-carrier that I am, I called him and it being Sunday morning.

"Casey."

"Coyne."

"Wasn't herself brilliant last night, dead friggin' brilliant!"

Mike likes a phony Irish brogue.

"Brilliant altogether . . . We have some matters on which we need your input."

"Why does that not surprise me?"

"Is there any reason to think that Joe McMahon has had recent contact with the Sabattini brothers out in Oakdale and secondly has he had recent contact with Lou Garner, a gombeen man who went to school with Jack Donlan?"

Nuala scribbled on a piece of paper. "Tell him about the Christmas plans."

"So that's the way herself is thinking? You're right about Lou being a gombeen man. Joey and the brothers out in Oakdale? That's an interesting idea. It will be a little difficult, but I'll see what we can find out."

"If you haven't risked your Sunday peace by reading the papers, you'll be pleased to know that Eyes and Ears reports reconciliation in the Donlan family and a planned Christmas dinner in Oakdale."

"Isn't that nice now!"

"An invitation to the bad guys. And they'll probably be quiet all week to lull us into thinking they have the Christmas spirit. . . . Joey would figure that he'd take over DAM, eh?"

"Wrongly, I think, though that would depend on how much money he has socked away. More likely it would be a target for a hedge fund or private company like Blackstone . . . Anyway we'll get on it first thing in the morning. . . . Don't forget to watch the Bears."

"Game doesn't matter. They're in the playoffs anyway."

"Anytime they play, the game matters."

"I figure that without Tommy Harris and Mike Brown they'll never win the Super Bowl."

There was a faint smile on me wife's face when I hung up.

"Don't bother watching them today," she said. "They'll lose."

"You don't have to be fey to figure that out."

"I don't know why I didn't think of an alliance between Joey and the brothers, Dermot Michael," Nuala said. "It fits perfectly. Crazy and sloppy."

"They'll probably do something crazy on Christmas, blow up the house maybe."

"Och, Dermot, this time won't they be more subtle?"

"What will they do?"

"Poison!"

"Poison?"

"Slip something deadly into what everyone will eat, something that might not show up in an autopsy."

"We'll have to stop them?"

"Faith, Dermot, of course we'll stop them, but this time we'll have to get the evidence against them."

The "dark" one was back. I shivered a little. That persona scares me a little anytime she sneaks into the house.

"Why don't you call your poor da, and himself knowing everything there is about medicine and everything else besides."

Poor in this case meant "long-suffering." He was the instant pediatrics consultant for all his children, though in his career he'd been a cardiac surgeon.

I called him.

"Doctor Coyne."

"Nuala's husband."

He loved all his children and their spouses, but he had a special soft spot for his own mother, Mary Anne or Nellie as she was always called. Hence our Nellie was the super favorite.

"I see by the papers that she will get great reviews for her special."

"Probably on Wednesday morning. It was the best yet. She improves with age."

"That doesn't surprise me."

"She wanted me to ask you a question."

"Something about a nefarious way to commit murder?"

"Just so . . . Imagine that she wanted to wipe out a whole family with poison at Christmas dinner. What would be a convenient and safe way of doing it?"

"Well, she might introduce a very powerful dose of E. coli into the dressing. We've had a lot of E. coli poisoning going around lately. It would be lamented as a tragic accident."

"Where would they get it?"

"Your local hospitals keep cultures around, for comparative purposes. They're watched pretty carefully. Still . . ."

"If someone wanted it bad enough . . ."

"That would be a simple way to do it. I hope you're able to catch them before they do any harm."

"Count on it."

Nuala, who had been listening on the other phone, looked glum.

"Didn't herself tell me that one of her nieces works at Kishwaukee Community Hospital, just down the river from Oakdale?"

"And I'd bet that a niece or a nephew works at the supermarket where the Connors do all their shopping?"

"This is too easy altogether, Dermot."

"Easy to know what they're doing, hard to stop them."

— Nuala Anne —

THE NEXT morning was another bad 'un for me. At my age in life I should know meself well enough to understand that after a successful show I would experience a deep letdown. But I always forget until it happens again. If the special didn't do all that well, I'd bounce back immediately, but when it is a huge success, as *Lullaby and Good Night* was, I go into a tailspin. This is very Irish of me, but as I've learned here in Yank land, I am very Irish—cheerful and brave in defeat, melancholy and depressed in victory. My poor dear husband has figured out through the years to put up with moods and bring me back to the real world. He let me sleep in this morning, made breakfast for the small ones, and then took them over to school. Then he's meeting with his publisher about the contract for the new novel which will be about me, like they all are and are very flattering, though no one recognizes me because the character in the story has such a stable disposition. I didn't even wake up to wish him good luck, not that he needs it because they are so desperate for a new story.

Poor Dermot needs a vacation away from this house, away from the kids, and away from me too. Except that would never work. So I would have to go with him. His parents would love to have the kids to themselves for a couple of weeks. I'll just have to talk poor Dermot into it.

Anyway thank you for sending me such a wonderful husband. Help me to be a better wife to him and help us solve this puzzle so Jack and Maria can have happiness together while there is still time. And themselves with at least thirty more years of life. We can't go to the Cayman Islands until we solve it. Now make me get out of bed and have some soda bread and a cup of tea and get to work. I love you and thanks again for me poor dear overworked husband.

The first thing I did after my breakfast was call that nice Mr. Casey. I chatted with his wife Annie Reilly for a couple of minutes. She's so sweet to me, though she thinks I'm round the bend altogether.

"Mr. Casey," I says to him, "I presume that me husband told you that I think there will be another assault on the Donlans on Christmas out beyond in Oakdale?"

"Woman, he did!"

"And he told you that I think there is a conspiracy between the Sabattinis and this rodent Joey McMahon?"

"Woman, he told me that you *knew* this to be true!"

He likes to imitate Dermot Michael when me poor husband tries to imitate me.

"So you'll be after monitoring his phone calls to the Sabattinis out beyond?"

"Haven't we started that already and doesn't it confirm what you *know*?"

Me heart jumped just a bit. So I was right after all.

"Sure was there ever a doubt?"

"Not at Reliable . . . He's making most of the calls from his office, which shows how reckless he is. Haven't I been talking to the sheriff out there who has no love for the Sabattini boys? Won't we be keeping an eye on them?"

"Good on you, Mr. Casey . . . You'll keep us informed?"

"Is the Pope Catholic?"

I hoped that I would be as lively as Mike and Annie when I'm that old and that me poor husband still loves me as much then as he does now. There's no good reason why he should and meself being such a nag. How much longer will I be a good lay? . . . Now that isn't fair to me poor dear Dermot at all, at all!

I thought about it all and decided I'd better chat with Maria Angelica again. I called her at her office.

"How are both of youse keeping?"

"I'm keeping fine, my spouse still hurts all over, but that doesn't interfere with his lovemaking."

"Still. And your company is doing well?"

"As good as ever, given the present state of the housing market. It's DAM we're worried about, but we'll know how much all this scandal stuff is hurting after the first of the year. My husband still has a few tricks up his sleeve."

"And you'll be feeding the whole clan on the feast of Our Lord's birth?"

"My daughters and stepdaughters will be doing most of the work. In the end I suppose I'll have to banish them all from my kitchen if I'm going to get any work done."

I sighed in loud protest. "'Tis the way of it all, isn't it? . . . No cousins invited?"

"We don't have any cousins. . . . Oh, you mean my brothers' kids. . . . They've all been raised to hate us. Won't speak to any of us. They're afraid of us too. . . . The sons are thugs like their fathers, except the one that's studying science at CalTech. The family doesn't like him either. Why waste your time with that stuff when you should be home helping us in all our small-time deals and crimes? . . . People tell me that they think now that they have the local franchise on the Sopranos."

"They kill someone every week?"

"They're too dumb to be able to do that. It would be nice if they went to Vegas or somewhere like that and leave this town alone."

"Isn't one of the daughters a nurse over at the hospital?"

"Camilla . . . or Cammy as they call her, sister to Tammy who works at our local supermarket. Steals from the store all the time. My kids tell me that Camilla is not all bad. Wanted to be friends with them when they were teens, but too shy to try it. Shy is not fashionable in that branch of the clan."

"Cammy and Tammy, sound like a sweet pair," I said.

"I wouldn't mind having them over for Christmas dinner, but Tammy would steal the silverware."

When we were finished with our gossip, I called Mr. Casey again on his mobile. He wasn't there, so I left my message about Cammy and Tammy.

Then me poor dear Dermot Michael called me.

"Nuala Anne."

"Me first wife, is it?"

"First and best!"

" 'Tis true."

"Did you get your friggin' contract?"

"Woman, I did."

"And?"

"Well, they actually want three books instead of one, though they all have to be about this ditsy woman."

"The one that's fey?"

"I wouldn't go that far. She thinks she is one of the dark ones."

"A lot you know about the dark ones . . ."

"They're petty good stretched out naked in bed, I'm told!"

"Give over, Dermot Michael Coyne! You have a dirty mind altogether!"

"I'm just saying what I hear."

"And?"

"And they have gorgeous tits."

"You know what I'm asking!"

"You mean the money?"

"I do!"

"You never tell me what Kosmic Entertainment is paying you."

" 'Tis a different matter altogether! You're not the family treasurer."

"I don't remember when we elected you. . . ."

"How much are they paying?"

When me dear sweet Dermot is teasing me and also trying to stir me up from a distance, he can be a desperate man!

"Well, since you put it that way, a lot more than you told me I should ask for. You can retire now, Nuala, and we can spend the rest of our lives making love all day on a beach in the Cayman Islands."

"You're round the bend altogether. . . . But congratulations anyway! You can show me the check when you come home!"

I told him about the developments on the Donlan case that morning.

"It looks like we'll be able to fly to Ireland after all," he said. "I'll be looking forward to my annual Irish cold."

"Well, I'll keep the bed warm for you won't I and make the soup!"

When the man is teasing me, he can be a real amadon.

Stretched out naked on a bed! Well, he will be waiting a long time for that to happen, won't he now!

Till tonight anyway.

Please God, don't let him get sick this time.

— Maria Angelica —

ON THE Wednesday afternoon before Christmas, the day before Christmas Eve, I returned to Oakdale to prepare the Christmas festival. At Jackie's insistence I went home in a Reliable limo. I made him promise he'd do the same. The bad guys were still around somewhere. I didn't think they'd take time off for the holidays. I stopped at the office where my son Pete was holding down the fort while reading the Barchester saga.

"Nothing happening," he said, barely looking up from the book.

"Go home to your family, Pete," I suggested. "I have some phone calls to make."

"Okay, but then I won't be able to finish this book today."

"Your daughter is more important."

His eyes twinkled mischievously.

"I guess so . . . How's Jackie?"

"Dutiful and obedient. He'll be out tomorrow."

"Maybe you shouldn't stay home alone tonight."

"No one would try to harm me here in Oakdale."

"If you change your mind, give us a ring. We'd be glad to have you share supper with your granddaughter who might even throw something at you if she's in a playful mood."

I almost said yes. I should have said yes, but then I wouldn't have met my late-night visitor.

There was a big stack of Christmas cards waiting for me. I opened them carefully and set aside those to whom I had not sent a card or those who merited a special note of sympathy or congratulations. There was one, astonishingly enough from Sterling Silver Stafford in which he congratulated me on my marriage and wished me many years of happiness. He added that he and his wife were going to settle down in Oakdale after the first of the year and suggested we all have dinner sometime later. It was a peace offering. I would reply that my husband and I would welcome a dinner invitation—a return offering of peace. I gathered up the cards and the other mail and asked the Reliable man to drive me home. Then I suggested that he could drive back to Chicago and collect my husband who had better feel as lonesome as I was. Well, I didn't say the last clause, but I thought it.

So when I entered our house two blocks behind the office and turned on the lights, it looked very empty and very old. Well, it should have looked that way. It was empty and old. And I was lonely. In all the years since Peter's death I had never felt lonely here. And it wasn't Peter's absence that made me feel lonely. I hoped that he wouldn't mind my bringing another man into his home and into his bedroom. The blessed in heaven are not jealous are they? I love him, Peter, I said. That doesn't mean I will ever stop loving you. But this is different.

I had yet to make love to Jack in our bedroom. I would certainly do it at Christmas, no matter how many people were in the house or in the charming motel down the street. We all had to move beyond such a critical symbol. It would be hard on Jack's daughters. Their love for me was genuine enough in the sense that they wanted to love me and had begun to love me, but still had some doubts. For that I couldn't blame them. Everyone would be on their good behavior, too good perhaps to relax. By next Christmas we would have bonded sufficiently to be able to argue and fight.

Enough philosophy. I was lonely and I wanted to tell my man that I was lonely.

"Jack Donlan."

"I think I may divorce you and yourself leaving me all alone out here."

"You're beginning to sound like that lovely Irish witch."

"I want you, Jackie, and I want you here."

"It was your idea that—"

"I know it was my idea, but you shouldn't have agreed with me. You know how besotted I have become with you."

"We'll make up for it tomorrow."

"I'll hold you to that promise. . . . I hope you have a difficult and lonely night."

"I'll try my best. I hope you have a good, quiet night with peaceful dreams about our first Christmas together."

"You too," I replied. "I didn't mean what I said. I love you."

"And I love you, Maria Angelica."

We both wept, more from love than loneliness and said good night. I made him promise to call me before he went to sleep.

I walked around the house, getting a feel for what it was like now that I had a new husband. The house was not interested in my changed state in life. It still tolerated me as did the ghosts of those who had lived in it for more than a century. I knew that their spirits checked in periodically to make sure I was being good to the house and departed approvingly. They did not live there anymore, but lived elsewhere. They were happy spirits.

Was this all my superstitious Italian soul, or my serene Catholic faith? I figured that the two were not all that far apart.

The phone rang and I jumped, startled out of my mix of nostalgic reverie and physical loneliness. It was the sheriff.

"Hi, Maria, good to have you home for Christmas. It wouldn't be Christmas here in Oakdale if you weren't with us."

The sheriff, Jake Danzig, was an elderly man, of my father-in-law's generation, but sharp and competent. Also a loyal Democrat.

"Thanks for the welcome, Jake. It is good to be back."

"We're looking forward to seeing your handsome husband."

"So am I! He won't be here till tomorrow morning. I miss him already. . . ."

"I'd say that's a pretty good sign. . . . I know that you're not the nervous Nellie type, but I thought I'd mention that the Oakdale chief of police and I have arranged to have cars cruise by your house alternately all night long. Just a precaution."

"Thanks for the reassurance, Jake. It is just a little scary being here alone on the darkest day of the year. I'll sleep more peacefully knowing that the cruisers are out there."

And thanks to Mike Casey for alerting you.

His call and his flat Midwestern voice brought everything back to normal. It was my house and my town and my county and I was perfectly safe. I took off my clothes and put on a nightgown, part of my quickly assembled trousseau, and made myself a salad and a cup of warm herbal tea and settled in to finish the mail.

The phone rang again. My husband going to bed and calling me to tell me he was lonely too.

A woman's voice on the other end of the line trying to find words.

"Uhm . . . I . . . Aunt Maria?"

"I think so . . ." I made a quick leap. . . . "Camilla?"

A rush of relief in the voice.

"Yes! Aunt Maria! How did you know it was me?"

"A pretty voice suggested a pretty young woman."

"Thank you . . . I have to talk to you, Aunt Maria. . . . Tonight . . . I'm sorry to bother you. . . ."

"No problem . . . Can you come over here?"

"I think I'd better . . . I'm out at the hospital. . . . I'll park behind your house in the alley and knock on your back door. . . . I hope you understand. . . ."

"Of course, hon. I'll be in the kitchen getting ready for Christmas, so I'll see the lights of your car."

"Thank you, Aunt Maria, it will be nice to talk to you."

I spent the quarter hour profitably preparing cranberry sauce. Almost to the minute a tiny car turned into our alley and stopped behind the garage. The lights went out and a slender figure emerged from the car. She was wearing a dark coat and huddling against the wind. I opened the back door as she approached it.

"Camilla," I said, opening my arms.

"Aunt Maria," she said, collapsing into them.

Inside the kitchen we both sobbed.

"Thank you for visiting me."

"Thank you for letting me into your house."

"Come into the parlor and sit down. May I get you something to drink? A glass of wine maybe?"

She hesitated.

"Just one glass. I have to drive back to the hospital. I live there now."

I took her coat and hung it in the closet, opened one of my bottles of Barolo, filled two glasses, and brought them back into the parlor. I turned on the gas fire in the fireplace, and offered a toast.

"Welcome, Camilla! You will always be welcome in this house."

She was wearing a nurse's uniform into which her young body fit neatly. She looked so much like a younger Maria Angelica.

"You are more beautiful than ever, Aunt Maria," she said. "You must be happy in your new marriage."

"Thanks, Camilla. I am very happy, happier than I ever thought would be possible for me."

"I am in love with a young psychiatrist on the staff, an Irish Catholic boy who is so good. He's in love with me too, I think. We are both very careful. I couldn't ask anyone to marry into my family. My father and uncle are both psychopaths. They have terrorized and brutalized my mom and my aunt. . . . My uncle has tried to assault me several times. I will not live in that house ever again."

"How awful, Camilla!"

"They are plotting with a terrible man from your husband's office to murder you and all your family here in your house on Christmas Day. I had to tell you."

"Joseph McMahon."

"Yes, that's his name. Like my father and my uncle he is on fire with hate."

"He has been behind several attempts to hurt us, hasn't he?"

"He is such an evil man. He and my uncles delight in the thought of torturing you. They were very angry when your friends thwarted their plot to kidnap you."

I shivered.

"We will thwart them again, Camilla, and we will protect you."

"I don't think I'm a psychopath. Yet I was caught up in their plan. I have to escape from the family."

"We'll protect you, Camilla, that I promise you."

"They want me to steal some poison from the hospital. I am to bring it on Christmas Eve and they will give it to cousin Tammy who will put it in the turkey dressing she will deliver here later in the day. You know what she's like. She has no conscience at all. Everything, no matter how cruel is a big joke. I'll take something harmless. If they find out, if they test the chemicals, they will rape me and kill me."

"They will do no such thing. You are under my protection from now on. . . . You have a cell phone of course?"

She gave me the number.

"You bring the poison to the house, early in the morning. Tell them you have to return to the hospital. And you come here instead. Will Mr. McMahon be in your house all day?"

"Yes, he wants to make sure nothing goes wrong this time."

"It will be the last time. . . . Do your mother and your aunt try to resist them?"

"Not anymore. They were peasants brought over from Italy. They have been beaten into submission. They hate their husbands and their sons, except for my cousin Nino who is at CalTech, but are afraid to try to break free."

"Terrible," I murmured. So much evil at this holy time . . .

"I must go back to the hospital, Aunt Maria. . . . This is very good wine."

"I promise I will take care of you, no matter what happens."

We hugged again and she slipped out the back door. I should call someone.

My husband? No, I wanted to tell him personally tomorrow and calm him down. Mr. Casey? I was afraid to call him. Who then?

The answer was obvious. Our good angel.

I punched in her number.

"Nuala Anne."

"Maria . . . I hope I'm not interrupting anything."

"In a half hour or so, you would be, but not yet."

— Nuala Anne —

I DIDN'T tell Maria Angelica the whole truth. She was interrupting us, just before what might be called the point of no return. It didn't matter because we knew how to slip back into the proper mood again.

I grabbed the pen and pad that Dermot keeps at bedside for any stray images that he might have in the course of the night. I scribbled down her report as me husband peered over me shoulder.

"Well done, Maria Angelica," I said when she finished. "We will stop them of course and get them with the evidence. Stay in close contact with that wonderful niece of yours. . . . She sounds like a junior Maria Angelica. Tell her that Nuala Anne and Dermot guarantee her safety. I suspect Mike Casey will want her to bring some deadly stuff so they will be able to make a good case against them. It will be the endgame for them all. Yes, we'll see that the women are protected.

"I was right, Dermot Michael, I was right. They were going to poison everyone at Christmastime and the rodent was part of the plot."

"You were right indeed, magical spouse. I never doubted you for a minute. I gave that up long ago. You'd better wake up Mike Casey. He will have to work this out with the Chicago cops and the local ones out there. Then we have some matters that you and I must finish."

"Well if you think I'd be letting you escape from your solemn duties, you're wrong altogether!"

So I called that nice Mr. Casey and spilled out the whole story.

"It's ball game, Nuala. We've got them all. I'll have to do some negotiating with the locals and the CPD. And we'll protect that brave young woman, never fear. I should tell you that we began listening in to your good friend the rodent yesterday and we already have enough to put him in jail for the rest of his life or perhaps the loony bin of our choice. I'll talk to you in the morning."

"Well, Dermot Michael, we'll go to Ireland on Boxing Day after all."

"I didn't know there was any doubt."

"Your health is the only doubt. I'll not force you to come home with me if your friggin' cold comes back."

"Nuala Anne McGrail, you and the kids are going home for Christmas regardless. . . . Now let's get on with our little pas de deux."

So we did and it was a grand dance altogether—even better because we finally had good news.

— Dermot —

THE NEXT day my good wife went off on patrol down Clybourn Avenue, the new shopping center for yuppies and other denizens of the North Side who needed to shop for a bunch of kids at the last moment. She wore her black boots, jeans, sweater, leather jacket, and ski cap, enough to strike terror in the heart of someone who would dare seize a present on which she had designs.

Since school was out, this was the assigned day for the kids to pack for the Irish venture. I was deputed to supervise this agony of choice with a strict set of guidelines that herself had provided. The harshest was that each child was permitted only one toy—Nelliecoyne's camera and the Mick's sketchpad did not count as toys. Socra Marie stubbornly refused to leave any of her dollies at home. They would cry themselves to sleep every night if they were rejected. Patjo claimed that he would bring all his toys.

I enforced the rules with the indisputable rubric of "Ma said." In Ma's name I triumphed in the end despite the tears. Moreover the young 'uns were mandated to bring only two changes of clothes—sweaters and jeans which are never dysfunctional in that wet and chilly island, especially in late December when the sun, having departed for the far horizon, tentatively explores the possibility of coming back and extends daylight by tiny increments, on those rare days when the weather permits daylight. The Irish compensate with warm peat fires, even in those places which have more advanced sources of warmth, which would include our three bedrooms in the new hotel in Clifden . . . as far west in Connemara as you can go without stepping on the sands of Long Island. Carraroe, as picturesque as it is, seems to be on a direct line for the winds and the storms which blow in off the Gulf Stream. In the hotel, one could have warm showers every day without paying more, wasn't the hotel designed for Yanks? In the homes of Connemara, that was often thought to be a needless expense, especially since it would involve removing one's long underwear.

I could feel my cold coming on.

The kids responded to their shrinking lifestyle by demanding to know why we had to go to Ireland for the week after Christmas when some of the other kids on the block or in the school were headed for warmer climes, like Florida or Puerto Rico or Arizona or Mexico. My response was that Ma had the right to be with her family at Christmas and to celebrate Mother's Christmas with her own ma. There were no assaults on the propriety of such a choice.

Mother's Christmas, aka Little Christmas, Twelfth Night, and the Feast of the Epiphany, which in the present state of the confused Catholic liturgy happens around or about January 6, usually earlier. However, the kids must be back in school on January 3, so in Connemara we reschedule Ma's Christmas to happen on December 31. It is called Mother's Christmas because it is supposed to reverse the protocol of Christmas Day on which mothers do all the work. On Mother's Christmas, the ma is not supposed to do any work at all, at all. Only one who knows nothing of the compulsions of Irish and Irish-American women will accept the possibility of such a phenomenon.

Anyway, while I was pondering these mysteries of our annual pilgrimage to the West of Ireland and wondering whether my sinuses were more clogged than normal, Mike Casey called me.

"Well, I've lined it all up," he said. "The arrest of the suspected perpetrators is in the jurisdiction of Kishwaukee County and its sheriff with help from the town police of Oakdale and back up from the Illinois State Police. However, since Chicago has a claim on some of the perps and almost a monopoly on the evidence, we will offer part of Tactical One—thirty sharpshooters who will be authorized to take out any perps who emerge from the house with human shields. The local cops will arrest all of the surviving perps, with the understanding that Joseph McMahon will be delivered to the sheriff of Cook County within the week."

"And the innocent women and children?"

"Everyone understands Camilla Sabattini is working with the police of her own volition and will be treated with gratitude and respect by arresting officers. We assume that she will be with Maria Connors Donlan. Reliable will have a cordon of armed cops at her home, just in case. The other women who may be in the Sabattini house will be taken into protective custody and perhaps brought to the local hospital for such treatment as is necessary."

"The local sheriff is in command?"

"Legally there can be no question about that. Your friend Terry Glen doesn't like that, but he knows he has to live with it. He also believes that there is enough evidence from the tapes of phone messages to obtain convictions in the courts of Cook County for all previous attacks. Finally, I am convinced that the sheriff is rock solid."

"Who authorizes the thirty snipers to shoot?"

"There will be only three, two primary, one secondary. The authority has been given to a consultant who has something of a reputation for coolness under fire."

"Michael Patrick Vincent Casey."

"And you're not even psychic!"

"What do we tell the heroic Camilla?"

"We tell her to deliver the harmless material she has obtained, no one wants to take chances with any foul-ups. We also tell her to leave her house and return to the hospital or to Ms. Connors's house. Under no circumstances is she to return to her family home until I personally tell Maria Angelica that it is secure. Moreover, under no circumstance is

Maria to leave her own home and the protection of the Reliables assigned there until she is authorized to do so by me personally. I will relay all these instructions to her, but you or your good wife should pass them on to her today. I will keep her informed on her mobile phone minute by minute."

"You're not going to activate Godzilla?"

"I wanted to, but the locals didn't like the idea. It's their turf."

"What time will this all go down?"

"Precisely at one P.M. and don't you dare show up. You've taken too many risks in this mess."

"Do the locals know that if this plan fails, our friends out on the West Side will handle it themselves?"

"I doubt it. No point in complicating their lives."

I wasn't a cop, never had been. Much less was my Irish Tiger. No way that Mike the cop would dictate to her where she should be and when.

— John Patrick —

I TRIED to persuade myself as we drove out to Oakdale that I would not climb all over my wife immediately upon arrival at her house. A proper and gentle lover should know when restraint is appropriate. However, my head throbbed as I walked up to the door of the house and my desire exploded as she opened the door and smiled at me. She was unbearably, intolerably attractive and I was wildly hungry for her. I crushed her in my arms, kissed her passionately, bore her to the floor, peeled off her red and green Christmas robe, and devoured her. We both laughed insanely as our game continued.

"Best yet," she sighed compliantly when I was finished. "Let's go to my bedroom and act like civilized people."

"I haven't had enough of you," I protested.

"I didn't think you had. But I have some news to report."

She told me that Joe McMahon, my trusted aide, was the architect of our problems and now with the eager and clumsy cooperation of her own brothers. I was dumbfounded.

"He thought the scandals would force you to sell the firm and that he could buy it for much less than it was worth. He was envious of your success and resentful of his, as he saw it, subordinate position. He became more and more obsessed with his anger as we fended off his attacks."

"He is good at what he does, I'll admit that. He saw in your firm a real bargain without reckoning that you would be part of the bargain. But he is incapable of making a decision. I often asked him bluntly whether I should buy or sell stocks which were on the edge. He saw both sides of the decision but couldn't move beyond that. That was my responsibility and, among other things, he probably resented the fact that I found it so easy. He did not want to make mistakes. I realized that making mistakes was part of the game."

"You liked him," she said.

"I did. I'll miss him. I took him for granted, but I paid him well, not well enough I guess."

"From what I'm told it was not the substance of the payment but the fact that you made it. . . . What are you doing to me, husband?"

"Amusing myself . . . What will happen to him?"

"He'll be tried and go to jail. Nuala apparently suggested to the cops that they check the number of calls from his phone in your office to my brothers' plant out here. Then they obtained permission for a phone tap. They're planning to poison the lot of us at dinner on Christmas Day. . . . I didn't say you should stop playing with me. . . . It was a long, lonely night without you."

Then she told me about the visit from her niece Camilla and her promise to, in effect, adopt Camilla as one of her own.

"I knew, Maria Angelica, when I married you that you were beautiful, brilliant, witty, and a good bedmate. I didn't know then that you were a great woman. I now know you are. You've absorbed my three daughters into your clan without blinking an eye and now you take under your wing a frightened young woman who was raised to hate you. You are, as the young people would say, like totally awesome. The longer I know you, the more I see in you all that is love."

"Just so you don't leave me in a lonely bed too often. . . . Now let's finish what you started out in the parlor before the crowds assemble."

We did finish it, but I wanted more. Perhaps I would always want more.

"I suppose young 'just marrieds' act like we do," I gasped.

"I don't remember, but they don't have the experience with the opposite gender that we do and they don't know how important it is."

"Also," I added, "just how limited time can be."

"Speaking of time, the throngs will arrive soon. I'd better be up at work when they come, instead of lolling around like a libertine. Make yourself at home. This is our bedroom. Unpack your clothes and things and put them anywhere you can find room. If you disrupt any of my stuff I may take you into court."

Naturally there was an empty closet and several empty drawers which had been assigned to me along with a place in the marital bed. I showered and dressed in corduroy clothes that said *rural gentry.* I ensconced myself in a rocking chair in an enclosed front porch where a rural magnate might belong and opened the *Times* and the *Journal* and a book about the Enron scandal. However, I could not dismiss Joe McMahon from my mind. My dad had trusted him completely. I inherited that trust. I had never seen any evidence of resentment or disloyalty. Yet his anger must have festered through the long years. And he must have resented Maria immediately. I was responsible in some way for him. The least I could do was see that he got a good lawyer. No, that wouldn't do. Conflict of interest. Would they plead him on insanity? Who was there to stand by him?

While I was pondering these painful problems, a young woman, clearly Italianate, clearly with Sabattini genes appeared at the door and pushed the bell.

I opened the door, smiled my best country gentry smile and said, "Yes?"

"I'm Tamrya. This is Mrs. Connors's usual Christmas order of turkey dressing."

I accepted the package.

"Thank you, Tamrya. I'll give it to Ms. Connors."

"Bye."

She disappeared immediately, as if she had never been there.

Young woman, you have just become an accessory before the fact to the crime of attempted murder.

I wandered around the house, which obviously had been built in many stages, in search of the kitchen which had been hidden in a new alcove. It was the kind of modern, hyperconvenient "elegant" kitchen that Maria Elegante would have built. She was in the kitchen, huddled over a huge table with several lists and two daughters, a daughter-in-law, and a granddaughter. The latter beamed and gurgled with pleasure, perhaps because her grandmother would occasionally pick her up and swing her into the air.

"A young woman named Tamrya delivered this turkey dressing by hand for Mrs. Connors."

"I thought we were making our own dressing?" one of the daughters said.

"We are. . . . Jackie, would you be a dear and take this package out to the man in the black car in the alley."

"Certainly! Good morning, ladies!"

"Good morning, Jackie!"

Knowing where I did not belong I made a quick retreat.

"I think, Sergeant, that Mr. Casey was expecting this evidence."

"Yes sir, he was. Turkey dressing. I'll see that he gets it."

I passed the kitchen, which was beginning to smell of many good things.

"Jackie, would you answer the phone for the next half hour please?"

"Happy to do something useful."

I did finish the *Times* and the *Journal* before the phone rang.

"Jack Donlan," I said, aware that this was not really my house, though as the spouse of the owner I had some minimal rights.

"Dermot . . . Nuala is on the other phone. We're calling to make sure you're there and all right."

"Never been better."

On reflection, I hoped that comment had not seemed too suggestive.

"We want to make sure you know all the details of what's going down tomorrow."

"I think so. The allegedly tainted but really not dressing has arrived. At herself's instructions I gave it to a Reliable who is standing guard in a limo out in the alley."

"And the arrest will be . . . ?

"Christmas at one P.M., not an ideal time for an arrest."

"Nor for a murder," Dermot said. "These are bad people, Jack."

"I know that."

"Me point, John Patrick Donlan"—Nuala's voice sounding like that of a worried member of the seraphim—"is that under no circumstance are you to be anywhere near the arrest when it goes down, do you understand?"

"I don't get to ask why?"

"Absolutely not . . . You don't argue with one of the dark ones when it's a matter of life and death, do you understand?"

"Yes ma'am. To tell the truth I have no desire to be there."

"'Tis a fine instinct altogether. Maria Angelica doesn't deserve to be a widow again quite so soon."

That was ominous. However, I had no desire to be present at the end of the chase and even less desire to disobey a witch, even if in this case it was the good witch of the West of Ireland.

I read the first two pages of the Enron book before the phone rang again.

"Jack Donlan."

"Uncle Jack, uh, this is Camilla. I'm a niece of Aunt Maria."

"I've heard of you, Camilla. It's a pleasure to hear you. I endorse my wife's promise to take care of you and protect you. . . ."

"Thanks, Uncle Jack . . . Could I talk to her for a sec? . . . I'm on duty at the hospital."

"She's meeting with the other magnates and potentates of this festival time in the kitchen and I'm the temporary switchboard."

"Well, she invited me to come to midnight Mass and stay over tomorrow. I want her permission to bring a guest. He won't need a room because he has to be back at the hospital by morning both days, so we won't need an extra room. . ."

"I'll tell my good wife and I'm sure she'll call you back. But I don't think there'll be a problem. . . . Might I tell her the name of this fast-moving guest?"

"Uh, he's Johnny Burns, M.D. Senior psychiatric resident. He's really cool."

"I'll tell the good Ms. Donlan and I'm sure she'll be back to you immediately."

"Thank you, Uncle Jack. Thanks a lot."

I risked my life by venturing back to the kitchen.

"There was a call for the woman of the house from a sweet young woman named Camilla. She begs leave to bring a guest to the midnight Mass and to the dinner, but not an overnight guest because he has to get back to the hospital both days. His name is John Burns, M.D."

"Thanks, Jack. I'll call her back right away."

"Camilla!" exclaimed the three young women.

"Why not!" their mother said. "What difference does one daughter more or less make, when we already have a horde of them."

As the sun set on the very short Christmas Eve day, the participants in the festivity began to pour in, including my daughters who swarmed around my rocking chair.

"What a gorgeous old house!"

"Did Maria redo it? . . . It's so *her*!"

"And the town is *her* today, picturesque but not quaint! No way!"

By repeating such assertions frequently enough, they would persuade themselves that they had been wrong about my new wife from the beginning. Evie went to her assigned room to put the baby down and unpack her and her husband's clothes. He would arrive later in time for the collation at seven thirty—hot dogs, hamburgers, pasta, wine, ice cream, an indoor picnic.

I suggested to Mary Fran that we take a walk before twilight turned into dusk.

"I'm abandoning my guard post at the door," I informed my wife and her helpers in the kitchen, "and going for a walk in the twilight."

"I'll have one of the cars follow you."

As Mary Fran and I walked down the steps from the porch and turned toward the church, a black car started up the street and followed us at a distance.

"Car following us, Dad."

"Security."

"Will that always be necessary?"

"Only a little while longer. The danger is almost over. We're going to have another M.D. here tonight, a shrink at that. . . . One John J. Burns, a senior resident at Kishwaukee Community Hospital."

"Johnny Jim, they call him. Brilliant practitioner and so gentle. Don't tell him I want to be a shrink. I'd be embarrassed. . . . Is he part of the family *too*?"

"Too early to tell."

I told her about the call from Camilla, leaving out the plot which was to be put down tomorrow.

"Maria is such a wonderful earth mother. . . . And funny too . . . I can tell you are still happy . . . even dizzy in love."

"Dizzier every day . . . How goes the stepmother crusade?"

"We're making progress. . . . Maria is so wonderful it was always hard not to like her. It's still a struggle for poor Evie. She is determined not to be wrong again. . . . Yet there are always little things that catch her up. . . . You'll be sleeping in Maria's room tonight?"

"If she'll have me."

"Oh, she'll have you. . . . But that's a little hard, for Evie, especially."

"Don't tell her, but I was in there this morning too!"

Mary Fran laughed.

"Of course you were, Daddy. Both of you are irresistible."

We had arrived at the church. Inside people were singing "Silent Night" and the stained glass windows were glowing. We turned to walk back to Maria's house. Our house now, I guess. Two family Christmas parties, I thought, one of them about murder, the other threatened by murder.

They were singing inside powered by a determined tenor voice, one that made most of the notes. Loud applause and then "O Holy Night!"

Inside the "collation" was being distributed and the guests were gathering around tables and TV tables.

"Mom said this was for you, Dad," Irene said as she pushed a platter of pasta Bolognese and a glass of wine. "It's Barolo."

I welcomed the red-haired Irishman who was obviously the tenor and the slender young woman who was leaning on his arm, Maria Angelica Sabattini of thirty years ago.

"Camilla," I said, "you look like my wife must have thirty years ago. God bless and protect you."

"I'll do my best to be as kind and good as she is and leave the looks to God."

"Johnny Burns, sir . . . And genes can be very powerful predictors, can they not?"

"Environment is equally important, sometimes more so," Nurse Camilla insisted. "That's why I'm so happy to be part of your family."

"I don't have much to say about it, but my wife says you'll be a great asset."

"And she's absolutely right." Johnny Burns consumed her with an adoring smile. "I've just met your daughter, though I've known her work for at least a year. Her paper on grace and therapy is brilliant beyond her years. We'd love to have her do her residency up here, but she is set on Loyola or Illinois at Chicago."

"I'm afraid that she's at the state now, Johnny Burns, where she analyzes everyone she meets."

"I did that till about eighteen months ago."

"More like six," Camilla murmured.

"You don't get respect anymore."

Then my wife appeared, freshly showered, sweetly smelling, and beaming in a long loosely flowing and yet closely fitting Christmas dress, dark green and trimmed in red. There were some gasps from the crowd at how beautiful she was. She took my arm in hers and waited till all the guests were quiet.

"I welcome everyone to our annual Christmas Eve collation and Christmas party tomorrow. As you know we have a ban on liquor from this minute until we return from midnight Mass. It is a bigger party this year and we fondly hope that it gets even bigger in the years to come. I welcome all of you, especially this gentleman here who captured me body and soul a few weeks ago. Pray for us as we all pray for you and welcome new family and old."

She kissed my cheek. Everyone applauded.

Yet more physical love for me tonight before the dawn of "Our Lord and Savior's Holy Birth" as Nuala Anne called it? Where was that Irish Tiger? I didn't feel secure unless she were around.

Evie took the floor.

"I'm the oldest of the new family and this babe inside of me is, as far as we know, the youngest for the moment anyway. I want to thank you,

Mom, for making my father blush with happiness and protecting us as the Bible says under the shadow of your wings. You can count on us."

Applause, hugs, and kisses.

"That is a very seductive dress you're wearing woman," I said to my wife.

"I thought you wouldn't notice."

She hugged me again, very suggestively I thought. My somewhat austere upbringing had not prepared me for such openly seductive behavior. Either no one else noticed or they expected it.

We all trooped down to the church and crowded into it when the doors opened at eleven o'clock. There were trumpets and cellos and cymbals to stir up our emotion of joy and sadness and triumph as we sang the traditional carols. Father Matt preached a beautiful and blessedly brief homily. We were home for wine and fruitcake by one fifteen. Joy and love were back in the world and as the night wore on in our bedroom.

God, you have revealed your beauty and love in the glories of my wife's body. Protect us from the terrors of the morrow.

— Dermot —

WE ARRIVED at the Sabattini plant at five minutes to one. It was at the far edge of Oakdale from the old Connors house. It consisted of two ugly modern homes (right out of *The Sopranos*) in front of a large storeroom and garage covering twice the distance of the combined length of the houses. While they had lost control of their casino to a Las Vegas company, they still received a large annual payment from the new operators and had messed around in various local projects, both straight and crooked, and made little money from either kind. The cops arrayed around the "plant" seemed disorganized, confused, and dangerously close to the house.

"A frigging mess," I murmured to Mike the cop.

"I told you two not to come, with these trigger-happy goofs, it could be dangerous."

Two characters were standing next to Mike, a study in contrasts in rural cop stereotypes, Sheriff Jake Danzig and Oakdale Chief of Police Covington Bell. The sheriff was a wizened little man in civilian clothes with a fedora that went out of style a half century ago. The chief ballooned in riding breeches and an Ike jacket with Sam Brown belt and a gun holster. He clutched a high-powered rifle with grim passion. He had come to shoot.

"Jimmie, Paulie Sabattini, Joey McMahon, we have you surrounded. We are holding warrants for your arrest on charges of conspiracy to murder. You are innocent until proven guilty. If you surrender peacefully now, you will have the right to consult your lawyers immediately. We beg you to avail yourself of this right. Please come out of the house with your hands in the air."

"Amateur night," Mike muttered. "Someone is going to get hurt."

"The men inside are frightened, terrified," Nuala said, her hands clasped in something like prayer. "They can't think straight, they're so afraid. Poor scared little forest creatures."

"These cops are clueless," Mike said. "You guys don't belong here."

"They're not cool," Nuala said, caressing her weapon of choice, her camogie stick. "The people inside. They are about to do something wild. Be careful . . . Mike, they are terribly scared and terribly dangerous. Warn them that there have been no killings. There are no murder charges yet. Tell them not to take any chances."

Mike reached for the PA microphone. The sheriff, confused and befuddled by it all willingly gave it up.

"This is Superintendent Michael Casey. I am talking to James Sabattini, Paul Sabattini, and Joseph McMahon. The warrants we are holding for you are for attempted murder. That is not a capital crime. Your plot has been frustrated. No one has died. No one needs to die. Please come out with your hands up. No one needs to die today."

"These locals will start shooting as soon as they come out the door," Mike whispered. "They're trigger happy, worse even than the Bureau."

The door of the house on the left swung open. Two men pushed out with two women in front of them, shields against the police bullets. Two cops, sheriff's deputies by the look of their uniforms, who had been standing casually at the door, pulled forty-fives from their holsters. Pistol fire crackled. Both cops reeled and fell to the ground. A fusillade rang out from all around the police circle.

"Damn it to hell," the sheriff screamed on his PA. "Cease fire. I told you no one shoots unless I give an order. The next one who fires a gun will be instantly dismissed from the force.

"I'm sorry, Mike," he said to Superintendent Casey. "I thought I could keep them under control."

The Oakdale chief standing next to the sheriff lowered his rifle reluctantly.

"Watch that man, Mike," Nuala warned. "He wants to kill someone!"

"I see that," Mike whispered.

"You fuckers move back and let us through to our cars or we'll waste these cunts. Anybody shoot again and they die."

The city chief raised his gun.

"I'll take those fuckers out."

Mike shoved the rifle out of his hands.

"Asshole! You are not authorized to shoot! Do that again and you'll never be a cop anywhere in the world."

"Cov, I'm in charge. You obey the rules or I'll destroy you."

He turned on his PA again.

"Jimmie, Paulie, don't do anything stupid. No one is dead. You haven't killed anyone yet. The charge isn't murder."

"Liar! They're all dead by now, that cunt Maria and all her friends! We have no choice! We gotta get out of here! We'll kill these cunts if anyone moves on us. They're fucking useless anyway."

"Hold your fire. I repeat, everyone hold your fire. . . . Jimmie, Paulie, we intercepted your poison."

"Go fuck yourself, liar!"

"I beg you," the sheriff pleaded, "give yourselves a chance."

"Just to show you I mean business, I'm going to kill this cunt. Then you get out of the way."

"Poor, crazy, stupid man." Nuala fell to the ground to pray.

"Jake?" Mike said.

The sheriff nodded his head.

"Do it, Mike!"

Mike nodded ever so slightly to three Chicago Tac men in grey who stood to one side by a tree. They raised their weapons, aimed carefully, and fired. Both Sabattinis folded up and collapsed on the ground with holes in the center of their foreheads. The two women were still standing, freed from certain death. Police began to pull weapons from their holsters and aim their rifles. Trigger-happy goons.

"Everyone hold their fire," the sheriff bellowed. "Put your guns back in your holsters, break open your rifles, and shotguns. That is an order. Both men are dead. No more shooting. Anyone who shoots I will have up on charges today. I repeat, they're dead. No more shooting. They're dead."

The cops reluctantly sheathed their weapons as the two women began to wail like banshees. That the dead men were about to kill them did not matter. We had killed their husbands. A younger woman, Tammy most likely, joined her mother wailing on the body of one of the dead.

"Get some ambulances up here so we can evacuate these survivors," the sheriff ordered. "Get them here right away."

The cops didn't seem to understand that the fight was over, they were milling around, looking for someone to shoot. Then I saw Joe McMahon shoot out of the back door running toward the woods. These stupid rural cops would let him get away. I took off after him. As I almost caught up with him I felt the whiz of a bullet as it rushed over my head.

— Nuala Anne —

"MIKE," I shouted, "this focking asshole is trying to kill my husband."

He raised his rifle to shoot again. I hit his right arm with my camogie stick with all my strength.

"Cunt!" he screamed as he fumbled for his pistol.

I smashed his hand and he dropped the gun. He bellowed curses.

"Cease fire," the sheriff begged, "no more shooting!"

The chief of policed lunged toward me. I hit him in his balls and he fell to the ground and groaned.

I glanced at where Dermot had been. He was standing up, holding the rodent. A line of grey Tac forces were deploying around him with their M-16s at the ready.

"That's enough, young woman!" the sheriff barked.

"It will only be enough when I beat his brains out and yours too. He was taking a second shot at my husband and you were letting him do it. You are as much guilty of attempted murder as he is."

"Casey here." Mike had taken the megaphone. "We have seized the principal coconspirator whom you were permitting to escape. I am a deputized officer in the Illinois State Police. I'm arresting the trigger-happy perpetrator that fired at one of my consultants as he captured the escaping Joseph McMahon. If there are any more random shots at any of my people I will authorize my men to shoot back."

My Dermot stood next to me.

"Is that the guy that shot at me?"

He pointed at the chief of police, still twisting in pain.

"Yes."

"I wanted to slug him. I see you beat me to it."

"You could always hit this asshole of a sheriff who let him do it."

My poor Dermot clutched his fist and then saw that the sheriff was sobbing.

"I'm sorry, Mike," he groaned. "I ordered them to cease fire and they kept on shooting."

"In my report on this I will say that you lost control of your men, that in fact you never seemed to have control of them and that you thereby endangered not only the success of the mission but the lives of my personnel. . . . Nuala and Dermot, get out of here. Report to Maria and her family what has happened. . . . Sergeant Reed, will you escort this couple to the red Lincoln?"

"Yes sir . . . Miss, could I carry your hockey stick for you?"

"Certainly, Sergeant! Only it's a camogie stick. My husband usually carries my weapons, but he has been rattled by the recent events. . . . And, Superintendent Casey, tell them back at the CPD that they should have sent that cute little Godzilla creature."

My spear-carrier took my arm.

"I'm glad you're on my side."

"Those poor men weren't meant to die, Dermot. They shouldn't have died. They were so frightened."

"And so stupid."

— Maria Angelica —

AS THE hands on our old grandfather clock moved from one o'clock to two o'clock, I became more uneasy. I knew that the war in heaven between good and evil—the historic conflict in my family of origin—was going on across town. I was afraid we'd lose. Yet we must begin to eat at two o'clock regardless, because some people had to leave. I moved back and forth from the parlor where our guests were sipping Cokes and coffee lest they ruin the meal that they would be expected to demolish. I was also exhausted from the trysts with my ferocious new husband. I knew what would happen when he came into the house, his eyes alight with hunger. I had brought it all on myself and loved every second of it. But I was tired.

At five to two I entered the kitchen.

"Are you ready, young people?"

"Yes, Mom!"

"Then let's eat!"

"Dinner is served!" I announced and the meal was carried out and presented on the table amid much deserved applause. The guests and young people swarmed to their places.

"Man of the house, will you ask God's blessings?"

I had warned him that I would assign the task to him.

"This is St. Brigid's grace which our friend and protector Nuala Anne taught me.

Bless the poor
Bless the sick
Bless the whole human race
Bless our food
Bless our drink
And all our families please embrace.
Amen."

More applause and then our happy young people began to devour the food.

Later, as my assistants began to remove the food plates and prepare for dessert, Mary Fran whispered in my ear, "Nuala and Dermot are in the study. They want to talk to you and Dad and Johnny Burns in the sewing room."

This was a room off the kitchen where a mother could retreat momentarily to sew or read or in this era watch TV. I caught Camilla's eye and nodded toward the sewing room. She inclined her head toward Johnny Burns. I nodded. We would surely need a psychiatrist.

I took my husband's hand and said to the assemblage, "We must see to some matters before dessert." His hand was as cold as mine. Nuala was pale and somber, her lovely face frozen in sadness. Dermot looked grim and determined. Granne O'Malley's crowd coming ashore from Galway Bay.

"The battle is over," she began as mechanically as a police spokeswoman on TV. "The area is now secure. James and Paul Sabattini are dead. They hid behind their wives as they tried to fight their way out of the police cordon. They shot and wounded two Oakdale police officers who were not prepared for the onslaught. Each held the other's wife in a firm grip and held a pistol at their throat. They said they would kill the women if the police did not back off. Both wives were screaming hysterically. There was no doubt that they meant what they said. They were both terribly frightened, indeed men with fright which had deprived them of all ability to consider what they were doing. There was no choice but for two officers with telescopic rifles to kill them both. The two men fell immediately to the ground. The women were not injured. They threw themselves on the bodies of their husbands wailing and sobbing their loss. Tamrya emerged from the house and similarly mourned her father. Mr. Joseph McMahon who had been hiding somewhere in the house emerged from the rear door and ran toward the woods behind the plant. He was apprehended by one of the officers, arrested, cuffed, and warned of his rights. He laughed hysterically adding some counterpoint to the noise. Ambulances were removing the dead and the survivors as we left to come here. . . . My husband and I want to express our sorrow to everyone. . . . I want to point out that everyone at this house was a target of a mass murder plot and yet you are all still alive for which we must thank God."

The room was silent. No one knew what to say.

"Are they at the hospital?" I said hoarsely. "We must go to them and console them."

"Yes," Camilla agreed. "They need us now."

"You must do what you have to do," Nuala said softly, in the tones of a gentle mother superior. "I would suggest that you give them time, lots of time before you attempt reconciliation. They have lost their husbands who, however cruel and brutish and however they would certainly have killed them, were still their husbands. They must grieve, perhaps for a long time. Perhaps they will return to Tuscany as rich women and begin to understand. Save your consolations until they are ready to hear them."

Johnny Burns broke the ensuing silence.

"I have to say that Ms. McGrail is correct. They must be given time to hate you and to move beyond it. I can't predict how long that will take. I will monitor their short-term recovery at the hospital and keep you posted. Camilla, may I suggest that you take a brief leave so that you will not be in the ward while your mother and your aunt and your cousin are there?"

"As you know, Doctor Burns, I am reluctant to admit that you might be right on anything. This time I'm sure you are." She began to sob. He put his arm around her and she leaned against him.

"And, Johnny Jim, isn't Ms. McGrail me ma and isn't she over beyond in Ireland? I'm Nuala Anne."

We all laughed and the tension eased.

She was crying, poor child, playing the role of the wise old great grandma. Dermot put his arm around her.

I was crying too. Where was my husband's arm?

There it was around me already.

We pressed them to stay for a bite but they had to pick up their kids back beyond in River Forest.

Camilla and I dried our tears and supported by our two men returned to the festive dinner as though nothing had happened. Life is stronger than death, that's what Christmas is all about.

— Epilogue —

THE TRIP to Galway was the disaster I predicted it would be.

It began with a teary walk down the street with the hounds to the Murphy house where the dogs were greeted with glee by Katiesue and Johnnypete. Our crowd, mother included and Patjo excluded, bid them mournful farewells. I tried to explain that dogs tend to be promiscuous with human friends. So long as there are friendly humans around, they don't much care who the humans are. However, the crowd did not accept this rationalization. The dogs would miss us every minute of every day.

Despite all our frantic efforts we boarded the plane just before the doors were closed, having suffered a long delay at the security barrier because our normally well-behaved children took umbrage at the representatives of Homeland Security. The latter I suspect had a purgatorial time during the holidays and were not sympathetic to pushy kids.

The plane sat on the runway at O'Hare for two hours because of wind problems. The kids demanded to know whether we could get off and go home. The first hour of the flight was bumpy and poor Socra Marie succumbed to motion sickness. With the same bravery that had kept her alive for several months in the hospital, she did not complain. Finally when we managed to rise above the worst of the winds, she collapsed in her mother's arms and slept the rest of the trip. Patjo and I were the only ones among the rest of the crowd who were unaffected by the milkshake ride. The good Nuala Anne and the equally good Nelliecoyne prayed rosaries with great fervor for our safe transit.

"You'd think we are on one of them coffin ships," I said.

"How do you know we're not?"

Then somewhere south of Greenland I began to sneeze.

"You're not getting your cold again!" Nuala protested as if that were an optional matter with my organism.

"Certainly not!" I lied.

Our van and driver were not waiting for us at Shannon because the plane was late. I argued with the attendant at the rental car counter that the driver should have noted that the plane was posted late. She responded with I thought a deliberately unintelligible brogue. My wife spit out a steady stream of Irish words. It worked. The van with a different driver would be back at eight o'clock sharp in the morning. They had reserved three "quality" rooms for us at the airport hotel and would notify the hotel up above in Clifden that we would be a day late.

The rooms were nice, if you ignored the jets screaming overhead, the kids piled into their beds, and Nuala and I staggered into our room, large, comfortable and stocked with notes from the management and complimentary fruit and drink.

She called her mother "up above" in Carraroe and explained in mournful Irish what had happened—while discarding her clothes and donning a warm winter nightshirt.

"Och," she concluded in English, "aren't they all great travelers and themselves in fine form!"

Even by the elastic standards of Irish truth, that statement was flat out false.

"Weren't you right all along, Dermot Michael Coyne?"

"Woman, I was . . . But about what?"

"That this trip is a daft idea, that we should have planned on sleeping here before we drove up to Galway and now yourself with your cold and you'll be sick for the whole week!"

"I shouldn't sleep in the same bed with you. I don't want to give you my cold and ruin your trip."

"You know I never catch your colds," she said, turning over and wrapping herself in the blanket.

It was a claim, I thought, to a certain moral superiority. I took my temperature—ninety-nine point eight, typical of my colds. Then I fortified myself with the cold medications that I had brought along and collapsed into feverish sleep.

The next day was bright and clear. The ride through Clare and Galway was spectacularly beautiful. It was a countryside easy to love, so long as you didn't plan to earn a living off its fields. My fellow travelers had recovered their élan and they marveled at the splendors of the West of Ireland and listened with rapt attention to the stories their mother told, in Irish now. Poor dear da, sitting dazed in the rear seat of the van, was an object of occasional sympathetic concern.

I wondered if I should carry a bell, like a leper.

Carraroe glowed in the rare winter sunlight and Galway Bay took on its Mediterranean persona. We were welcomed enthusiastically at the new bungalow which had replaced the old stone house with a thatched roof, though the latter remained in the backyard because of the Irish conviction that it is bad luck to destroy a home. "You can never tell when you might need it again."

Nuala's ma had "just the thing" for a cold. I knew from experience from my own "ma" (grandmother actually) that it would be a concoction of whiskey (Irish), hot water, and lemon juice, with some other mysterious things added. I agreed to drink it, every last drop. It would not help my cold at all, at all, but it would kill the pain. The days in bed would pass seamlessly without a care or worry. Chicago? Where was that? Joey McMahon? Who he? The hounds? Cindasue and her crowd could keep them. My novel? The check with the advance? It had been duly put in the bank. Me wife and gossons and colleens? There was enough in my accounts so the kids could attend college. So why not go back to sleep?

My family had a great time without me, all of them babbling in the Irish language, even my poor little second son. The trip was, I was assured, "great craic." My wife was attentive and caring, as though she were ministering to someone in his final agony.

The last day or two I pulled out of the worst of the cold and some of the self-pity and insisted on hosting a dinner in a Norman restaurant on the very edge of the bay, a few miles west of Galway Town, called that by the locals, though it was now the fastest growing city in Europe.

We had dinner at the house in Carraroe the night before our departure. There was much singing and dancing and storytelling and lullabying from me wife and no wasting of a single drop of the creature. Nuala had but one splasheen of the drink, because she had to drive us home in the dark.

The next day our departure from Connemara and Shannon and our flight home was uneventful, if it seemed to me interminable. The hounds did not seem nearly as happy as they should have been on our return. Why should they be? The Murphy clan had indulged them shamelessly.

The Chicago scene had not changed much. Joey McMahon was in the psychiatric unit at Cook County Hospital, set aside for patients from county jail. It was not certain that he would stand trial. The brothers Sabattini were buried from the parish church and in the little parish cemetery behind the church. Father Matt had preached powerfully about God's mercy and love. The widows had refused to recognize Maria and her sister Gina at the wake or the funeral. However, they permitted Camilla to stand in the mourners' line, but did not speak to her. Young Dr. Burns attended her with respectful attention.

The two wounded cops were recovering from their wounds. Chief Bell had retired. The capture and charging of Joseph McMahon had been reported in both the Chicago and Rockford media, but with few details.

A week after the funeral the two widows and Tamrya had departed on Alitalia for Italy, leaving no indication that they would ever return. There was apparently lots of money in the family construction business which they had promptly sold.

The now more relaxed merger of the Connors and Donlan families were proceeding and Camilla Sabattini had been included in it. John Patrick

Donlan had added two employees to his team, both graduates of the University of Chicago Business School. He and his new wife had finished a belated honeymoon in the Caymans and continued to be radiant in their common life. I had left my cold behind in Ireland, where it belonged and began my new novel. Mike the cop and his wife Annie Reilly celebrated Twelfth Night with a party in honor of me wife and meself in which a number of our cop friends were among the guests—John Culhane, Nikos Mashek, and Terry Glen included. Nuala had changed back into her Irish Tiger life. She sang of course, a whole new line of songs she called "police songs."

I worried about her. She had thrown herself back into her pre-Christmas lifestyle, without ever taking the vacation she needed. I debated within myself how to bring up the subject.

She saved me the trouble.

One night in mid January with a new blizzard assaulting our old house while we were lying in bed almost asleep, she said, "Dermot love, the small 'uns are all worried 'bout you. They think you've worn yourself out. Doesn't Da need a vacation? I say he does, but he'll never take one. They say I should make him. So I've reserved a suite in the Caymans, the same one that Maria and Jack stayed in, for two weeks. Your parents will move into our house. . . . You know how much they love being with the kids and the mutts. I'm sure you won't catch cold down below. I'm going, Dermot Michael Coyne, even if you don't come. . . ."

More Irish fibbing.

What would, in the circumstances, be a wise reply?

"Well, I've been feeling tired a lot lately. I guess I need a vacation. . . ."

Never argue with an Irish Tiger!

— Note —

The North Central section of Illinois in this story is mostly fictional. I think I have crossed the Fox River no more than half a dozen times in my life. Oakdale is entirely fictional. The Kishwaukee County and River, Rockford, DeKalb, and Northern Illinois University actually exist but my rendering is fictional. Do not search for Oakdale because, alas, you will find it only in my imagination. The tactics of the Chicago police presented in this story are also completely fictional as well as various police officers. Neither the Reliables nor Godzilla actually exist. Indeed everyone in this book is fictional. It does not follow, however, that they do not exist vividly in my imagination and haunt my dreams

God is not fictional.

Tucson
Vernal Equinox,
St. Patrick's Week
2007